Who Kidnapped Holly Gold?

ANGEL JONSON

Who Kidnapped Holly Gold?

Published by Angel Jonson.

Cover design by pro_ebookcovers.

Book design by Angel Jonson.

ISBN-13: 978-0-9983341-1-0

Printed by CreateSpace, An Amazon.com Company

Dedicated to God,
who has been with me
in the most difficult times of my life.

CONTENTS

CHAPTER 1

I am sitting in my office. I am thinking about my vacation with Holly. We are going to Florida next week. I bought an engagement ring. I am not ready to ask Holly to marry me but my mom pushed me to do it. I don't understand, why Mom wants me to marry Holly. Holly and I, have never spoken about marriage. We have been together now for one year and seven months. I met Holly when I bought her apartment. I put down a lot cash when I was buying it. I was living in that apartment for two months, when my agent called me.

"Do you remember Holly Gold, Paul?"

"Of course, Monica. Holly is a model and she is very beautiful."

"She wants to see you, Paul"

"Why didn't Holly call me Monica?"

"She is a model and she is rich, Paul."

"Did she tell you that Monica?"

"I am kidding Paul. I think that Holly is afraid to call you."

"I think that models are outgoing, Monica. They show their bodies almost naked for many people to see. They are smart, because they know how to make millions of dollars."

"Do you think that Holly is smart too Paul?"

"I bought her apartment, because Holly needed a bigger and more expensive apartment. I make good money, but I don't have money to buy a more expensive apartment."

"If you meet Holly you may have a chance to move to a bigger apartment."

"I don't even dream that Holly will invite me to live in her apartment Monica. She is surrounded by many men. They have higher chance to be in her apartment."

"Maybe Holly is tired of them and she want you Paul. Maybe you are right Monica."

"What do I need to do?"

"Call her." Monica gave me Holly's phone number. I didn't think much and I called Holly. "I am Paul Morgan, Miss. Gold. Call me Holly, boy."

"Why do you want to see me, Holy?"

"Maybe I want to offer you to live at my apartment. If I have problem to pay my mortgage you will be able to help me with that Paul."

"I don't have enough money Holly."

"You are lying to me Paul. You put down a lot of cash, when you bought my apartment."

"Why did you do that Paul?"

"I work at an investment company. Every day I invest millions of dollars. I put down a lot of cash, because I wanted to invest in the property."

"I don't understand you Paul. Could you come to my apartment to explain to me what I need to do with my money?"

"I will be waiting for you on Saturday at 7:00pm" and Holly gave me, her address. "Are you coming Boy?"

"I will be there Holly."

You aren't going to be happy to see me boy.

"I am afraid to think for that. You are beautiful Holly."

"I am twenty-eight years old Paul."

"Women don't tell, their age, Holly."

"I have nothing to hide. I know who I am, boy."

"Why are you calling me boy?"

"Do you call that every man who was with you Holly?"

"I call them men, boy. I want you to be different from them."

"What do you want me to call you?"

"I told you boy. Call me Holly. I like the way you call my name. You are from New York, Paul.

"I was born in New York and have lived there my whole life."

"Are you from New York too?"

Many people think that I am French. I live in New York and Paris. I had an apartment in Paris, but I sold it. I love both cities.

See you on Saturday boy and Holly hang up.

I bought a perfume and flowers. I was at the front door of Holly's apartment at 7:00 o'clock. I pushed the bell. Holly opened the door. I gave her the flowers and the small box with the perfume. "You are a gentleman" and she kissed me.

"I bought a present for you, because I made good deal when I bought your apartment, Holly."

"This is in the past boy, I forgot how much you gave me. I was happy that you bought my apartment fast.

"I wanted to buy this apartment."

"I want to open the present boy. Oh, my God. Who told you that I love and use this perfume Paul? You surprised me. She kissed me. I cooked for you Paul."

"You know how to cook?"

You will tell me after you try the food Paul. I told you, Paul, because you took my heart.

"Because I bought a perfume?"

"No, because you didn't know me, but you bought the perfume that I love. What do you want to drink?"

"Glass of whiskey with two pieces of ice."

"Full or half glass?"

"Full. I am a man." Holly gave me a full glass with whiskey.

"Do you like to drink?"

"Sometimes after work I drink, but mostly on Fridays."

"After you drink, do you want to be with a woman in bed?"

"I am a man Holly." We laughed. "I like to drink wine, two or three glasses."

We sat and ate. "Your cooking is good Holly."

"I learned to cook in France, when I was young. Now, I don't have time. Sometimes I cook for me."

I looked at my watch. It was after midnight. "I need to leave Holly. I had a good time with you."

"I am leaving for Paris tomorrow Paul. When I return to New York, I will call you."

"I will be happy to see you again Holly." Holly called me after one month.

"I am in New York Paul. I want to see you tonight. I will be waiting for you in my apartment." After three weeks, I moved in with Holly in her apartment. I stay in my apartment when Holly travels.

3

I was surprised when Judy asked me "What are you thinking about Paul? I was thinking of Holly, Judy. I will ask Holly to marry me next week."

"Roy wants to see you."

"Do you think that Roy will fire me Judy?"

"I don't think so, Paul. You make a lot money for Roy's company. If everybody that works in the company makes the same money, Roy will be happy. You know that Roy loves to make money."

"Do you think that Roy is greedy Judy?"

"I think that Roy is my boss Paul and I want to work in Roy's company. You ask Roy, Paul."

"I will Judy."

"Everybody in the office thinks that you don't have zipper on your mouth Paul and you tell the truth when you speak."

I entered Roy's office and asked him "Are you greedy Roy?"

"Why do you want to know?"

"Because I want you to fire me."

"I will be stupid if I fire you Paul. You are a golden chicken for my company. I will fire everybody that works in the office, but I will never fire you."

"You didn't answer me Roy."

"I asked you to come here, because I want to speak with you about Miss. Nancy Jones, Paul.

"What do you want to know?"

"How did you convince her to become your client?"

"I tried to work with Miss. Nancy Jones twenty-five years ago."

"Did you try again?"

"I tried, but she told me that I am greedy and stupid to work with her money. I don't understand why Nancy is working with you, because she knows that you work in my company Paul."

"If I leave, Nancy will follow me Roy. Don't say that Paul."

"Do you care about me at least a little, Paul?"

"Hey Roy, Susan will be a widow and I will marry her."

"Susan is old too for you, Paul. What is Holly doing?"

"I will ask Holly to marry me next week Roy."

"Oh my God. Susan will be so happy to hear that Paul."

"Aren't you Roy?"

"I am too. You know that I am different. I know, that you think only for your business Roy."

"How did you have three children Roy?"

"When you are young you think for money and sex, Paul. I had a good result. I have three children and I have money."

"Thank you for the good advice Roy. If I marry Holly, I need to work hard in bed and in the office."

"Young people do that good Paul. You are young so you should not have problem doing that, but I want to hear what happened between you and Nancy, Paul?"

I went for lunch in a restaurant. An old lady carrying a little dog was speaking with the waiter. The restaurant didn't allow dogs. The waiter told the old lady to go to another restaurant. She told him that she will pay one thousand dollars if she and the dog can eat in the restaurant.

"I am sorry lady. I don't want to have a problem with my boss."

"I and my broker want to eat in this restaurant, waiter." I saw that the broker didn't take any sides.

I walked to them and said "I will take care of your dog lady. You need to speak with your broker."

"Who are you boy?"

"It doesn't matter, I just want to help you, lady."

"Would you like to give me the dog?"

"Where are you going to take my dog, boy?"

"In the waiting area, lady."

"Call me Nancy, boy."

"What is your name, boy?"

"Paul Morgan, Nancy. "

"My dog's name is Bandit. You must be careful with Bandit."

"Maybe me and Bandit will robe a bank, before you come to get him, Nancy."

"I like you Paul. You are a funny boy. Do you have a business card?" I gave her my business card.

"Can you tell me what Bandit will like for lunch Nancy?"

"Bandit is a man. He eats everything, Paul." I sat with Bandit in the waiting area. I ordered food for me and Bandit. I eat with my hands, because I gave food to Bandit too. When Nancy came to get Bandit, he wanted to stay with me.

"O boy, you took the heart of my dog. Bandit wants to stay with you, Paul. He never wants to stay with strange people, any time I wanted to leave him with them. I will call you Paul."

Nancy called me after four months. She wanted to have lunch

with me and her broker, but she didn't want her broker to know that I am a broker too. "You are in the same business, Paul. I would like to talk to you after the lunch."

We had lunch. I saw that her broker was greedy. After the lunch Nancy asked me what I thought for her broker. "I am not greedy and you will have more profit if you are with me, Nancy.

"Many of my friends told me the same Paul, but they aren't in this business. I believe now, because you are in this business. Thank God that I met you Paul."

"You need to tank Bandit too Nancy."

"Bandit is a good boy, you are too Paul."

Three months Nancy called me. I wanted to meet with her in my office, but she preferred her apartment. Now I know why Nancy didn't want to meet me in the office. Nancy didn't want to see you Roy. Nancy hurt me, when she declined to work with me, but I am happy that she chose to work with you Paul. "Of course Roy, I work in your company."

"How do you manage take women's hearts Paul? Every woman in the office loves you.

"Hey Roy, I am planning to marry Holly soon."

"Holly is beautiful Paul. Susan will happy when you marry Holly. Susan loves Holly and you Paul. I asked Susan. Why do you love Paul, Susan?" She told me "Paul is a man Roy."

"What am I for you Susan, we have three children?"

"You are my husband Roy."

"Susan didn't tell me that I am a man Paul."

"Women are different Roy." I want to tell you what happened when I was in college. We were in class. I saw that Lisa looked at me. After class I asked Lisa to drink coffee with me some day and she said "We will have coffee now Paul."

We started to date. I invited her in my dad's apartment. Dad and Mom were on vacation. She told me that she isn't ready to have sex. We continued to meet, but my goal was to have sex with her. Lisa's goal was to marry me. I told her that I am too young to marry. Lisa left me.

One day when I was having lunch in the cafeteria. A beautiful woman sat next to me. She asked me "Why did you stop meeting with Lisa, Paul?"

"How did you know my name lady?"

"My name is Kelly, Paul. Many women know you, because you

are from New York city. Many women want to marry you so they can live in New York."

"Do you?"

"Of course Paul."

We started to meet and we had sex. Kelly was happy with me. I was happy that she didn't ask me to marry her. One day, a man stopped me and he wanted to speak with me. "My name is Lee, Paul. I love Kelly and I want to marry her, but I am not from New York. I will give you ten thousand dollars, if you stop to meet with Kelly." I thought that Lee was joking with me and I told him "Twenty thousand". "OK Paul" and Lee gave me twenty thousand dollars.

"I am from a rich family and I want to marry a beautiful woman, Paul."

"Lee, I need time."

"I will wait Paul. Keep the money."

Kelly told me that her Mom will come to see me and her. I met with Lee and I told him where he needs to come tomorrow. I and Kelly met her Mom. Lee came too.

"What are you doing here Lee, I don't want to marry you. You aren't from New York?", Kelly said.

"I am not, but I am rich Kelly. Paul isn't rich. I love you Kelly."

"Sit next to me Lee" Kelly's Mom told Lee. The next day Kelly told me that she is divided between me and Lee. Kelly continued to meet with me, but she was meeting Lee too. While this was going on, Lisa asked me to meet in the apartment of my dad. We had sex there and I asked her "Why did you have sex with me now Lisa?"

"I know that you are having sex with Kelly. She is beautiful. Since, I had sex with you, I am feeling beautiful too Paul."

Kelly married Lee, Lisa married her boyfriend Roy.

"You will never understand what women want Roy."

"You are right Paul. Holly has a lot of men around her, but she wants to live with you."

"It has been one year and seven months, Roy."

We laughed when the phone rang. Roy picked up. "For you Paul."

"What are you doing boy?"

"Roy and I were talking in his office. I told him that I don't understand women. Why do you live with me Holly, because you are surrounded with many good looking men?"

7

"You are right Paul. I am going to see one of them in Paris."

"Aren't there enough men in New York for you? "

"I have one in New York."

"Is it me, Holly?"

"Of course boy. You know that I love you very much."

"When we are on vacation next week, I will tell you how much I love you Holly."

"I told you that I am going to Paris tonight Paul. You need to tell me now how much you love me now."

"Are you kidding me, Holly?"

"I am not Paul."

"If you go to Paris, I don't want to see you!"

"What is your problem Paul, we have changed our schedule many times when I needed to travel?"

"I want to be with you on vacation Holly."

"It isn't possible Paul. I must go to Paris. I worked very hard to be where I am. I want to be on the top in the next twenty or thirty years in this business."

I know that Holly did what she said, but wanted to scare her so I said "If you don't come with me, I don't want to see you Holly". I hung up, before Holly answered me.

"Do you have a problem, Paul?"

"I don't know Roy." The phone rang.

"Holly wants to speak with you Paul."

"I am going to Paris, boy."

"Good luck Holly" and I hung up.

"I will leave the office Roy. I will return later today or tomorrow. I am not taking my cell phone with me, because I don't want to speak with Holly." I saw Judy in the hallway and I gave her the engagement ring. She was so happy, "It is so beautiful Paul. Why did you give me this ring?"

"The ring was for Holly. I wanted to marry her next week, but she prefers to go to Paris. If someday I decide to marry, I will buy a new one, Judy."

"Thank you so much Paul."

"I don't have time to speak Judy" and I left the office. I returned to the office at 7:00PM. I checked my cell phone. I had many massages from Holly. I didn't listen to them. I erased them. It was 8:15, when Holly called me again.

"I thought that you have left for Paris, Holly. My flight leaves one hour from now Paul."

"What do you want?"

"Why did you give my engagement ring to Judy?"

"How did you know?"

"I went to your office late this afternoon Paul."

"Why didn't you tell me that you want to marry me, Paul?"

"I was surprised when Judy told me."

"I wanted to surprise you in Miami Beach, Holly."

"We never spoke for marriage Paul."

"You are right Holly."

"Frankly, I wasn't ready to ask you to marry me. My mom pushed me to ask you Holly."

"Do you think that Janet loves me Paul?"

"Of course Holly. I don't see that you have problem with my mom."

"Your Mom hates me Paul. I have had many problems with your Mom in the last six months." "Don't tell me that Mom hates you, because you want to go to Paris."

"Paul, I will marry you. I don't care what Janet thinks of me. I know that Henry loves me and he wants me to marry you."

"I know that my dad loves you Holly. What is the reason my mom to hates you Holly?"

"I don't know Paul. I was surprised that Janet wants you to marry me, because she hates me. If you don't believe me, ask Henry."

"My mom and dad will be with us when I ask you to marry me Holly."

"Why are you going to Paris?"

"I have to sing a contract for my future Paul. I told Roy, why I have to go to Paris."

"Do you love me boy?"

"Of course Holly. I am little surprised at what my mom did. She hates you, but she wants me to marry you, Holly. Do you want me to ask Mom?"

"When I return from Paris, we will speak Paul. Your Mom isn't a problem for me, because Henry is behind me."

"I will surprise Mom, Holly. I will call you on Sunday, Holly."

"I am kissing you, boy."

I was in a crazy situation. I can't go to Florida to see Mom and Dad. I decided to go on vacation in the Caribbean. I called my travel agent "Hi Bobby. Hi Paul".

"Are you ready for your vacation?"

"I want to change my plan Bobby. I want to go to Puerto Rico instead of Miami beach, but I don't want anybody to know, where I am. I want to leave this Saturday and return next Saturday. I will be alone."

"O boy, you are going to see a mamacita in Puerto Rico?"

"Hey Bobby, maybe I will be back with a mamacita." We laughed.

"I will call you later Paul."

Bobby called and sent me a fax with my reservation to Puerto Rico. I told Bobby that I will ask my friend Roy to go to Florida and that he needs to help Roy, if he wants to go there.

It was Friday. It was hot in July in New York. I went to the office. I saw Judy.

"Good morning Paul."

"Did you have good time last night Judy?"

My friends asked me, "Who bought the ring?", Paul.

"What did you say to them?"

That you gave me the ring, but you will marry Holly.

"Are you sure that I will marry Holly, Judy?"

I spoke with her yesterday and I told her that you gave me the ring Paul. She loves you so much.

"Was Holly angry, when she saw the ring?"

Holly laughed Paul. I was surprised.

"You are a lucky, that Paul gave you the ring, he is a rich man." I wanted to give Holly the ring Paul.

"What did Holly tell you?"

"Keep the ring Judy. Paul will buy a new one for me."

"Holly took my heart Paul."

"Why did you want to give the ring to Holly?"

"I got scared when I saw her."

"Why did you put the ring on your right hand?"

"I don't want people to ask me when I am getting married. I don't have a boyfriend. Hey Paul, I am an expensive woman now. People will think that I am rich too. What do you want for lunch Paul, I will buy for you?"

"The same you are buying for you, Judy." The phone rang. Judy picked up.

"Roy wants to see you Paul. I will bring the lunch at 12:00

o'clock in your office Paul."

"Thanks Judy."

"Hi boss."

"Did you speak with Holly?"

"She was in my office yesterday after 5:00 pm. Holly was crying Paul. I didn't know what to do."

"You should have hugged her and kissed her, Roy."

"I couldn't believe that Holly was crying, because you refused to speak with her. I told Susan what happened in the office. Susan laughed and she told me "Paul is a man, Roy. I will cry too if he doesn't want to speak with me." Susan was joking with me, Paul."

"Don't worry, everything is OK Roy. I spoke with Holly."

"Hey boss, do you want to go on vacation in Miami Beach? My mom and dad will be there."

"Why not Paul. I like your father. I am sure that Henry and I will have a good time Paul. Your Mom is little different because she is younger than Susan and me."

"Hey Roy, my dad is fifteen years older than my mom, but he has been with her thirty-four years. Call Bobby is my travel agent and he can give you the details. I have already paid for Holly, Mom, Dad and me? Don't call me after tomorrow, because I will be on vacation, but I don't want anybody to know where I am."

"Go to Paris, Paul. "

"I will think about that Roy." Judy came with the lunch at 12:00.

"Can you clean the desk Paul?"

"I will Judy. "

"I will close the door Paul."

"If you are going to ask me something that you don't want people in the office to hear, then that is a good idea."

We started to eat our lunch when Judy said "I want to tell you about my life Paul."

"Why don't you want people from the office to hear about your life Judy?"

"You are different from them Paul. You never ask people in the office about their life."

"I don't have time Judy. I am busy with my life."

"I see that Paul."

"You work hard and you speak with people in the office for business."

11

"My dad taught me that I needed to help people when they had problem, but I didn't need to ask about their life." He said "If they want to share, they will tell you Paul."

"Your Dad is right Paul, but people have different life. For example, I use to hate Holly."

"Why did you hate her, Judy?"

"You met Holly three or four times. Holly never said anything bad about you. Honestly, Holly and I never spoke about the people working in the office. Holly knows well Roy and Susan. Frankly, Susan is a good friend of Holly."

"I hated Holly, because she is the reason I lost my boyfriend."

"Did Holly take your boyfriend?"

"I don't know Paul. I thought that maybe you know something."

"Holly has a lot of men that work for her, Judy."

"What kind business is your boyfriend in?"

"He owns a flower shop."

"I don't believe that Holly has an afire with your boyfriend Judy. If your friend was a millionaire or billionaire, maybe Holly met him."

"Why my boyfriend stopped to meet with me after Holly spoke with him?"

"Can you tell me what happened Judy?"

"As part of my job, I have been ordering flowers for your girlfriends. I have sent flowers to Holly too. Holly met with my boyfriend and she asked him, if he has good business with you and how many times he has delivered flowers for your girlfriends."

"What did he say?"

"That you had a lot beautiful girls, but Holly is above them. After that Holly started to use the store to send flowers for her friends. He stopped to invite me to drink coffee with him."

"Having coffee was your relationship with him?"

"Yes, Paul."

"He used you Judy. He invited you to for coffee, because you were helping him get more business. He wasn't your boyfriend. I invite my clients to have lunch or dinner, because I have business with them. I am sure that he is afraid to invite Holly to drink coffee with him. Go and tell him, that Holly will stop to order flowers if he doesn't drink coffee with you."

"I will never go back to his store Paul. You had many girlfriends and you never went back to see them. I need to look for another man. Hey Paul, I have an expensive ring now. Maybe somebody will think that I am rich and he will want to be with me."

"This is a good decision Judy."

"Do you still hate Holly now?"

"I will hate her, if she wants to take the ring from me."

"Holly will never do that Judy. Holly likes to give presents and she has a big heart. "

"Yesterday, I saw that she is not what I thought of her Paul. I will clean the desk Paul."

Judy was on the door leaving my office when she said "Let me know if you need anything Paul".

"I will Judy." I was in my apartment when Mom called me.

"Why did Holly go to Paris, Paul?"

"Why didn't you ask me what I am doing Mom?"

"It isn't important now Paul. I want to know what will Holly be doing in Paris."

"Call and ask Holly about that, Mom."

"You are her boyfriend, and you need to know Paul."

"Holly has business in Paris, Mom."

"Holly and you were supposed to be in Miami Beach, Paul. Do you think that Holly wants to marry you, Paul?"

"I don't know Mom. You need to ask Holly."

"I don't like Holly anymore, Paul."

"Why did you push me to ask her to marry me when Holly and I were coming to Miami Beach?"

"I knew that Holly was going to go Paris."

"You are crazy Mom."

"Don't call me crazy Paul. Holly is the crazy one."

"How did you know that Holly was going to Paris, Mom?"

"I booked our vacation a month ago. Holly left to Paris at the last minute yesterday."

"I found out that Holly had a schedule to see her old boyfriend in Paris, Paul."

"Do you know my schedule for next week Mom?"

"Of course Paul. You are coming to Miami next week. We need to speak for your future Paul, because Holly left you. You need to find another woman and marry her."

"I don't think so Mom. Maybe I will never marry. I was happy before I met Holly, because I had many women. Holly stopped me from looking for other women, Mom. She took all my energy in bed."

"Did Dad do that for you Mom?"

"I am your mother Paul. You have never spoken with me for sex before."

"I didn't have problem like this before Mom. Holly left me and my life changed. I am not sure what I am going to do. Do you think that I need to kill myself?"

"Stop joking with me Paul. I am sure that you had another plan if Holly leaves you."

"Holly surprised me, Mom. I was ready to ask her to marry me."

"Did Holly know that you wanted to ask her to marry you, when you were coming to Miami Beach?"

"Holly didn't know when she decided to go to Paris. Holly was in my office and Judy told her. I gave the engagement ring to Judy and she told Holly that this ring was for her, Mom. If I want to marry, I don't have money to buy a new engagement ring. I need to work ten years and save money to buy a new engagement ring." Mom understood that I was joking with her and she hung up. My dad called me after thirty minutes. He was laughing.

"Do you need money for a new engagement ring son?"

"Hey Dad, are you busy with Mom?"

"If you are asking me for bed, I am not son. You forgot that I am seventy years old."

"Did you ask Roy if he is busy with Susan?"

"I didn't Dad, but you will have a chance to ask Roy next week. Roy and Susan will come to Miami Beach. I will not."

"Did you tell your Mom?"

"I didn't and I don't want you tell her. I want to surprise Mom, when she sees Susan and Roy."

"I will not tell her, Paul."

"Do you know what happened between Holly and Mom?"

"I know that Janet suddenly started to hate Holly, but I don't know why. Holly is a very good woman Paul. I love her Paul."

"Holly loves you too Dad."

"Do you think that you will have problem with Holly, because she left to Paris, Paul?"

"I don't know Dad. I spoke with Holly before she left to Paris.

Holly told me that she has a problem with Mom, but she will still be with me."

"Do you think that Mom will ever come to see me when I marry Holly?"

"I will ask her Paul, but I will come son."

"Thank you. You are a good Dad."

"Holly will be a good wife and Mom, Paul."

Henry hung up. I thought for Mom and Dad. They have been living together for thirty-four years. I never thought for them before. I never saw them arguing. I remember that Mom wasn't at home for two months when I was six years old. My dad told me that Mom was for two months in Ohio to see her relatives. When I grew up I went to Ohio to meet my mom's relatives. They told me that Mom hasn't been in Ohio, after she married Dad. I never asked Dad why he lied to me. I didn't what to hurt him, because he loves me very much. Henry will do anything for me. Henry was the best Dad. I love him very much too. For the first time in in my life I realized that Mom and Dad are different people. I called and ordered taxi for the morning at 8:00 o'clock. I woke up at 5:30 am. I drank coffee. It was 7:00 am when my mom called me.

"What are you doing Paul?"

"I woke up early. I am going to drink coffee somewhere. I don't want to stay alone Mom."

"You need to find another woman Paul."

"Why don't you like Holly anymore, Mom?"

"Holly isn't the right woman for you Paul. You need to listen to me because I have taken care for you for thirty-three years, Paul."

"You are lying Mom. In the last ten years I have been living alone and I have been taking care of myself. I pay my rent and my bills. I bought an apartment. I never asked you and Dad to help or give me money in the last ten years. I have made all the decisions for my life."

"Of course Paul. That explains why you are living with a prostitute."

"Do you know how many abortions has Holly had?"

"Holly didn't have an abortion for the last one-year and seven months Mom. I don't know if Holly had before I met her. I didn't ask her. If it happened it is in her past."

"Did you speak with Henry last night Paul?"

"I didn't Mom."

"Don't listen to Henry! I know that Henry loves Holly."

"Are you jealous Mom?"

"Henry is seventy years old. He will die if he has sex with Holly."

"Now, you are going too far Mom. Holly is my girlfriend."

"She is a prostitute and she sleeps with many different men Paul."

"I am surprised that you know what Holly does."

"I live with Holly, and I know her well." I understood that Mom wanted to hurt me and I asked her.

"Did you have an abortion before you married Dad, Mom?" She hung up. I knew that Mom will call later. She will never stop hurting me, because I didn't tell her that I will leave Holly. I was in the airplane. I had my cell phone handy in case Holly, Roy, Dad or my clients call me. I was not going to speak with Mom. I am going to Puerto Rico. I need to enjoy my vacation.

CHAPTER 2

I arrived at San Juan airport in the afternoon. I took a taxi and I was in Hotel International. Pedro who was on front desk asked me which floor and view I prefer. "I want a higher floor and I want to have a view so that I can see far in the ocean, Pedro. I don't have problem to pay more for that."

"You look like you have money Mr. Morgan."

"I work to have money Pedro. I spend a lot time in my office and my clients make good money. I am making good money too Pedro."

"I spend a lot of time in hotels too, but my clients forget to give me gratitude often Mr. Morgan."

"I don't Pedro" and I gave him three hundred dollars. Pedro was surprised. "It is OK Pedro."

"If everybody shows me the same gratitude, I will be rich Mr. Morgan."

"What are you going to do if you were rich Pedro?"

"I will buy an expensive house and I will spend time with girls."

"If you do that, you will finish your money pretty fast Pedro."

"When I finish the money, I will start to work again Mr. Morgan." We laughed.

"I like you Pedro. You are a funny man."

"Thanks Mr. Morgan."

"Call me Paul, Pedro."

"Where is your girlfriend Paul?"

"If you need one, I know a lot of girls. They aren't expensive

Paul."

"If my girlfriend doesn't come, that may be a good idea Pedro."

"They speak good English, Paul."

"You forgot to tell me that your girls know well to count money."

"First they look at the man. If the man is old, they will work less, but they will count more."

"Oh my God. You took my heart Pedro."

"Hey Paul, I am a man and I know what man want."

We laughed a lot. I gave one hundred dollars more to Pedro.

"I am the manager Paul. If you have any problem at all, call me."

"I will Pedro." I took the elevator. Pedro set me up on an apartment on the top floor. Pedro's choice was perfect. The apartment had two bedrooms with two baths, a big living room and a kitchen. I went on the terrace. The view was beautiful.

I checked my messages. I had many messages, but fifteen of them were from Mom, one was from Holly. Mom's messages were funny. In some of them she cried in some she laughed. She wanted me to call her, because she wanted to divorce my dad. This may be good for Dad, I told myself. Next message. "Please don't marry Holly, Paul. She is a prostitute". I understood that Mom had a problem. I never noticed before that may be Mom has a mental problem. Mom and Dad had a normal life. My dad never mentioned to me that Mom had a mental problem. "What do you want Mom, I told myself?"

I checked Holly's message she said "Call me boy". I called her back.

"Where are you Paul?"

I will tell you, but you can't tell if anybody asks you.

"I can't believe that your Mom doesn't know Paul?"

"Nobody knows where I am Holly. I don't want anybody to ask me where you are."

"I didn't think about that when I left for Paris, Paul."

"You had been many time in Paris alone Holly, but now is different."

"What is different Paul?"

"I wanted to you to marry me next week, but I am in Puerto Rico and you are in Paris."

"Why did you go to Paris?"

"We were together until last Thursday morning. You didn't tell me that you had to go to Paris." You called me in the afternoon and told me that you have to go to Paris."

"What was that Holly?"

"Do you think that I am your little dog and you will do what you want to do with me?"

"Oh my God. I never thought that Paul. You know that I respect you a lot. I am with you, because you are the best man for me. All my friends know that you control my life and you decide for many things in my life. I am happy that you do that Paul, but I told you that my emergency trip to Paris is for my future. I spoke with Giles at 10:00 am on Thursday morning. I work with him in Paris. He told me that Marcel will come to my apartment in the afternoon and I need to go to Paris with Marcel. By the way, Judy likes Marcel. He was in your office with me."

I didn't know why, but I felt little nervous when I heard that Judy likes Marcel.

"Are you jealous Paul?"

"No Holly. I don't have problem to sleep with Judy. She isn't my type, so it will not be Judy. If you get in bed every man who wants to be with you, then this is your problem."

"Your Mom told me that I am a prostitute. Do you think that I am Paul?"

"I can't be with you if you were Holly. People sleep with them for one night. I am with you one year and seven months. It is a very long time for a prostitute."

"O boy, you are killing me."

"Why did you call me Holly?"

"I called you, because I have problem with Janet, Paul. I had many messages from her."

"I have too Holly."

"Do you think that Janet has a mental problem Paul?"

"I thought about that before you called me. Janet was a normal person Holly. I don't know what happened to her. If Mom has a boyfriend and she wants a divorce, she needs to speak with Dad and me. Do you have any idea why Janet hates you? What is my mom is speaking against you, Holly? You are my girlfriend. First, Janet pushed me to marry you, now she wants to separate us. I work with many people and I understood them when they had problem. I don't understand what the problem of Mom is. I had message that she will divorce my dad."

"I have spoken with Henry many times Paul. I never heard that Henry had problem with Janet and Henry never said anything against Janet, Paul. Why does Janet want to divorce Henry, he is the perfect man, Paul?"

"Because you left for Paris, Holly. Mom loves me and she doesn't want me to stay alone. Mom told me that I need to find another girl."

"Do you?"

"I am thinking about that Holly. I will tell you when I am ready."

"Can you come to Paris, I want to be with you, Paul?"

"I can't come Holly. Maybe it is good for us to be separated right now."

"I will be back next Saturday in New York, Holly. If I don't sign the contract next week, I will be back on Sunday in New York. Do you love me boy?"

"Of course Holly. You hurt me, but I love you. It was crazy idea to leave so fast to Paris."

"We will speak tomorrow Paul. Maybe I will have more information for my contract. Go to the beach. I love you so much boy. I am kissing you."

Holly hung up. I was on the beach. There were many unoccupied chairs and umbrellas, so I chose one of them. I saw that a girl was waving her hand at me.

"Come and sit next to me man. I need somebody to help me."

I walked to her.

"Are you alone?"

I turned around to look. "I don't see anybody with me lady."

"My name is Gina."

"Call me Paul, Gina. You are a pretty young Gina."

"I am twenty years old Paul. My dad told me that I am too young to stay alone on the beach."

"Do you think that he is right?"

"Depends on what you want Gina. Some girls make business on the beach."

"You talk the same way as my father Paul."

"What do you want Gina?"

"Can you put some sunscreen on my back, Paul?"

I put sunscreen on her back and was ready to leave when Gina asked me "Can you stay with me Paul, you seem like a good man?"

"Are you afraid Gina?"

"I am Paul. I am alone and many men want to speak with me."

"This is normal Gina. You are a pretty woman."

"I don't want men who want me to go to bed with them the Moment they meet me."

"You tell them that you need to swim for two hours and run for three hours. When you are finished exercising, you will go to bed with them. I think that they will go to look for another girl."

"This is very funny Paul, but if they wait for five hours, what I should to tell them?"

"That you are tired from all the exercise Gina." We laughed.

"Do you have a girlfriend Paul?"

"She left me, because I didn't wait for her five hours. It is a long time Gina."

"Are you joking all the time Paul?"

"I am busy with my job and when I am not working I like to joke."

"Why did you look at me, after that you were looking for somebody on the beach?"

"Are you waiting for somebody?"

"I arrived yesterday at hotel International. I had dinner. A man was watching me the whole time when I was in the restaurant. He asked for me at the front desk. He followed me this morning on the beach."

"Why didn't you tell the front desk, that the man followed you in the restaurant and on the beach?"

"I told them. They told me that it was normal when you were alone in the hotel."

"Of course Gina. You saw me alone and you wanted to be with me."

"I was speaking about the man who followed me Paul. I didn't want him. I think that people who work on the front desk know this man well and he knows them too. I am afraid, because Dad told me that people sale drugs or kidnap young girls. I think that this man wants to sale me drugs or kidnap me. My father is a detective and I believe him. My mom and dad are in Ponce now. My dad didn't want to leave me alone, but Mom told him that I am a big girl. They will come to hotel International on Wednesday. I want to stay with you, because I am a little scared for my safety."

"Don't be afraid Gina. I am alone and I will be with you."

"Thanks Paul. My dad was right Paul. He told me "If you have problem Gina, you need to call me or you find man who you can trust".

"Do you think that you can trust me Gina?"

"Yes, if you stay with me Paul. "We laughed. She kissed me. "Hey man, this is my boyfriend. Do you want to fight with him? Yesterday you followed me in the restaurant and on the beach. Now you will have to follow me and Paul."

I turned and I saw a man walking away very fast.

"Why are you leaving man, I want you to stay here, so you can see Gina kissing me?"

The man started to run. Gina kissed me again. "It was funny, but I wanted to kiss you, Paul. "

"You will have a chance to kiss me many times, if you come to my apartment tonight Gina."

"Do you want me in bed Paul?"

"I will save your life Gina."

"I want to be with you tonight Paul, but you don't think that I want to go in bed with you. I know you for a very short time."

"Less than one hour, Gina."

"Are you from New York, Paul?"

"Yes, I am from New York. Your father is a detective, but I think that you are too Gina."

"I am from Philadelphia, Paul."

"How do you know that I am a good man and I will be willing to help you?"

"Every single man who comes on the beach looks to sit next to a young single girl. You didn't look for a young girl. You looked for a free chair and an umbrella Paul."

"I am on vacation Gina. I didn't come to Puerto Rico to work at night. Many men go single on vacation, because they want to be with a young girls Paul. I don't understand, why do they spend a lot of money for a vacation to be with young girls Gina? They can be with young girls where they live."

"Usually they don't want somebody to see them, because they are married or have a girlfriend. You are alone too Paul. Why did you say that you don't want to work when you are on vacation Paul? Do you think that the sex is work?"

"For some of people sex is work, for some it is a feeling."

"I don't want to be a work for you, Paul."

"Of course Gina. Feeling is better."

I don't understand when you are telling the truth and when you are joking Paul.

"Why do you speak for sex with me, I am a young girl Paul?"

"Why did you ask me to put sunscreen on your back Gina? My fingers touched your soft and beautiful skin. My hand took a lot energy from your body Gina."

"I have energy, because I stayed on the beach the whole day."

"Tomorrow, I will not touch your body. I will stay the whole day on the beach to get energy too Gina."

"I am going for a swim Paul."

"If you have problem in the water, I will help you Gina. I swim well."

She walked to the water. I looked at her back. She had a fee more pounds that she needed, but her ass was beautiful. She moved her ass very interesting. Holly moved her ass the same way, but she is a model. If Gina loses some pounds, she can be a model too, but she is pretty anyway. Holly is a beautiful woman. I started to think for Holly and me. If Gina was right, Holly left to Paris to see her boyfriend there. I came in Puerto Rico to find a young girl. Maybe Gina is the young girl for me, if she comes and stays tonight in my apartment. What will I tell Holly if she asks me tomorrow, what I did on Saturday night? Why will Holly ask me after she left to see her boyfriend in Paris?"

My life was so simple after I started to live with Holly. I did two things. I worked hard at my job and relaxed with Holly when I didn't work. She wanted to be with me in her apartment. Holly didn't want to go out. I thought that Holly didn't want her friends to see her with me. Holly laughed a lot when she heard what I thought.

"O boy, I spent a lot of time with many people, because of my job Paul. I am tired to be all time with many people. I am feeling good when I am alone with you."

Holly wanted to cook for me. She wanted to spend long hours with me in bed. Holly wanted me to feel good when we were together. Honestly, I was feeling good, when Holly and I were together in her apartment. I am sure that one hundred per cent that Holly wasn't in Paris to see her boyfriend, because I am her boyfriend. I didn't understand why Mom told me that Holly has a boyfriend in Paris. "If she has, then why did she call me today and she wanted to speak with me?" Holly would want to cook and spend time in bed with her boyfriend in Paris. I saw that Gina was waving her hand.

"Come in the water with me, Paul. The water is hot." She was right. The water was hot.

"I felt that you looked at my back Paul."

"I looked at your ass Gina. You move your ass very good."

"Did you try to be a model?"

"I tried to be a model. I tried to sing. Every teenager does that Paul."

"I didn't Gina. My dad pushed me to spend more time to read books and play tennis, run and swim."

"My dad too Paul." He told me "Gina your body isn't the model type. Your voice isn't good enough to be a singer. You need to get a good education. There is your power."

"My body is like my dad's. My mom has the perfect body. Hey Paul, you will see her on Wednesday. You don't try to flirt with her, because my dad is jealous. He has a pistol and he will kill you."

"Will your father kill me if your Mom wants to be with me?"

"Do you like to flirt with women that are forty-five?"

"I don't, but I will have a chance with your Mom."

"What are you going to tell your girlfriend, if you are in bed with me and my mom, Paul?"

"I want to know what is the difference between twenty years old girl, thirty-year-old woman and forty-five-year woman."

"Your girl is thirty years?"

"Yes, and her name is Holly."

"Do you love her?"

"I am with you Gina."

"You don't love me, because you don't know who I am Paul."

"You are right. I need to spend more time with you."

"If you want, we can spend four nights together, Paul. I am leaving on Friday, but I don't know what will happen, when Mom and Dad come on Wednesday. It will be OK for Mom, but Dad is different. Are you going to have a problem if your girlfriend finds out that I am sleeping in your apartment Paul?"

"I don't know Gina, she is in Paris."

"Holly will not know that you are with me. Nobody knows me here, so there is nobody to tell her, that I am with a pretty girl. Do you have a boyfriend Gina?"

"I left him four months ago. My dad found that he uses drugs."

"It isn't good to have a father detective Gina."

"My dad knows everything I do."

"Maybe he will kill me if I sleep with you Gina."

"Don't be afraid Paul. I am not a virgin."

When I had sex for a first time, my dad came in my bedroom and he asked me "Why did you have sex with him, Gina?"

"I am eighteen years old Dad and he is my boyfriend."

"Did he push you to have sex daughter?"

"No Dad. I pushed him, because he was scared that you would kill him."

My dad didn't know what say. I asked him "Are you going kill him, Dad?"

"It is too late to kill him now Gina. You aren't a virgin anymore and he left my bedroom."

"After that, I had sex with one more boy."

"Is that the boy that uses drugs?"

"Yes, Paul. My dad was right when he stopped me to continue meeting with him. Maybe I will start to use drugs too Paul."

"Do you work Gina?"

"In August I will be in my third year at the University of Pennsylvania."

"I assume, your ex- boyfriend studies there too. I met him there."

"My dad was right that I need to get a good education."

"My dad told me that too Gina, but I wanted to get good education. Now I work in a good company and I make good money."

"Do you think that the money is most important think in your life Paul?"

"Money is important to live good Gina."

"My dad told me the same."

My mom told me "If you marry a rich man, you don't need to work Gina. I married a detective and I need to work. Don't marry a detective Gina."

"Your Mom is a funny woman."

"She is a like you, Paul."

"Maybe her big heart saved her marriage?"

"My parents are different, but I love them."

"Are your parents different too, Paul?"

"I don't know Gina, but I love my dad more than my mom. Maybe, because I am a man."

"Some boys have good relationship with their Moms. They listen to what their Mom tells them, because they want their Mom's approval. The fathers want the boys to grow to be strong man."

"Maybe you are right Gina. I listened to my mom and now I have a problem with my girlfriend."

"Don't be afraid about that Paul. I am with you."

"Do you want me to leave my girlfriend?"

"You need to decide that Paul. You are thirty-three years old. I am twenty. I don't have to tell you what you do with your girlfriend. I left my boyfriend, because my dad wanted me to. You need to ask your Dad, Paul."

"I know what will my father say. He loves Holly. He will tell me that I need to marry her."

"Are you ready to marry her?"

"I was, but now I don't know. I know that Mom hates Holly."

"Your Mom must support your girlfriend, because they are women."

"The problem is, that Mom liked Holly before. Now she hates her."

"Do you know what happened between them?"

"Last Thursday was the first time I understood that Holly had a problem with Mom, but she didn't know why Mom hates her."

"You need to speak with my mom, when you see her on Wednesday. Maybe my mom will help you, Paul."

"She won't help me if she wants me and you to be together."

"It isn't possible, Paul. I and you have different lives. My dad will tell me that I am young to marry and I think that he is right Paul."

"Why do you want to be with me Gina?"

"To get little experience in bed Paul. You had a lot of women in bed. I am kidding Paul, but I want to stay in your apartment, before Mom and Dad come to the hotel."

"Do you want to do that Paul?"

"Sounds good Gina. I have a chance to be with a young girl."

"Don't think about bed Paul."

"I will be dreaming about that Gina."

"Sounds good Paul. The life is so easy with you Paul. Now is 6:30 pm. We need to return to the hotel Paul."

We were in the elevator. "You need to come with me in my room Paul. I will get some of my things and we will go to your apartment."

"Why don't you cancel your reservation Gina?"

"I don't want to look chip in your eyes Paul."

"You want to keep your room, because if something happens between us, you will back in your room Gina."

"I need to be ready for everything Paul. Maybe your girlfriend will tell you that you need to kick me out from your apartment."

"Holly won't know that you are in my apartment and she is busy with her boyfriend in Paris."

We entered my apartment. "Oh my Gog. The apartment is huge Paul. I want to look around. You have two bedrooms and two bathrooms Paul."

"One for me. One for you Gina."

"If you want something, you can come to my bedroom Paul." Gina embraced and kissed me.

"You are rich Paul. I can't marry you, doesn't matter that you are rich. I think that there will be a problem when you meet my mom. She will push me to marry you, Paul. You must tell her, that you have a girlfriend and you will marry her."

What should I tell to your Mom if she asks me "Why did you go with Gina, when you plan to marry your girlfriend?"

"I invited me to my apartment to save her life." I know that my dad will tell Mom, that I made a good decision when I moved in your apartment. He is a detective and my life is more important for him, Paul. My mom doesn't know that I have slept with boys. My dad didn't tell her. It was a secret between me and Dad.

"I am hungry Paul. We need to get ready for dinner."

I was ready and waited for Gina in the living room. Gina looked different when she came from her bedroom." You surprised me Gina. You look so good with clothes." She laughed.

"I need to turn the light off, before you see me naked Paul, because you may run away fast."

"Why don't you go and ask something the lady at front desk Gina?"

Gina walked to the front desk. The same man that was following her before, tried to speak with Gina again. I walked to the front desk. When he saw me he turned and walked to the elevator. I approached the front desk and said "Hi lady. My name is Paul Morgan. Gina is my girlfriend. She has problem with the man who tried to speak with her, but when he saw me, he went to the elevator. May I speak with Pedro?"

"He left and he will return on Monday, Mr. Morgan."

"I don't want to call the police, but if I see this man at the hotel or on the beach, I will call the police myself."

"Call me Maria, Mr. Morgan. The man stays in the hotel Mr. Morgan."

"He is selling drugs in the hotel Maria. You need to call and tell Pedro what I told you. Pedro knows well who I am. Do you understand Maria?"

"I understand Mr. Morgan. You don't want to call the police, because you don't want to create a problem for me and Pedro."

"You are a smart girl Maria." Gina and I left the front desk.

"You scared me, Paul."

"Why did I scare you Gina?"

"Have you been in an expensive hotel before, Paul? The people who work here, have big power. You need to listen to them."

"Who told you that you need to listen the people that you pay, Gina?"

"The people that work in the hotel are here to serve and help us. We pay them for that."

"My dad told me that I need to listen to the people who work in the hotel, because I will have a good service."

"I travel everywhere in the world and the people in hotels do what I want Gina."

"But you never stayed in expensive hotels like this Paul."

"This hotel isn't expensive Gina. Sometimes I have stayed in a five-star hotel where I paid one thousand or two thousand per night."

"Oh my God. You spent for four nights the money that Mom and Dad make in a month."

"How much do they make in a year Gina?"

"Both, no more one hundred thousand."

We were in the restaurant. I told Gina that she needs to order what she wants. I told her that I will pay for the dinner. I was surprised that Gina ordered different food, I think that fish and chicken are different food for dinner Gina. "I am hungry Paul." I laughed and told Gina that if Holly was here, she will have eaten ten percent of this food. "My mom told me that if I cut in half the money that I spend for food, I will be rich."

We laughed and I told her, "Your Mom loves you very much Gina. She wants to save your life. Now you are young and you spend a lot of energy. You will have problem after you become thirty years old Gina."

"Maybe I will stop to eat after I get to thirty Paul."

"I hope so Gina."

"Can you order another bottle wine of Paul?"

We finished dinner. We had a lot of food and wine Paul. I am feeling full. We stood up. I feel a little drunk Paul. We were in the apartment.

Gina kissed me and she told me "Can you get ready Paul? I will be waiting for you in my bedroom."

When I entered her bedroom, I heard Gina snoring. I woke up at 6:40am. For almost ten years I have been waking up between 6:30 and 7:00am. Sometimes Holly was disappointed with me and she wanted me to stay in bed late in the morning on Saturday and Sunday. She will tell me "Can you do something to make me feel good Paul?" Holly never said that she wanted sex. Holy didn't want to speak for sex.

I took cup of coffee and went on the terrace. I looked at the ocean. The water was flat and perfect for swimming. "Maybe tomorrow I need to wake up early and go for a swim", I told myself. If Holly was with me she will push me to go early on the beach. Holly wants to run for one hour early in the morning. I prefer to swim. My cell phone rang. It was Holly.

"How was last night boy?"

I was thinking of you Holly. I am sitting on the terrace and drinking coffee. If you were with me I would have been in the ocean swimming.

"You don't want something in bed Paul?"

"I don't Holly."

"Hey boy, do you remember Turks and Caicos?"

I told you in the morning that it was raining and we needed to stay in bed. After bed we were on the balcony. The weather was great. You laughed and told me that I lied to you, because I wanted you in bed. After fifteen minutes the weather changed and started to rain. You wanted to go back in bed, but I told you. I don't want to, because I lied to you and you wanted to drink your coffee.

"How is the weather Paul?"

"Perfect Holly."

"Good morning Paul." I turned my head and saw Gina.

"Good morning Gina."

"Who is Gina, Paul?"

She slept last night in my apartment Holly.

"Did she come with you from New York?"

"I met Gina yesterday on the beach. She was afraid to be alone, so I invited her to come with me."

"Did you sleep with her?"

"This is my privacy Holly. I didn't ask you what you did in Paris."

"May I speak with Gina?"

"Are you jealous Holly?"

"I am a little disappointed with you Paul. You never did that before."

"You never left me at the last minute before Holly. Come here Gina. Holly wants to speak with you." I gave her the cell phone.

"I am going to the beach. Don't answer if somebody calls me Gina."

"You don't want people to know where you are Paul. Nobody knows where I am."

"Does Holly know?"

"She knows."

When I left the apartment, Gina continued to speak with Holly. Gina gave me my cell phone when she came on the beach.

"I know Holly Gold, Paul."

"Did you meet or speak with Holly before Gina?"

"I didn't, but my dad had business with Holly Gold. It was three years ago. Dad spoke a lot for Holly Gold when he returned to Philadelphia. Did Holly tell you about my dad, Paul?"

"Holly meets a lot people and we never speak for our past and business. It is a rule, between us. I meet many people every day too. If Holly and I speak about them, we will never speak for us."

"My dad and Mom speak every day about thinks that happened in their jobs. Some time I was tired to listen to them."

"Did your Mom and Dad spoke about the people in their jobs too Paul?"

"I don't remember, because I was busy with my life and I didn't spend a lot time at home when Mom and Dad where together. I spent more time with my dad, Gina."

"You didn't ask me what I and Holly spoke about, Paul."

"I don't care."

"You may have a problem with Holly, because I slept in your apartment. Are you angry that I spoke with Holly?"

"Holly wanted to speak with you Gina. I gave Holly a chance to speak with you. Holly never gave me a chance to speak with her boyfriend in Paris."

"Holly doesn't have a boyfriend in Paris, Paul."

"Of course Gina. Your father is a detective. You are too. Have you been to Paris, Gina?"

"My father has a friend in Paris. We have been many times there. Paris is an expensive city and hotels are expensive. We slept in the apartment of my dad's friend. Do you sleep in your parents' friends' places, when you and your parents travel Paul?"

"My mom and dad didn't want to do that. Me too. Dad and I slept in my relatives houses in Ohio only."

"Where did your Mom sleep?"

"She didn't come with me and Dad when we went to Ohio. When Mom, Dad I went to see their friends, we always slept in hotels."

"My parents and I sleep in the houses or apartments of their friends. Sometimes my mom wasn't happy, but Dad told her that we saved money that way. Are you going to sleep with Holly in your friends' places, when you marry her?"

"I don't think so, because I will not marry Holly and I prefer hotels Gina. I have enough money."

"Holly has too Paul."

"Holly's boyfriend in Paris needs to think for her money."

"Holly was right when she told me that you are a bad man."

"Why do you stay with me Gina?"

"There are a lot free chairs and umbrellas on the beach."

"So I can sleep in your apartment Paul. Your apartment is too big for one person. Holly stays in a big apartment too."

"Did Holly tell you that she was with her boyfriend in an apartment Gina?"

"You want Holly to be with a man, because you are with me Paul."

"I am with you, because you had a problem yesterday and you wanted to be safe Gina. Is this correct?"

"You are right Paul. I was scared yesterday."

"How do you feel today Gina?"

"I am feeling good with you, Paul."

"Did you tell Holly that?"

"I didn't, but tomorrow I will tell her."

"I will not give you my cell phone Gina"

"Holly has my cell phone number. She asked for the number of the cell phone of my dad too. I gave her the number of my dad too."

"Did Holly give you the cell phone of her boyfriend, I want to speak with him, Gina?"

"He doesn't have time to speak with you, because he is busy with Holly, Paul."

"You forgot to tell me that he is busy in bed with Holly."

"You are a smart man, Paul. I didn't need to tell you that. You can figure it out yourself. Are you happy about that Paul?"

"Of course Gina. Now I am not afraid that somebody will kidnap or sale drugs to Holly. Holly's boyfriend will save her."

"He may do something in bed Paul."

"This is a problem for Holly. I didn't have this chance with you, Gina. You were sleeping when I came in the bedroom. It is good that Holly doesn't drink a lot of wine. Her boyfriend needs to be happy for that."

"I drank last night Paul. I don't usually drink, because I am twenty years old Paul. I don't know why I drunk last night. Maybe I wanted to have courage to go in bed with you, Paul."

"Did you tell Holly what happened last night Gina?"

"I told Holly and she laughed. Holly told me that you wouldn't go in bed with me because you love her and you stopped to chase women after you met her. Is it true?"

"Holly is right Gina, but after last Thursday I am not sure that I can't go to bed with another woman."

"I promised Holly that I can't have sex with you Paul. I have a lot of respect for her."

"Why?"

"How is that possible? You spoke with Holly for the first time, this morning. You didn't know Holly before."

"I have known Holly for three years, Paul. I was seventeen, when I watched interview with Holly. We watched the interview with Mom and Dad. I promised them that someday I will make a lot of money too." Mom told me that Holly isn't a serious woman and I don't need to listen to her. Dad told Mom that Holly works very hard to make money. He said "I will be happy if Gina works hard and make good money."

"When I finish with college, I want to work hard and make money too. I am not happy that Mom and Dad don't make good money."

"Why don't you tell them?"

"I can't tell them, because they are my parents."

"Did you tell Holly that you watched her interview three years ago?"

"She was very happy when I told her. Holly is a good woman. Why do you want to leave her, Paul?"

"Holly left me, Gina."

"This is not true. Holly went to Paris for business Paul. Holly wants to sign a contract for the next twenty or twenty-five years. When I finished my conversation with Holly, she wanted to tell you something, but you already left for the beach. You need to call and apologies to Holly."

"I don't think so Gina. I am going in the water."

"Do you want to come with me?"

"No, Paul. Holly may call. I want to be able to pick up the phone. I will tell her that you are in the water."

"Holly won't call me Gina. She will be waiting for me to call her. I know her well. You are on vacation Gina. You need to relax and enjoy. I am with you and nobody will be bothering you or trying to sale you drugs. I don't understand why are you thinking about Holly?"

"I don't know Paul. I am a little nervous. I will go to buy something to drink. Do you want a beer Paul?"

"It is too early for beer Gina. I will drink after six or seven o'clock. I never drink in the morning, at lunch or in the afternoon."

"My dad starts to drink after 10:00am, when we are on vacation."

"Does your father have belly?"

"He has and Mom jokes with him. She says "When Scott married me I felt one thing when we were in bed Gina. Now I feel two things. Scott's belly and something else."

"Maybe after thirty, my husband will feel two things too, if I don't stop to eat a lot."

"You are so funny Gina."

"Did I snore last night Paul?"

"Many people snore Gina."

"My mom joked with me that my husband will have to sleep in another bedroom, because of my snoring."

"You will need to buy a house with four bedrooms Gina. Two for your children, one for your husband and one for you Gina."

"Mom told me that I need to lose some pounds, if I want to sleep with my husband. Do you think that she is right Paul?"

"I don't know Gina. You need to speak with a doctor."

"Do your parents have bellies?"

"They don't. Dad is around one hundred seventy pounds. Mom is around one hundred forty-five pounds, and they are tall."

Gina went to buy something to drink, I went in the water. I noticed, that Gina spoke a lot for her parents. Holly never spoke for hers or any of her relatives. I have never met any of Holly's relatives. Holly told me that she didn't have parents for twelve years, but didn't tell me what happened with them. I assumed that they were death. If Holly calls me tomorrow, I will ask for her parents, even if it is painful for her. She forgot that I am Paul Morgan. The family name Morgan is very popular around the world. The Gold family name isn't. Maybe Holly's great grandfather had a gold mine and came from Klondike, where people tried to find gold. Maybe Holly don't want to speak for her family, because she didn't want me to know that her family has tons of gold in the banks. I laughed at my joke. I felt good thinking of Holy while I was swimming. She hurt me, but I feel that I still love her. I will have to stop thinking about Holly, if I decide to separate with her. I am not sure what I will tell my dad if I decide to leave Holly. My mom hates Holly. She has lived with my dad for thirty-five years. Mom know well Dad.

I haven't checked how many messages Mom has left me, but I don't want to call her. For the first time in my life I didn't call my mom after she called and she left a message. I will check my cell phone when I return to my chair. It may be good, if Gina speaks with Mom. Mom will think that Gina is my new girlfriend. The problem is that Gina speaks a lot and she will tell Mom where I am with her. I don't want Mom to know where I am. I returned back to the chair. Gina gave me a cold water bottle.

"I didn't ask you what you like, so I brought you some water Paul."

"It is OK Gina. Why do you talk all the time Gina?"

"I love to talk to people Paul. Sometimes Mom tells me to shut up, because a fly may enter my mouth since it is always open. My dad laughed and told her that it may work out good, because I am hungry all the time and he doesn't need to buy lunch for me." Gina and I laughed.

"Do you think that we are a funny family Paul?'

"You are Gina. I didn't remember my mom and dad joking, when we were together."

"You are joking all the time Paul."

"I started to joke after I left them."

"How old were you?"

"Twenty-three. Mom didn't want me to move out, but Dad supported me."

"Who paid your bills?"

"I paid everything. It was a deal between Dad and me. I didn't need to leave the apartment of my mom and dad, because the apartment has three bedrooms."

"Why did you leave?"

"I wanted to build my own life. Mom was giving me advice all the time. I told her that I am not a child and I know what to do". She told me "You live in my apartment and you need to listen to me. I pay the bills for the apartment".

"I had enough money so I left after two weeks. Mom cried. Dad was happy. You are the same as Holly."

"She was younger that you when she left her parents."

"How did you know that Gina?"

"Holly told me yesterday, but she didn't want to speak about them."

"I am scared to think that someday I need to leave Mom and Dad, Paul. I depend so much on my parents."

"If you want to make good money Gina, one day you will have them."

"Why do you want to live with your parents? Do you plan to marry?"

"I love them. I will buy a big house and I will live there with my husband, children, Mom and Dad."

"What If your husband doesn't want your parents to live with you in the same house?"

"I won't marry him. I think that Holly will like to live with your father. Holly told me that she loves Henry. Is that your father's name?"

"Yes, Gina. Holly told you a lot for her and my family."

"Holly wanted to speak for herself, your Mom and Dad, Paul. I think that Dad can't separate with Mom Gina. Holly doesn't have a chance to live with me, my mom and dad, because of my mom. Maybe your Mom will divorce your father."

"Can you think for your family Gina?"

"I will go to buy something to drink Gina."

"Looks like you want to be alone Paul. You are thinking now for your Mom, Dad and Holly."

"Of course, you are a daughter of a detective. You know what I think. Frankly, I didn't think for them." I knew that when I go in the water, Gina will call Holy and tell her what we spoke about.

I am not ready to speak with Holly if she calls me. I will be ready to speak tomorrow. I want to put my cell phone in my hotel apartment safe box and get a break from everything. I know that Holly will call Gina's cell phone and she will like to speak with me, but I can't speak with Holly today. Tomorrow is Monday. I usually make many decisions on Monday. I left Mom and Dad on Monday. I started to work at Roy's company on Monday. I bought Holly's apartment on Monday. Maybe tomorrow I will tell Holly, that I can't see her anymore. Doesn't matter that she will cry and I will have a problem with my dad.

CHAPTER 3

The alarm clock rang. I set it last night for 5:30 am. It was Monday. I made a plan yesterday. I needed to wake up early. I need to be on the beach at 6.00 am. I will call Holly when I walk on the beach. Gina wanted to stay and speak with me last night, but I told her that I was tired and I was in bed by 9:30pm. The whole day she wanted to ask me, why I didn't want to speak with Holly. Gina tried to give me her cell phone when Holly called, but I didn't get take the phone. I took my cell phone and left the apartment. I was in the hotel lobby when my phone rang. It was Holly.

"Hi Holly."

"Why didn't you want to speak with me all day yesterday, Paul?"

"This was yesterday Holly. Today is a new day and I want to speak with you, but I don't want to speak for marriage."

"What is the difference between yesterday and today Paul?"

"I wasn't ready to speak with you yesterday. I needed to think."

"Are you ready to marry me today Paul?"

"I was ready and I bought an engagement ring, but you went to Paris. I don't understand what you want for me Holly. You are in Paris. I am in Puerto Rico."

"I am wearing your engagement ring."

"I gave it to Judy, Holly."

"I bought a new one this morning and I put it of my finger. My friends asked me, who bought the ring. I told them that you bought it and you asked me to marry you. I said yes Paul."

"This is a funny story Holly."

37

"It isn't a story Paul. I will marry you for new year."

"Do you marry me, Paul?"

"Oh my God. Say yes Paul."

"I want to know more for your family, before I say yes Holly."

"My family is so rich Paul, but I don't want to speak about them. When I return on Sunday to New York, I will tell you for my family, but you must say yes. Deal Paul?"

"Deal Holy, I am saying yes. Are you happy now?"

"I am Paul. Hey boy, how was last night with Gina?"

"You need to ask Gina, because I will lie to you Holly."

"Did you order flowers for her?"

"I don't know where the flower shop is here, Holly. I didn't ask you, if your boyfriend bought flowers for you."

"He left me after he saw the engagement ring. Paul, I need to tell you about Marcel and Giles. I don't want your Mom to tell you."

"My mom doesn't know who Marcel or Giles are, Holly."

"This morning Marcel was in my apartment. I was taking a shower. I wanted to ask Marcel where should we go to choose my clothes. I heard that Marcel saying to somebody "When we receive the money, we will do what you want Miss. Morgan".

When Marcel saw me he said "Holly is here Miss. Morgan and he hung up".

"I didn't ask Marcel who was Miss. Morgan."

"Do you think that it was Janet?"

"Mom knows that you are in Paris, but how does she know Marcel? Mom has never been in Paris with you Holly."

"Why didn't you ask Marcel?'

"I have a problem with Marcel. He was my boyfriend six years ago. Marcel introduced me to Giles. I understood that Marcel listens to Giles.

"And you jumped in bed with Giles."

"I never asked you how much money and how many flowers you sent to your girlfriends in the past, Paul. If I knew that I will meet you, I would have kept my virginity for you Paul. Are you happy now Paul?"

"Do you have problem with Giles, Holly?"

"I have, so that is why tomorrow I will meet with his wife. It was wrong when I slept with Giles. He was married and with two children Paul. Marcel is single."

"Why are you telling me now about Marcel and Giles?"

"I know that Janet will tell you. It is better that I tell you."

"Why didn't you tell me before?"

"I didn't tell you, because, you and we agreed not to speak for our past Paul."

"What do you think Paul?"

"You are right Holly. It isn't good to speak for your ex-girlfriends or boyfriends."

"I want to speak for business with you Paul. You have a lot of experience, because you sign many contracts with your clients. I signed a contract with my agent but I didn't understand everything that was written in the contract. I am not a lawyer Paul. Do you think that I will have a problem with Giles, because I want to send the contract to my lawyer before I sign? Giles told me that my lawyer doesn't need to read the contract, because is simple. It is strange that I have been in Paris for four days now but Giles never showed me the contract. We have met every. I asked myself, why am I in Paris? When I left New York, I thought that I will finish on Friday or Saturday. Today is Monday, Paul. I think that Marcel and Giles are not being honest with me."

"Maybe they want to sleep with you, before you sign the contract. I thought about that on Sunday and on Monday I bought the ring. This morning and told Marcel and Giles that you are in Paris, but you staying in another hotel. You don't want to meet Marcel and Giles. After I told them that, I saw that two men followed me everywhere. Marcel and Giles told me that this was for my safety."

"Are you afraid for your life Holly?"

"I am little disappointed with Marcel and Giles. I spoke with Scott. He is Gina's father. I met him in New York. He was in charge of my security. My agent was afraid for my life. I spoke with Scott yesterday and today."

"What did Scott tell you?"

"He advised me, what to do if I have problem with somebody. Marcel and Giles are somebody, Holly. I am not sure I can believe them. I am so sorry Paul. You are on vacation and a young girl is waiting for you. I will call you tomorrow boy. I am kissing you."

I returned to the hotel. Gina was on balcony and she was drinking coffee.

"Did you spoke with Holly, Paul?"

"Yes, I did."

"I spoke with my dad last night. He told me that Holly will have problem with Marcel."

"How does Scott know Marcel?"

"I told you that my father has a friend in Paris. He is a detective too."

"Does Holly uses drugs?"

"I never saw her Gina, but Holly travels a lot."

"You don't use drugs Paul?"

"I don't, but if you don't believe me, Scott will come on Wednesday. He will investigate me. Scott needs to be sure that I don't use drugs, but I am not your boyfriend Gina. Scott doesn't need to look into my life."

"My dad need to be sure that you don't use drugs because you are Holly's boyfriend. She is a friend of my dad."

"Are you sure that Scott don't use drugs Gina?"

"Of course Paul, and you stop to joking, because drugs aren't a joke. Many people die after they use drugs."

"Many people die when they drive a car. Maybe we need to stop to drive cars. If people walk they will get more exercise and they will lose more calories Gina. Everybody will be tin and fit. Do you think that I am right Gina?"

"You are joking with a serious problem Paul."

"The drug isn't a problem Gina. The people are problem, because they buy and use the drugs. The people spend money to kill themselves. It is so crazy Gina. I don't understand people who use drugs."

"Maybe cars too Paul."

"The car is different. I was joking when I compared the drugs with the cars. I will get ready and go to the beach Gina. We will continue our conversation there."

I was in the water. I saw that Gina waived her hand. I thought for her. Gina want to be with me, because she is feeling safe. Gina knows that nobody will touch her if she stays with me. The question is what I want from her. I understood that Gina wouldn't sleep with me. When Gina moved in my hotel apartment, I wanted her in bed, because Holly left me. Now I don't want to sleep with Gina. We had a chance to have sex the first night, I didn't know who Gina was. She was happy that she moved in a safe place. The bed was good place for both. Now Gina and I think that the bed isn't a good place, but Gina and I want to be together. When I return on the chair I will ask Gina, if she want to leave me and stay far away from me. I knew Gina's answer, but I will ask her. I sat on the chair.

"Do you want to go away from me Gina?"

"Why Paul?"

"Can you answer my question Gina?"

"I want to stay with you and your hotel apartment. When Mom and Dad come, I will move in my hotel room."

"Do you have more questions Paul?"

"I don't and I am happy that you want to stay with me Gina. The sex isn't important for our relationship Gina."

"Are you afraid that Holly will know Paul?"

"Holly is my ex-girlfriend Gina. She wants to return in my life again, but I don't know if Holly and I have a future. Now many things stay between me and Holly."

"Your Mom is number one Paul."

"She is Gina, but whole my life I have listened to my dad. He was close to me all my life. I don't remember that Mom was close to me my whole life. I remember that Mom was not there all the time."

When I was in sixth grade I asked my dad, why my friends were dropped in school by their Moms? "You are a man Paul. I am a man and I am dropping you." My dad didn't want to speak a lot. He wanted to listen to me. I told him everything that happened at school or when I played with my friends. Sometimes Mom told me" Your father is tired to listen to your stories Paul". My father told her "I am not tried to listen to my son, Janet. I will be tired if I have more children."

"Why didn't you have brothers or sisters?"

"I don't know Gina. I never asked my parents."

"I am alone too Paul. I asked Mom and she told me that Mom and Dad wanted, but Mom had problem."

"Maybe I didn't ask, because I am a man Gina."

"I will ask Holly, if you are a man Paul."

"You have will have a chance to understand, if I am man to-night Gina."

"First I will ask Holly. I don't want to try before I am certain."

"I know that Holly will tell you that I am a man, but you need to choose another man, because she wants to marry me."

"What are going to do, if I want to marry you too after we have sex Paul?"

"I don't know Gina. It is better if we don't have sex." We laughed. I was surprised that Gina ate fruits for lunch.

"You aren't hungry Gina!"

"I am, but I will try to lose pounds."

"Did Holly tell you what you need to eat?"

"Holly is a model. I need to listen to her if I want to be a model too."

"Maybe when you are model, you will get me in bed Gina."

"I don't know Paul. I will have a lot of men around me. I am young and I will prefer young man."

"Oh my God, I understood why Holly wants to be with me and she wants to marry me. Because she is thirty years old."

"You are right Paul. Holly doesn't want to miss the last train."

"I will ask Holly tomorrow."

"You will be stupid if you ask Holly that Paul. Why ask Holly, if you don't plan to marry her?"

"You are right Gina. Holly is beautiful and rich. She doesn't have problem to marry anybody. Holly wants to marry me, because she loves me, Gina."

"Finally, you have a light in your head Paul."

"Do you think that I am stupid Gina?"

"I don't think that Holly wants to live with a stupid man. Maybe I am the last train."

"If you think that you are the last stupid train for Holly, that is OK for me Paul. Tomorrow I will tell Holly that she need to look for new a train in Paris. You are old and stupid train for her. Are you happy now Paul?"

"I am happy that you told me the truth Gina. I forgot that I am thirty-three."

"It is OK for Dad, because he married Mom, when he was thirty-seven. You have four more years Paul. I don't want my wife to look like my mom. Holly is different and she is a good choice Gina. Don't tell Holly that I am the last train."

"Are you joking or you are serious Paul?"

"It is my problem, because I don't know when I tell the truth, when I am joking Gina.

"You will never stop to joke, but I will tell Holly to leave you."

"Do you want to be with me in bed with me after Holly leaves me Gina?"

"I told you that you are an old train."

"I understood you Gina. I need to keep Holly for me."

"You are right Paul. I am going in the water, but I don't want the old train to follow me."

Gina went to the water. I lay and laughed on the chair. I had a very good time with Gina, she makes me happy when I speak with her. I don't regret that I got her in my hotel apartment. I can't have sex with Gina, but I will have a good time with her. Gina returned.

"May I go in the water now Gina?"

"I won't follow you Paul. So many questions Paul."

"I have one more.

"Are you going to follow me tonight?"

"Do you have a dream to be somewhere with me, Paul? I don't think so Paul."

"If don't you want to come with me for dinner tonight Gina, then I am happy that I will save money."

"Can I take my words back Paul? I want to come with you for dinner, because I will have good time with you. And you know I will save money, because you will pay my bill. Do you think that I am honest with you, Paul?"

"You are Gina. I don't care for money. I don't want another girl to spend my money. You have chance to continue with her in bed Paul."

"I don't want Holly to know, because you will tell her."

"You are right. I will tell Holly that you were in bed with a woman. Maybe I am stupid, because I know Holly for three years, but I spoke with her for the first time yesterday. If Mom was here she will tell me that it isn't my job to tell Holly what you are doing."

"What does your father tell you?"

"Detective will tell you that you need to know what other people do. Dad saw one of my mom's friends was with another man. He told her husband and they divorced. Mom didn't speak with Dad two or three months. It is good that Holly is my girlfriend. I will tell her what we talk about, but I will never tell Holly, if you are with another girl Paul. I don't want you to separate with Holly. Holly must know what kind of man you are. I don't need to tell her. I like you Paul. You spend time and money for me, but I don't want to hurt Holly. You were ready Saturday night Paul."

"I was Gina. I didn't think for Holly on Saturday night. I was ready to be with any woman in bed."

"Holly told me that you changed your life after you met her."

"It was hard for me Gina in the first three, four months. I didn't believe that I needed to be with Holly every night. I never had a long sexual relationship with a girl."

"Why Paul?"

"I don't know Gina. Maybe I waited to meet Holly. After I met Holly I was not interested to meet another woman. I had a chance Saturday night, but you were drunk."

"Do you want to go in the water Paul?"

"No, I am ready to go."

We left the beach at 6:15pm. We were in the restaurant at 8:00pm. Gina ordered light dinner and she didn't drink wine.

"I will save money Gina."

"You are rich, because Holly doesn't eat a lot Paul."

"No, it is because she paid when we went out Gina. Holly never counted how much she spent when we were together."

"Do you want to speak with Holly tomorrow Paul?"

"I will speak with her every day, if she wants to. Holly is coming back to New York on Sunday. I feel that something isn't right because she is staying longer in Paris than she planned to."

"Why don't you tell her to come back to New York?"

"I will tell Holly tomorrow morning. I will try to find out, why she is extending her stay when Giles isn't showing her the contract she went to sign. Maybe your father knows something Gina."

"You ask him when he comes here Paul. You know that Dad will ask you for Holly. You need to be ready with your answer Paul."

"Why do I need to answer to your father?"

"Because you are boyfriend of Holly's. If something happens in Paris with Holly, the policemen will come and ask you, where you have been."

"I am with you Gina. Do you thing that I need to lie to the policemen?"

"Dad will tell them that you were with me Paul, but this is a stupid conversation. Holly is OK in Paris. You are Ok with me in Puerto Rico. Aren't you Paul?"

"I am feeling good with you Gina and I want to stay with you, because I will have an alibi. If a policemen ask me "Have you been with Gina in bed?" I will tell them that this is my privacy and I need to speak with my lawyer before I answer." Gina and I laughed.

"My dad told me that sometimes people need to lie to save their life. I believe my dad, because he is a detective."

We left the restaurant at 10:30pm. On the way to the elevator I asked Gina "Do you think that I need to stay in your bedroom for my alibi?"

"I will tell them that you were Paul."

"You will lie to the policemen?"

"Of course Paul, but Holly will be happy that I didn't sleep with you."

"Good night Paul."

Gina entered in her bedroom. I walked in my bedroom. I thought about what Gina told me "I believe my dad, because he is a detective". If I tell Holly that she needs to return to New York, she will ask Scott. Holly won't believe me. She will believe Scott, because he is a detective. I have to figure out what Holly is thinking tomorrow. Holly called me at 8:00 o'clock in the morning.

"Do you think that you are save in Paris, Holly?"

"Scott told me that I don't have anything to be afraid of. If I have a problem, Scott will come to Paris from Puerto Rico. Don't be scared for my life Paul. I called you, because I will meet Estelle at 4:00 o'clock in the afternoon."

"How is your life with Gina?"

We have fun time Holly. We are joking a lot. Scott is coming to your hotel tomorrow.

"Where is Gina staying?"

"Gina needs to decide Holly. If Gina leaves my apartment I will be happy. If she stays in my apartment I will be happy too. Gina isn't the problem for me, Holly. You are my problem, because I am afraid for your life."

"I will call you on Thursday Paul" and Holly hang up. I understood that Holly didn't want to speak with me for her safety. Holly believes in Scott. I wasn't happy when Gina asked me "Do you have problem with Holly, Paul?"

"Holly believes your father and Holly didn't want to speak for her safety with me."

"That isn't right Paul. You know well Holly. She must believe you, doesn't matter that my dad is a detective. I know that my dad will try to keep Holly close to him, because Holly will pay him good."

"How do you know that Gina?"

"He is my dad and I know that he wants to be rich. He told me" I will be rich someday Gina and I will give you a lot money to you to live good. I want you to be proud of me, Gina." My mom laughed and told him "Gina is proud that she has a father, who is a stupid detective."

"Are you proud Gina?"

"We laughed, but I love Dad, Paul."

"The problem is that your father tells Holly that she doesn't have problem in Paris. Holly didn't want to speak with me, what the problem is. She hung up the phone Gina. Holly wants to marry me, but she doesn't want to speak with me."

"Do you think that Holly is right Gina?"

"No Paul. My dad is a detective, but Holly must listen you."

"Do you think that Scott is manipulating Holly for money?"

"Scott is my dad and I don't want to take a side Paul. If you think that Dad will do something wrong, you need to tell Holly."

Gina and I were on the beach, but we didn't speak. After we returned from the beach, Gina entered her room. I knocked and asked Gina, if she was ready for dinner. Gina told me that she wants to stay in her bedroom. I was in the balcony drinking coffee. It was 7:45 in the morning. Gina came to me. She kissed me and said" Thank you so much Paul. I will be going to my hotel room."

"Is anything wrong between me and you Gina?"

"No Paul. You are a good man. I will remember this time when I was with you in your hotel apartment."

"Are you coming to the beach?"

"See you there Paul."

"Are your parents coming to the beach?"

"I spoke with Mom. They will come to see me on the beach. If you don't want to speak with my parents, I will tell them."

"I don't have a problem with your parents Gina. Who are they for me? You your Mom and Dad will leave on Friday. I will never see you after Friday."

"You will see my father Paul."

"Why do I need to see Scott?"

"I asked my dad for Holly. He told me that Holly is OK. I understood that Dad lied to me. Dad changed his voice when I asked for Holly."

"Did you speak with Holly today?"

"I will speak with her tomorrow."

"Tell her that she must return to New York. I feel that somebody will kidnap Holly, Paul."

"Holly doesn't have enemies in Paris, Gina. Marcel and Giles are her enemies. I asked Dad, who was with Holly at the hotel. My dad told me that Holly met with Marcel and Giles at the hotel where Holly stays. Scott didn't want to tell me more about them."

"Do you think that Marcel and Giles are lovers of Holly?"

"Holly slept with them, but many years ago."

"My dad told me the same story Paul. When I asked Scott if Holly depended on Marcel or Giles, he told me that they depend on her. Scott lied to me Paul. Marcel and Giles must do what Holly wants, if they depend on her. Marcel and Giles are keeping Holly in Paris for something. I think that they are waiting for somebody to give them money. Marcel and Giles will kidnap Holly, after they get the money."

"They will need to kill Holly, Gina. If they need to kill her, they can't meet with her at the hotel. The policemen will arrest them, if something happens with Holly."

"Why doesn't Scott tell Holly?"

"Scott will investigate what happened with Holly and try to save her Holly. Scott will be a hero and Scott will get good money from Holly."

"Scott is your father Gina. You are imagining this."

"The future will tell who is right Paul. You don't tell my story to my dad. I want my dad make to money, but I don't want Marcel and Giles to hurt Holly. That is why I told you this story. If we don't speak about Holly, it will be good for both of us Paul."

In the afternoon, Gina's parents came to the beach. Gina introduced me to Scott and Cindy. "You are beautiful Cindy" I told her.

"Finally, a man told me that I am good looking."

"Do you think that Paul is right Scott?"

"Paul was with Gina. Maybe Paul wants to be with you now. This is a great idea honey."

"Are you jealous Gina?"

"No Mom. Paul is a free man."

"He isn't Gina. Paul has a girlfriend. Her name is Holly. Holly is in Paris with Marcel and Giles."

"If Mom wants to be with Paul, I will support her."

"I am her husband Gina."

"I won't tell Mom, that she need to divorce you Dad. Mom wants to have a good time like do."

"Did you sleep with Paul, Gina?"

"What is your problem if I have slept with Paul, Dad? I am twenty years old."

"Isn't Holly's your friend Gina."

"I spoke with Holly, but I never met her. Maybe Holly is happy that I was in bed with Paul."

"I will ask Holly."

"This is a good idea Dad, but you need to tell Holly that Mom wants Paul too."

"Are you going to tell Holly that?"

That was funny. I and Cindy laughed.

"Why aren't you laughing Dad? Of course you never laugh. You are a serious detective."

"Why do you hate me Gina?"

"I will hate you if something happens with Holly. You keep her in Paris. I spoke with Holly she said that she has business with Marcel and Giles."

"Holly will never make business with them, Dad. You know that well, but I don' like to speak for Holly, Dad. You have business with Holly. You will make good money, aren't you?"

"I don't want to discuss my business with Holly, Gina. Paul doesn't give information how much money he makes from his clients. Paul makes millions of dollars per year, but he never tells how much he makes."

"This is business Gina. I am speaking with you for a first time Scott. How do you have this information about me?"

"I am a detective Paul. You are boyfriend of Holly and Holly is wearing your engagement ring."

"Are you going to marry Holly, Paul?"

"It isn't your business what me and Holly will do in future Scott."

"Maybe you are right Paul. I didn't need to tell you what I know about you, but I think that we need to be friends, because nobody knows what will happen with Holly in Paris. Marcel sales drugs. He is Holly's friend."

"Do you think that Holly use drugs Scott?"

"I don't know everything about Holly's past, but Holly and

Marcel are longtime friends."

I didn't tell Scott that Holly slept with Marcel. If Holly told Scott, that isn't good for Holly. I felt a little nervous. I saw that Scott looked at me. "I am so sorry, but I need to leave" and I took my things.

"Did you know that Holly slept with Marcel, Paul?"

"Marcel didn't sleep with me. I didn't meet or speak with Marcel, Scott."

"You gave me good information Paul. I thought that you are a friend of Marcel and Giles. They are with Holly in Paris."

"Do you know Giles, Paul?"

"I didn't answer."

I left the beach. At this Moment I hated Holly. Scott is her detective, Holly didn't need to tell Scott, who I am. Oh my God. I am so stupid. I was with Gina for the last five days. Maybe Scott got my information, from Gina. She understood that Scott used her. Gina knows that Scott isn't honest with Holly. Gina understood that something will happen with Holly and Scott will make money. Gina tried to open my eyes. She wanted me to get Holly to return to New York. Gina didn't want to tell me everything, because Scott is her father. I was in the lobby. I saw Pedro. He looked at me.

"Are you OK Mr. Morgan?"

"I had problem with Gina's father on the beach Pedro"

"Scott is a detective and he wanted to know, if I will marry Gina. I am not ready to marry Pedro."

"Thanks so much Mr. Morgan. I need to be careful with Gina's father. Scott will be looking if somebody is selling drugs here."

"You are right Pedro. Scott has investigated, if I use and sale drugs."

"Scott is stupid Mr. Morgan. You are a businessman."

"It is hard to tell that to Scott, Pedro "

"Gina is a good girl Mr. Morgan."

"She is Pedro. Hey Pedro, I need a taxi. I want to go to the old city."

"What time Mr. Morgan?"

"At 5:00pm. I hope I will feel better after that. Call me Paul, Pedro."

"The taxi will be here at 5:00 o'clock Paul. I will give you a map of the old city."

I was in the lobby at 5:00, ready to leave. Pedro gave me the map. I saw Gina Cindy and Scott. Cindy came to me and said" I am so sorry Paul. It is hard to control a stupid detective." I laughed.

"It is OK Cindy."

"Where are you going?"

"To the old city of San Juan. The taxi is waiting for me."

"Scott has a rental car. You don't need to get a taxi. You will save money Paul."

"I felt better for one hour, because I didn't see and speak with Scott, Cindy."

"You are right Paul."

I entered the taxi. I walked and shopped in the old San Juan. I understood that if I want to see well the old San Juan, I had to come tomorrow too. It was good idea, because I didn't have to see Scott. I know that Scott will try to find me on the beach. Gina knows that I love to stay for a long time in the beach. I will surprise Scott. Frankly, I had a good time when I was with Gina. Cindy is OK too. But to see Scott's belly on the beach isn't good idea. The belly of Scott isn't the problem. Scott's mouth is the problem. It was 7:30pm. I decided to eat. I chose a restaurant. I sat outside. I ordered white wine and fish. I ate. I heard the voice of Scott.

"May I sit next to you Paul?"

I turned my head. Cindy and Gina are better looking Scott.

"You want to look at my face when you speak with me, so will be better if you sit on front of me. Two beautiful flowers will sit next to me and one dung on front to me." Cindy laughed and applauded me.

"Finally, you told him the truth Paul."

"I want to sit on another table Mom."

"Sit with me Gina. I will pay for the dinner. Scott will save money. I work with people and make money. Scott investigates people and he doesn't have enough time to make money. Do you think that I am right Scott?"

"Do you have fifteen million dollars Paul?"

"I never counted my millions Scott, but I think that I have more."

Cindy sat next to me and asked me "Will you marry me, Paul?"

"You need to divorce Scott first, Cindy."

"Gina will not be happy if you divorce him. You are right Paul. I wanted to divorce him ten years ago, but Gina stopped me. Now is too late to divorce with Scott. Sit down Gina."

"I will Mom."

"You to Scott I told him. Holly told me that she has a good relationship with Henry, but Janet doesn't love her. Do you love Holly, Paul?"

"I have two beautiful women sitting next to me Scott. I prefer to love them. I don't know what Holly is doing in Paris."

"Maybe she is busy with Marcel and Giles, Paul. For that reason, I want to be with Cindy and Gina, Scott. Gina is young and single. Cindy is old and married. Cindy will teach me what I need to do with Gina, Scott."

"Cindy is my wife Paul."

"I will marry Holly, Scott. You must think before you open your mouth. If you use your mouth to eat is better. You don't speak Scott. What do you like for dinner Scott.? You don't look for price. I will pay, doesn't matter that we don't have a pleasant conversation? I forgot what I said to you Scott. You are the detective of my future wife."

"Holly told me that she will marry you when she returns to New York."

"Do you know when Holly will return to New York, Scott?"

"On Sunday afternoon Paul."

"What, If Holly doesn't sign the contract?"

"Holly is sure that she will sign the contract Paul."

"I don't believe that Scott. Somebody is keeping Holly in Paris. I don't know why. You need to know, because Holly didn't want to speak with me yesterday. Maybe you want to make problem between Holly and me."

"I spoke with Holly about her problem in Paris. We didn't speak about you or your family Paul."

"You are lying to me Scott."

"How did you know that Henry loves Holly, if you didn't ask Holly? I am sure that Holly wouldn't tell you, if you didn't ask her. Did you ask Holly where I live?"

"In her apartment, but you keep your own apartment too Paul."

"Can you tell me where my mom and dad live?"

"In Florida."

"Why did you need this information Scott?"

"Me, my mom and dad aren't in Paris to investigate us. Maybe you want to know how rich my family is, because you want me marry Gina."

"That sounds good Paul."

"Shut up Mom."

"Paul will marry Holly."

"You need to think for you Gina."

"Holly is doing well in Paris. I thought that Dad is greedy, but I didn't know that you are too Mom."

"I am thinking about your future Gina. Paul is a good man. If you marry Paul, you will be rich too."

"Oh my God. Paul will never marry me, Mom. He is joking."

"Are you joking Paul?"

"Of course Cindy. I don't have future with Gina."

"You don't want Gina, because I am a detective."

"What should I tell Holly, if I want to marry Gina, Scott? I know, you will tell me that Holly has been with many men in bed and Gina is a better choice for me. Did you speak with my mom, because she thinks like you Scott? If you didn't I will give you her cell phone number."

"I have Janet's number, but I didn't speak with her. If I need, I will speak with her."

"Do you have Henry's phone number Scott?"

"I don't need the phone number of Henry, Paul."

"Of course Scott. Henry loves Holly. Janet hates Holly. Maybe you want to know how much my mom hates Holly. If you tell Janet that I was with Gina, she will tell you that Gina is better for me. Mom doesn't want me to marry Holly. Holly told you everything that happened last week Scott. You have a lot information. I hope that you will help Holly to return to New York."

Everything depend on what Holly wants Paul. Holly wants to marry Paul, Dad."

"How do you know that Gina?"

"Holly told me. She paid you Dad."

"Did you know how much Holly paid me?"

"Holly didn't want to tell me."

"It isn't your business to ask Holly, Gina. You need to take care of your life. You don't need to know what I do. My money is your money Gina. Many times I told you that someday I will be rich Gina."

"I am sorry Dad."

Cindy laughed. "I have heard that for twenty years. Maybe I will have to hear that for twenty more years Scott. Are you going to divorce me when you are rich Scott?'

"We will count together the money Cindy."

"I don't have a chance to divorce daughter." We laughed.

I paid for the dinner and we took Scott's car. We didn't speak in the car. We were in the lobby. We took the elevator. The elevator stopped first at Gina's floor. I told her good night.

"See you tomorrow on the beach Paul."

"I don't know what time I will come on the beach Gina. I need to speak with Holly."

"Say hi to her from me."

"I will Gina." She kissed me and exited the elevator.

"Why did you kiss Paul, Gina?"

"I love Paul, Dad."

Cindy and Scott told me good night and they exited the elevator. I entered my hotel apartment. I was alone. I never been alone when I was on vacation before. I was seventeen when my dad told me that I am a big man and I needed to go with my friends on vacation. My mom didn't agree. My dad told me "She is a woman, you don't listen to her." This was the first time when Dad told Mom "Shut up Janet. You needed to take care of Paul, when he was a little boy. You didn't do it. You were busy with your life. Let Paul to do, what he wants to do. Did your lover leave you and now you have time to look at what Paul is doing?"

My mom didn't answer Dad. After that Mom wanted to give me advice, when Dad wasn't with us. After eighteen, I decided everything for my life. Dad told me "Freedom is responsibility Paul. You must think before you do something. I don't want you to drink before you become twenty-one. I don't want you to use drugs and I don't want the policemen to arrest you." I started to drink after twenty-one, doesn't matter that I was on vacation with my friends and Dad wouldn't see me. My friends drank. I didn't. I love my dad, because he knew, what to tell me when I was growing up. I know that I am this Paul, because Dad did everything for me. He was a god teacher. I was a good student. I didn't remember what Mom did when I was growing up. I remember that Mom missed two months when I was six years old. Oh my God, this happened twenty-seven years ago and I remember it.

I woke up at 6:35 in the morning. I was in the bed. I decided not to go to the beach, but go to the old San Juan. I will leave the hotel after 8:30am. I took my cell phone to check my messages. I had many messages, but five were from Mom and one was from Judy. I erased Mom's messages. Judy left me a short massage "Call me Paul". It was early to call her in the office. I called Judy's cell phone.

"What are you doing, I am so happy that you called me Paul?"

"I am OK, Judy. I am in bed."

"Is Holly with you?"

"This is personal Judy. Maybe Holly will not be happy, if I tell you what she is doing."

"You are right Paul. I asked you, because Marcel called me and he asked where you are staying in Paris. I told Marcel that you are with Holly. Marcel told me that you didn't stay in the same hotel where Holly was. He didn't see you with Holly too."

"She is busy and I prefer to stay in another hotel Judy. Holly called me and we met somewhere in Paris or she comes to my hotel."

"How did you know Marcel, Judy?"

"Marcel was with Holly at our office. I didn't tell you that Marcel was in your office, when Holly spoke with Roy?"

"Did Marcel asked you for me?"

"Do you think that Marcel wanted to know who you are Paul?"

"Holly told him who I am Judy, but if somebody wants to see my office, I will not be happy. I have many documents in the office, but it is OK, because I will return to the office on Monday."

"When you left on Friday I locked your office. You forgot to locked Paul. I know that you were busy and you thought for Holly. You are a good friend Judy."

"Did my mom call the office?"

"Roy called me and he told me that he was with your Mom and Dad in Miami Beach."

"Did Roy ask for me?"

"He didn't."

"See you Monday, Judy."

"I will be happy to see you Paul" and she hang up.

I left the hotel at 8:30am. I walked and look for a taxi. I didn't ordered taxi from the front deck, because Scott will ask the people at front deck, if they have seen me. Scott will be nervous the whole day, because he won't know where I am. The taxi dropped me in the old San Juan. It was 9:30am. Holly didn't call me. Maybe she was waiting for me to call her. I called.

"Did you want to hear me Paul?"

"If I was with you in bed would have been better Holly. I don't know for how many days I didn't have sex."

"Maybe you didn't think for sex, because you were busy."

"Why did you take Marcel to my office?"

"He wanted to see where you work. I called you to ask, but you didn't pick up your phone. Marcel told me that your cell phone was on your office desk."

"I don't understand, last week Marcel, this week Scott wanted to know who I am."

"Why did you give Scott the phone number of Mom?"

"Scott wanted to know her phone number. I told Scott that I have problem with Janet. I didn't tell Scott that she hates me."

"How much did you pay Scott?"

"Fifty thousand."

"It is a lot of money Holly."

"My life is more expensive Paul."

"Did Scott ask you to pay him fifty thousand?"

"He told me that I need to pay this money, because he will be on call if there is any emergence in Paris, and I need his help. Scott asked me a lot for about your family. Maybe Scott asked me, because you were with Gina. He loves her very much."

"Scott needs to love that much Cindy, Holly."

"Scott loves Cindy too Paul."

"Does Scott love me Holly?"

"I love you boy."

"Of course Holly. I don't want a man to love me."

"Henry loves you, Paul."

"He is my dad Holly. Does your father love you?"

"I don't want to speak for my parents Paul."

"Do you have parents Holly, because we never spoke about them?"

"You know Mom and Dad."

"I fell Henry like my dad, Paul."

"I can't marry you if Henry is your father Holly."

"I feel like that Paul. It is different than he being your Dad."

"How does Cindy look?"

"She is beautiful for her years. Cindy is forty-five. I and Cindy joke a lot when we are together Holly. Cindy is a funny woman, but

I saw that she isn't happy with Scott. Cindy wanted to divorce him ten years ago. Gina saved the marriage of Cindy and Scott. Cindy will be so happy if I marry Gina."

"Do you?"

"I may consider it if we separate Holly."

"I think that we will marry Paul."

"Oh my God. I won't have a chance to marry Gina."

"You don't boy. I will be your future wife."

"Do you agree?"

"Do you think that something will happen with you in Paris, Holly?"

"Tomorrow afternoon I will sign the contract. On Sunday I will be in bed with you in New York."

"Sound is so good Holly. I will think for you the whole time, before I get you in bed."

"Are you happy when you are with me in bed?"

"I am enjoining when I am in bed with you Holly. I am ready Holly. We need to stop speaking for sex I am on the street of old San Juan, Holly."

"I am so sorry boy." We laughed.

"I was scared to call you Paul, because I didn't have news for you, but you made me feel good. You do that every time when I am with you."

"You told me that you will sign the contract tomorrow afternoon Holly."

"Every day I hart the news that I will sign tomorrow Paul. I am tired to listen to this news. If I hear that again I won't sign, I will get on the plane and return to New York. I had a problem with my business, because people lied to me. I will change my life when I return to New York. I will travel less and I will spend more with you, boy."

"Did meet with Estelle on Tuesday, Holly?"

"It was stupid thinking that Estelle will help me. She told me that Giles needs to prepare the contract. I asked her if she knew that Marcel came and he took me from New York, because Giles wants to sign the contract for our business in future."

"I didn't know that Marcel was in New York, Holly. You need to ask Marcel, because he was your lover. You were with Marcel for a long time few year ago. You must know him well."

"I looked so stupid. The words of Estelle killed me Paul, but she was right. I left Estelle's house fast. I think that Estelle knows that I had sexual relationship with Giles. I am ashamed of my past, because I knew that Giles was married with two children."

"You must think for your future Holly."

"With you or single Paul?"

"With me Holly."

"Thanks Paul. Henry was right. You have a golden heart. O boy, I will listen to you for everything in the future. I am Holly Gold, but you are Paul golden boy."

"That sounds good Holly."

"I will call you on Saturday Paul."

"I hope that everything will be OK."

"Everything will be OK, when you are next to me Holly."

"I understood that Paul. I am kissing you golden boy."

I walked and laughed. I will tell Roy that I am a golden boy and I will put my body on Wall Street. I am one hundred seventy-five pounds. This is a lot of gold.

I had coffee and then I started shopping after 10:30 am. I wanted to buy something for Holly, Mom, Susan, Judy, Dad and Roy. Holly thought me how to shop. Paul, when you go shopping you need to know what you will buy and you must negotiation the price. I told her that I have money. You work hard to make money Paul.

"Why do you want to spend your money without getting the value? Somebody else will get your money and live good with them."

Holly was right and I stared to listen to her when I do shopping. I saved a lot of money when I was shopping with Holly. I bought what I needed and I paid less. Holly wanted to count how much we saved, after shopping.

One time I asked Holly "Why did you count every penny when you were in the shop, when you pay a lot money to the people that work for you Holly?"

"You are right when you said that they work for me and they are my friends Paul. I work with them every day. They help me to make money. I want to give them, the money that we make together. Your boss Roy is greedy Paul. You make a lot money for Roy's company, but Roy don't give you enough money."

"How do you know that Holly?"

"I asked Susan."

"She told me "I am Roy's wife, but I will tell you that Roy don't give enough money to Paul. He deserves to get more money Holly.""

I was surprised when Roy gave me a raise because I didn't ask Roy for money. I had lunch. I walked and looked at the old San Juan after the lunch. I returned to the hotel at 7:30pm. I was in the lobby. Maria came to me. "Scott has been asking Pedro where you are Paul whole day. Pedro left the hotel after 5:30pm. Scott called several times at front desk and asked for you after 5:30pm. Pedro told me that Scott is a detective Paul. You were with Scott's daughter Gina."

"Maybe Scott is angry that I have a new girlfriend Maria."

"You are rich Paul. You don't have problem to get two or three girls in your hotel apartment. I have idea Paul. If Scott calls and ask for you, I will tell him that you came in the hotel with three girls. They are in your hotel apartment now."

"Tell that to Scott, Maria. I am a free man. I want to be with girls. I don't want to be with his family. Gina is young, Cindy looks good Paul. The problem is Scott, Maria. Scott will follow Gina and Cindy to see what they do with me."

"Pedro was right when he told me that you are a funny man Paul." I gave Maria two hundred dollars and told her that she needs to order fish and white wine for me in my hotel apartment.

"I will not leave the apartment tonight Maria."

"You are afraid that Scott will ask if you ordered food from your hotel apartment."

"I am not afraid. I don't want to see Scott's face Maria."

"Maybe Scott will have Gina and Cindy with him."

"Of course Maria. Scott will tell me that I need to order food for them."

"But Scott will not be happy if you and Gina go in bed together."

"That is the point Maria. I will spend money for nothing." Maria and I laughed.

"What time they you want the dinner?"

"At eight o'clock."

"I will call you three times at your hotel apartment, but you don't pick up. If somebody knock on the door after five minutes, you need to open the door. Somebody will bring the dinner."

The fish was delicious. The white wine was good quality. I felt asleep.

I was drinking coffee in the living room when somebody knocked on the door. I looked at my watch. It was 8:15 in the morning. I heard the voice of Gina.

"Paul, it is me, Gina. Could you open the door?"

"What are you doing so early in the morning here Gina?"

"It is 8:15 Paul. I was afraid that you will go on the beach. I will leave at 10:00 o'clock. I want to see you before I leave."

"Do you want coffee Gina?"

Yes, Paul. My dad was looking for you all day yesterday." Gina saw the shopping bags on the sofa.

"You went shopping yesterday. I don't believe that you went shopping Paul."

"I bought something for Holly and my family and friends Gina."

"May I see what you bought for Holly?"

"Check this shopping bag Gina. I bought her three different blouses."

"They are so beautiful Paul. Oh my God. The blouses are expensive."

"You can choose and take one of them Gina?"

"You bought them for Holly."

"Holly doesn't know that I bought three Gina."

"May I take this?"

"It is yours Gina. Hey Gina, if you want to go shopping with Holly, come to New York. Believe me, Holly will buy a lot of clothes for you."

"Because I didn't sleep with you?"

"No Gina. Because your father is detective and Scott works for Holly."

"You don't like my dad."

"I prefer you or Cindy, Gina."

"You need to be careful with Mom, Paul. I am not dangerous." We laughed.

"I need to leave Paul. If I come to see you and Holly, I will wear this blouse. I am so excited that I saw you Paul. I forgot to ask you Did you speak with Holly?"

"I spoke with her yesterday and she will call me on Saturday. I will be with Holly on Sunday afternoon Gina."

"Why did you ask me?"

"I heard when Scott was speaking with Holly. When you speak with Holly tell her that she must return to New York on Sunday." Gina kissed me and she left.

"Why didn't Gina tell me what she heard?"

I went on the beach. I chose a chair and umbrella close to the water. A woman around thirty came and asked me "May I lie next to you Paul, because I didn't see your girlfriend Gina? Gina is young, but she isn't beautiful. My name is Lena. Why did Gina leave you?"

"Her Mom and father don't like me. I am not rich enough for them."

"You stay in an expensive apartment Paul?"

"How much did you pay to get information for me and Gena, Lena?"

"I will pay them if I am with you tonight. You will pay me one thousand if I stay one hour in your apartment Paul. For the whole night two thousand."

"I don't have cash Lena. I will pay you two thousand with a credit card. I don't want you to tell me how I need to get cash Lena."

"You don't want me Paul."

"I had a good time with Gina. She was an attractive girl. Gina wasn't a professional and she didn't ask me to pay her. Gina wanted to be with me in bed. You will not be the same as Gina and I don't want to pay you, Lena. You will have to find another man?"

"I will Paul. I don't want to have problem with you, because you will leave tomorrow and Lena left."

Two old people sat next to me. They were from Boston. I spoke with the man for business and Wall Street. We had dinner together. They didn't ask me why I was alone. I checked out at 8:30 in the morning. I was expecting Holly to call me, because she promised me to call me on Saturday. I was at the airport. It was 9:45am. Holly didn't call me. I decided to call her. Holly didn't pick up. The cell phone was turned off. Before I entered the airplane I called again. The same. We flew. My cell phone was turned on. We arrived at Kennedy airport. I was afraid for Holly because she didn't call me. I left two massages.

"Why didn't Holly call me?"

I called again. It seemed that Holly didn't turn on her cell phone. I called in the morning from Puerto Rico. It was the afternoon and I was in New York. It was seven hours later. I didn't know where Holly was staying in Paris. I never asked when Holly traveled, where she stayed. I will call Dad and ask him. Maybe he knows something.

"Hi Dad, did you speak with Holly, Paul?"

"I tried, but her cell phone has been off for seven hours Dad."

"I am concerned for Holly, Paul. I spoke with Holly yesterday morning."

"You called or she called you Dad?"

"I called her Paul. Janet spoke about Holly on Thursday night. We had dinner with Susan and Roy. Janet told us that Holly is having a good time with two men. Janet hurt me when she told that you are Holly's little dog, because you are with Holly in Paris, but Holly was with you during the day to spend your money. At night Holly was with two men in bed. "Holly needs two men Susan. I am a woman, but I never been with two men in bed. I think that Paul isn't the man for Holly, Susan."

I was surprised that Susan told her "I don't believe that you haven't been with two men Janet. You have two now Janet."

"My whole life I had two men Susan, but one is stupid."

"It was hard for me to listen that you are stupid Paul. You are her son. I know that you are the man for Holly. She loves you so much Paul. Holly wants to marry you."

"My mom spoke against Holly, because she doesn't want me to marry her, Dad."

"I know that Janet started to hate Holly in the last six months Paul. I don't know why, but Janet spoke against you on the table while Susan and Roy were with us. Roy is your boss Paul. Roy must have respect for you."

"Don't worry about that Dad. Roy knows who I am, but Mom went too far. I know well Holly Dad. Can you give me the phone number of the hotel where Holly is staying, if you have it?"

"Holly gave me the phone number of the hotel Paul. Just a Moment. Dad gave me the phone number."

I called the hotel. "My name is Paul Morgan, lady. I am the boyfriend of Holly Gold. I am calling from New York. May I speak with her?"

"I don't have a permission to give you information about people who stay in the hotel Mr. Morgan. But I know that Marcel is Holly's boyfriend. Detective Scott Hunter has more information for Holly. Mr. Hunter is from America. You need to speak with him. I will connect you to his room."

"What are you doing in Paris, Scott?"

"Who are you to ask me?"

"You know well Scott. You recognized my voice."

"I didn't sir. It is Paul Morgan Scott. You know that I am Holly's boyfriend. You should have called me before you left to Paris, Scott. Everybody in hotel Le Royal Monceau Raffles thinks that Marcel is Holly's is boyfriend. What did Holly tell you Scott?"

"That you are her boyfriend and she will marry you Paul."

"Are you going to marry Holly, Paul?"

"Of course Scott. I want to know where Holly is."

"She left with Marcel and Luca last night. I was surprised that the people in hotel Le Royal didn't know your name Paul. Maybe they lied to me, Paul."

"They didn't know me, Scott. When Holly travels I speak with her on her cell phone. I never call the hotel. This was the rule between Holly and me."

"How did you know the phone at hotel Le Royal?"

"My dad gave me the number."

"Do you want me to come to Paris, Scott?"

"It is early Paul. I don't have a lot of information. I will tell you to come to Paris, if you need you to help me, Paul. I have a friend in Paris. He is a detective. We will work together. I will call you if I have information as to what happened with Holly."

"Do you think that Holly was kidnapped Scott?"

"Holly was happy when she left the hotel with Marcel and Luca. The people who were at front desk last night, didn't see that Holly was afraid. They thought that Holly left for dinner with Marcel and Luca. The problem is that Giles came in the hotel Le Royal and told the front desk, that Holly will stay ten more days in the hotel. Giles paid for Holly's apartment."

"This is not good news for me Scott, because Holly had to return to New York on Sunday."

"Did you speak with Giles?"

"My friend will speak with him tomorrow. He told me that we don't need to involve the police."

"If you receive information about Holly's location, call me Scott. I will come to take her."

"What do you think about Marcel, Paul?"

"You are the detective Scott. We know three people. Marcel, Luca and Giles. The fourth person I heard about is Estelle. She is the wife of Giles. You need to ask this people, where Holly is. They met and spoke with her." I hung up. I don't know why Scott asked me. He was in Paris to investigate what was happened with Holly. She paid him fifty thousand dollars. I called Dad.

"I spoke with detective Scott, Dad. He told me that Holly left the hotel with Marcel and Luca last night."

"I don't think that Janet is right Paul."

"I know that you love Holly very much, but it is true Dad."

"I will come to New York, Paul."

"You need to stay with Mom, Dad. Maybe she knows where Holly is spending good time with Marcel. We may be able to find out where Holly is."

"This isn't a joke Paul" and Dad hung up.

"You are right Dad, but Holly left me before ten days", I told myself. The fact is that Holly wasn't with me. Holly left with two men. I wish you good time with them Holly. Maybe Marcel and Luca are better men in bed. "I must stop to think for Holly", I told myself.

CHAPTER 4

It was Monday. I woke up at 6:30 in the morning. I was getting ready to go to the office. Mom and Dad called me several times yesterday, but I didn't pick up my cell phone. I didn't listen to the massages either. I knew that Dad would asked me what happened with Holly. I didn't have any information to tell him. I will call Dad if I have. Mom hates Holly and she was happy that Holly left with two men last Friday. I know that Mom would have asked me why Holly left me. I didn't want to tell Mom, that Holly slept with Marcel, but Holly wants more men in bed and she left with two men. I was in the office at 9:00am. Judy was at the front desk.

"How was your vacation in Paris, Paul?"

"Was Holly happy to be with you, Paul?"

"I think so. You never know what a woman thinks Judy. Holly was busy with her business."

"Did you return with Holly from Paris?"

"I don't have time to talk, Judy. If I don't work and make money, Roy will not have money to pay the rent. Roy will need to close the office. You will need to work for another company Judy."

"Do you want to have lunch with me Paul? I will buy lunch and we will eat together."

"I don't know now Judy. I will tell you latter if you need to buy lunch for me."

I entered my office and I closed the door. I didn't want other people that work in the office to ask me for my trip to Paris. Everybody in the office knows that when my office door was closed, I

64

didn't have time to speak with them. If they wanted to ask me they called my phone. My cell phone rung. It was 10:00am. I picked up.

"If you want to see your girlfriend, you need to pay thirty million dollars."

"Why do I need to pay. I don't have a girlfriend man?"

"Holly Gold is your girlfriend and you are planning to marry her, isn't that right?"

"She isn't my girlfriend anymore. Holly lives with Marcel now. Call and ask Marcel to pay, if you want to get thirty million. My name is Paul Morgan."

"I know that you are Paul. We will kill Holly if you don't pay."

"Can you call me when you kill Holly? I will be free and I will find another woman to be with me in bed. How much I need to pay you If you kill Holly?"

"Thirty million dollars Paul." I laughed.

"Don't call the police Paul. We will kill Holly if you call the police."

"You are a stupid man and I closed my cell phone."

Roy called me and told me that we will have lunch together.

"I had very good vacation with Susan, Janet and Henry, Paul. I want to tell you, what happened last week in Miami Beach."

"Hey Paul, why did you tell Judy that I will close the company?"

"She asked me for my vacation and Holly. I have problem with Holly. I don't want to speak for that now. I will come at 12:00 o'clock in your office and we will speak."

I entered Roy's office at 12:00. "I bought chicken for lunch Paul. I am sorry that I didn't asked you what did you want."

"It is OK Roy." Roy and I sat and ate.

"Henry is good man Paul. We spoke a lot for you and Holly. Henry loves Holly. I don't know why Janet hates Holly. Janet had problem with Susan. You know that Susan loves Holly too. Do you know something Paul?"

"You wanted to have lunch with me, because Susan wants to know Roy. I know that you want to know how much money I will make for the company this week."

"You are right Paul. I promised Susan."

"I don't know why Mom hates Holly, Roy."

"Do you think that somebody will kidnap Holly and I need to pay a ransom for her?"

"Whoever kidnapped Holly needs to ask her family for a ransom Paul. You are her boyfriend. She is rich. Holly doesn't have problem to pay, if somebody wants to kidnap or kill her."

"They asked me to pay thirty-million-dollar ransom Roy."

"Are you serious Paul?"

"Yes, Roy. Holly disappeared on Friday night. Frankly she left the hotel with two men. Nobody knows where Holly is now. Holly were supposed to call me on Saturday. She didn't. I called, but her cell phone was off. Holly was planning to return yesterday to New York. She didn't."

"Did Henry know that somebody asked you to pay a ransom for Holly?"

"I spoke with Dad on Saturday. We didn't have good conversation and Dad hung up."

"You need to call the police Paul. They will kill Holly if I involve the police."

"What are you going to do Paul?"

"I spoke with Scott Hunter on Saturday. He is a detective from Philadelphia. Scott is in Paris. Holly known Scott and they spoke last week. Do you think that I need to listen to Scott?"

"I don't know Paul."

"Do you know well Scott, Paul?"

"I saw and spoke with Scott when I was on vacation. We stayed in the same hotel. I know Scott's wife, Cindy and daughter Gina. They were in the hotel too. I like Gina and Cindy. Scott is a stupid and he asked Holly a lot of questions about my family."

"Why did Scott ask Holly questions about your family?"

"I don't know Roy. He was with me at hotel. Scott should have asked me for Mom and Dad."

"How did you meet them Paul?"

"When I arrived I offered Gina to stay in my hotel apartment. She is twenty years old and she was afraid. She is a good girl."

"Did you sleep with her?"

"I didn't."

"What does Cindy think of you?"

"She thought that I was a good choice for Gina to marry me."

"Because you are rich."

"I am not rich Roy. I have enough money to live good. You are rich Roy. I need to introduce you to Cindy. You will have two choices. Cindy or Gina."

"You shouldn't talk like that, because you will have problem with Susan."

"You forgot that Susan is my best friend Roy."

"What should I do Roy?"

"You need to call Henry and tell him, that somebody wants you to pay a ransom. Call now Paul."

"Do you want to listen Roy?"

"If you have problem with Henry, I will help you Paul."

I called. "Hi Dad."

"Did you speak with Holly, Paul?"

"I didn't Dad."

"You don't love Holly?"

"She doesn't love me Dad. I didn't go anywhere with two girls. Holly went to Paris to see her lover Dad."

"You are so stupid Paul. Holly loves you so much. If you leave Holly I don't want to see you Paul."

"Hey Henry, don't say that. Paul loves Holly. He doesn't know what to do, because somebody called Paul and asked him to pay thirty-million-dollars ransom for Holly's freedom. Paul doesn't have the money and he asked me to help him. Paul loves Holly. She is only his girlfriend, but Paul wants to pay. You know that the family needs to pay the ransom Henry. Paul thinks that Holly is family Henry."

"Holly is Roy. I love her like family. I know why you love Holly, Henry. I have six grandchildren. You have a son, but you don't have a grandchild yet. Am I right Henry?"

"You are right Roy. Paul will never marry if he and Holly separate. Holly is the first woman who has had a long relationship with Paul. It was a miracle that I married Roy. Paul is like me."

"How much do you have Paul?"

"I will be ready with seventeen-million-dollars Dad."

"I will give you thirteen million Paul. I will come tomorrow in your office. You tell them that you will pay thirty million dollars for Holly's freedom. See you tomorrow Paul and Dad hung up."

"Oh my God. Henry is crazy man Paul. Thirty million are a lot of money Paul. I will tell Susan, that Henry wants to pay thirty million. Susan loves Henry. I will ask her. Do you want to marry a man who wants to pay thirteen million dollars for his future daughter in law Susan? I know what Susan will tell me that Henry is a man. Honestly, I will never pay Paul."

"Do you think that I need to pay Roy?"

"You must listen to Henry, Paul. He is your father."

"Thank you for speaking with my, Roy. I would never have paid the ransom and I would have had a big problem with Dad. I love him, but I work so hard for my money."

"I see that Paul. Sometime life is more important. Henry wants to see grandchildren. You need to spend more time in bed with Holly."

"If I see her, Roy."

"You will Paul."

I was in the office when Scott called me "Do you have information for Holly, Paul?"

"You need to tell me Scott. You are in Paris."

"My friend spoke with Giles and Estelle. They don't know where Holly is."

"You need to call and ask Marcel, Scott."

"Marcel's cell phone is off Paul. If Marcel kidnapped Holly, he has to call and ask you to pay for Holly's freedom."

"Somebody called and asked me that I need to pay thirty million dollars if I want to see Holly alive."

"Did you call the police Paul?"

"No. I will pay the ransom Scott."

"This is a good decision Paul. You love Holly and you want to save her life. When are you coming to Paris to pay?"

"The man didn't tell me where or when I need to pay. How did you know that I need to pay in Paris, Scott?"

"Holly disappeared from Paris, Paul?"

"Maybe I will have to pay him in New York."

"You need to get Holly when you pay Paul. I think that Holly is in Paris."

"Maybe you are right Scott. I will call you when the man calls me again." I was ready to live the office, when Mom called me "Hi Mr. Paul Morgan".

"Hi Mrs. Morgan."

"Why didn't you call me for one week Paul?"

"What do you want to know Mrs. Morgan?"

"I am not Mrs. Morgan. I am your Mom, Paul."

"I am sorry Mom."

"Are you going to marry Holly?"

"I don't know Mom."

"You were with Holly in Paris last week Paul."

"I am in New York now. Holly stayed in Paris."

"Holly is wearing the engagement ring that you bought for her."

"Many women wear engagement rings, but some women return them Mom."

"Did Holly do that Paul? I will be happy if Holly returns the engagement ring that you bought for her in Paris, Paul."

"I don't want to make you happy Mom and I won't tell you what happened between me and Holly."

"Holly spent a good time with two men Paul."

"Did you call me to tell me that Holly doesn't love me?"

"Of course Paul. Holly loves Marcel."

"How do you know Marcel, Mom?"

"He is with Holly in Paris."

"Are you with Dad in Florida?"

"I know everything about you and Henry. You are my son. Henry is my husband. Why do you want my money Paul?"

"I never asked you in the last ten years for money Mom."

"Henry told me that you want to invest our money Paul." I laughed.

"Why did you laugh Paul? It isn't funny if you lose seven million dollars?"

"You are right Mom, but Dad wants to be richer, so I will invest your money."

"Are you going to be happy if you get someday ten or twelve millions?"

"I believe you Paul. Roy told me that you know how to work with money. Henry will come tomorrow to New York."

"Why don't you come with Dad?"

"I want to stay in Florida, Paul. Now is hot in New York."

"You are right Mom. It is so hot. You are a good woman. I don't understand why you hate Holly. You loved Holly and you were happy when you went shopping with her. What happened between you and Holly?"

"Holly didn't come to Florida with you Paul. I wanted to be there when you asked her to marry you Paul."

"You are lying to me Mom. Holly told me that you started to hate her six months ago."

"I am not lying."

"Holly lied to you Paul and Mom hung up." I laughed. If Mom knows that Dad wants to give me thirteen million for Holly's freedom, she will kill him. Mom told me that they have seven million. I was wondering "How does Dad have six more million and Mom doesn't know about this money?"

I thought that Dad told Mom everything. Dad will surprise me if he has six million that Mom doesn't know about. I will ask him, if he is ready to divorce Mom. I will ask Dad, what happened between Mom and him, when I was six years old. I never asked Dad before, because I didn't have reason to ask him. Now, Holly disappeared and Dad wants to help Holly. Mom hates Holly and Dad will have a big problem with Mom, if she knows that Dad wants to give me thirteen million for a ransom. I think that Dad doesn't care what Mom thinks about Holly. Mom and Dad know Holly for one year and six months. They were happy when I introduced Holly to them. Now Dad has one goal. He wants me to marry Holly. Mom has another goal. I don't marry Holly. Mom and Dad have lived together for thirty-four years. They need to know each other well. "If Mom and Dad have problem with their marriage, why do they live together?"

Maybe Mom and Dad have a secret and they are keeping this secret from me. Cindy told me that she wanted to divorce Scott ten years ago, but Gina saved their marriage. I never heard that Mom wanted to divorce Dad. The question is, "Why did I remember that Dad was always available for me my whole life?"

I didn't remember Mom being there for me as much as Dad, but Mom, Dad and I lived together for twenty-three years. I need to look into the past and the people who have lived with me, so I can predict the future. I am alone now. Holly left me. I left Mom and Dad ten years ago. Maybe I need to ask Mom and Dad for our past and Holly for her life before I met her. The problem is that I don't want to know anything about the past of the closest people to me. I want to know what will happen in future. I need to connect the past, the present and the future of Holly, Mom and Dad, if I will marry Holly. Tomorrow I will ask Dad for his past with Mom. When Mom calls me I will ask her what she did before she married Dad. When I see Holly, I will ask for her family, because I thought that her parents were death and she didn't want to speak about them. I didn't know if Holly has brothers or sisters. Holly knows that I don't have other siblings. Holly knows everything about my family, but I don't anything about hers. If Holly doesn't want to tell me, I can't marry her. If Dad pushes me I will tell him that this is my life. If he loves Holly, he needs to divorce Mom and marry Holly.

Oh my God. If I spend all my time thinking about Holly, Mom and Dad, I won't have time to work. Roy will fire me. I will be poor and I will be homeless. I will tell that to my dad tomorrow. Maybe Dad has enough money to support me and I don't need to work. I will live with Dad, if he divorces Mom. I will tell Dad what I thought tonight. Dad will be in my office tomorrow. Mom has never been in my office. When I asked her to come she told me that she will not feel good. She said that she prefers to see me at a restaurant.

When my dad was working I have been in his office many times. I didn't remember Mom ever being there with me. I don't remember Mom going to work and me being in her office. I will ask Dad why Mom didn't work. I don't know if wives of rich people need to work. I don't know if Dad was rich. He has an apartment in New York and house in Florida. Dad wants to give me thirty million dollars for a ransom. Maybe Dad is rich, but I and Dad never spoke for money. I had everything when I grew up. When I was in college, Dad paid everything and gave me money. I had scholarship for college. I worked too, but I didn't make enough money. Frankly I depended on my dad, before I started to work in Roy's company. Dad never gave me money, after I took my first pay check from Roy's company.

When I was growing up Dad taught me to save money. I remember that Mom wanted to spend money in the shopping center. Mom has a lot of clothes. Dad joked that he needs to buy a new bigger apartment for Mom's clothes. I never heard Dad asked Mom why she spends a lot of money shopping. My dad was joking when Mom was shopping "Your Mom needs to look good Paul, if she wants to marry another man." I was young and I didn't understand Dad, because I never saw that Dad had problem with Mom. The parents of my friends divorced and their Moms married again. My friends joked with me "Paul, you have one Mom and Dad. I have two Moms and Dads. Why doesn't your Mom divorce your father, he is too old for her? We think that your father is your grandfather." I never been angry when my friends joked with me. I told them that my dad is the best father and a husband. Mom will never divorce Dad, because she will need to go to work. My friends told me "You are right Paul. Our Moms told us that they were stupid when they decided to marry for men that don't have enough money to support their family and the women need to work." They weren't right, because I saw many women in my dad's office and they were happy working. I know that if I marry Holly she will work too. I will ask Dad why Mom never worked. I was in bed when my cell phone rung. I looked at my watch. It was 6:15 in the morning.

"Are you ready with the money Paul?"

"Oh man. It is 6:15 at morning. I am in bed."

"Did you sleep last night man?"

"I didn't."

"You are right man. You will sleep after you get thirty million."

"I will not sleep after I lose thirty million man."

"You will make money again Paul. Your business is to make money."

"Is your business is to kidnap people man?"

"Holly makes money. She will give you the money that you pay me, after you get her alive. Holly has money man."

"Why don't you ask her to give you the money?"

"Holly will be your wife and her money is your money Paul."

"First, I need to pay ransom to get Holly. Second, I don't know if Holly will marry me and I don't know if Holly will give me the money. May I speak with Holly, I need to ask her, man?"

"You will speak with Holly, after I get the money."

"Why do I need to pay ransom man?"

"If I don't receive money before Saturday, I will kill Holly, Paul."

"Don't get angry man. We are having a good conversation."

"Why do you want to kill Holly. She is a beautiful woman?"

"Every man wants to be in bed with Holly. If you don't believe me, you need to ask Marcel. He is with Holly now. Maybe you need to ask Luca, he is with Holly too. Did you sleep with Holly, man?"

"I prefer to get thirty million dollars Paul."

"Because you didn't sleep with Holly I will give you the money man, but I don't know when. Call me after 2:00 o'clock in the afternoon. I will call you at 2:00 o'clock, but you must tell me which day you will give me the money."

"I called Scott. They called me again. In the afternoon I will know if I will pay or not."

"They will kill Holly if you don't pay, Paul."

"How did you know that Scott? Are you working with them, Scott? Maybe Holly will make a deal with them. Holly has money Scott. Why should I pay if Holly will pay them?"

"Holly needs to go to the bank to get the money."

"I need to get the money from the bank too Scott. I don't keep thirty million in my apartment." "Holly doesn't have a chance to give them the money. You know well Paul."

"Why doesn't Holly call me and tell me that I need to pay a ransom for her freedom Scott?"

"I have not heard from Holly since last Thursday."

"Do you know that Holly's family is rich?"

"We never spoke for her family, Paul?"

"What did you talk about?"

"For you, Janet and Henry. I will call Henry and tell him that you don't want to pay for Holly's freedom Paul."

"I understand Scott. You want me to pay. You don't need to call Dad. I will call you tomorrow and tell you, when I will come to Paris."

"How much do I pay you Scott?"

"Holly paid me. You need to pay the ransom."

My dad was in my office at 10:00am. "Do you have news from them Paul?"

"I have Dad. The news isn't good. They want thirty million or they will kill Holly."

"We will pay Paul. I want to see Holly alive."

"I have many questions Dad."

"You don't want to pay Paul?"

"No Dad."

"You will see Holly alive, if she is alive. If you want to ask me for my and Janet's live, I don't want to speak here. We will speak in your apartment Paul. I will stay with you tonight."

"They will call me at 2:00 o'clock. I will tell them that I will be in Paris on Friday morning."

"Thanks Paul. You need to work. I will go to see Roy."

Dad left. Roy and Dad came to my office.

"Let's go for lunch together Paul." Roy, Dad and I left the office.

We went to a restaurant near the office. There was Susan she greeted me and said "Nice to see you Paul" and Susan kissed me. "Do you need money Paul?"

"No Susan. It is enough that I will lose Dad. Mom will kill Dad, if she knows that Dad gave me money to pay the ransom for Holly. Roy will kill you if you give me money Susan."

"You are right Paul."

"You will save the life of Holly, Roy."

"This a problem for Henry and Paul, Susan."

"Why don't you want to help Paul, Roy?"

"I don't want to be involved Susan. If I give my money, I will give Paul advice, because I will be investing my money."

"Oh my God. This is different Roy. You will give money to help."

"I have never done that in my life Susan."

"What if somebody kidnaps our child or grandchild?"

"What are you going to do Roy?"

"I will decide when it happens Susan. We are here to have lunch Susan."

"Of course Roy."

"Do you count your money, when you have lunch with people?"

"When I am with a client, I count how much my client will invest Susan."

"When I am with Paul or people who work in my company, I speak for business."

"What do you do, when you are with me Roy?"

"When I and you were young, I thought for bed. Honestly I and you were in bed after we were in a restaurant and we had results Susan. We have three children. If Henry did the same, he would have had more children." I and Dad laughed.

"You are right Roy. You need to give this advice to Paul, when he is in a restaurant with Holly. I want to have two or three grandchildren. Do you think that Janet will be happy too Henry?"

"I don't care for Janet, Susan."

"You are right Henry." I saw Janet with her lover. Last week I saw Janet with a man while she kissed him. I followed them. They went to a hotel. I entered the hotel and asked the people who work in there for Janet and her lover. They told me that Janet has stayed many times with her husband in their hotel. They told me that Mrs. and Mr. Goldbear love to stay in this hotel, because they met in this hotel thirty-five years ago. "His name is Alan, Henry."

"Do you know him, Henry?"

"Roy was right Susan. We are having lunch. We finished the lunch. We left the restaurant."

"Do you want something for dinner, I will cook for you Paul?"

If you cook fish and buy white wine it will be good for us Dad."

"I will Paul."

"Hey Dad, we will be just two of us like old times."

"This was so long ago Paul. I will never forget Dad. I love you so much."

"Me too Paul."

"I am so sorry if I hurt you Henry."

"You didn't hurt me Susan. You opened my eyes. Thank you for telling me about Janet and Alan." Dad and Susan wanted to walk. Me and Roy took a taxi.

"Oh boy, you have a golden father. Henry will do everything for you."

"Do you think that I am a golden boy and I told Roy my story?" We laughed a lot.

"You are golden boy for me Paul. You work so hard. Someday you will be the of boss of my company. When I was in Miami Beach, Henry spoke a lot about you. He is so proud of you Paul. I have three children. I have a good relationship with them, but you and Henry have the best father and son relationship I have seen."

"Thanks Roy."

The man called me at 2:00pm.

"I will be in Paris on Friday morning. I will stay at the same hotel where Holly stayed."

"Are you going to bring the money Paul?"

"I will, but If you decide to kidnap me, my family doesn't have money to pay. You must be ready to kill me. You don't need to lose time with me. It is different if you want me in bed, but you need to pay me, man."

"He told me that you are a funny man, but you will pay the ransom for Holly."

"Who told you? Marcel, Luca or Giles?"

"Marcel" and the man hang up.

I didn't know Marcel. I didn't meet or spoke with Marcel, Luca and Giles. The only man who know me in Paris was Scott. "Does the man know Scott?"

I will not be surprised if he knows Scott. I called and bought ticket for Thursday to Paris. I will fly at 7:30pm. I called Scott. And told him, that I will fly on Thursday and I will arrive on Friday morning. "You need to pick me up from the airport." I told him my flight number and airline.

"Everything is OK. I have the money Scott, but I want to speak with Holly, when I arrive in Paris."

"You must tell them, Paul."

"If the man calls me I will ask him, Scott."

"It is good idea Paul. You will give thirty million dollars."

"See you on Friday Scott."

I called Gina. Maybe she knows something. Gina will help me, because she loves Holly. Maybe Gina will not tell me, if she knows that I will pay thirty million ransom for Holly's freedom.

"Hi Gina, this is Paul."

"You sound happy Paul."

"Is Holly OK?"

"I don't know Gina. I spoke with Scott and he told me that Holly left the hotel with two men. Maybe Holly is happy with them."

"I know that my dad is stupid Paul, but you are stupid too. When I spoke with Holly, she never told me that she had another man. Holly told me that she loves you so much and I shouldn't sleep with you, because I would hurt her. If Holly had another man, she wouldn't care if I slept with you. Why didn't you push Holly to come back to New York? Maybe you were waiting for somebody to kidnap Holly so that you will be a free man. Do you have a new girlfriend Paul?"

"I am going to Paris on Thursday Gina. You are right that I didn't push Holly to return to New York, so I can go to Paris. I felt that something wasn't OK in Paris."

"Did my father tell you what happened on Friday night?"

"He didn't."

"Do you have pen and paper?"

"I have Gina. I will give you the phone number of my dad's friend. He is a detective in Paris. I don't know why my father didn't tell Holly that she needs to speak and use Morel if she was afraid for her life. Dad was in Puerto Rico. Morel was in Paris. Are you ready Paul?"

"I am Gina" and she gave me the phone number of Morel.

"Do you think that I need to call to Morel now Gina?"

"When you are in Paris call Morel. If you call now, Morel will ask Dad, about who you are. I don't know what Dad will tell Morel. When you speak with Morel and tell him that you are Holly's boyfriend, he will help you. Maybe Morel will not ask you to pay him, but you give him money. You are rich and smart Paul. You need to decide how much you need to pay Morel. Don't forget. Morel is a good man and he has a beautiful wife and two boys."

"Do you think that Morel's wife will help me too Gina?"

"It isn't funny that Holly disappeared, but I am happy that you are joking. It will help you to find Holly alive Paul. You don't tell my father that you spoke with me Paul. Are you regretting that you met me in Puerto Rico, Paul?"

"We had a good time Gina. We will be friends forever."

"My father may hurt you Paul."

"Scott can't hurt me Gina. You gave me a good advice. Morel is a detective in Paris. I need to use him in Paris. I won't use Scott and Morel's wife." We laughed.

"You need to listen to Morel. He is smart."

I will Gina. I left the office at 6:30pm. I was in my apartment. Dad was in the kitchen. "The dinner is ready Paul."

"Do you like glass of whiskey Dad?"

"A little Paul. You forgot that I am seventy years old. Cheers Paul."

"Cheers Dad. Sometime I miss you, but I know that you are a big boy and you need to build your live alone."

"You forgot Holly, Dad. You are a man and you must build your family Paul. Holly will be next to you to help you."

"Do you think that Holly will marry me?"

"Why did you ask me that Paul?"

"Because she left to Paris and she didn't tell me why. You spoke latter with Holly and she told you, Paul."

"Why do you support Holly, Dad?"

"I can tell you about my past, but I can't tell you about Holly's."

"If you aren't ready you don't do Dad."

"Maybe your Mom has a role in Holly's disappearance Paul. I want to tell you for me, Janet and Alan, Paul. This is long story that has been written for thirty-four years now."

"How did you meet Mom, Dad?"

"Don't ask me Paul. You need to listen."

"Do you want to tell me after dinner Dad?"

"The story is long. We will eat and I will tell you my life." I and

Dad ate and drank wine.

"It was Friday. Every Friday after work I wanted to drink. I sat on the bar and ordered vodka. I saw woman's items on the chair next to me. Few minutes later a woman came and sat on the chair. Her eyes were red. The bartender asked her If she wants one more cocktail."

"I will pay your cocktail lady", I told her. "My name is Henry."

"My name is Janet."

"Why are your eyes red Janet?"

"My boyfriend left me. He didn't want to marry me."

"Maybe he isn't ready to marry, Janet. I love him, Henry and I want to marry him."

Janet told me that her boyfriend lives in California. She was from Ohio. It was around midnight when Janet and I left the restaurant. I asked her where she will sleep.

"I and my boyfriend were in expensive hotel. He is rich and he paid everything when I am with him. I don't have money to stay in this hotel."

"My apartment isn't big, but it has two bedrooms Janet. If you want, you can sleep there."

"Tomorrow you will leave."

"I was surprised that my parents were there. You know that they lived in Connecticut. Mom exited the bedroom Janet was supposed to sleep in. I told her that I am sorry Janet and I didn't know that my parents were coming from Connecticut."

"It is OK Henry. I will sleep in your bedroom."

"We had sex. I didn't use condom. I woke up in the morning. Janet wasn't in the bed. I thought that she left the apartment. I went to the kitchen and Janet was there. She was talking with Mom and Dad. They invited me and Janet to go to Connecticut the following week. I didn't know how tell them that I saw Janet last night. I didn't know who she was. Janet answered that we will be happy to see them next week."

"Oh my God. Paul, she knew the names of my mom and dad. I wanted to say that I was busy next weekend, but Dad told Janet "Finally Henry will come in my house with a beautiful girl". I will be happy if you marry Henry, Janet. Henry is thirty-seven and he doesn't need to wait to get forty to marry. I married Kelly when I was forty Janet. "Old man is better than a young man John", Janet told Dad. Janet and I married next month."

"My life was a disaster the first three months, but she was pregnant and I decided to live with Janet, Paul. I never lived with a woman before. The women stayed not more than three or four days with me. They left me. Janet didn't Paul. After nine months you were born. I was a father Paul."

"You are a good father, Dad." I and Dad laughed.

Paul, you changed my life. After work I wanted to come back at home and play with you. You were everything for me. Your grandfather told me that he was the same when I was born.

"Do you think that I will be a good father Dad?"

"Of course Paul. You are like me and your grandfather. You will be the best father when Holly delivers your children."

"Do you think that Mom will be happy?"

"Who cares Paul. Janet is busy with Alan now?"

"Did Mom tell you who was her boyfriend?"

Once Janet told me that If she married Alan, her life would have been better. If Janet continues to love Alan then she has to marry Alan, because Janet was with Alan in Miami Beach.

"Is this the same Alan that Mom was before she married you?"

"He is. Oh my God. This is thirty-five-years Dad. Are you going to divorce Mom?"

"I will never ask her for a divorce. If Janet wants I will divorce her Paul."

"Why don't you divorce if you know that Mom is with Alan?"

"I don't want to pay a lawyer."

"What If Mom wants?"

"I will tell her that I don't want to involve a lawyer. We will be both agree to divorce and she will go to live with Alan."

"I will be a free man Paul."

"Oh my God. You are so funny Dad, but you are right. Why do you need to pay a lawyer if Mom wants to live with Alan?"

"Hopefully Alan is rich. He needs to support Janet. Mom wants to spend money shopping Dad."

"Alan needs to think about that Paul." We laughed.

"Can you tell me what happened when I was six years old Dad?"

"This is different story Paul."

"I remember something Dad."

"Of course Paul." I had to lie to you for two months. It was hard time for me Paul. You know that I don't lie. "Do you remember what was the season Paul?"

"I remember that it was spring."

It was Saturday. It was a beautiful day outside and I decided to go to the park with you. Janet told me that she will stay at home. We returned in the afternoon at home. Janet wasn't at home. I thought that she was outside with her friends. It was 9:00pm. She didn't return. I called and asked her friends if they knew where she was. Nobody knew where she was. You and I left at 9:00 am that morning. Some of Janet friends called at 9:30 am, but she didn't pick up the phone. Your Mom didn't come back and I called my mom to come to the apartment. Your grand Mom came and I told her that Janet has disappeared. Janet didn't return or called on Sunday. I called Ohio. I asked Janet's sister Becky, if she has spoken with Janet today or yesterday, because Janet left my apartment on Saturday and she has not returned. I asked her "Do you think that I need to call in police Becky?"

"Ask them what do you need to do Henry, but I think that Janet is with her ex-boyfriend Alan. She called me at Thursday and told me that she will marry her rich ex-boyfriend. I told her that she was married to you and has a boy from you Henry. She told me that, but his father will be Alan."

I asked her "Did you speak with Henry that you want to leave him Janet?"

She replied "I am kidding Becky" and Janet hung up Henry.

"I didn't call you, because I thought that Janet was joking. Janet was in Ohio with Alan, but she married you. You and Janet have a smart and beautiful boy. You don't worry about Janet. I will try to find out where she is. You need to think for Paul. Somebody needs to take care for him."

"My mom is here Becky."

After four days Becky called me" Janet is with Alan, but they are traveling around in America. Are you going to divorce her Henry?"

"I don't know Becky. I will have a problem with Paul. He keeps asking where his Mom is. If Janet returns home, it will be good for Paul. If I divorce, Janet she will take Paul with her. I love Paul so much and I don't want to lose him."

"Can you find and speak with Alan, Becky?"

"If Janet calls me I will want to speak with Alan."

"After fifty days, I found out that Alan and Janet were in Los

Angeles. Becky told me where they were staying. I flew to Los Angeles. I found Janet and Alan. I followed Alan when he was alone, I stopped him and he asked me what I was doing in Los Angelis."

"You know who I am Alan?

"Of course Henry."

"You are with my wife Alan."

"I am with her for almost two months Henry."

"Are you going marry Janet, Alan?"

"Hey, I am a married man Henry. I have a three years old daughter."

"What are you doing with Janet then, she is my wife?"

"Do you want me to live with your wife Alan?"

"Why not, if she wants Henry."

"Where did you take Janet with you Alan?"

"I was in New York and I called Janet. Janet came to my hotel room. She told me that her life with you isn't good and she prefers to come with me."

"Did Janet know that you are married Alan?"

"Janet knows everything for me Henry. She loves me and she wants to hear from me all the time. Janet called and told me that she married you, but she still loves me. I was angry that Janet married you, Henry. Janet was my girlfriend."

"You left her, Alan."

"Why did Janet married you one month after I left her?"

"Janet needed to wait. When I was ready to marry her, I would have called and got her from Ohio."

"What are you going to do with two wives Alan?"

"Janet is your wife Henry. I just have a good time with her."

"What does your wife do Alan?"

"Lori is happy that she is rich Henry. She is busy with our daughter."

"Janet and I have a son. He asks where his Mom is, Alan."

"This isn't good for Paul, Henry. Janet must go back to New York. I promise you that Janet will be back in your apartment after two days Henry. I need to leave, because I don't want Janet to see me with you. This will not be good for Paul. He is a smart boy."

"Paul is six years old Alan. He looks a like his father Henry."

"Alan left. I was scared for you Paul. I thought that Alan was your father. Alan is a crazy man, Paul. I returned to New York. I checked your DNA at two laboratories. I was so happy when my friends told me that you are my son. I thought for you, Paul. I didn't care for Janet. She returned after two days. We didn't speak for one week. You were happy that Janet was at home and I started to speak with Janet."

"Alan is crazy Dad. He came back for Mom after twenty-seven years."

"Maybe your Mom called Alan. It isn't import now Paul. We need to think for Holly. She disappeared. You need to find where Holly is and bring her back with you Paul. Do you have a plan?"

"Tomorrow I will make a plan Dad."

"I have seventeen million dollars in the bank, Paul."

"You told me that you have seven million, Dad."

"I checked in the bank and I understood that I have ten million more Paul."

"You are joking with me, Dad."

"I am not joking with you Paul."

"When you were one-year-old your grandfather was in New York. Janet and Mom were shopping. I and Dad sat and drank coffee. You were playing on the floor. My dad told me "Paul look likes me and you Henry. I would like to give a present to Paul". Dad gave me a check. "Keep this money in the bank Henry. You give the money to Paul when he goes to college". I left that money in the bank as my father requested. I made good money, so I never needed this money. I thought to give you this money when you marry."

"Dad, I was eight years old when my grandfather died. I was ten when my grand Mom died. I didn't understand when my grand Mom told me that she wanted to go to see my grandfather. He was death."

"It was big problem between me and Mom, Paul. I wanted to get her to live in New York with me, you and Janet."

She told me "I don't want to be far away from your father Henry". I told her" Mom, Dad is death".

"You need to think for your future life. I don't have future, Henry. I want to live with your father. We lived forty-eight years together."

"Why didn't you have brother or sister, Dad?"

Mom told me that she had a problem when I was born.

"Did Mom had problem too Dad?"

"Janet didn't want to have more children after you were born."

"I didn't want after you were six years old. You didn't want to take care of two children Dad. You are right Paul." We laughed.

"I was the only child in my family as you are. I hope that you and Holly will have two or three children Paul."

"Now is 12:00 o'clock. You need to sleep Paul."

"I am going to sleep, because I will be busy tomorrow Dad." I was in the office. The man called me again.

"I told you that I will come on Friday man. I bought a ticket and I will fly on Thursday night. I will give you the money, but I will want to speak with Holly on Friday."

"You don't need to speak with Holly. She will be with me when I get the money." "We have a deal Paul" and he hang up.

I called Citibank International in Paris.

"May I speak with Norman Pepin?"

"It is Norman."

"Hey man, this is Paul Morgan."

"Oh my God. I haven't spoken with you in a long time Paul."

"What are you doing?"

"I will be in your bank on Friday morning. I will transfer three million dollars. I will need two million in cash."

"Can you buy a bag that can carry thirty million dollars Norman?"

"You need to buy books and put them in the bag. You will cover the books with two million dollars."

"Do you need to pay a ransom?"

"My girlfriend disappeared in Paris. I need to pay thirty million to get her back."

"We will speak when I see you Paul. I will be ready with the bag and the books."

"See you on Friday Norman. See you Paul." Gina called me in the afternoon.

"Did you speak with my father today Paul?"

"I didn't Gina. I will see Scott on Friday in Paris"

"If Dad calls and asks you for me, you need to tell him that you spoke with me last in Puerto Rico. After that we have not spoken. My dad was happy when he called me."

I asked him if he found Holly. He told me, "Holly won't have a problem Gina, if Paul comes to Paris with money. I will be rich after Friday, Gina."

"Did you promise to pay good money to Dad, if you get Holly

back, Paul?"

"I never told Scott that I would pay him, Gina. I spoke with a man who asked me to pay thirty-million-dollar ransom. Scott will be rich if he takes the ransom and I get Holly back."

"What will Dad investigate if he gets the ransom Paul?"

"That is a good question Gina. Looks like Scott and the man that asked me to pay the ransom are connected. I haven't spoken with Holly after last Thursday."

"Do you think that this is normal Gina?"

"No Paul. You need to speak with Holly before you give the ransom. Maybe somebody wants to get the money, but he doesn't know where Holly is. Why would you pay a ransom to him, if you don't get Holly back?"

"You are a smart girl Gina. I think that my plan is right. They will not get money if I don't have Holly. Do you think that I can trust your father?"

"It will be better if you meet and ask Morel. He knows well my dad and he will help you Paul. You need to tell Morel about your plan to Paul. It will be good if you see Morel alone."

"I will call Morel when I arrive in Paris Gina."

"Good luck Paul. I hope to see you and Holly together soon."

"Thanks Gina."

I left my office at 8:00pm. I was at the main door of the building when Mom called me "Hi Mom".

"Who is Scott Hunter and what is he doing in Paris, Paul?"

"I don't know Mom."

"You are lying to me Paul. You will meet with Scott on Friday in Paris."

"Somebody else lied to you Mom, not me. If you want to know who Scott is, you need to ask Holly, Mom. Scott is a detective and he works for Holly."

"I don't have a way to ask Holly, because she is busy with Marcel, Paul."

"Why do you want to hurt me all the time, when you speak with me, Mom?"

"Holly isn't the right woman for you Paul. Holly had a lot of men before she met you and she will have a lot of men after you marry her."

"This is my problem Mom."

"You are my son and I need to think for your life Paul."

"Why are you flying to Paris tomorrow? "and Mom told me number of the flight number.

"Who gave you this information Mom?"

"I have people who are looking for your safety Paul."

"You are crazy Mom. I am not afraid for my life."

"I am afraid, because Holly will pay and somebody will kill you Paul."

"Holly doesn't have time Mom. She is busy and happy with Marcel."

"You didn't tell me why you are going to Paris."

"I want to ask Holly, if she want to stay with Marcel or she wants to come back to live with me Mom. If Holly prefers to live with Marcel, I will marry another woman."

"Don't waste your time and money, Paul. New York has a lot of beautiful women. You can choose one of them."

"Maybe you are right Mom. When I see Dad I will ask him."

"Henry loves Holly, and he will tell you to go and speak with Holly, Paul. I understood why Henry wanted to come to New York. After Henry came to New York, you want to go to Paris. You were in Paris last week. You were with Holly, Paul. Why did Holy leave with Marcel, she needed to return in New York with you Paul?"

"I don't know what I need to tell you Mom."

"Do you have an answer to my question Paul?"

"I don't Mom. You can't be stupid like your father Paul."

"Do you think that Dad was right when he married you Mom?"

"You need to ask Henry. I have a man that I love my whole life. He is next to me Paul."

"Dad is in New York Mom." She hung up.

I started to think about my life. Maybe Mom and Alan want to take control of my life. Janet is my mom. Alan thinks that he is my father. Maybe they want me to marry a woman that they want. Alan is rich. Maybe he has a rich friend who has a daughter and Alan wants me to marry her. Alan has a daughter. He needs to think for his daughter, because I am one hundred percent a son of Henry. I look like my dad and my grandfather. Mom knows that.

"Why doesn't she tell Alan that I am Henry's son?"

Maybe Mom wants to control Alan, if he thinks that I am his son. Many people tried to take control of my life, when I started to work in Roy's company. They wanted to tell me that they were my bosses and I needed to listen them. Including Roy who is my boss. I put them on their place. They understood that I was a man and I didn't need to listen to them. I told them that I know who I am and I don't need to listen to their stupid advice. It was good that Roy staid neutral. He didn't take sides, otherwise I had to leave the company. Now the same people are listening and asking me for advice when they have problem with their clients. Now they love me and support me. Oh my God. I love Holly, because she is a like me. Holly never lied or misled me and the people who work for her. I entered my apartment. Dad, I love Holly and I will marry her.

"Did you speak with Janet?"

"Yes, I spoke with her."

"Don't take seriously what Janet told you, Paul. I understood that Janet is crazy, when Susan told me that she saw Janet with Alan."

"Dad, do you think that Mom depends a lot on Alan?"

"Yes, I think so. I also think that Alan is the problem between Holly and Janet."

"Do you think that Holly was with Alan. Alan is rich. Maybe they met many years ago. Alan is fifty-seven. Holly is thirty. Holly travels to a lot of different places in the world. Maybe Alan travels too. You think that Alan was an ex-lover of Holly and Mom has learned about it and that is the reason she doesn't want me to marry Holly."

"Janet isn't the wife of Alan, but maybe she wants to divorce me and marry Alan."

"How would Janet feel, if you marry Holly, Paul?"

Holly will tell Mom "Hi, mother in law. How do you fell with my ex-lover Alan?"

Do you think that I taught Alan to have better sex with you, because you were with Alan before me and after me?"

"You are so funny son, but you told a joke that was true. Janet was with Alan, thirty-five years ago and she is with Alan now." I and Dad laughed.

"Mom knows that I will fly tomorrow to Paris. Do you think that Mom uses Alan's money to spy on me, Dad?"

"Why not if Janet wants to separate you with Holly. You need to ask Holly when you are with her, if she had a sexual relationship with Alan in her past. It is possible that something else is the problem between Holly and Janet. Can you tell me about your plan Paul?"

I transferred three million dollars to Citibank in Paris. Norman Pepin works there and I have known him for seven years. I met him when he was in New York. We are good friends. I met Gina in Puerto Rico. She is the daughter of Scott. Holly paid him fifty thousand, before she disappeared. Gina called me and told me that I need to use Morel when I arrive in Paris. Morel is a detective in Paris.

"Tomorrow I will give you the fifteen million Paul."

"Dad, I haven't spoken with Holly for one week. Her cell phone doesn't work. Holly didn't call me after last Thursday. Nobody know where she is. I don't want to risk thirty million dollars. You will stay in New York. If I need to pay the thirty million, I will call you. The good news is that we have the money to pay the ransom. The bad news is that we don't know where Holly is. I feel that Holly isn't in Paris. The man who asked me to pay the ransom, wants me to pay in Paris."

"I assume they will bring Holly when you pay them Paul?"

"I will know that on Friday, Dad. I need to speak with Scott and Morel. I need to prepare for my trip to Paris. We can continue our conversation in my bedroom Dad. If Mom calls you and asks you to return to Florida, you tell her that you must stay in New York."

"What do I do if Janet want to come in New York?"

"I am sorry Dad that I am the one that has to tell you that Mom has loved Alan her whole life. Janet never loved you."

"How do you know that Paul?"

I provoked Mom and she told me that she loves the man who was next to her. I told Mom that you were in New York. Mom hang up. Alan was with Janet. Maybe when you return to Florida and you see Alan, you will have a chance to tell him" Hi Alan. Did you have a good time with Janet?"

"Why not Paul? Can you take Janet with you? Janet has loved you for thirty-five years. She wants to live with you, because I am an old man." I and Dad laughed.

"I am so happy for you Dad. You opened your heart and you are joking with your life."

"You are the same as me Paul. Holly disappeared and you need to pay thirty million, but you are joking all the time."

"We need to be in control of our life Dad. So many crazy people are around us."

"Starting with your Mom Paul."

"Next, to her is Alan, Dad."

"When you marry Holly, I want to live with you and Holly, Paul."

"Holly doesn't like me to joke with her, but she will be quiet, because you will be with me, Dad."

"What are you going to do, if Janet wants me leave New York Paul?"

"I will tell her that you will stay with me and Holly. Holly is a good woman, Dad. Today I understood why I love Holly. She is the same as me. I think that Holly will joke with me and you when we live together."

"That sounds good Paul."

"I am not coming back to my apartment tomorrow Dad. I will get my luggage with me to the office."

"You don't have to do that. I will bring luggage for you to the airport Paul."

"OK Dad. You want to wish me good luck, before I leave to Paris."

Scott called me on Thursday morning and he asked me if I have spoken with Gina. I told him that haven't after she left Puerto Rico.

"What is Gina doing, Scott?"

"Gina has a new boyfriend. She met him last Monday in the university and Gina is busy with him. Are you jealous Paul?"

"Why should I be jealous Scott?"

"Because Gina has a boyfriend. I think that Gina loves you, Paul."

"Why does Gina have boyfriend if she loves me? If I want Gina to be my girlfriend, why am I paying thirty million ransom for Holly? I will be with Gina or another woman, if Gina doesn't want me."

"I am joking Paul."

"I am not joking Scott. Do you have news about Holly, because I am coming to Paris to bring her back home?"

"You will get Holly on Friday, Paul."

"Are you sure?"

"Of course Paul."

"It is Ok, because I will carry thirty million with me?"

"Are you caring the money from New York?"

"You are crazy Paul."

"The man who asked me to give him thirty million in Paris, is crazy Scott. I don't have time" and I hang up. After one hour the man who asked for the ransom called me.

"Are you coming tomorrow Paul, because I don't want to kill Holly?"

"I will be in Paris tomorrow man."

"Thanks Paul and he hung up."

I understood that Scott knows the man who wanted to get the thirty million dollars. They were working together. Scott wasn't doing anything to help me find Holly. Scott was working to get the ransom. Morel might be my only chance to find Holly. I will know that when I meet and speak with him. I arrived at the JFK airport. Dad was waiting for me.

"Janet wants me to return to Florida" he said.

"You must stay in New York, Dad."

"I can send you the money from Florida, Paul."

"It's not about the money, it is for your safety Dad. When I return from France, we will decide what to do with Mom."

I entered my gate. I saw a man that was looking at me. He entered the airplane with me. I will not be surprised if he sits next to me. He didn't, but he was in first class. He sat behind me. We were going to fly together. It will be better if he was she and sat next to me. I would have had good time. We flew to Paris.

CHAPTER 5

I was happy that nobody sat next to me in the plane. I turned my head towards the man that was looking at me before we boarded the plane. He was looked at me too. I didn't want to speak with him. I wanted to sleep. The air hostess approached me and asked me "Do you like something to drink sir?"

"I would like to sleep lady. I had a busy day today and will have a busy day tomorrow as well. If I sleep it will be better for me." I closed my eyes.

I looked at my watch when I woke up. I slept for five hours. I stood up and walked to the restroom. The man that looked at me wasn't at his seat. His jacket was on it. I saw that his ticket was in his jacket. I took the ticked and read his name. His name was Duke Oran. I put the ticked back in his pocket and walked to the restroom. When I returned to my seat, Duke Oran was on his seat and his eyes were closed. I sat down on my seat. The air hostess came to me and said "I want to speak with you sir. Please follow me." We walked to the service area and she asked me "Why did you check the ticket of the man who is seating behind you sir? If you wanted to know his name you need to ask him."

"My name is Paul Morgan, lady. I saw that this man looked at me when we were at the airport. He is flying with me and sitting behind me. I felt that he was watching me when I sat on my seat. Why didn't Duke Oran ask for my name or tell me his name when we were at the airport or in the plane?"

"Many people were at the airport, before you entered in the

plane Paul. It is normal that somebody looks at you."

"I would have been happy if a girl was looking at me and followed me in the plane. But Duke looks like a strong man. If he wants to fight with me I need to know at least his name."

"They will arrest him if he wants to fight with you Paul."

"You are right lady."

"Call me Marion, Paul."

"You have a beautiful name and you are beautiful too Marion."

"I think that you have many women a like me, Paul."

"I lost one of them in Paris, so I am going to Paris to find her."

"Are you joking all time Paul?"

"No Marion. My girlfriend, Holly Gold, disappeared in Paris last Friday."

"I know Holly Gold, Paul. I read about her and saw her in many magazines. She is beautiful."

"Every model is beautiful Marion."

"You told me that I am beautiful, but I am not a model Paul. Do you think that Holly can help me to work as a model?"

"I don't know Marion."

"You are her boyfriend."

"I am, but I never follow her when she has a show. I stay far away from her business."

"Aren't jealous Paul?"

"I am not Marion. Maybe Holly has another man."

"That is what it looks like. She left with Marcel last Friday night and she hasn't call me since."

"Maybe Holly is having a good time with Marcel."

"He is French and lives in Paris."

"Well in this case you and I can have a good time in Paris too Paul. I have another trip after three days, Paul. You can stay with me. You don't need to pay for a hotel. You can stay in my apartment."

"That sounds good Marion, but I will have a big problem with my father. He loves Holly and he wants me to marry her."

"Do you have a Mom, Paul?"

"She doesn't love Holly and she doesn't want me to marry her."

"You need to listen to your Mom, Paul. If I listen to my mom, she will tell me to be with you Marion. Mom will be so happy."

"Me too Paul."

"The problem is that I love Holly. I have been with Holly now for one year and seven months. We had a very good live, before she left to Paris."

"Maybe Holly has only business with Marcel, Paul."

"She came to Paris for business to sign a contract with Giles. I am guessing that Giles is the boss of Marcel."

"Does Holly know well Giles and Marcel?"

"She slept with both of them."

"Oh my God. I have never met a man like you before."

"Why do you want Holly back after she slept with Giles and Marcel?"

"Holly slept with them before I met her. I had a lot of girls before I met Holly too Marion."

"Then, why don't you want to be with me Paul?"

"After I met Holly, I stopped sleeping with other women. Holly is everything for me. Holly is good in bed."

"I am good too Paul."

"I don't care who is better Marion. If I don't find Holly I will call you."

"I will give you my phone number Paul. I will be waiting for your call Paul."

"Hey Marion, this is my business cart. Call me when you are in New York. I will be happy to see you." I returned to my seat. I saw that Duke was reading a magazine. We arrived in Paris. Marion kissed me, and said that she will wait for my call.

I called Morel. "My name is Paul Morgan. I am in Paris to pay a ransom. Scott Hunter is waiting at the airport for me. I want to speak alone with you. Gina told me that you are a good detective and I can use your help." Morel laughed.

"Why are you laughing Morel?"

"Because I am the one waiting for you at the airport Paul." I was walking out from the gate and talking to Morel. I asked "Where is Scott?"

"He is waiting for us at the hotel. Scott is my boss Paul." Morel continued to laugh.

"You are a funny man Morel. Looks like I will have a good time with you in Paris."

"Gina told me that you are funny too Paul. I hope to have a good time too."

"Scott destroyed my life in one week."

"To be a detective isn't a funny job Paul, so I try to joke about it. If you joke, you can resolve the problem easy."

"That is what makes you a good detective Morel."

"You don't tell that to Scott, because he must find where Holly is."

"I don't think that Scott is looking for Holy, he is waiting to get thirty million dollars Morel. He doesn't know where Holly is."

"Are you a detective Paul, because Scott told me that you are very good with money? Scott and I are detective, but we don't make good money."

"I am not detective Morel, but I work and make money. I need to give thirty million to Scott, because he wants to be rich like me."

"Does Gina know that Paul?"

"Gina told me that Scott will be rich after he sees me in Paris."

"What do you think about her?"

"Gina is a good girl. She told me to call you when I arrive in Paris. Gina was afraid that her father will tell you something against me."

"Gina is right Paul. Scott told me that you aren't a good man, but you need to pay a ransom. I saw that a man was weaving his hand. O boy, Scott was right that you are a dangerous man. You look very strong Paul." We shook hands.

"Do you think that it will be easy for me to kill Scott, Morel?"

"I am not going answer, because I will have to investigate who killed Scott."

"You don't have to investigate just ask Gina. She will tell you."

"Paul killed my dad, because he didn't know where Holly is, but Dad wanted to be rich Morel."

"How was your trip?"

"I met a girl on the plane. Her name is Marion. She invited me to go to her apartment. If I don't find Holly, I will call her. Marion wants me to spend time with her in her apartment. She is a pretty girl."

"What are you going to do if we find Holly?"

"My dad wants me to marry Holly."

"You don't?"

"Hey Morel, if your girlfriend left the hotel with her ex-lover and she didn't call you eight days, what would you do?"

"I am a married man with two children Paul, but you are right. If I had a girlfriend and she left me with another man. Maybe I will find and ask her why she wants to live with another man. Does she think that I am a bad man?"

"You forgot to tell in bed Morel."

"It will be hard for me to ask her who is better in bed Paul."
We laughed.

"Can you tell me what your plan is Paul?"

"I have a friend that works in Citibank. He will give me a bag
full with two million dollars and books. "

"Do you love to read books Paul?"

"I will give the books to Scott. Maybe he will spend a lot of
time in jail. Scott will read the books."

"You are funny, but you are smart Paul. Do you think that Holly is in Paris, Paul?"

"I don't Morel. If Holly was in Paris, Marcel and Luca would
have been in Paris too. It has been eight days. Somebody would
have seen them. Holly, Marcel and Luca are out of Paris. They can't
risk to be seen, if they want to get thirty million, but I think that
Marcel and Luca kidnapped Holly for another reason."

"We need to go to Citibank, Paul. I will drive you there, while
you explain the plan to me Paul. I will tell you if you are right or
wrong."

"I think that Marcel and Luca kidnapped Holly, because my
mom don't want me to marry her. She is with Alan. Mom has had a
sexual relationship with Alan for a very long time. He is a very rich
man, but Dad married Mom, thirty-four years ago."

"You spoke so easily about your Mom's long time relationship
with another man. Does your father know about it Paul?"

"He found out last Tuesday."

"My dad doesn't care for that. His name is Henry. My dad's goal
is for me to marry Holly. Henry will give me fifteen million dollars
if I need to pay the ransom. Holly and Henry have a good relationship."

"Your Mom doesn't."

"Yes that is correct. My mom's name is Janet. She loved Holly,
but six months ago something happened and Mom started hating
her."

"Maybe Holly had a sexual relationship with Alan, Paul."

"Me and Dad think that too Morel. Janet is married to Henry.
Maybe she wants to divorce Dad and she likes to marry Alan."

"I don't understand why Janet has a problem with that?"

"It is my problem that Holly slept with Alan. Holly slept with

Marcel and Giles too. Everybody slept with other people before they marry. I can't be surprised if Holly had more men in bed. I had many women too, before I met Holly."

"People are different Paul. You think like my wife. My wife and I have panned a vacation with children but Scott called me on Saturday."

"I am in Paris, Morel."

"Do you want me to pick you up from the airport Scott?"

"No. I am in hotel Le Royal Marceau Raffles."

"Do you want me to pick up you from there?"

"I will stay in the hotel." I was surprised because when Scott was in Paris he always stayed in my apartment.

"You have become a rich man Scott, because Le Royal is a very expensive hotel."

"I have a rich client. If you want to be rich, you need to help me, Morel." I met with Scott in the hotel. He gave me a magazine and told me.

"Do you know who this woman is?"

"This is Holly Gold, Scott."

"She disappeared last night from this hotel. I need somebody to help me, Morel."

"I will help you Scott." He gave me two thousand and said "When Holly pays me, I will give you more money Morel."

"Holly paid Scott fifty thousand Morel." He laughed.

"Now I understand why Scott was staying in Hotel Le Royal."

Morel showed me a picture. I asked him "Is that my picture, Morel? Who gave it to you?"

"Scott." He told me, "Paul Morgan is rich. He makes a lot money in New York and Paul Morgan is the boyfriend of Holly Gold".

"Where did you get the picture of Paul, Scott?"

"I was on vacation in Puerto Rico. I met Paul there. He was with Gina."

"You will have a rich son in law Scott."

"Gina didn't like Paul. She told me that Paul is old for her."

"What did Cindy tell to Gina?"

"Cindy liked Paul, but I didn't."

"I understood that Scott lied to me. Gina loves Scott and Cindy, but she listens to her Mom. My wife is a good friend of Cindy and Gina. My wife laughed a lot when Cindy told her that she was stupid, when she married Scott. Cindy joked that at her house live two stupid people, but she is happy that Gina is smart."

"What do you think about Gina, Paul?"

"Gina is a pretty and an honest girl, Morel. I had good time with her."

"Did you sleep with Gina?"

"I was ready the first night, but next day Gina spoke with Holly and we decided to be friends."

"Why did Scott tell me that you slept with Gina?"

"Gina was right that Scott will describe me as a bad man, when he speaks with you, Morel."

"Scott spoke a lot against you, Paul."

I told Scott a lot of truths and I and Cindy joked with Scott when we were in the old San Juan.

"Can you tell me what happened when you met Giles, Morel?"

"My wife doesn't love Scott." I told her that I need to meet Giles at his house. My wife knows well the wife of Giles, Estelle. She is from the family of Cote. The family is very rich. My wife is from a rich family too, but Cote's family is richer. Estelle and my wife were in the same high school.

"Did your wife tell you that she was stupid when she married you, Morel?"

"I never had problem with her. She had problem with her family when we decided to marry, but we have two children and we have a good relationship with her family. I showed her your picture and told her that you are the boyfriend of Holly. She told me "You must be honest with Paul. You need to tell him everything that happened between Scott and you, Morel. If you take the heart of Paul, he will help you to make more money. Scott will try to lie to you and Paul." She was right Paul."

"I didn't understand, why Scott didn't want to meet and speak with Giles. Scott is investigating what happened with Holly. Giles was in the hotel on Saturday and he paid for Holly's apartment for nine more days. Giles must have told Scott where Holly was, because he met with Holly many time last week and Holly left the hotel with his friend Marcel. I met with Giles. I didn't push him. I waited for him to tell me what happened with Holly. Giles told me that Holly and Marcel are old friends and they have a sexual relationship. It was so stupid Paul."

"Why does Scott need to investigate where Holly is, if he knows that they are lovers and they want to be somewhere alone?"

"I have a man that works for me. His name is Lamar. I told him that he needs to go to the hotel and follow Scott if he leaves the hotel. I left the house of Giles. After two hours Lamar called and told me that Scott met Giles. Scott didn't tell me that he met Giles. I met with Giles two more times. I asked Scott if he spoke with Giles. He told me that he doesn't want to meet or speak with Giles. I have informant in the hotel. He told me that Scott speaks regularly with Giles. A man met Scott in the hotel. His name is Dex Benet. Lamar saw Scott, Giles and Dex together in the coffee shop." Morel stopped at the bank.

"I am sure that Scott, Giles and Dex want to get the thirty million dollars Morel. We will continue our conversation after I return from the bank Morel." Norman Papen was waiting for me.

"Are you busy Paul?"

"I am Norman. Morel is my detective. He is waiting in the car." We entered the office of Norman. I signed the paper he gave me.

"Do you need I come with you Norman?"

"Sit and wait for me in my office Paul." He returned in few minutes and gave me two million and one hundred thousand.

"Can you count the money Paul?"

"I don't have time Norman."

"Where is the bag for the money?"

He pulled the bag from under his desk. I covered the books with the money.

"Do you think that this bag can carry thirty million dollars Norman?"

"Believe me Paul. Whoever wants to get the money won't have time to count them. He will look in the bag."

"Why did you say that your girlfriend disappeared in Paris?"

"Is it Holly, Paul?"

"Yes."

"I haven't heard that Holly Gold has disappeared Paul. She is very popular in Paris. If Holly disappeared it would have been big news in Paris."

"The problem is that she left the hotel with two men and hasn't call me for eight days. I spoke with Holly before she disappeared. Holly was a little scared. Last Monday somebody called and asked me to pay a thirty million ransom, if I want to see Holly alive. If I need to pay this money, my dad will transfer fifteen million dollars to your bank Norman. I will transfer additional thirteen million here."

"At this point you don't want to risk thirty million."

"You are right Norman. I will pay when I am sure that I will get Holly with me."

"I know that you will get Holly back Paul."

"I need to leave."

"I will have ready thirty million dollars in cash Paul."

"Thanks Norman."

I was in the car of Morel. "Oh my God. You are carrying thirty million for Scott, Paul!"

"If Scott gets two million is it will be OK Morel." I and Morel laughed.

"The man who asked me to pay the ransom will call me. I don't know what I need to tell him, Morel."

"You need to tell him that you are ready with the money, but you want to speak with Holly."

"What should I do, if he tells me that I will speak with Holly when I pay?

"He needs to tell you where you will meet him. I will make a plan after I know the place." I took twenty thousand and said "I will pay you this money now Morel. When we find Holly I will pay you more."

"Why are you paying me, Paul?"

"Because you will work for me. Scott will not be your boss, because he paid you two thousand."

"I need to tell Scott that he isn't my boss, because you paid me more Paul."

"No Morel."

"If I get the money I can't speak against you, Paul. Scott thinks that you will kill him."

Scott told me "If I didn't save life of Holly, Paul will kill me Morel."

"I have never killed a person Morel."

"I need to use Scott. I think that I need to speak with Giles Cote or Dex Benet. Maybe they know where Holly is. I think that Scott planes kill me after he gets the money."

"Why does Scott wanted me to work for him Paul?"

"You are a detective and Scott thinks that you will never speak against him. You are an old friend of Scott's family. I pay you, because you need to pay your people that will work for you to find Holly. I will give you more money if you need. If I spend one hundred thousand and I save the life of Holly, it will better for me. Otherwise, I need to pay thirty million."

"I understand Paul. You pay me and I must work hard to save Holly's life."

"Can you take the money Morel?"

"I promise you that we will find and save the life of Holly, Paul."

"This is what I wanted to hear Morel." We arrived at the Le Royal Hotel. We were in the lobby. I saw Duke Oran. He was at the front desk.

"Do you see the man on the front desk Morel?"

"His name is Duke Oran. I want to know more about him. I will wait in the lobby. You need to get more information for Duke." I sat and took to read a magazine. Duke couldn't see my face. Morel returned.

"He isn't Duke Oran, Paul. The name of this man is Kevin Cole. He has an Australian passport."

"Are you sure?"

"This is what the people on the front desk told me. Keven is leaving tomorrow."

"I think that something is wrong Morel. I saw the ticket of this man in the airplane. His name is Duke Oran."

"I will arrest him if you want Paul."

"It is too early to arrest Duke, Morel. I need to speak with Marion, before we decide to arrest Duke or Kevin, because he uses two names. One when he bought the airplane ticket. Another when he got the hotel room."

I checked in. Me and Morel were in my hotel room.

"I will call Scott and tell him that we are in the hotel, Paul."

"I need to make a call too, Morel." I called. "Hi Marion. This is Paul."

"Are you coming to my apartment Paul?"

"I can't today".

"Why did you call me?"

"Listen, you saw me when I looked at ticket of Duke Oran. I am in hotel Le Royal and Duke Oran is here too. Maybe he will be coming latter to my room Marion.

"Is that why you don't want to be with me, Paul?" We laughed.

"Do you want to find more information for him?"

"I need to know if Duke Oran is sick Marion."

"I am not sick Paul." We laughed again.

"You think that Duke Oran followed you from New York, Paul."

'I am sure Marion."

"I need time Paul. I may be able to help you with that."

"Do you want me to call you on your cell phone or at the hotel?"

"Doesn't matter for me Marion."

"The information for Duke Oran is important for me and Morel."

"Who is Morel, Paul?"

"He is a detective and will help me to find Holly. Morel is from France and lives in Paris, Marion."

"Will Morel call the police Paul?"

"Why?"

"Because I will give you a privileged information for Duke Oran."

"Can you speak with Morel, Marion?"

"This is a business between me and Paul, Marion. I will be happy if you can help us. Thanks Marion."

"She will call Paul. Why did you tell her that I am with you, Paul?"

"You are a detective Morel. I never lie to people. I will go to take a shower. You call Scott to and ask him to come here."

"Can you get the bag with you in the bathroom, Paul?"

"You are scared that Scott will kill you and disappear with the two million. Scott will think that he got thirty million Paul. He doesn't know that there are only two million dollars in the bag."

"It will be sad for me, if Scott killed me for two million. You are right Morel. Thirty million is better."

"When Scott kills you, Paul, I won't tell him that he took a lot books for reading. He didn't get thirty million dollars." We laughed.

I took the shower, dressed up and entered the room. Scott was there. "Nice to see you, Paul. I can't believe that you came. I asked Morel to pick you up from the airport."

"Why did you tell Morel to come in airport, if you weren't sure Scott?"

"I am kidding Paul."

"Are you ready with the money Paul?"

"I am ready Scott."

"Where are you meeting them to give them the money?"

"They will call me around 11:00am. Now is 10:55am Scott." Somebody called Morel.

"I need to meet my friend in the lobby" said Morel and left the room.

"I have the money, but I am not ready to give them the money Scott."

"Did Morel tell you that you didn't need to pay, before you hear Holly?"

"Morel didn't want to tell me what happened with Holly, because you are his boss."

"You are right Paul. Morel needs to listen to what I tell him. Did Morel tell you how much I paid him Paul?"

"I don't care how much you paid to Morel. I know that I need to pay thirty million ransom for Holly, Scott. Can you tell me how much Holly paid you Scott?"

"This is business between me and Holly, Paul."

"Why do I need to pay a ransom, if you have business with Holly?"

"You need to pay the ransom Scott, because you spoke with Holly and you gave her advice. Thanks to your advice Holly disappeared. Frankly, Holly left with two man, but I need to pay a ransom."

"You are her boyfriend. You need to pay for her freedom Paul."

"Are you sure that I will get Holly when I pay ransom?'

"They need to bring Holly when you pay."

"How do you know that Scott?"

"Everybody does that. I am a detective and everybody in Hotel Le royal knows that I have been investigating what happened with Holly."

"What are you trying to tell me Scott?"

"You will pay and they will bring Holly, Paul."

"This isn't a movie Scott. I need to be sure that I will get Holly when I pay. The hotel knows that you are a detective, but you don't know where Holly is. I prefer that nobody knows you, but you knew where Holly is.

"What did you tell them when they asked you where Holly is

Scott?"

"You are Holly's detective. That is the reason I came in Paris to meet with you Scott. That is why I came to pay the ransom. I know that you investigate very well the boys, who were with Gina, but they sold drugs. Holly isn't a drug dealer. She is a model. Holly was in Paris for business."

"Do you know why Holly was in Paris, Scott or your goal is to get money?"

My phone rung.

"Are you in Paris, Paul?"

"I am in Le Royal Hotel."

"Do you have the money?"

"I want to be sure that Holly is alive. I want to speak with Holly, man."

"You will speak with Holly when you get here. I don't believe you man and I hung up."

"Why did you hung up. They will kill Holly?"

"I will not pay the ransom if they kill Holly. I will be happy if they kill Holly, Scott."

"I want to be sure that you have the money Paul. I went to the bathroom and got the bag.

"There are thirty million dollars in this bag Scott." I opened the bag. Scott saw the money that covered books.

"You are crazy Paul. You have the money, but you want them to kill Holly." Scott left my room. I knew that Scott will tell them, so they will call me latter. I understood that Scott was with them. Their goal was to get the money. They didn't know where Holly was. Morel entered my room. I told him "I think that we have to deal with two groups Morel. One that kidnapped and is holding Holly somewhere in France. One that doesn't know where Holly is, but they want to get the money that I need to pay for Holly's freedom. I think that Scott, Giles and Dex are the people who want to get the money from me. Marcel and Luca are the people who kidnapped and are holding Holly. Alan or Mom paid them. I don't know yet what Kevin or Duke want from me."

"Why is Duke using an Australian passport and why did he followed me from New York? He lives in Brisbane, Australia. Why did he used a British passport with the name Kevin when he checked at the Le Royal?"

"He lives in London, Morel."

"Who paid him?"

"I think that Alan or your Mom paid him, Paul. You were right when you told me that Scott, Giles and Dex want to get your money. They will kill you after they get the money."

"Why will they kill me. I will pay Morel?"

"Because, you know Scott."

"They need to kill you too Morel. You know Scott and Giles."

"Scott will never kill me, because I am a detective. Scott will use me to cover for him, when he kills you, Paul. I work with Scott. If I tell the policemen that Scott killed you, they will suspect that I helped Scott to kill you, because I work with him. They will expect that since I am a detective I should have known what kind of man Scott is."

"Do you think that I am a killer and I will kill Scott, Morel?"

"I will tell to policemen that you killed Scott to save your life Paul."

"You didn't answer my question Morel."

"It is hard to kill somebody, if you aren't a professional killer, but I think that Scott is afraid. He thinks that you will kill him if something happens with Holly."

"Is that why Scott thinks that he needs to kill me?"

"Scott has killed people before. You haven't Paul."

"Have you killed people Morel?"

"I am a detective. I have a lot of enemies. I have a beautiful wife and two children. I had to save my life."

"I am not afraid to be with you, Morel."

"Thanks Paul. I have news for you. Kevin was in the office of Giles. When Giles left the office, Kevin followed him. Giles met with Dex. When Giles and Dex separated, Kevin followed Dex. I think that Dex is the one that is calling you, Paul."

"Maybe Kevin is that one that is calling me Morel. Kevin didn't know Scott, Giles and Dex. They didn't know Kevin too. Because Kevin followed Giles and Dex."

"Of course. If Kevin knew them, he didn't need to follow them. Kevin would have spoken to them. Where is Scott, Paul?"

"I told Scott that I will not pay the ransom. Scott became angry and he left my room."

"Maybe Scott is speaking with them now Paul. I will call Scott's room. The phone is busy. Scott is probably speaking with them right now Paul."

"Do you think that I need to speak with Scott, when he returns to my room Morel?"

"You told me that we need to use Scott to find where Holly is. Scott doesn't know where Holly is." "He doesn't, but Scott met with Giles. Maybe Giles knows where is Marcel. Holly left with Marcel last Friday. If we find Marcel, maybe we will find Holly, Paul."

Scott entered my room. I told him "I will pay the ransom Scott."

"Did Morel tell you to do that Paul?"

"Yes. We are detectives. You need to listen to us, Paul."

"I will do what you tell me to do, because I want to get Holly back Scott."

"What are you going to tell them, when they call you Paul?"

"I will meet with them and I will pay."

"Do you want to speak with Holly, before you pay them?"

"No. I will speak with Holly when they bring her to me. I will order lunch for three people. We will sit, eat and wait until they call me. Do you think that this is a good idea Scott?"

"It is Paul."

I ordered lunch. Scott stood up and said "I need to use the bathroom. I will go to my room, Paul." He left my room. Morel and I laughed.

"Scott went to tell them that everything is OK Paul. I will call Scott's room again. The phone is busy Paul. Scot is dangerous."

"I must listen you what you are telling me, Morel, if I want Holly and I to be alive. I never thought that someday I will need to listen to somebody else, because my father taught me that I needed to decide for my life. I don't need to listen others."

"Did you listen older employees when you started to work Paul?"

"It was different Morel. I always taught how to be more productive at my job. I listened to the people that worked with me, but I made the decisions when I met with my clients. Now I fight for mine and Holly's life. Job and life are different Morel. I had many problems when people told me what I to do. I didn't understand them, because they were asking me to help them, but they expected me to listen them."

Scott entered my room. I and Morel stopped our conversation. "Why did you stop to speak Morel, Scott asked?"

"We were speaking about Gina. Morel was disappointed that I asked Gina to live in my apartment. Morel told me that Gina is too young for me."

"Don't worry about Gina, Morel. Gina needs to decide for Paul. Paul, you and I need to find Holly.

"Do you think that they will call again Scott?"

"They need to call if they want to get thirty million Paul."

"Are you ready to give them the money?"

"I am ready Scott, because if I don't they will kill Holly."

"They will call you and you will save Holly." I saw that Morel was almost ready to laugh. I was too. Somebody knocked on the door. I jumped to open the door. Morel started to laugh.

"Why are you laughing Morel, Scott asked?"

"I laughed, because Paul is hungry. We are lucky that the lunch arrived before Paul started to eat us Scott." Paul and Scott laughed. We ate. I ate fast.

"You are right Morel. Paul refused to give the money to the people, because he was hungry."

"I was nervous too Scott. After the lunch I will be OK." We drank coffee. My phone rang.

"How did you feel now Paul?"

"I am feeling very good man. I am so sorry that I hung up, but I was hungry. I didn't think for Holly. Now I had some food and I am thinking for her. Can you tell me where I need to give you the money?"

"I will call you at 5:00pm." and the man hung up.

"What did he say you Paul?"

"He will call me at 5:00 o'clock. That isn't a problem Scott. To-night he will get the money and I will get Holly."

"Why did you say he, Paul, there must be more than one person?"

"I spoke with one person Scott. I don't know how many will come to get the money."

"Are you going to save my life if they want to kill me, Scott?"

"If course Paul. I am in Paris to save the life of Holly too Paul."

"What will Morel be doing then Scott?"

"You decide for Morel, Paul. You and I will be busy tonight Paul. I will go to relax in my room. I will be back in your room at 5:00pm" and Scott left. Morel and I laughed. "You took my heart Paul. I have never met anyone like you in my life."

"Do you want to relax Morel?"

"No Paul. I will not relax, because I have to think about what they may do tonight."

"Can you tell me more about Giles, Morel?"

"Everybody thinks that Giles is the boss of the company with which Holly has business in Paris. In reality the boss is the wife of Giles. Estelle controls the money in the company. Giles is from a poor family. Everybody was surprised when Giles married Estelle."

"Why did Estelle marry Giles?"

"If you see her, you will understand Paul."

"Holly met with Estelle."

"Did Scott tell you that?"

"He didn't. Holly told me that Estelle knew, that Holly slept with Giles."

"Why did Holly meet with Estelle, Paul?"

"Holly told me that it was a stupid decision."

"Which day did Holly meet Estelle?"

"On Tuesday last week."

"Estelle knows that Giles sleeps with many young girls who want to be models."

"Why doesn't Estelle divorce him?"

"Giles and Estelle have two children. The children love Giles. Estelle will have problem with them if she wants to divorce him."

"If somebody kills Giles, it will better for her. Do you think that I am correct Morel?"

"Absolutely Paul. The family of Estelle doesn't like Giles, but they don't want to pay." We laughed. "If Estelle meets you, she will want to get you in bed Paul."

"Why not. Holly slept with Giles."

"You will have hard time before you go in bed with Estelle, Paul."

"I will close my eyes Morel."

"You can't open your eyes before Estelle leaves the bedroom. You will be OK, if the bedroom is on the first floor. You will not hurt yourself."

"What will I do if Estelle want to meet with me?"

"You will need to drink one bottle of vodka. That will make Estelle look beautiful in your eyes." We laughed. We had tears in our eyes.

"I am rich, because I don't need to drink vodka, when I go in bed with Holly. I saved my money. You will not be rich after Scott get your thirty million, but I have a plan. I will marry Gina. I know that Scott loves Gina and he will give the money to Gina."

"What if Scott gives the money to Cindy?"

"Then, I will marry Cindy, Morel. She is forty-five. I am thirty-three."

"What happens to Scott?"

"Cindy will kill Scott to marry me."

"That is why Scott will kill you tonight Paul."

"Do you think that Gina and Cindy will cry Morel?"

"They will forget for you when they see the thirty million dollars Paul."

"Dad was right when he told me that Holly is may last chance to be married. We need to save Holly, because I will never marry."

"My wife will laugh a lot when I tell her about our conversations in Hotel Le Royal. She likes to joke with people, but you are on the top Paul. Does Holly like to joke with people too?"

"She doesn't. She discourages me when I joke with people, especially if don't know them well. Holly told me that I need to respect people."

"Why does Holly live with you?"

"I don't know. I love her and she love me. That is, it."

"Maybe the money you have is the reason you live together Paul."

"I don't think so Morel. Holly has a lot of money."

"I have money too"

"Do you think that Holly will pay thirty million dollars, if somebody kidnaped you Paul?'

"I am sure that Holly will pay Morel."

The phone of Morel rang. He spoke for a short time. He said "I need to leave. I will return at 5.00 o'clock Paul." I was alone. I will ask Holly if she will pay thirty million for my freedom.

Dad called me.

"Hi Dad. Do you think that Holly would pay for my freedom if I was kidnapped?"

"Holly loves you and she will pay Paul."

"Thanks Dad."

"I called you, because I spoke with Janet."

"Does Mom ask you for divorce her Dad?"

"Janet told me that they will kill you tonight Paul."

"Why didn't Mom call me?"

"Janet knows that you will laugh, if she tells you."

"Mom is right Dad."

"Are you afraid for your life Paul?"

"They will try to kill me to get the money Dad."

"You will pay them Paul. I will not, because they will not bring Holly when I pay. Nobody knows where Holly is, Dad."

"You need to call the police Paul."

"Holly's detective Scott Hunter should have called the police when he came to Paris. Scott spoke with Holly the whole week. He would have had information, if Holly was afraid before she disappeared. Now is to late Dad."

"I spoke with Holly last week too Paul. Holly told me that she was stupid when he left to Paris and Holly was disappointed with her decision."

"I think that Mom knows where Holly is, but she will never tell me or you Dad."

"I don't believe that Janet knows Paul."

"Mom hates Holly and she spoke with Marcel. Holly left the hotel with Marcel. Nobody saw or heard from Holly after that. I promise you that I will be back with Holly in New York. I will marry Holly to punish Mom."

"Call me if you need help. I will come to Paris, Paul."

"You must stay in New York, Dad."

"What do I tell Janet if she calls me?"

"That I will back with Holly."

"I will be waiting for you and Holly, Paul." Scott entered my room. I looked at my watch. It was 4:30pm.

"Where is Morel, Paul?"

"Somebody called him and he left?"

"When will Morel return?"

"At 5:00 o'clock."

"What do you think about Morel, Paul?"

"You know Morel better Scott. He is your friend. You, Cindy and Gina had been many times in Paris and slept in his apartment."

"He is from Paris. You need to listen to Morel, Paul."

"I don't know well Morel, because I met him this morning. I will listen to Morel, because he is your friend Scott. What are you going do Scott?"

"I will come with you when you carry the money. It will be at night. It is dangerous to carry thirty million dollars alone in Paris."

"Nobody will know that I carry thirty million in a bag Scott."

"Maybe the people that call to meet them somewhere in Paris, will follow you when you leave the hotel.

"Do you think that they will want to kill me and get the money?"

"You figured out fast Paul what might happen."

"You will be with me when I give the money."

"No Paul. I will be behind you when you give the money." Scott walked and picked up the bag. "The bag is heavy Paul. If you run with the bag, you need to be a strong man."

"Why do I need to run with the bag Scott?"

"I will give the money to them and I will get Holly."

"Maybe they will run Paul." Morel entered the room.

"Did you speak with Gina, Paul?"

"What?"

"Doesn't matter Paul." Morel looked at me and Scott.

"I will leave if you need to speak, something that I don't need to hear."

"I want Morel to stay in the room. I and Scott will continue tomorrow Morel. Gina is in America. We need to think about Holly." My phone rang.

"Do you have a pen and paper?"

"Just a Moment. I am ready man. I will wait for you at Park Monceau. The park is five hundred meters from your hotel. You must walk at Allee de la Comtesse de Sequr."

"Can you repeat that again?"

"Alle de la Comtesse de Sequr. OK. Before you across Avenue Ferdouse, you will see me and Holly. You must be there at 8:45."

"Man, I will carry with me thirty million in cash. If you aren't there, I need to keep the money at the hotel. It is too dangerous man."

"I will be there Paul."

"Holly too man."

"She will be there too."

"Do you think that I need to get a map from front desk of the hotel?"

"This is a good idea. You don't know well Paris, Paul. You will find the directions easy, but if you have a map will be better for you and me."

"For Holly too man."

"You are right Paul. I don't want somebody to be with you or follow you Paul."

"I will be alone man. See you there" and he hang up.

"I need to go to get a map from front desk. I want to see where is Park Monceau. You stay here with Morel."

"I will go to get the map Paul." Scott left the room.

"May I see the paper with the directions Paul?"

"I will be there at 8:30 pm Paul."

"I don't believe that Holly will be there Morel. "

"We know that Paul. I need to arrest Giles. He will be there with a woman that look the same as Holly. Giles will tell us where Holly is."

"I don't want to carry the bag Morel. I think that Scott will kill me before I enter in the park."

"I will take the bag with me Paul. Somebody will give you the back, before you enter the park."

"Thanks Morel." He left with the bag.

Scott entered and handed me a map. "This is the map of Park Monceau, Paul. Where is Morel?"

"He left. I don't know why."

"Where is the bag with the money?"

"Morel took the bag. He will give me the bag, before I enter the park."

"You are stupid Paul. Morel will disappear with the money."

"First Morel is your friend. Second, you told me that I need to listen to him. Morel asked me to give him the bag and I taught that it is good idea, because somebody may kill me before I give the money and get Holly. I will lose my life, Holly's life and the money Scott. If Morel steals the money, I will save my life. I will meet and tell them that Morel stole the money and Holly has money. She will pay them."

"Why did you rape Gina?"

"Gina told you that"

"Cindy told me. Gina is scared to tell me, because she was a virgin."

"What do you want from me, Scott?"

"To marry Gina."

"Why did you tell me that I needed to come to Paris?"

"I should have gone to Philadelphia. I think that Gina lives there or Gina should have come to New York. I will not go in Park Monceau. I will return to New York. I will call Gina to come to New York, Scott. Don't you think that this would have been better for me and Gina?"

"You don't think for Gina. You are in Paris to save the life of Holly. You need to go to the park. Maybe Morel will bring you the money before you enter the park Paul."

"Are you going to follow me in the park Scott?"

"Why do I need to follow you in the park Paul?"

"Because I will carry a bag with thirty million Scott."

"I will call Morel and ask him, if I need to follow you in park."

"Can you call and tell Morel that he needs to come back to the hotel Scott?"

Scott called. "Morel didn't pick up Paul."

"You are right Scott. Morel stole my money. I will call the police."

"What are you going to tell them?"

"That Morel stole my money."

"Morel didn't stole your money Paul. You gave the money to Morel. He is a detective and a good man."

"Thanks Scott. Now I am sure that Morel will give me the money."

"I will try to speak with Morel later Paul" and Scott left the room. It was good idea that Morel got the money. Scott didn't know that Morel got two million. I looked at my watch. It was 6:15pm. I had two hours until the meeting. I called at asked how long I need to wait if I order dinner.

"Thirty minutes sir." I ordered dinner. Mom called me.

"Did you speak with Henry, Paul?"

"I spoke with Dad, Mom."

"Why didn't you call me?"

"I am busy Mom."

"Of course you need to finish everything, because they will kill you after two hours."

"How do you know that and why somebody wants to kill me?"

"To get your money Paul."

"I will get Holly Mom."

"Holly isn't in Paris, Paul."

"Do you know how much money I am carrying?"

"I don't know, but Scott called me and asked me to pay him

thirty million dollars.

"Why do you need to pay Scott, Mom?"

"Because you raped Gina. You know that Gina is Scott's daughter."

"Where did I rape Gina?'

"In Puerto Rico. Everybody thought that you were with Holly in Paris."

"This is my alibi Mom."

"Don't be stupid Paul. Scott is a detective."

"What does Scott want?"

"Scott and Cindy want you to marry Gina."

"Do you want me to marry Gina, Mom?"

"Of course Paul. Gina is young and a good girl. I never saw her, but it will be better if you marry Gina."

"Because you hate Holly, Mom."

"I told you many times that Holly is a prostitute. Gina was a virgin when you raped her."

"Do you want me marry Gina because she was a virgin Mom?"

"Yes, Paul."

"Did Dad marry you because you were a virgin Mom?"

"Why did you lie to me, Mom?"

"Alan was your boyfriend before you married Henry. You are with Alan now Mom, doesn't matter that Henry is your husband. Susan followed you and Alan. The people in the hotel know Alan as your husband. For thirty-five years you live with two men. Can you tell me why did you do that Mom?"

"Alan is rich. When I marry Alan, you will be rich too Paul."

"I don't need Alan's money Mom. I have enough money to live good. Holly has a lot of money too. I want to marry her. I don't want you marry Alan. Hey Mom, you must divorce with Dad."

"Henry told me that he doesn't want to divorce. Henry loves me Paul."

"Does Alan love you too Mom?"

"I love Alan. You love Alan's money too Mom. Henry told me that Alan is better in bed and you like to be with Alan, because Alan is twelve years younger than Dad."

"Henry is right Paul."

"Hey Mom, I will have two fathers when you marry Alan. Henry, who isn't rich as Alan is, but he loves me very much. Alan, who is rich, but doesn't love me."

"I am your Mom, Paul and I know who is your father Paul."
Mom hang up before I told her that Henry is my father.

They brought the dinner. I ate and thought about my future. I
must save my life tonight, if I want to find Holly. I know that I
need to walk to the park, but I don't have idea, what I need to do,
when I enter the park. Maybe Morel or his friend will tell me when
I get the money. The hotel phone rang. I thought that Morel was
calling me.

"Can you come to my room?"

"I want, but I am far away from Paris. Oh my God."

"Why did you call the hotel phone Gina?"

"I was afraid that you won't pick up when you saw that I was
calling you Paul."

"Because you told you Mom that I raped you."

"I didn't say that Paul. My mom and dad want me to tell the police that you raped me in Puerto Rico. They want to get money
from you or your Mom, Paul. You must understand. I taught that
Mom and Dad love me and I love them. I never believed that Mom
and Dad were greedy people. They are not thinking about me Paul.
First, you never had sex with me and I need to lie that you raped
me. Second, all my friends will know that you raped me. How can I
marry anyone else? What will I tell my children, if they ask me why
you rape me?"

"If you marry me, you don't have problem Gina."

"Why do I marry you if you raped me Paul?"

"Because your parents want to get money from me or my
mom."

"If I marry you, your money will be my money Paul. My parents
didn't get any money. You must be very careful with Scott tonight
Paul.

"Are you afraid for my life Gina?"

"I am scared for your and Holly's life Paul. You are a hero for
me, because you are risking your life to save the life of Holly. I will
be so happy when I see Holly and you alive Paul."

"Are you going to tell Holly that I raped you Gina?"

Gina laughed. "Holly won't believe that Paul. Holly will believe
if somebody tells her that I wanted to be in bed with you."

"Why didn't you do that in Puerto Rico, Gina?"

"When I spoke with Holly I understood that Holly loves you so
much Paul. I didn't want to hurt her."

"Were you ready to go in bet with me Gina?"

"Of course Paul."

"Hey Gina, now I will tell your parents that you wanted to be in bed with me."

"It wasn't a joke. It was true Paul, but I don't want to tell that to my mom and dad. They wouldn't understand me. They would be happy if I married you, because you are rich."

"Do you know how much Holly paid Scott?"

"Scott didn't tell me Paul."

"Fifty thousand Gina. Now I need to pay a lot of money to save her life."

"Scott was right when he told me that Holly has a lot of money and she doesn't care for her money when she needs to pay somebody."

"Scott lied to you Gina. He asked Holy to pay him fifty thousand."

"Dad isn't a good detective, but he is a good professional liar Paul. "Gina and I laughed.

"I need to leave the hotel Gina. I am happy that I spoke with you before they kill me."

"I will be happy if you get Holly back, Paul."

Thanks Gina. I hung up the phone and left the hotel.

CHAPTER 6

I left the hotel at 8:00 o'clock. I was walking on Allee de la Comtesse de Sequr. When I checked the map, it was five hundred meters between the hotel and the park as the man said on the phone. I noticed that everyone walking on that street was walking, then stopping to look around quite often. I decided to do what the same, so that I will not attract attention. That way I would had a chance to see if anyone was following me. I didn't carry anything in my hands. I stopped and turned my head. I didn't see Scott. I didn't see anybody stopping and watching me. I knew that Scott will be careful if he followed me. I was close to the park. I saw the same car that Morel was driving. I stopped close to the car. The window of the car opened. Come in the car Paul. I didn't know who you are man. I work for Morel, Paul. I entered the car.

"Where is Morel man?"

"Call me Lamar, Paul. Morel is in the park. He will be on the left side before Allee de la Comtesse across Avenue Ferdousi. Morel doesn't want anybody to see him when you meet with the people that want the ransom."

"Can you tell me what I need to do when I enter the park?"

"You will carry the bag with the money. Don't turn your head to look behind you. We know that Scott will be waiting for you, but he doesn't know if Morel is watching your back. When Morel is sure that nobody is behind you, you will be at the place you need to give the money. Morel is at the place you need to be at. If he sees that Scott wants to kill you, he will stop him. Morel will kill Scott, if he tries to kill you."

"My life will not be safe between here and the people who are waiting for me."

"You are right Paul."

"Why shouldn't I turn my head to see, if Scott is behind me, Lamar?"

"If you do that, Scott will know that nobody is covering your back and he may decide to be more aggressive and kill you and get the money before the meeting place."

"I understand Lamar. If I am not scared, then Scott will be scared and he will not try to kill me. Scott will not risk to get the money alone. Scott will follow me, but he will wait Dex or Giles to get the money. Scott will divide the money with them, because Scott didn't have a chance to get the money alone."

"Morel told me that you are smart Paul. You understood quickly what I wanted to tell you."

"When I see the people that are waiting for me, I will see Morel to the left of me. You are right Paul."

"Can you put on this jacked, cap and gloves?"

"It is so hot Lamar. It is good for your safety Paul. I will move so you can exit the car from my door. If Scott is watching, he will not know who is carrying the bag with money. Remember, you must start to walk fast after you enter the park."

Lamar moved and I exited the car. I took the bag and walked toward the park. I entered the park. I started to walk fast. My life depended on how fast I was able to walk to the people that were waiting for me, because Morel was there. I felt that somebody was walking behind me. I didn't turn my head. I started to walk faster. I saw three people around sixty meters on front of me. It was forty meters to get to them when a man told me that I need to stop. There were two men and a woman. I stopped. I was feeling good, because I was alive. I didn't believe that Scott will kill me and get the money, because this people were here to get the money too.

I said "Hi Holly."

The women replied "Hi honey."

Holly never called me honey. I was sure that they didn't know where Holly is, but now I was sure one hundred percent. The man told me that I need to throw the bag. I saw Morel. He was behind some bushes. They didn't see Morel. He gave me a signal with his hand that I need to throw the bag, so I threw it.

"Can you come with Holly when you get the money man. I want to get Holly before you get the money?"

"I will check the bag before Holly to comes to you Paul."

I recognized the voice. It was Dex. He walked to the bag. I saw that Dex carried a pistol in his hand. I asked him "Are you going to kill me Dex?"

"How did you know my name Paul?"

"Many people who have been working to find Holly know your name Dex. You are working with Giles and Scott to get my money. I think that Giles is with a woman that looks like Holly. Why did you lie to me so many days that I will get Holly when I pay the ransom, Dex?"

"This was the idea of Scott and Giles. They used me to speak with you Paul. I don't know where Holly is. Giles knows her location."

"Do you think that Scott knows that too?"

"Scott and Giles spoke alone. Maybe Giles told him."

Suddenly the body of Dex dropped. I didn't understand what happened. I heard that Scott run and said behind me "You aren't an honest man. You killed Dex, because you don't want to pay. I will kill you and I will get the money Paul."

I walked closer and knelt to check pockets of the dead body for information that may help to find Holly. I heard sound above my head. The bullet missed my head. My eyes looked at Morel. I heard Morel telling me "Don't get the bag Paul. You must run fast towards me Paul. Scott will kill you." I was surprised, because the bag had two million dollars. I didn't take the bag. I run as fast as I could to bushes where Morel was. When I run, I saw that the body of the woman that called me "honey" was on the ground and the man who was with her disappeared. I saw that Morel carried a pistol. Morel fired in the direction where I heard the voice of Scott. He said "follow me Paul. We need to leave the park fast. Scott is wild because he didn't get the money. He will kill us."

"Didn't you kill Scott?"

"I fired in air to scare him."

"Why didn't I get the bag. Somebody will get two million Morel?"

"Don't be afraid for the money Paul. You didn't lose the money."

"What will Scott do now Morel?"

"He will be laying on the ground for a while. Before Scott is certain that I will not fire again, we need to leave the park." Morel was running fast. I followed him. We were outside the park. Morel and I started to walk on the street. He said" Take off your jacked and cap Paul. The people are looking at you. It is hot." I took off the cap, gloves and the jacked. "Now you look better, but little wet."

"Who killed Dex, Morel?"

"Why did you talk for so long with Dex, Paul?"

"I asked Dex if he knew where Holly is."

"This was dangerous for you, Paul. Scott was very close to you."

"I didn't believe when Scott fired at me Morel. Holly paid fifty thousand dollars to him."

"You want to pay Scott thirty million Paul."

"I thought that Dex would get the money. I heard when Scott and you fired, but I didn't hear any sound when the body of Dex dropped. I think that Keven killed him. I think that Kevin is a professional killer. Why did Kevin killed Dex and who paid Kevin, Morel?"

"It looks to me that somebody paid Keven to save your life Paul. The person that paid Keven knew that Dex was supposed to kill you, when he gets the money, because you would see him. If you are alive, you will tell the policemen, who got the money."

"Dex carried a pistol, but he spoke friendly with me, Morel."

"Dex is death, Paul. Nobody will know what Dex thought when he was to you. We will go to check the apartment of Dex. He lives close to the park."

"Why did Dex and Giles used this place to get the ransom Morel?"

"His apartment is close. The subway is close and there are usually many people on these streets. It was a good place to get the money and disappear pretty easy."

"What will Scott do?"

"Scott was out of the game after I took the money. The plan of Scott was to kill you when you walked with him on the street.

"That means that Scott needed to kill me between the hotel and the park Morel."

"Yes."

"What will Scott do with the money Morel?"

"He was probably planning to take train to Geneva and put the money in a bank there. The he would have returned to America."

"I will never give the money to Scott. He will have to kill me to get money. People at the front desk of the hotel would have seen that he left with me the hotel and they would have told the policemen that Scott killed me."

"Scott isn't stupid. He would have told you that he would wait for you outside on the street. The people on the street would have seen that Scott killed me."

"There are many benches between the hotel and the park. Scott would have told you that you need to sit on one of the benches for few minutes. Scott would have killed you on the bench placed your body to look like you were sitting and relaxing."

"How did you figure this out Morel?"

"My people saw that Scott walked the distance between the hotel and the park three times. He sat on a bench, but he was choosing very carefully which side to sit on. Scott was choosing based on the hand he would carry his pistol with. If he used his right hand, Scott had to use his left hand to keep your body from falling from the bench after he killed you. Scott was trying to see which hand will better to use, the left or the right hand. Scott needed to keep your body on the bench. If your body dropped on the ground, the people would have tried to help you and they would have seen that you were dead."

"Did you think that I would be safe, when I walked with Scott to the park, because I knew that Scott wanted to get the money?"

"You didn't have a chance to be alive Paul. You saw that Scott fired at you in the park. Scott would have fired on the street too. The goal of Scott was to get the money. Scott didn't think for your life. The money was more important for him."

"Thanks Morel. It is early to think that you will be alive tomorrow Paul. Scott is somewhere alive. He must kill you because he missed in the park and he didn't get the money. We must be careful with him, before the policemen arrest or kill him."

"Why did you checked the pocket of Dex, Paul?"

"I was looking for information that may help us find Holly. I found a wallet in his pocket. I took it. Can you check the wallet Morel? Maybe we will find where he lives.?"

"I know where he lives Paul."

"Dex lived Morel. The body of Dex is in the park. Dex will

never return in his apartment to live. His apartment is in the cemetery. He will relax there forever. I saved my life, because I squatted Morel. Are you going to call the police to tell them what happened in Park Monceau, Morel?"

"If we don't know where is Holly tomorrow afternoon, I will call the police. I will tell them that they need to arrest Scott Hunter and Giles."

"Why do the policemen need to arrest them?"

"Scott killed Dex Benet and tried to kill Paul Morgan."

"I think that Kevin killed Dex, Morel."

"Nobody saw that Kevin fired at Dex and killed him, Paul. Giles killed a woman in Park Monceau. If Scott leaves France, I will not call the police. I will need to speak with Giles. Maybe it will be better if you speak with Giles, Paul. I will be with you, but you will speak with him. Giles is your partner in bed or he is your friend. Giles needs to tell you where Holly is, because you what to know who was better in bed with Holly. Maybe you and Giles will travel together to see Holly."

"What should we do, if Holly tells us that Marcel is better than both if us, Morel?"

"You will call Scott and tell him that you can't pay thirty million, because Holly loves Marcel and she wants to stay with him."

"Hey Morel, Holly will be happy, me too, because I saved my money and I will be a free man."

"Why are you trying to find Holly, Paul, if she loves Marcel?"

"I need to be sure that Holly loves Marcel, Morel." We laughed.

"Where are we going Morel?"

"I want to check the apartment of Dex. Maybe I will find information for Holly there."

"Dex told me that he didn't know where Holly is."

"Maybe I will find addresses, names or phone numbers of other people that may have information. I will ask them if they know something about Holly. When you investigate you must check everything Paul. You don't know who will give you information."

"You are the detective Morel. You know what to do. I don't care when you are asking Paul. I am happy that you are alive and I have a good time with you."

"You told me that I didn't lose the money, but I didn't get the bag."

"The bag was full with books. I changed the plan when my

people told me that Scott would be in the park. I knew that Scott would try to kill you to get the money. So, Scott got the bag, but not the money. When Scott opens the bag and he sees the books, he will throw the bag. When the policemen come in the park, they will find the body of Dex and the bag. If Scott didn't use gloves when he was looking for the money in the bag his fingerprints will be on it. This will be a problem for Scott."

"I think that Scott isn't stupid. He most probably was wearing gloves, Morel."

"Why did you change your mind. You thought that Scott was stupid?"

"After I heard that Scott had a plan to kill me on the street, I changed my mind. People who are stupid, can't have that kind of plan. They will kill anywhere to get the money. Scott made a plan where he needed to kill me to get the money. Scott wanted to be clean after he killed me."

"Who made the plan that I meet Dex in Park Monceau, Morel?"

"Scott did everything Paul. He met Giles. Scott asked me for Giles when he came to Paris. I told him that Giles is greedy and he will do anything for money. When I told that to Scott, I thought that he will meet and ask Giles about Holly, because somebody paid Giles for her disappearance. Holly met with Giles every day that week. He must know where Holly is, because he paid for her apartment in the hotel, after Holly disappeared on Friday. When Scott told me that I need to meet Giles, I understood that Scott wasn't in Paris to help Holly. Scott was in Paris for another reason. I told my people to follow Scott, everywhere in Paris."

"I had a big question, why didn't Scott tell me that he met Giles and Dex?"

"Now I know. Scott promised them that they would get thirty million dollars. Dex was a criminal. He was selling drugs. Dex died. Giles killed the girl that was with him in the park pretending to be Holly. Scott took the bag with the books."

"I am alive. You finished a good job Morel."

"It wasn't good Paul. Two people died for nothing. Frankly, I didn't believe that Giles would kill the girl and somebody would kill Dex. The person that killed Dex finished the good job, Paul"

"Maybe you are right, because he carried a pistol, but I don't believe that Dex had to kill me. He wanted to speak with me longer when Kevin killed him."

"The job of Kevin was to kill the person who wanted to get the money. Somebody told Kevin that this person would kill you."

Morel stopped and said" This is the building where Dex lived. Are you coming with me or you are staying here Paul?"

"I am coming with you Morel."

"Are you scared that Scott will kill you?"

"I want to find Holly, Morel." He laughed.

"If Scott killed you, Holly would not have a chance to be free Paul."

"You are joking with me, but this is true Morel."

We entered the building. Morel found on which floor was the apartment of Dex. He said "We need to climb the stairs to the third floor Paul."

"The building has elevator."

"Somebody may see us if we use the elevator Paul."

"Somebody may see us when we climb the stairs, Morel."

"Most people think the same as you, Paul. They use the elevator."

We were on the third floor. Morel opened the door easy. We entered the apartment of Dex. "You are a professional thief Morel. You need to use your skills to open doors more often. You will make some money."

"If Scott kills you and they take my license, I will take your advice Paul."

"I hope that they will not take your license Morel."

"If you want to be alive Paul, stay here and you don't touch anything. I will be looking for information."

"Do you think that Dex lived alone Morel?"

"He wasn't married, but I am not sure, if somebody is here Paul. If Dex had planned to come back with the money here, I think that he wouldn't wanted people in the apartment. Don't open the door if somebody asks for Dex."

"The apartment has a doorbell Morel."

"I know, I said that in case, a neighbor knocks on the door."

"Do you think that neighbors spy on each other?"

"Some of them don't have anything else to do.'

"If somebody knocks I will tell him "Hi neighbor, I am Dex and I am busy now. Call me tomorrow."

"She will call the police Paul."

"It could be he Morel."

"The men prefer to drink wine. They don't want to spy. Can you stop to ask questions for the Moment Paul? I will never finish my job if I stay and speak with you. Can you zip your mouth Paul?"

"It would have been better if Scott killed me. I wouldn't have a chance to ask you, Morel."

"Sit on the chair and be quiet Paul."

Morel had a lantern. He didn't turn off the lantern even though the apartment had light from a street lamp. I sat on the chair. I looked around me. Morel went to another room. I was thinking about what happened in the last one hour. It was a miracle that Scott didn't kill me. If I didn't squatted Scott would have killed me. If Dex squatted, Kevin wouldn't have kill him. Dex carried a pistol, but he didn't look dangerous. He didn't point the pistol at me. Dex didn't tell me, "I need to kill you Paul." Now I was in his apartment. He should have been here. Morel returned back to the room I was waiting for him in.

"What happened to you Paul. You look strange?"

"For the first time in my life I saw a man that was killed on front of me Morel. I was thinking for Dex. Why didn't he knell?"

"If Dex tried to get the money, he had a chance to be alive, because Kevin would have missed." "First Dex didn't know that Kevin was there to kill him. Second, Dex saw that you didn't carry a weapon and he didn't have a problem to kill you and get the bag with the money. Third, Kevin is a professional. He will never miss when he fires to kill. Dex had a zero chance to be alive Paul."

"Did you find anything Morel?"

"I found a lot of information, but for people who buy drugs from Dex, I will check this room too Paul."

Morel checked the room fast. We need to leave, because the policemen will come here any time now. We were on the street.

"How do you know that Kevin killed, Dex?"

"My people saw that Kevin entered the park at 8:00pm."

"Do you know where is Kevin now?"

"My people will tell me. Kevin isn't dangerous Paul. He finished his job and I think that he will leave for England. Kevin came to the park with a car. He parked the car nearby. Maybe Kevin is driving to England as we are speaking."

"Did you have a plan when Scott tried to kill me?"

"I didn't believe that Scott wanted to kill you in the park Paul. Scott tried to kill you when he saw that Dex was killed. Scott thought that I gave you a pistol and you killed Dex."

"You gave a pistol to Scott too."

"It is my problem."

"I was the one with the problem Morel. You, Dex, Scott, Kevin and Giles had weapons. I didn't. Why didn't you give me a pistol Morel?"

"I wanted Scott to kill you Paul."

"If Scott killed you, now I didn't have to answer your stupid questions. Do you have more questions Paul? Why did Giles kill the girl?"

"The girl saw what happened in the park."

"Who does Kevin for work, Morel?"

"For Janet and Alan."

"Janet is my mother Morel."

"That is why Kevin killed Dex. He didn't kill you, Paul. They paid Kevin to save your life."

"Who told you that Morel?"

"Hey Paul. I am a detective. You wanted me to help you. Do you want to find Holly alive Paul?"

"I want Morel. That is why I am in Paris."

"Your Mom spoke with Scott, before he left for the park. Scott told her where they will kill you. Scott told her that he spoke with you, but you didn't believe that somebody wanted to kill you, because you were carrying the money to pay the ransom."

"Why did Scott tell Mom?"

"He is stupid because Mom will tell me."

"Your Mom didn't have a chance to tell you. Scott knew that Dex or he would kill you in the park. Janet didn't call the police. She called Kevin. Scott didn't think when he spoke with Janet. Scott is thinking now Paul. He must kill you, before French policemen arrest him. How much are you going to pay me to save your life Paul?"

"You got already two million Morel."

"Do you want more?"

"You are so funny Paul. I will keep your money in my apartment. I will never take this money. If Scott kills you, your family will get the money back. Nobody knows that you got this money from me. Do you think that your wife is stupid Morel?"

"She is smart Paul. You are right. She knows that I work with you. If Scott killed both of us, my wife would know who killed us."

"Did you tell her that Scott wants to kill us?"

"I told her that Scott wants to kill you to get thirty million dollars. You were carrying the money to pay for Holly's freedom."

"Do you know what she told me?"

"This is a man Morel. Paul is risking his life and wants to pay for Holly, because Paul loves her. Would you pay thirty million for my life Morel?"

"I love you, but I don't have this money honey."

"You are a smart detective Morel. You will kill the kidnappers and take me. I love you that you are a man Morel."

"Do you think that I am a smart detective Paul?"

"Of course Morel. You took two million, but you saved my life."

"Do you think that your live is worth two million dollars Paul?"

"Holly's life is more expensive Morel. Thirty million dollars."

"You didn't answer my question Paul."

"I think that my live is more than that Morel. Holly told me that I am her golden boy." We laughed.

"What is the name of your wife Morel?"

"Margot. You will sleep in my apartment Paul. There are Margot and two children Morel."

"I am not Scott."

"Margot would have been happy to meet you, Paul, but she is on vacation with boys."

"Why didn't you go on vacation with them?"

"I was busy saving your life Paul. If I was on vacation, Scott would have killed you and he will never come to sleep in my apartment, because he will be rich. I would be lonely, if Scott, Cindi and Gina are in Paris and I didn't see them."

Morel picked up the phone to talk to Lamar. They spoke in French. "Lamar is waiting for us Paul."

"Lamar was in your car Morel."

"I need to get my car." We didn't walk too long. Lamar was outside the car.

"Do you know where is Scott, Morel?"

"We will speak in the car Lamar. You need to drive, because it will be easy for you to find where you parked your car Lamar."

We entered the car. Morel said "The last time I saw Scott was in the park, when he fired at Paul."

"Did Scott try to kill Paul?"

"Scott missed Lamar."

"Scot is crazy Morel."

"Scott went wild when he saw that somebody killed Dex, Lamar."

"Kevin killed Dex, Morel. Kevin is a dangerous like Scott now Morel."

"I don't think so Lamar. Believe me, we will hear that Kevin left for London. He finished his mission in Paris. Kevin wasn't in Paris to kill Paul and get the thirty million dollars. Scott came in Paris for that."

"Do you think that Scott will try to get on an airplane to America?"

"Scott will stay in Paris. He didn't kill Paul and he didn't get the money."

"What is your plan Morel?"

"At this point I don't have a plan Lamar. Paul will sleep in my apartment, because Scott could be waiting for Paul in the hotel or somewhere around the hotel."

"Hey, Morel and Paul, maybe Scott is reading a book somewhere in Paris. Do you think that Scott took the bag with the books?"

"I have never seen Scott reading a book when we were together Lamar. I don't believe that he got the bag with the books."

"Scott knows that you got the money from the hotel Morel. Maybe he is waiting somewhere around your apartment."

"Maybe you are right Lamar, but I am not afraid to meet Scott. I fired one bullet in the air to scare him in the park. I will fire one at his head to kill him, if he wants to see me. Scott knows who I am Lamar. Scott used me to kill Paul and get the money. Scott is a detective and he was in Paris to investigate what happened with Holly. Scott lied to me for one week. Scott knows that I will never forget that. I have a wife and two children. I don't want to finish my life in jail. Scott wants me to finish my life there."

I was with Morel the whole day. For the first time since I met Morel I saw him angry.

"Don't you try to joke with me right now Paul? I am not happy at all right now."

"I see that Morel." Lamar stopped the car.

"What do I need to do after we separate Morel?"

"You know the address of Kevin in London. Tonight you must go to London. You need to find Kevin and speak with him. If he doesn't want, you tell him that he killed Dex in the park and you saw it. Tell him that I will call in policemen in Paris to call the police in London and ask them to arrest Kevin there. I want to know who paid Kevin to kill Dex. I don't want to know who is he. It isn't my job."

"Do you want me to ask Kevin, if he knows where Holly is?"

"The people that paid Kevin know that Lamar. I will ask them. Tell Kevin that my business is to find Holly alive. That is why I am asking him for the people that paid him."

"You can tell Kevin that I will give him additional money that he saved my life Lamar."

"Paul is right. Tell him that, Lamar. I think that Kevin can't be afraid when he hears that, because he was in the park to save Paul's life. Paul's Mom called Kevin to go to the park."

"I will call you from London, Morel. I know that you will have fun time with Paul, but sometimes look at your phone Morel." We laughed. Lamar exited the car. He got his car and left.

"Do you like Lamar, Paul?"

"He is young, but he is a smart guy Morel."

"I love Lamar and I want him to stay to work for me Paul, but I think that Lamar can't stay for a long time, because I will not have enough money to pay him."

"I will help you, if we find Holly alive, Morel. I will ask Holly to work with you in Paris. Holly isn't a cheap woman Morel. She will pay you good money."

"You are like my wife Paul. Margot told me the same."

"I never listen to Holly, because we have different business Morel."

"Margot is my wife. Holly isn't your wife Paul. Are you going to marry Holly, when we find her?"

"I would like to marry her, because my dad loves her, but I don't know what Holly will decide. I will never ask Holly to marry me."

"How are you going to marry Holly, if you don't ask her?"

"Holly needs to ask me, because I was ready to ask her, but she left to Paris. After that Holly left the hotel with two men, Marcel and Luca. Why didn't Holly leave with one-man Morel? I was hurt when Scott told me that Holly was with two men. One was OK. But two More? Oh my God." We laughed.

"Maybe Holly needs two men Paul."

"When we find Holly I will ask her."

"Are you joking with me Paul?"

"Of course Morel. I understood this morning that Holly has a big problem. We need to find Giles, Morel. I think that Giles got money from Mom or Alan. Last time when I spoke with Holly, she told me that Marcel was happy. Holly told me that she will be back in New York on Sunday, doesn't matter if she had signed or not the contract. The next day Holly left the hotel with him and Luca. Nobody saw or heard from her after that. If Holly wants to be with Marcel, she would not have told me that she loves me and I need to wait for her at the airport. Scott told me that Holly had a plan, but after two ours she changed the plan."

"Paul, you never knew what Holly thought and what Holly did."

"That isn't true Morel. I have been with Holly for one year and seven months. Holly never changed her plan. Holly did what she said. Holly wanted to tell me."

"You are like me Paul. You never lied and you never changed your plan. You know well Holly."

"Yes, Morel."

"I asked Scott to tell me for Holly's family. Scott didn't have information for them."

"Did Holly speak with you about her family?"

"She told me that something happened with her parents when Holly was seventeen or eighteen. I thought that her parents were death and I never asked her again. When I was in Puerto Rico I asked Holly for her family. She told me that they are rich, but she will talk to me when she returns to New York. I feel that the parents of Holly are alive Morel, but I am not sure one hundred percent."

Morel stopped the car. He said "I will exit. You need to stay in the car Paul. I must be sure that Scott isn't here." Morel returned and he opened the car's door.

"Come with me Paul." We took the elevator.

"My apartment isn't big, but it is good for four people. It was good that my wife delivered two boys. If we had a boy and a girl, I had to sleep with the boy, Margot needed to sleep with the girl.

Otherwise, I needed to buy a new apartment with three bedrooms. I needed to get money from a bank, because I don't have money to pay for a new apartment."

"You must love Margot that she saved your money Morel."

"I love Margot that she married me Paul. She is a beautiful and from a rich family. I am from a working family."

"The rich people work too Morel. They work, but they know how to make money. You have money to pay thirty million for ransom. I don't." We entered the apartment.

"I need to tell you that my dad will give me threaten million dollars, if I need to pay the ransom, Morel"

"Where is your father?"

"He is waiting in New York. His name is Henry. Henry will transfer money in Citibank, if I need them. The big joke is that Mom hates Holly and she doesn't want me to marry Holly. Dad loves Holly and he will pay thirteen million, and will I marry her."

"This is normal Paul. Margot's Mom supported her to marry me. Her father didn't want me and he was against our marriage."

"How is your relationship with the father of Margot now Morel?"

"He is happy that he has two grandchildren. Hey Paul, because I worked hard to had two boys, he loves me now." Morel laughed.

"I think that you made Margot happy when you worked hard in bed too Morel."

"I never asked Margot, but she told me that I made her happy when I was with her in bed. You must make Holly happy too when you marry her and spend time with her in bed."

"I will ask Holly if she is happy Morel." We laughed.

"When I met the father of Margot, he asked me. What will you work after you finish college Morel?"

"I will investigate people."

"This isn't a job to look what people do Morel. I don't want you in my house, because you will look all the time at what I do. Margot, I don't you invite Morel here."

"For a long time, I didn't visit his home. Margot's Mom came to the wedding when we married. Margot and the boys were going to his house. The children asked me why I can't come with them in the house at their grandfather. Margot told them that I was busy."

"When Estelle married Giles, my father in law came in my office and told me "You are a good man Morel. I want you come in my house next weekend." When I went there he asked me "Did you know why I invited you Morel?" I told him that I don't have any idea. He said "Cote's family is richer than my family, but my daughter married a better man. Giles asked Cote to give him money to open a business. Of course, Cote told him that Giles needs to listen to Estelle. She will control Giles and the money of the Cote family. I love you that Margot have two boys and you never asked me for money Morel." After that we became good friends. He loves me now Paul. Maybe your Mom will love Holly too, after she delivers two boys and you didn't ask her for money Paul.

"Who knows Morel?"

"I will prepare dinner for us."

"What do you want for drink?"

"I am in France. It is polite to drink French wine". I saw a picture of Margot. She was beautiful.

"Can you tell me more about Margot, Morel?"

"Are you surprised that this beautiful woman is my wife?"

"No Morel. I am surprised that Margot turned her back on her rich family to marry you."

"Margot was a powerful girl when I met her."

" Isn't she now?"

"No. Margot is the same, but now she has two boys. The boys changed her life. She needed to take care of the children and go to work. Sometimes Margot told me "If I die it will be good for me Morel. I am feeling so tired.""

"The family wanted to help her and they tried to give her money. Margot told them "You don't want Morel. I don't need your help. I live with the man that I love." The family asked Margot to work in the family's business. She would make more money there. I pushed her to work for their family but Margot told me "If I work with them, they will speak the whole day against you. They will try to separate us. They don't understand that I don't want their money. The power of money is everything for my family Morel.""

"I didn't understand Margot. Everybody wants to have a lot of money. Everybody likes to be rich. I asked her "Do you like to be rich Margot?" She said "I am rich Morel." I thought that she spoke for her family. Margot told me "Don't think that I am rich, because my family is rich. I am rich, because I have two boys and you Morel. I know that we will not be rich, but we will have a good life." Margot was right Paul. Margot and I never had a problem between us. The boys are growing very well."

Morel looked at his watch. It was 12:30am. "We need to get a good sleep Paul. Tomorrow will be a busy day. I will show you where you need to sleep. This is the room of the boys. Margot changed the sheets. If you want something, you need to tell me."

"It is OK. I will feel that like a boy, when I sleep in the bed of a boy." I slept very good. I felt like a young boy when I woke up. I entered the kitchen. Morel was preparing breakfast.

"How are you feeling Paul?"

"I am feeling like a young boy Morel. May be Mom will tell me.

"Paul, you are a young boy. Holly is an old woman for you. Can you choose a young a girl to live with you?" We laughed.

"Do you think that Mom is right Morel?"

"May be Holly will tell to your Mom "I want to live with a young boy. Paul is good choice for me."

"I have good news for you Paul. I spoke with Margot early this morning. I told her what happened last night. She told me that you and I must use Estelle to find Holly."

Margot told me "Maybe Estelle knows where Holly is. You must scare her. Tell Estelle that Giles killed a woman in the park. Her family will be scared if the news goes to the newspapers or TV. To cover this story, Estelle will help Paul to find Holly. Estelle will want somebody to kill Giles."

"I told Margot that Giles and Estelle have two children. Do you know what Margot told me?"

"Estelle depends on her family. If they get the money from the company that Estelle controls, she will be nothing. What will Estelle do with her two children and no money? They are more important for her. Estelle will try to kill Giles."

"Would you kill me Margot I asked her?"

"I don't depend on my family. You will never kill somebody for nothing Morel. Now you have a chance to be a good detective. You don't lose your chance Morel. "Margot hang up Paul.

"Do you think that Margot is right?"

"She is smart Morel. We need to use Estelle. You need to tell me what I need to ask Estelle."

"Estelle is smart too Paul. If I tell you what you need to ask her, she will understand, that somebody told you. Estelle will not be honest with you. She will not make a deal with you Paul. You work with people every day. They are different, but you need to make a deal with them. Estelle is your client. You must make a deal with her Paul. This is the phone number of Estelle. Call from my home phone, Paul. If Estelle asks you where you are, tell here that you are in my apartment."

I called. A man answered the phone "This is house of Estelle Cote, may I help you?"

"My name is Paul Morgan. I am from New York. I want to speak with Estelle Cote."

"Are you calling from New York, Mr. Morgan?"

"I am in Paris and I want to speak for business with Ms. Cote."

"What kind business do you have Mr. Morgan?"

"I am an investor sir."

"Hi Mr. Morgan, this is Estelle."

"Nice to speak with you Ms. Cote."

"Call me Estelle. May I call you Paul?"

"Of course Estelle. When I met Holly, she wanted to call me Mr. Morgan, because Morgan is a popular family name."

"What is beautiful Holly doing, Paul?"

"Your voice is beautiful Estelle. If I was beautiful, it would have been better for me Paul. I would not have married Giles."

"He is Holly's a partner, Estelle. Holly never spoke against Giles."

"I don't believe that Holly talk to you for somebody in her business Paul. Holly is a smart woman. Are you going to marry Holly?"

"I was ready to ask her, but Holly left for Paris. She needed to sign a contract with Giles."

"What happen with her Paul?"

"Giles told me that Holly left with Marcel somewhere. They have an old sexual relationship Paul. May be Holly wants to marry Marcel?"

"I want to find Holly and ask her."

"Who is better in bed. If Holly tells me that Marcel is better, I will leave her alone?"

"Do you want to be in bed with me, Paul?"

"You are married for Giles, Estelle. He is your husband. What do I tell Giles if he asks me why I am with you?"

"Giles isn't here now. Where are you Paul?"

"I am in the apartment of Morel."

"May I speak with Margot?"

132

"She isn't here. Margot is on vacation with the boys."

"What are you doing in Margot's apartment?"

"Last night somebody tried to kill me. Morel saved my live. You know that he is a detective. He is investigating what happened with Holly."

"Everybody knows that Holly is with Marcel, Paul. What is he investigating?"

"Why did they want to kill me last night in Park Monceau? I was carrying thirty million dollars to pay a ransom for Holly's freedom."

"Are you are joking with me Paul?"

"I am not Estelle. Giles was in the park too. Giles did something there. I don't want to tell you what Giles did on the phone."

"I want to meet with you in my house at 11:00am. Are you coming Paul?"

"I am Estelle."

"I will give you the directions for my house."

"I will get them from Morel, Estelle."

"I don't want to see Morel, Paul. He is married for my good friend Margot, but Morel is a stupid detective. Nobody wants to have anything to do with a detective. Do you think that I am right Paul?"

"I will come alone Estelle."

"See you at 11:00" and Estelle hang up.

"Oh my God. You had a very good conversation with Estelle, Paul."

"I will go to see her Morel. Don't run away when you see her Paul."

"Do you think that I need to drink one bottle of vodka before I go Morel?"

"It is too early for vodka Paul, but if you drink one bottle vodka, Estelle will look like a princess to you."

"Estelle will take me easy in bed Morel."

"You will not save the life of Holly, Paul. You will kill Holly and Giles."

"I will never kill people Morel."

"Estelle will pay to somebody to finish this job Paul. I will drop you at Estelle's house. When you are done, I will pick up you. I will call the hotel and ask them, where Scott is."

Morel called. "Scott checked out Paul. The people that work in the hotel are so happy that Scott left. They told me "Morel, your friend Scott is a stupid detective. Don't tell him not to return to this hotel. We will leave the hotel.""

"May be Scott left Paris, Morel."

"I think that Scott is still in Paris and he will try to meet with Giles. I will call and tell my people to look around Estelle's house. Estelle told you that I am a stupid detective and she doesn't want to see me with you at her house."

"I am so sorry Morel."

"Estelle is right Paul. The living room of her house is bigger than my apartment. Estelle was disappointed when I met with Giles in her house. When Estelle left the house she told me" I don't want to see you again in my house stupid detective.""

"Did Giles heard that?"

"He laughed and told me that Estelle was angry when Giles told Estelle that I want to speak with him in the house."

"Why did you see Giles there?"

"I wanted to meet him at his office or somewhere else, but Giles told me that he wanted us to meet in his house. Giles did that to hurt Estelle. They are like a mouse and cat, but they live together. I don't know how they have sex, but they have two children Paul. We need to have a plan Paul."

The phone of Morel rang. "This is Morel. For you Paul."

"I will meet you at 2:00pm. Is this OK?"

"I will come at 2:00 o'clock Estelle. May I bring Morel with me, Estelle?'

"They told me that you are a funny man, but you know my answer Paul."

"I will be alone Estelle. Why did you change the time?"

"My children will leave the house at 1:00 o'clock Paul. You want us to be alone Estelle?"

"Of course Paul. You don't want somebody see what we will do. They told me that you are a smart man too. I want to know who is better in bed Paul. See you at 2:00o'clock" and she hang up.

"Estelle wants to have sex with me Morel."

"Estelle wants you to forget Holly after had sex with her, Paul. I don't believe that, because Holly is beautiful, but it is your decision Paul." Morel laughed.

"Do you think that this is funny Morel?"

"Of course Paul. You will have one more woman in bed. May

be Estelle is an attractive woman in bed. Call and ask Giles. He will tell you who is more attractive Estelle or Holly."

"You are right Morel. Giles has been with both them in bed. I haven't."

"Well, this is your chance Paul."

"Do you think that Estelle will tell Giles and Holly?"

"One hundred percent Paul. Estelle wants to hurt Giles and Holly."

"Hey Paul, if Estelle divorces Giles and she marries you, you will be a rich man."

"And I need to work for the Cote family Morel."

"You work for somebody now Paul. What is the difference."

"Holly will miss me very much Morel."

"Holly will find another man Paul."

"She doesn't need to find Morel. Holly is with two men now. Marcel and Luca."

"What is your problem to sleep with Estelle, Paul?"

"I will decide what I need to do when I see Estelle, Morel."

"You are almost ready to go in bed with her, Paul."

"I will know that after 2:00 o'clock Morel."

"What are you going to do if Estelle tells you that she will tell you where Holly is only if you have sex with her?"

"That is good Morel. I will tell Holly that I slept with Estelle, because I needed information to find her. It was so hard for me to be in bed with Estelle, Holly. Maybe Holly will tell me "You made a good decision Paul. You saved my life." Hey Morel, I will call my dad."

"Are you going to ask your father what you need to do with Estelle?"

"If Dad is happy I will ask him."

"Hi Dad."

"Oh my God. You are alive."

"I am Dad. Janet scared me last night. She told me that I didn't love you Paul."

"Why did Mom tell you that Dad?"

"Because I didn't stop you to go to Paris. I told her that you are a big man. Janet told me "Paul is a boy for me Henry. You had to stop him.""

"Did your Mom called you Paul?"

"I spoke with her yesterday. Mom was right Dad. They tried to kill me. God saved my life."

"If you have problem in Paris, you need to return back to New York, Paul."

"I will be back with Holly, Dad. I know that you will keep your promise, but your life is more important for me, Paul."

"Dad, what do you do, if you need to have sex, but you don't like the woman? What do you do with her?"

"If she wasn't a pretty woman, you have sex from behind, Paul. This way you don't see her face. It will not be good if Holly finds out that you had sex with another woman, Paul."

"Holly left with two men, Dad."

"Holly was kidnapped Paul. Holly didn't go to have sex with them."

"How do you know Dad?"

"Janet wanted to hurt me last night. She told me that Holly was raped and you are stupid that you want to marry her."

"Did Janet tell you who raped Holly?"

"She didn't, because I hang up. Dad, if Mom calls you again, you need to speak with her. May be Mom will tell you where Holly is with Marcel and Luca."

"Why did you ask me that you need to have sex with a woman that is not pretty?"

"Her name is Estelle. She is the wife of Giles."

"Why does she want sex with you Paul?"

"Holly slept with Giles four years ago".

"Why do you want to have sex with Estelle, Paul?"

"Holly didn't know you when she slept with Giles. It is normal for twenty-six years old woman to have sex. Did you have sex when you were twenty-six Paul?"

"Maybe I will sleep with Estelle If she tells me where Holly is."

"This is different Paul. You will have sex to save the life of Holly."

"Thanks Dad. Hey Dad I will call you after I meet Estelle. Don't be afraid, because Holly's life is more important Paul."

"What did your father tell you?"

"I need to use everything I can to save Holly."

"Your father is a good man Paul."

"He is Morel."

"Do you need to go to the hotel to change your clothes Paul?"

"I am OK. I will take a shower before I leave your apartment.

Dad told me that Marcel and Luca raped Holly."

"How did he know?"

"My mom told him."

"I want to know more about Janet and Alan, Paul. Janet spoke with Scott, Marcel and Giles. She knows Kevin. Your Mom has information about what happened with Holly."

"She will never tell me, Morel. I know that you want me to call her."

"We will talk about that after you meet Estelle."

"We know where Estelle is and I will meet with her, but we don't know where are Scott and Giles, Morel. I think that Giles knows where Holly is. Estelle doesn't. Scott left the hotel. He has two choices. To leave France or try to kill you and get the money. If Scott stays in France, I will know where he is after two hours or before you meet Estelle. Scott isn't a problem, because he isn't from Paris or France. Scott doesn't have friends in France to help him. He has one person who will help to kill you. This person is Giles."

"Do you think that Estelle hates Scott, Morel?"

"I think that Estelle hates Scott, because he is a detective and Estelle thinks that Scott wants to find Holly."

"Estelle didn't know that I wanted to pay a ransom for Holly. Giles didn't tell her, because Giles, Dex and Scott needed to divide the money. Estelle would have called the police if she knew that you need to pay a ransom. Estelle will never involve her family. She has enough money. Giles is a cheap man. He needed to get ten million."

"Scott is a cheap too Morel."

"I know that Paul. That is why Giles and Scott started to work together for the ransom. They thought that you are stupid and they will get easy thirty million dollars. Scott and Giles used Dex. Maybe they would have killed Dex after they got the money. Dex sold drugs. The policemen knew that. They would have thought that another drug dealer killed Dex. Giles and Scott would have gotten fifteen million each."

"Giles disappeared very quickly from the park Morel."

"He is from Paris. I think that Giles had a plan to kill Scott to get the thirty million. Now Scott is alive and you keep the money Paul. If Giles meets with Scott, we will arrest him, but I think that Giles is at the same place where Marcel and Holly are. This isn't good for us Paul. Giles will try to kill Holly. I am sure that Giles spoke with Estelle, before he disappeared. Estelle told you that she will be alone. She knows that Giles isn't in Paris. Estelle knows where Giles is. You need to do everything to get from Estelle the location of Giles. If you don't want to meet Estelle, I will go to speak with her, Paul."

"I will meet and I will do everything Estelle wants me to do, Morel."

"I want to know more about Alan, Paul."

"The first time I heard Alan's name was last Monday. I think that Dad knows more about Alan." "Because Alan is lover of your Mom. Henry knows Alan for more than twenty-seven years Morel, but I don't think that Dad has information for Alan. Dad knows that Alan was a boyfriend of my mom, before Dad married her. We had family problem when I was six years old and last Monday Dad understood that Mom was with Alan. Alan is rich. I think that my boss Roy Bell will know more for Alan, because Roy is rich too."

I called Roy. "Hi boss."

"Are you alive Paul?"

"I am calling you boss, so I must be. I spoke with Henry last night. He was afraid for your life." "Everything is OK Roy. I want to know what kind of man is Alan."

"Why did you call me, Paul?"

"You need to call Florida. Janet is with Alan. She can tell you anything you need to know about Alan."

"Mom will not tell me, because she will think that Dad wants to know more for Alan."

"Of course Paul, If Alan marries Janet, Henry is a free man and he will need to find another woman."

"It isn't time for joking Roy. I have a problem in Paris. They tried to kill me last night."

"Oh my God. I will lose you, Paul. You are a golden chicken for my company. I will try to help you. When I have information for Alan, I will call you."

"Thanks Roy."

"Hey Paul, did you find where Holly is?"

"Your information can help me find Holly, Roy."

"I will do everything to help you Paul."

"Roy will call me when he has more information on Alan, Morel."

"I need to give you the bag with the money Paul."

Morel returned to the living room. He carried the bag.

"You need to show Estelle that you wanted to pay money for Holly's freedom, but don't tell Estelle how much money is in the bag. If Estelle told you that thirty million are a lot money for the freedom of Holly, you need to understand that Estelle is working with Scott and Giles. You must be carefully with Estelle. I don't believe that Estelle knows for the ransom, but we need to be ready for everything Paul."

"Thank you for thinking for my safety Morel."

"Kevin killed Dex, but Giles thinks that I killed Dex, because Dex was with me. Maybe Giles told Estelle that I killed Dex in the park and she may call the police to arrest me. What do I tell the policemen, Morel?"

"Don't be afraid when the policemen come to arrest you. Giles doesn't know that I was in the park too. I saw everything. I will tell the policemen that you carried money to pay a ransom, because your girlfriend was kidnapped. I will tell them, that you didn't carry a pistol. How did you kill Dex if you didn't have a weapon?"

"I am a detective. The policemen will believe me. But I think that Giles didn't tell Estelle what happened in the Park Monceau. Estelle will ask Giles what he was doing in the park at 9:00 o'clock at night, because a woman was killed there at that time. Giles isn't a problem for me and you, Paul. The big problem is Scott, if he comes to Estelle's house when you are there. I think for that and I am trying to have a plan about what I need to do if that happens. We don't know where Scott is. How did Scott know Holly, Paul?"

"Gina told me that Scott had business with Holly three or four years ago in New York. Gina didn't sleep with me, because she has a big respect for Holly. Gina loves Holly. Gina was the first who understood that Holly has a problem in Paris. Gina told me that Holly needs to return to New York, before something happens with her in Paris."

"Do you think that Gina knows something that may help us Paul?"

"Gina spoke with Holly and Scott when I and Gina were together in Puerto Rico. Maybe Gina understood that Scott wasn't helping Holly, but creating a problem for her. Now we know what that problem is Morel."

"Why don't you call and ask Gina, Paul?"

"I think that Gina feels that something will happen with Holly. Gina is a sensitive girl. She lives with two different people. Cindy didn't love Scott. I don't know if Scott loves something Morel." "Scott loves money Paul. Scott wants to get my money, because he wants to show Cindy and Gina, that he is a smart detective. Gina knows well her Mom and Dad. Gina stays between them and creates a balance. Gina doesn't want them to divorce. I thought that Scott and Cindy have a sexual problem, but I understood that they have a financial problem. Scott and Cindy never told me that they have a problem with money."

"Of course Morel. It is OK for Scott and Cindy to have seven people sleeping in your apartment. For me isn't Morel."

"Margot told me that Scott is chip, but I never thought that he has problem with money."

"I saw that when I was with Gina, Morel. Gina is a pretty girl and she saved me from many problems."

"What happen between you and Gina? You told me that you didn't have sex with Gina."

"Scott and Cindy pushed Gina to ask me, to marry her. If I didn't want I had to pay money to her, because Gina will call and tell the police, that I raped her."

"Oh my God. Scott and Cindy are crazy Paul. They don't think for the future of Gina."

"Who told you that first Paul Scott or Gina?"

"Scott. I called Gina. I didn't ask her. Gina told me that her parents are crazy and I shouldn't listen to them. "I will never go to the police and say that you raped me Paul. I will tell them that I raped you. I love you and Holly very much Paul.""

"Did you understand, how many problems Holly created for me when she came in Paris, Morel?"

"I understood Paul. Scott tried to kill you and get the money. Scott and Cindy wanted you to marry Gina and get your money. The Hunter family wanted to get your money Paul."

"Gina didn't want that Morel. She was happy with me in Puerto Rico and she was ready to have sex with me, but she got drank. Gina was sleeping when I went to her bedroom. The next day Gina spoke with Holly and everything changed."

"Did you regret that you didn't have sex with Gina?"

"If I had, now I don't need to have sex with Estelle. I never saw Estelle, but you told me that I needed to be ready when I see her.

Gina is pretty and young. She doesn't have a boyfriend and Gina doesn't have children. Estelle is married with two children. It will be good, If I marry Estelle, because I don't need to work for children." We laughed.

"Life is funny with you Paul. I will be lonely after we find Holly and you and Holly leave to New York."

"I will see you, because you will keep Holly, when she travels to Paris, Morel."

"Do you think that Holly will return to Paris after we find her?"

"Holly will have business in Paris. Holly is nuts. She will never give up Morel. I love her, because I am the same. I am not scared for my life. I care for Holly's life. Holly will do the same, if I have the same problem."

"You are crazy people Paul."

"We are Morel. You will understand Holly when you see her."

"Do you hate Scott and Cindy, Paul?"

"No. If Holly came with me to Florida and I asked her to marry me, I would not have seen or heard of the Hunter's family. I met them in Puerto Rico. You need to know that I will kill Scott if he tries to kill me again."

"You don't have a pistol."

"Do you want one?'

"No. I will kill Scott with my hands. I will look Scott in the face and tell him that I am happy, because I will kill one stupid detective."

"Now is 12:00 o'clock Paul. We need to eat something."

The cell phone of Morel rang. He spoke in French. We left the apartment of Morel at 1:00 o'clock. I carried the bag with books and the money. I and Morel were on the street.

"I will not drop you at Estelle's house Paul. My plan changed after I spoke with my people. You will get a taxi." Morel stopped a taxi for me. He spoke with the driver of the taxi. I entered and opened the window.

"Don't be afraid Paul. I will be behind you. You must be a man when you see Estelle." Morel laughed when the taxi left to the house of Estelle.

I don't know if I will see Morel again, because I don't know what will happen in Estelle's house, but he is right. I must be a man.

CHAPTER 7

I was seating in the taxi thinking about Estelle. It was good that taxi driver didn't speak with me. I always have a plan when I meet with my clients. It became easier for me when Morel told me to think of Estelle as my client. I know what I need to tell Estelle, if she wants to invest money. This shouldn't be a problem for Estelle, because she is from a rich family. I am sure that a broker is working with the family Cote. My business with Estelle Cote is to understand where Holly is, if Estelle knows and she wants to tell me. Maybe I need to speak with Estelle for business. I do this very well. When Estelle understands that I am a good broker and I take her heart, I will ask if she knows where Holly is. May be Estelle will take me in bed when I enter her house. I need to make deal with Estelle, before she takes me to the bed. She needs to tell me where Holly is, after that we can have sex. It isn't problem for Estelle to tell me that Holly was with Marcel and Luca, somewhere in France. After the sex she may tell me that she doesn't know where Holly is. Estelle will lie to me, because she wants to have sex with me. Estelle may tell me "Holly slept with Giles. I slept with you, Paul. That is, it. I don't know where Giles is. He is my husband, but he didn't come home last night or call. Giles disappeared. Maybe Giles is with Holly and Marcel, but I don't know where they are." Estelle will be right. Giles left Park Monceau last night and Morel didn't know where he is. It is good if I stop to think about Estelle. I will figure it out when I meet her.

"Do you have a problem a sir? Your friend spoke with me and

told me where I need to drop you. He told me that you don't speak French. He didn't know that I speak well English. If you want, I will speak with you sir. Many people know well Estelle and Giles, because Estelle is from a rich family, Giles is from a poor family. It was big news in Paris when Estelle married Giles. Don't be scared to meet Estelle. She isn't pretty, but she has a good body and she is rich. Estelle is a married woman. Giles doesn't care for that sir."

"My name is Paul Morgan, man. Call me Paul. Can you tell me more about Estelle?"

"My name is Murk, Paul. Estelle has a good heart. She is rich, but she never shows that. Everybody wants Estelle to pay when she is with Giles and the children at a restaurant or a shop. Estelle gives good tips. Giles is chip. He doesn't. Your friend told me that you have business with Estelle. You need to be happy that you don't have business with Giles." We laughed.

"Your accent is from New York."

"I was born and live in New York, Murk."

"In the last two weeks two people were for business in the house of Estelle."

"Do you spy on Estelle or Giles, Murk?"

"No. My friend picked up Holly Gold from hotel Le Royal. She met with Estelle to speak with her for business."

"Why did your friend tell you that Holly Gold went to meet Estelle?"

"We were together that night. He told me that Holly Gold was his client."

"Do you know Holly Gold, Paul?"

"I know her. She is from New York."

"Holly is beautiful Paul. Every man in Paris wants to sleep with Holly, Paul."

"Did your friend picked up Holly from the house of Estelle?"

"He did. Holly had tears in her eyes when she entered the car. My friend asked her if Estelle hurt Holly. She said that she didn't, but she told her the truth. My friend dropped Holly in hotel Le Royal."

"Who was next Murk?"

"I dropped Scott Hunter. Scott told me that he is a businessman from New York. Scott's accent wasn't from New York. I have many clients from New York, Paul. They speak different English."

"Did Scott meet Estelle?"

"She left when I arrived at the house. Giles was waiting for Scott outside."

"Did you pick up Scott?"

"No. Scott told me that he didn't know how long he will stay in the house of Giles. Scott didn't know that this house was Estelle's. She lived in the house before she married Giles."

"Do you want me to pick up you, Paul?"

"I am in the same place as Scott. I don't know how long I will stay." We arrived at the property of Estelle. I saw a woman outside the house.

"This is Estelle, Paul. I will give you one thousand dollars Murk. When I finish with Estelle I will call you to pick me up."

"I will wait for you outside on the street Paul." I walked to Estelle. I kissed her cheek.

"Did Morel tell you about me?"

"I was ready to see your face Estelle. You didn't lie, because you kissed my cheek Paul. I am thirty-three, but it is a miracle when somebody kisses me.

"How old are you?"

"Thirty-three too Estelle. You kissed me, because you are my age."

"Are you?"

"I didn't know your age when I kissed you Estelle."

"The taxi that dropped you was the same that dropped another businessman from New York last week. He met with Giles. Do you know the name of that businessman Paul?"

"I don't Estelle. There are many businessmen in New York. I didn't understand why the businessman spoke with Giles. Giles doesn't have money. This man needed to speak with me. I met a businessman from New York in hotel Le Royal. The name of that businessman is Scott Hunter. I told him that I will see you, but he didn't tell me that he was here."

"When did you meet Scott?"

"After I spoke with you I was in the hotel to take a shower. I saw Scott in the lobby."

"Giles meets with a lot of trashy people, but I don't care. I need to approve the money Giles wants to spend."

"What do you do when Giles pays girls?"

"Giles doesn't pay them. He promises them that they will be models."

"Who decides for Holly's business?"

"Of course, I decide Paul. Giles checks them in bed, but Giles has sex with me too. I have two children."

"Do they kiss you?"

"Sometimes. They kiss Giles more. The children want to go out with Giles. They love him. I am not jealous Paul. I know who I am."

"I understand that Estelle. You have money and you have power."

"Do you think that I am not correct?"

"Why don't you think for your future Estelle?"

"If you lose the love of your family, you will lose their money too."

"What are you going to do when you don't have money?"

"Everybody in my family loves me Paul. What do you want to drink Paul? Coffee, tea or alcohol?"

"I don't need to drink alcohol, if you want to go in bed with me Estelle. Give me coffee. I want to speak with you before we go to bed."

"You aren't afraid."

"I am not Estelle."

"Do you want sugar and milk Paul?"

"No. I want dark coffee." Estelle gave me a cup of coffee.

"You want to speak for Holly, but I don't want now."

"Did you know that Holly had sex with Giles?"

"I know."

"Did Giles tell you!"

"I never spoke with Giles. Holly told me."

"How did you feel when Holly told you?"

"We have been living together for one year and seven months. She slept with Giles four years ago."

"You don't want to know what Holly did in her past?"

"I don't. Holly told me that Marcel was her boyfriend."

"Holly is having a good time with Marcel right now Paul."

"Where are they Estelle?"

"I don't know. If you ask me more about Holly, you will need to leave my house Paul. I don't want to call the police."

"I am not afraid if you call the police. I saw that you are angry that Holly had sex with Giles. Many girls had sex with Giles."

"You are right when you said many girls Paul. They are eighteen, nineteen or twenty when they have sex with Giles. They want to use Giles for their future. They are young and aggressive. Holly was twenty-six when she slept with Giles. Holly has money and a good business. Why did Holly had sex with a married man?"

"Holly knew that I was the wife of Giles and we have two children. I didn't have a lot of men in bed and I didn't have a lot of experience in bed. I love Giles, because he married me. Maybe I will not be married now. I will not have two children. You aren't stupid and you know who told me that many times."

"Giles told you Estelle. I want to speak for your face Estelle."

"What is your problem with my face Paul?"

"You have money Estelle. Why don't you have a plastic surgery on your face? There are many good plastic surgeons in the world today. They will not make your face to look beautiful, but they will make your face pretty. Can you show me your naked body?" Estelle took off her clothes.

"Your body is perfect Estelle. Every man will want to have your body in bed. You will have many men in bed after you change your face."

"Why men don't want me Paul? I am keeping my body in perfect shape."

"Because people see first your face Estelle. If you cover your face and walk naked on the street, thousand men will be walking after you."

"Oh my God. I never thought that I need to have a plastic surgery on my face. Paul you changed my life. I will try to find a good doctor on Monday. I will try to change my face. You are right. I have money. I will surprise my children and Giles. I am naked Paul. Come with me in the bedroom. I want to have sex."

I heard a voice "Bravo Estelle. Giles was right that I need to kill you and Paul in bed." It was Scott. Estelle put fast her clothes on.

"My name is Scott Hunter, Estelle."

"What are you doing in my house Scott?"

"I told you that I am here to kill you and Paul?"

"How did you know that Paul is here?"

"You spoke with Giles and told him that Paul will come in your house at 2:00 o'clock. You wanted to hurt Giles when you told him that you will have sex with hm."

"Is this true Estelle?"

"How much is Giles paying you to kill me and Paul?"

146

"Thirty million dollars Estelle. I know that Giles doesn't have money, because Giles wanted Dex to kill Paul. Giles, Dex and I will divide the thirty million that Paul carries to pay the ransom for Holly's freedom."

"Do you know where is Giles, Scott?"

"I think that Giles is having sex with Holly now. Giles knows that Paul is here and you have sex with him."

"Where are your thirty million Paul?"

"The money is in the bag Estelle."

"Can you open the bag and show the money to Estelle?"

I opened the bag. "Oh my God. It is true."

"I am not kidding Estelle."

"How much do you want for mine and Paul's life Scott?"

"You don't have a chance to be alive, because you will call the police Estelle."

"I want to speak with Giles, Scott."

"The cell phone of Giles doesn't work Estelle. Giles gave me this phone number to call him after I kill you and Paul."

"Can you give me the number Scott. I want to speak with Giles?" Estelle called.

"Can you put the phone on the speaker Estelle? I want to listen what Giles tells you. Marcel on the phone."

"May I speak with Giles, Marcel?"

"How did you know that Giles is here Estelle?"

"Scott Hunter is in my house. He gave me this number Marcel."

"Did Giles have sex with Holly, Marcel?"

"You need to ask Giles, Estelle."

"Estelle wants to speak with you Giles."

"Hi my husband. Scott is in my house. He wants to kill me, because you will pay him thirty million to kill me. Are you paying with French francs or dollars?"

"How does it matter to you after Scott kills you, Estelle?"

"Scott needs to kill Paul too. Paul brought thirty million dollars in my house to pay a ransom for Holly."

"Scott will not kill Paul, because he will get this money. If Scott kills me our children won't have a mother Giles."

"You know that the children love me, not you. You are so ugly Estelle. I will marry a beautiful woman, after Scott kills you."

"Are you going to marry Holly?"

"Paul is next to me and he wants to know."

"Give me Scott, Estelle. Why did you call me Scott?"

"Estelle called you Giles. You need to kill Estelle and Paul, if you want me to pay you" and Giles hang up.

"What now Scott?" I asked.

"I want to see you have sex with Estelle."

"What If I don't?"

"I will kill you. I want you and Estelle to be happy, when I kill you."

"Where do you want to have sex Paul?"

"In the living room, bedroom or the kitchen?"

I understood that Estelle had a plan. "In kitchen will be better Estelle."

"I think so too Paul." We walked to the kitchen. Estelle took off her clothes. She was naked. "You have a good body Estelle."

"I don't want to take off my clothes."

"You need to be naked too Paul." Estelle took off my clothes.

"Paul isn't ready Scott. I will make a French love to him. I need to squat." I saw that Estelle opened a drawer and got a knife. Scott walked towards me and Estelle to see what Estelle was going to do. Estelle jumped and stabbed Scott on the shoulder. He dropped the pistol. Estelle jumped and took the pistol. I saw that Morel entered kitchen. He carried a pistol too.

"What are you doing in my house Morel?"

"Oh my God. You have perfect body Estelle."

"Did you came here to see me naked Morel?"

"I came to help you and Paul, because my people told me that Scott is here. Scott tried to kill Paul last night."

"Is it true Paul?"

"Yes, Estelle."

Estelle laughed. "For the first time in my life three man saw me naked. You are right Paul. When I change my face I will have more men who want to see me naked. Get this pistol Morel" and Estelle threw the pistol to Morel.

"Take you clothes and follow me Paul. You need to take a shower." We entered a bedroom.

"Do you want to find Holly, Paul?"

"I want Estelle."

"You need to have sex with me."

"Do I have a choice Estelle?"

"I will never tell Holly that we had sex Paul. I don't want to hurt Holly. I want to have sex with you, Paul. We will take a shower together. You can be behind me because I am afraid that you will not be ready if you look at my face." I was behind Estelle. I felt good. I turned her body and took her legs. I raised the legs of Estelle and I kissed her mouth. Estelle moved her ass. I helped her. "Don't stop Paul. I don't care that you don't have a condom. I will never follow you Paul." When I finished I kissed many times Estelle's face. Estelle kissed me in the mouth for a long time. "You are the first man who kissed me so many times Paul."

"What are you going to do if you get pregnant Estelle?"

"It isn't your business Paul? I wanted to have sex with you and I did. I have enough money to raise many children, but nobody wanted to have sex with me. I loved Giles, because he did."

"Why did you say loved Giles?"

"Giles wants to kill me Paul. For many years I thought that he loved me at least a little. Now I know that Giles hated me the whole time. He used me to live good with my money. We don't have time to speak Paul. I want to help you find Holly." Estelle and I entered the living room. Morel held his pistol pointed at Scott. Scott and Morel didn't speak.

"Are you ready to kill Scott, Estelle asked Morel?"

"I will call the police to come here and arrest Scoot."

"If you do that, Giles will kill Holly. Paul wants to find Holly alive, Morel."

"We don't know where Giles and Holly are, Estelle."

"I know Morel. I know that I need to work with two stupid detectives, but I don't have a choice, if I want to help Paul. Scott was OK Paul. He wanted to get thirty millions after he killed us. How much money do you want to find Holly alive, Morel?"

"I know that Margot and Morel aren't greedy Estelle."

"They aren't, but Morel is stupid."

"Do you think that I am stupid, Morel asked me?"

I didn't answer. "Paul can't answer you, Morel. He doesn't want to take sides, because Paul knows, that I will not help him, if Paul takes your side Morel. Frankly, I think that Paul is stupid too Morel. Paul listens you. Paul needs to listen to Margot. She is smart Morel, but you are afraid to meet Paul with Margot, because Margot is beautiful and Paul will get her in bed. Paul was afraid to have sex with me, because Paul knows that he will be not ready for sex when he looks at my face Morel. If Paul looks at the face of Margot, Paul will be ready. Margot too Morel. Finally, Margot will be with a man in bed Morel."

"I will arrest Giles. He killed a woman in Park Monceau last night. I will create a big problem for you, Estelle."

"You need to arrest Paul too, Morel. He killed Dex."

"Did you see that Scott?"

"I saw that Paul killed Dex, after that Giles killed the woman."

"To arrest Paul isn't a problem for you, Morel. Paul is in my house. You need to arrest Paul, because when he entered my house, Paul told me that he will rape me if you don't tell him where Holly is. I told Paul that he didn't need to rape me, because I want him in bed."

"What did Paul tell you Estelle, Morel asked?"

"Scott entered the house and Paul didn't have a chance to answer Morel."

"Did you think that Paul would have raped me if Scott didn't enter?"

"Paul raped Gina, Estelle. Paul rapes every woman he meets. Holly told me that Paul raped her the first night they were together."

"Why did Holly sleep again with Paul, Estelle asked Scott?"

"Holly loves Paul." Morel laughed.

"You are right that Scott and I are stupid detectives."

"Can you tell us what we need to do, because you know where Giles is, Estelle?"

"Estelle spoke with Marcel, Morel."

"Shut up Scott, Morel told him."

"You spoke with Giles, Scott. Giles will pay you thirty million dollars to kill me and Paul. Why didn't you ask Giles, where Holly is, she paid you fifty thousand dollars to help her, Scott? You use the money to kill Paul and steal the money that Paul wants to pay for her freedom. I think that you aren't a detective. You are killer Scott. Why are you working for Scott, Morel? Maybe you are a killer too Morel."

"I am not Estelle."

"You are right that Scott used the money Holly paid him to kill Paul."

"When did you understand that Scott didn't want Holly to be free Morel?"

"Paul's Mom hates Holly. She spoke with Marcel and Scott.

Marcel and Luca kidnapped Holly. Marcel listens to what Giles tells him. Somebody paid Giles, Marcel and Luca to kidnap Holly. Maybe somebody paid Scott too."

"How much did Janet pay you if you or Giles to kill Holly, Scott?"

"Janet doesn't have money Estelle. She wants to pay after we kill Holly. I don't know where Holly is, so I can't kill her Estelle. My goal was to get the ransom that Paul wanted to pay."

"You are a criminal Scott."

"Are you going to call the police Estelle?"

"I won't. I will use you to save the life of Holly." The phone in the house rang. Giles is calling Scott. He wants to know if you killed me and Paul. I will not pick up so Giles will call your cell phone Scott. Are you ready to tell Giles, what you did?"

The cell phone of Scott rang. I and Morel looked at Estelle. Our mouths were opened.

"May I speak with Estelle?"

"Of course, but I want to tell you that I didn't kill them Giles. I need to receive the money that you promised to pay me. I know that today and tomorrow the banks are closed. I will keep Estelle and Paul alive. If I don't receive the money on Monday, I will leave to America. I have thirty million dollars Giles. If I kill Estelle and Paul now, you will call the police to arrest me. I am not stupid. I am not afraid for my life Giles. I am a detective. Morel is detective too. He works for me. The policemen will believe Morel and me. They will arrest you, because you killed that girl in the park last night. Holly is your problem Giles. You need to ask the people that paid you, Giles. I will leave France on Tuesday. You can speak to Estelle now."

"Hi Giles. You need to save my life honey. I and Paul are tied. Scott will kill us, if you don't pay. I don't have a chance to go to the bank on Monday. Scott will keep me and Paul alive until Monday. Do you want our children to have a Mom? We had sex and we have two children. I think that you love me Giles. Did you kiss me and had sex, because you wanted to use my money Giles?"

Giles said something to Estelle and she replied "Of course, I am ugly. Thanks for telling me the truth Giles. I will never forget what you told me." Giles hang up, and she gave the cell phone back to Scott.

"He told me something that I wanted to hear."

"I didn't kill people Estelle. I tried to kill Paul, but he is alive. I tried to steal the money that belong to Paul, but he was smart and kept the money. I will stay with you until Tuesday and I will do everything what you tell me Estelle. I don't want to stay in a French jail."

"I will arrest you Scott."

"You will be stupid if you arrest me Morel. Giles will know that I didn't kill Estelle and Paul. Giles works with many people who sale drugs. Giles will kill Holly and Marcel and disappear. Estelle will tell you where Giles and Holly are. You and Paul must go and save Holly's life. After Monday night or Tuesday, Holly will not be alive. Do you think that I am correct Estelle?"

"You are correct about Holly and you are right that Giles has people who will help him to disappear.

"What do we need to do Estelle?"

"I will stay in my father's house with Scott. When Giles calls and asks Scott what happened, Scott will tell him that he killed Paul, because Paul tried to fight with him. Scott is keeping me alive because he is waiting for the money. Giles is in Marcel's house. Holly, Giles, Marcel and Luca are there. Marcel loves Holly and he will keep Holly alive, but not for a long time. Scott was right. You and Paul must go and get Holly."

"Where are they Estelle?"

"In Corsica. Marcel has a house there. I have been there two times on vacation with Giles and the children. The house has two floors. There is a studio on the second floor. I think that Holly is staying there. The first floor has a kitchen, living room, one bedroom and a garage. Marcel never closed the garage door when we were there. Since they are keeping Holly there I don't know if the door will be open."

"Does the kitchen has a door to the outside?"

"Yes, Morel. Give me the address Estelle."

"Route the Mozzo street, Ajaccio, Corsica. You need to go to the house of Marcel, before you enter and get familiar with it. It is summer. A lot of tourists are in Ajaccio at this time of the year. If somebody asks you what you are looking for, you tell them that you are looking to rent a bedroom for one week. If they give you a room, then Holly isn't there. You need to call me Morel. I want to speak in my office with you, Paul. Follow me." Estelle closed the door. "I am sorry that I raped you Paul. I hated Holly when I understood that she slept with Giles and many people knew that. If something happened with Holly, they will think that I am behind that."

"What did you tell Holly when you met with her?"

"What I thought of Holly, Paul. Giles told me that you were in Paris, but nobody knows where you were and Giles wanted me to helped him. For that reason, I met with Holly. She thought that I will help her, because Giles listens to what I tell him. I asked Holly which hotel you are staying in in Paris. Holly told me that you aren't in Paris. I thought that Holly lied to me. I told her that she had to think, before she had sex with Giles. Holly started to cry and she left my house."

"What did you tell Giles?"

"That Holly lied to me. I didn't know that Giles and Marcel wanted to kidnap Holly. Now I know and I will fight to save the life of Holly, Paul. Holly is a good woman and she never lied."

"I was in Puerto Rico when Holly was in Paris, Estelle. If you don't believe me ask Scott. I was with his daughter."

"Did you sleep with her?"

"I didn't. Gina and I are good friends."

"Is she is beautiful?"

"She is pretty and sexy. Gina is twenty years old. I want to tell you that you didn't rape me Estelle. I was little afraid before I entered the bath. After, I felt very good."

"I understood, when you kissed me many times Paul. I felt that you are the first parson who wasn't afraid to kiss me. You know me for one hour Paul. I am a Mom with two children. I am not for you Paul. I will be happy if you marry Holly. I want to see you with Holly when you come to Paris. I will prepare a contract for her. I and Holly will work together. I will never go in bed with you again. You will busy with Holly, because you and Holly need to have children." Estelle laughed.

"I am thankful that you don't want to have future with me. I love Holly." I kissed her.

"Ask Morel to come to my office." Morel entered Estelle's office. I was alone with Scott.

"Did you tell Gina what happened in Paris, Paul?"

"No Scott. You were right. I am alive and I still have the money. Why did you ask me for Gina, Scott?"

"I spoke with her this morning. Gina told me that I am a greedy and my goal was to get money from Holly and you, Paul."

"Did you tell Gina that you are in Paris to pay a ransom?"

"I didn't. Gina doesn't know what I am doing here. Gina helped me when she told me that Morel is a good man. He is Scott."

"Of course Paul. I would have disappeared with the money. Morel didn't. What are you going to tell of Holly when she asks you, what I did?"

"That you helped me to find where Holly was."

"You will lie to Holly. Who cares if I find Holly alive Scott. Estelle stabbed you, but I don't see blood on your shirt."

"Estelle didn't hurt me deep. When you and Estelle were in the bedroom, Morel helped me. I am OK now."

"Why didn't you fight with Morel?"

"Morel is younger. I didn't have a chance to be free Paul. I understood that I lost, after I saw that Morel entered the kitchen. I thought that Estelle would kill me when she took the pistol. I was ready to die Paul. You didn't think for Cindy and Gina! I wanted Estelle to killed me, because I didn't want Cindy and Gina to read that I was arrested in Paris. I don't understand why Estelle didn't kill me."

"Because the policemen would come and investigate what happened in her house. She doesn't want that."

"Your Mom isn't a good woman, Paul."

"Do you think that you are a good man, Scott?"

"I am like your Mom, Paul." Scott and I laughed. I saw Estelle and Morel. They came to me and Estelle asked "What is funny Paul?"

"Scott didn't want me to marry Gina, Estelle."

"Because you love and want to marry Holly, Paul?"

"No, because I didn't want to give money to Scott, Estelle." She understood that I was joking.

"It is good that you are joking Paul. I thought that you hate Scott, because he created many problems for you."

"Scott didn't Estelle. Giles and Marcel had a plan to kidnap Holly. Scott didn't."

"Scott tried to kill you Paul. Scott thought to kill Giles too, but Scott's plan changed after he missed my head."

"Why didn't you kill Giles, Scott?"

"I would have given you a lot of money if you killed Giles."

"I am sorry that I took Giles for a partner. If you are my partner I will never miss to kill Giles, Estelle." Everybody laughed.

"Are you planning to get me in bed after you killed Giles, Scott?"

"I will call and ask Cindy."

"What will Cindy tell you?"

"When Cindy understands that you gave me a lot of money, she would tell me that money are more important for us."

"Don't hesitate to go to bed with Estelle. I will not tell Gina, that you had sex with Estelle, because Estelle is a rich woman. You will go to bed again with Estelle, when we finish the money."

"Oh my God. This is so funny Scott. We will be together three days at my father's house. You will have a chance to make money." I and Morel laughed. Estelle and Scott didn't.

"I think that this isn't funny, Morel and Paul. It is funny is that three men saw me naked, but nobody jumped through the window or broke central door running away." Estelle laughed.

"Why are you joking like that about your face Estelle?"

"Did you tell Margo that you saw me naked Morel?"

"I can't tell her that Estelle."

Are you afraid that Margot will ask you if you like what you saw, Morel?"

"You won't know what to tell her, Morel."

"You are right Estelle. If I say I like Estelle, Margo will tell me that I need to leave her. If I say, I don't, Margo will tell me "Can you leave me, because Margot is my friend?""

Everybody laughed.

"You didn't ask Paul what Holly will tell him."

"First we need to find Holly. When I see Holly, I will tell her what happened in my house. Do you want to call for a taxi Paul?"

"A taxi driver is waiting for me Estelle."

"I will come get you from the hotel Paul. I will be there after one hour and a half. You must be ready. I need to check out from the hotel Morel."

"Don't check out Paul", Estelle told me "I think that Giles called and asked this morning If you are staying in the hotel. They told Giles that you haven't check out. Giles spoke with Scott and he knows that you are in my house. Giles must think that Scott, you and I are together in my house." "You and Scott will go in the house of your father. What are you going to tell Giles when he calls your house or the cell phone of Scott?"

155

"That Scott doesn't want me speak on the phone at the house, because he doesn't know who is calling me. You don't ask Morel, when you are with him. Morel is from France and he has people that will help him, Paul. You need to leave. We don't have time to speak now. When you return with Holly, we will speak."

"You are right Estelle. Do you want to read books?"

"I love to read books Paul. I want to clean my bag. I have a lot of books in the bag that will give you."

"Where do you want me to leave the books Estelle?"

"On the table."

I put the money and the books on the table. I returned only the money in bag.

"You didn't carry thirty million dollars Paul?"

"Of course Scott. I am not crazy to walk on the street of Paris with thirty million."

"Why didn't you put magazines or newspapers?"

"You needed to read books when you were in jail Scott. Before I left New York, I knew that your future was in a French jail. You must love Estelle because she didn't want the policemen to arrest you. It was good that you want to help me and Holly. I told you what I will tell Gina, when she asks me for you Scott."

"How much money did you carry in the park?"

"Two million Scott. You tried to kill me for two million. I think that my life is more than that Scott."

"If you told me that you carried two million I wouldn't have fired at you Paul. You are right. Two million is nothing for your life. Why did you lie to me that you carried thirty million Paul?"

"I wanted you to kill me Scott, because you told me that Holly left the hotel with two man. It hurt me when I heard two men, but I want to ask you Scott. Why did you lie to me, that I would get Holly, when I pay?"

"This is enough Paul. Get your bag and come with me." I followed Estelle. She opened the central door and we exited the house. I saw that Murk was waiting in the taxi. Estelle embraced my neck and kissed me.

"I kissed you, because I loved you Paul. I will never forget that you kissed my face so many times."

"Why did you say "I loved you"?"

"Because next time when I see you, you will be married to Holly. I will kiss a married man. You are sure that I will find Holly alive and take her with me."

"One hundred percent, if you listen to Morel."

"You instructed Morel, what to do?"

"Yes, Paul."

"Thanks Estelle." I walked to taxi when I heard "Don't be afraid for Holly, Paul". I entered the taxi.

"Did you know Holly, Paul?"

"She is my girlfriend Murk."

"Where is Holly?"

"She is on vacation in the south of France."

"Why did Estelle say, don't be afraid for Holly?"

"Holly is alone on the beach and many men will be around her. You know what men think when a woman is alone."

"It is not a problem for Estelle, if she is alone on the beach, Paul."

"It is a problem for Holly, because she is beautiful."

"I think that Estelle loves you, Paul."

"Why, because she kissed me?"

"I saw that her eyes looked at your back lovely. I think that her eyes were taking off your clothes."

"You think that I was naked in her eyes."

"Almost Paul." We laughed.

"Do I need to take you back to hotel Le Royal?"

"Yes, Murk. I need to get my things and go to the south of France."

"Do you need a taxi to get to the airport?"

"My friend who stopped you will pick me up from the hotel. We will travel with his car."

"Your bag isn't full Paul."

"Why did Estelle get the money from you Paul, she is rich?"

"Estelle and I will have business Murk."

"She is smart Paul. You will never lose money, if you have business with Estelle."

"You know a lot for her. Many people in Paris know that Paul. I saw that Scott entered the house after you Paul. Why was Scott in the house?"

"Scott, Giles and Holly have business together. Holly is my girlfriend. Scott spoke with Giles about the risk that Holly has."

"You will have business with Estelle. Giles will have business with Holly. I understand now why you have money and I don't have money Paul."

"What did you understand Murk?"

"That money make money. I don't have money. My friends don't have money. We don't have a chance to have and make more money. My friends hate rich people. They told me that rich people need to give them money, because they are capitalists."

"What kind people are your friends Murk?"

"Of course, they are socialists Paul. I told them that they need to go to school and get the education, that rich people have." They told me "We aren't stupid to lose time in school." Frankly they don't want, but they don't have enough brain to go to college. My children didn't want too. I had big problem with them, but my wife told them "If you don't want to go to college, you need to go to work." "We will not find good job Mom", they told her. "That is why your father told you that you need to go to college and get good education. After you finish the college you will find a good job."

"What are they doing now Murk?"

"They are in college and they work part time."

"Your wife is smart Murk."

"She is Paul. It isn't easy for her. She works and two boys and one girl to take care of. I need to work. She works too Murk. She works morning at the store of my friend. I work day and night Paul. Sometimes I don't see my children for three days. When they were sleeping I was working. When I was sleeping they were at school. I told my children that their Mom is a hero. They love her very much and they have a big respect to her. They listen to her. It was good for me, because they will never listen me to go to college." We arrived at hotel Le Royal. I gave Murk ten thousand dollars.

"I am rich Murk. I need to help to people that don't have enough money. Give this money to your wife. I think that she knows what to do with the money."

"Thanks Paul. God bless you."

"Give me more of your business cards Murk. I will give them to my friends that live in Paris."

"Can you tell the people that work on the front desk of the hotel to call me when they need to order a taxi Paul?"

"I will Murk."

I was at the front desk. I told the clerk "I will not be back at the hotel for few days, but I will check out when I am back. My name is Paul Morgan" and I told them my room number.

"Do I need to pay now?"

"You don't Sir."

I gave them my credit card information. "You need to sign that you will stay three more days." They gave me a receipt and I signed it.

"My friend will come to pick up me. Call me when he comes in. This is the business card of the taxi driver that dropped me at the hotel. His name is Murk. When he picked me up from the airport, I didn't have idea where to get a hotel. Murk told me that hotel Le Royal is the best to stay in Paris. Murk understood that I have money to pay and stay in hotel Le Royal. I will tell my friends to stay in hotel Le Royal when they travel from New York to Paris. My girlfriend Holly Gold stays in this hotel too. She used Murk to drop her in hotel Le Royal. Frankly, Murk does everything to bring people to stay in hotel Le Royal. Can you use Murk, when people ask for a taxi?"

"I will Sir. My name is Jay. I know Holly. She is beautiful and many people in Paris know her. I will use Murk when I need to order taxi and tell other people that work at the front desk to use him too, Mr. Morgan."

"Call me Paul, Jay."

"Where is Holly, Paul?"

"She is in the south of France. I will go to get her."

"Why did you ask me for Holly, Jay?"

"I am afraid for Holly, Paul. I saw Holly when she left the hotel with Marcel and Luca. They work with drugs. I never saw Holly taking drugs. I and Holly have a good relationship. Sometimes we drink coffee together. Holly wants to be with me Paul and we have good time when we are together."

"Are you jealous that Holly was with Marcel and Luca."

"I don't want to speak for me, Paul. When you see Holly, you ask her. I am afraid, because the next day Giles paid for Holly's hotel apartment for nine more days. If Holly wanted to stay for nine more days, she would have called or Holly would have paid before she left the hotel on Friday. She didn't call after Friday. That is why I am afraid for Holly. This morning a woman called and asked for you, Paul. She told me that she is your Mom."

"Was her name Janet Morgan, Ray?"

"Yes. I understood that Janet is your Mom, Paul. She speaks perfect English and she called from Florida. Your Mom is smart Paul. She took my heart easy. I didn't lie to her when she asked me."

"What did Mom ask you, Jay?"

"If I saw you this morning and if you left the hotel. I told her that you didn't check out. Janet asked me if Scott Hunter stays in the hotel. I told her that Scott left the hotel. I was surprised that your Mom asked me for Giles. Janet wanted to know if Giles was in the hotel this morning. I told her that I haven't seen Giles in the hotel after he paid for Holly. Your Mom wants me to call her when you return to the hotel. Janet sent me a kiss. She was so polite with me, Paul."

"What do I need to tell her if she calls?"

"That I want to know where is Scott Hunter."

"He is detective Paul. We are so happy that Scott left the hotel. I need to lie your Mom."

"Yes, Jay. If you want to help Holly and me, you need to lie to my mom."

"I know what I need to tell Janet, Paul."

"I am sorry Jay. I need to get my things from my hotel room."

I went to my room and got what I needed. I was ready, I sat and waited for Morel to call me. The phone rang. "I am in the lobby Paul."

I was at the lobby. Jay came to talk to me and Morel. "He is a detective too Paul." Morel laughed. "I told Paul that your friend Scott is a detective Morel and we are happy that he left the hotel."

"I will leave too Jay, but with Paul. Don't tell the police that I kidnapped Paul."

"Do you like Paul, Jay?"

"Paul loves Holly, Morel."

"I am so sorry Jay. I understood that Morel was joking with Jay."

"What is your problem Morel?"

"I paid you to help me. I don't want you to speak with everybody."

"It is OK Paul. Morel joked with me many times, but he is a good man. Do you love me Jay?"

"Margot will kill me if I say yes Morel." We laughed.

"Have a good trip and I want to see Holly, Paul."

"You will see Holly on Tuesday, Jay."

"Kiss her Paul."

"I will Jay."

We left the hotel. Murk came towards Morel and me. He tried to kiss the hand of Morel.

"What are you doing man?"

"I want to kiss your hand Sir. You stopped me to get Paul. Paul paid me well and Jay called me to get a client from the hotel. I am waiting for my client and I saw Paul and you Sir."

"Do you love Morel, Murk?"

"We are men Paul."

"I wanted to thank your friend Paul."

"You need to be careful with Morel. He is a detective Murk. I don't sale drugs. I haven't done anything wrong Paul. I am not afraid that Morel is a detective. Maybe Morel will be my client in the future. This is my business card Morel. Call me. I will be ready for you when you call me."

"I need to be ready too Murk."

"Of course, I will get your things."

"You don't need to carry my bags." I laughed. Morel and Murk didn't. Morel and I entered the car. I continued to laugh.

"What is so funny Paul?"

"You will be a good client of Murk."

"Oh my God. I didn't think about that Paul. You need to be ready for everything Morel. Who knows what Murk has in mind for you. You look good Morel."

"I like Jay more than Murk Paul." We laughed for a long time.

"I will drive for five or six hours Paul. If you feel tired, you need to sleep, I will drive. Maybe I will try to sleep after we leave Paris. Estelle was so happy when she left the bedroom. What did you do with her?"

"This is my privacy Morel."

"Tell me Paul, I will not tell Holly that you were in bed with Estelle."

"I never been in bed with Estelle, Morel. I took a shower."

"With her or alone?"

"Why did you carry a small bag when you left the office of Estelle, Morel? Did she paid you for a job well done?"

"Hey, Paul this is my privacy."

"Tell me Morel."

"I will not tell Margot that you were in the office with her and she gave you good money for a good job."

"I carried papers in that bag. Estelle drew for me the house of Marcel."

"I thought that Estelle gave you a little model of the house of Marcel and told you where you will find Holly. The bag was small, but full Morel."

"It was paper Paul."

"Of course. The checks and the money are paper Morel. They aren't wood or iron. Estelle paid you half cash and half with a check."

"How do you know Paul?"

"Estelle was happy and she winked at me. I understood that Estelle paid for a job well done and for my safety. Did you save my life, because Estelle paid you, Morel?"

"Estelle was happy, because we saw her naked Paul."

"You are right Morel. Next time we will have sex with Estelle. We left Paris, Paul."

"I don't want to sleep Morel. I have a good time and good conversation with you. I need to look at your cell phone. If Margot calls you I need to talk to her.

"What are you going to tell her?"

"That you will save my live and I will pay you good. If Margot finds the money that Estelle gave you, she will think that I gave you the money. I will save your marriage Morel."

"Life is good with you, Paul. We were speaking for Estelle, Paul. Margot isn't happy when people joke with Estelle. Margot's father likes to joke a lot with the family of Cote. He says that Cote is richer, but he sold his daughter to a poor man, because Cote has a beautiful daughter. Margot told them that Estelle isn't beautiful Dad. He laughed and told Margot "Estelle is ugly, Margot". Margot replied "Estelle has perfect body and sharp brain Dad. Estelle makes the business of the family Cote. Estelle's father believes that Estelle knows what to do with the money of the family. They never lost money. You gave my brother to work with your money. Your son didn't make good profit for your family Dad.""

"You are in my family Margot."

"You will never give me to work with your money father. Because I am a stupid daughter that married to a stupid detective, but I don't want your money father. Morel and I are happy and some day we will make money."

"Your husband will never make money Margot."

"He was right Paul, but now I have a chance to make good business. I need to save Holly. The money will come late."

"Maybe you are right Morel. You never know what will happen in the future. I want to sleep. We will continue when I wake up." I closed my eyes.

CHAPTER 8

I felt that somebody shook my shoulder. I opened my eyes. I saw Morel.

"You slept very deep Paul. You were smiling when you were sleeping. Did you dream of Holly?"

"I dreamed about Estelle. She told me that you will save my life and I was happy."

"Why do I need to save your life. I need to save the life of Holly? Maybe you dreamed that Estelle loves you, Paul. You were in the bedroom with her."

"If I love Estelle why are we going at Ajaccio, Morel? I don't think that we are going to Ajaccio to save Holly. Maybe you are going to save Giles."

"Do you think that Marcel or Luca will kill Giles?"

"Giles must be afraid after he killed the girl in the park. He had to disappear and wait. Ajaccio is the best place for him. Everything will be OK for him, if Scott kills you and Estelle. Marcel and Luca aren't killers. I think that Giles will kill them."

"Why does Giles need to kill them?"

"If the people who paid him want to kill Holly, Giles will kill Marcel and Luca too because they will know that he killed Holly. I would have been more certain of my hypothesis if I had more information for your Mom. Since she is with Alan you need to call and ask him. Your father should know well your Mom like I know well Margot."

"My mom wants to be in the same situation as you Morel. You

164

are married to a woman from a rich family. Alan is rich and Mom wants to marry him."

"I don't agree with you. I have two children with Margot. Janet have one stupid son with Henry. She would have had a smarter son if she had a child with Allan."

"I don't care what you think for me Morel. Why did you wake up me?"

"To tell you what kind man you are."

"I know now Morel. I want to get more sleep."

"We need to find more about Alan, Paul. May be Alan had a sexual relationship with Holly. Are trying to tell me that Mom is jealous and she paid Giles, Marcel and Luca? I think that Alan should be the one that is paying if he had something to do with Holly in the past."

"Do you know somebody that will give us information for Alan?"

"I will check with Roy if he has found information for us."

I called. "Hey boss."

"You are alive. I spoke with Henry, Paul."

"Did you find any information about Alan?"

"I have made some calls to people that know him, but since your Mom is with Alan she should know. I don't understand why you don't want to ask her."

"Mom will not tell me, because she will think that I am spying on her for my father."

"You ask her how much you will get if she marries Alan because he is a rich man."

"It isn't time to joke Roy. I want to save the life of Holly." I need some more time Paul. I am waiting for calls from some people that work on Wall Street and as you know they work around the clock. I will call some of them back this morning"

"Call me as soon as you hear anything for Alan and his family. "

"How is your relationship with Roy, Paul?"

"I have been working in his company for ten years. Everybody in the office thinks that I am a strange man."

"Why?"

"I speak with my colleagues for business only. I never speak with them for theirs or mine personal life. There are many pretty women in the office, but I never invited them to go out. I am in the office to make money."

"So where do you meet women to go out with Paul?"

"I meet a lot of beautiful woman in the bars, restaurants or while shopping Morel."

"How did you meet Holly?"

"I bought her apartment. Holly was happy and she convinced me to live in her new apartment. Now I have two apartments."

"Does Holly have relatives Paul?"

"I never saw or heard of them. She has many friends."

My cell phone rang. "It is Roy, Morel."

"Did you get information for Allan? Looks like you want to help me boss."

"The good news is that Alan is rich. But I think that you already suspected that Paul. The bad news is that Alan is sick. He has a mental problem. Sometimes he spends a lot of time in a hospital, but Alan is still in control of the business of his family. The Goldbear family has billions of dollars Paul. I was not able to find out how Alan works when he is sick. Alan has a wife, Lori and a daughter, Hana, but nobody has seen his daughter in the last ten years. He is a strange man like you, Paul."

"Hey boss, I am not married and I don't have a daughter. I am healthy man too Roy."

"You never had sex with a woman in my office Paul."

"I don't want them to sue me for a sexual harassment Roy. You will have to fire me."

"Did you have sex with women in the office Roy?"

"Don't say things like that Paul. Susan will kill me."

"I asking if you did that in the past. Now you aren't dangerous for girls in the office."

"I am not Paul, but you are dangerous for Estelle."

"If you love her, why do you want to save Holly? Are planning to come back to New York with Estelle and Holly. I am confident that you can handle them all, Paul. You are a man for three women."

"How do you know that Roy?"

"About Estelle or the three women?

"About Estelle."

"Her father, Cote is an old friend of mine, but you need to think for Holly. Estelle is a married woman. You will not get her money. Cote decides for the money of the family Cote."

"Do you know who is Giles, Roy?"

"Giles married Estelle to get the money of the Cote family but he creates many problems for them. He isn't happy that Estelle continues to live with Giles. Giles is the father of her two children. Cote wants Estelle to divorce him, but Estelle doesn't want, because nobody will marry her. Giles is a good man for Estelle but everybody calls him Madam Cote, Paul." Roy laughed.

"You needed to tell me more for the Alan Goldbear family Roy."

"Don't forget that I am your boss. I will tell you what I want. Good luck Paul." Roy hang up.

"Do you have problem with Roy, Paul?"

"He knows that I was in Estelle's house Morel. Roy is a good friend of Estelle's father Cote. I think that Roy is hiding something for from me about the Cote and the Goldbear family. Why did Roy tell me that Giles is Madam Cote?"

Morel laughed. "When Giles married Estelle, he wanted people to call him Giles Cote. The people started to call him Madam Cote, because the wife usually takes the family name of her husband. Giles took the family name of his wife, Estelle. I asked Margot, how Estelle was feeling about that. She told me that Estelle didn't care, because she was married for the man that she loves. I told Margot that I didn't think that Giles loves Estelle. Margot is always on Estelle's side. They grew up together. When somebody wanted to joke with Estelle, Margot was angry. Frankly Margot is the same as you, Paul."

"You are right Morel. I have a sympathy for Estelle. I told her what she needed to do something with her face."

"If I tell Margot what you said for Estelle, Margot will love you, Paul.

"Will Margot leave you Morel?"

"You need to ask her, but you don't forget to get the two boys with you."

"What do I tell Holly, Morel?"

"That you are ready to marry Margot and she needs to think for Marcel."

"I prefer Estelle, Morel."

"What is the difference between Giles and you, Paul?"

"Estelle will be Madam Morgan. I will not be madam Cote."

"Are you serious Paul?"

"I am joking Morel. I love Holly. You didn't tell me where we are going."

"To Marseille Paul."

"Is somebody waiting for us there?"

"Lamar has friend in Marseille."

"Do you know him?"

"I don't, but Lamar grew up with this friend. He will drop me and you at Ajaccio."

"Do you know the name of this man?"

"Gaston is his name. Why do you want to know everything Paul?"

"I want to help you if you are wrong Morel. We are partners. I need to save the life of Holly. You need to save or kill Giles. I will marry Holly. Estelle will be your boss. Do you think that Estelle's father will love you Morel?"

"I don't need Cote to love me. I will not marry Estelle."

"You will work for the family of Cote, Morel. You forgot that you are a detective. The rich people don't like detectives to enter their houses. I am sure that Estelle will say," Father this is Morel. He is a stupid man"."

"Why do you invite a stupid man in my house Estelle. Giles is enough?"

"This man did something with Giles, father. Now I am a free woman."

"The father of Estelle will tell you "Come to me smart man and he will kiss your head. You will work in my family, because Giles left Estelle.""

"Giles didn't leave me father. He disappeared and nobody know where he is."

"What is your name boy?"

"Morel Sir."

"Call me Cote, Morel. You will be my son" "and he will kiss your head again."

"Did you give money to Morel, Estelle?"

"I gave him father. I needed to be sure that Morel will finish a good job."

"Do you think that I am right Morel?"

"If Estelle and Cote offer me to work for them, I will be happy Paul. I will make good many for my family."

"I am joking Morel. I like this story Paul." We laughed.

"Are you going to kill me when we are in Ajaccio, Morel?"

"Why do you think that I will kill you?"

"I was surprised that Roy knows Cote. He has one goal. To separate Estelle and Giles. If Giles dies, it is good for Cote. Estelle gave you money. Mom wants to separate Holly and me, but she will never pay somebody kill me."

"You are right. Your Mom paid Kevin to save your life."

"Why does Cote paid you to kill me and Holly, Morel?"

"May be Holly knows something for the family Cote." Morel laughed.

"Estelle loves you so much Paul. She gave me money and she told me. I want to see Holly alive in Paris, Morel, but I don't want to see Giles."

"Do you believe me?"

"Why does Estelle wants to save life of Holly, if she loves me, Morel?"

"I don't know Paul, but Estelle told me "Paul will stay forever in my heart Morel. He is a great man and I will be happy when Paul marries Holly." Honestly I didn't understand Estelle. Maybe you did something good to Estelle in the bedroom, but I don't want to know Paul. If everything is OK with Holly, Estelle will take me to work for her."

"Do you think that something will go wrong in Ajaccio?"

"Estelle told me that I need to call her if we don't find Holly at Marcel's house. If Holly isn't there, Estelle will try to find where Holly is. Are you OK now Paul?"

"Yes, I am feeling better. Holly will use you when she has business in Paris."

"We need to find Holly alive before Tuesday, Paul. Scott was right when he said that Giles will kill her after Tuesday."

"Hey Morel, maybe Estelle has a good time with Scott."

"If Cote doesn't kill Scott when he finds out that he is a detective. I need to make a call." Morel stopped the car at a gas station. He spoke for a short time with someone in French. When he came back to the car he said "Gaston is waiting for us. He gave me the directions to his house."

"I don't understand you, Morel. You never saw Gaston, but you think that he will help us."

"I don't think that we have a choice Paul. I might be able to find somebody who I know in Marseille, but in two or three days. It is a miracle that Lamar grew up in Marseille and knows people that he trusts."

"Why didn't you take Lamar with us?"

"He drove to London. Lamar told me that Gaston will do what I tell him."

"Are you going to pay Gaston good money? Everybody works for money."

"You don't need to pay Paul. It is my and Estelle's business." My cell phone rang. It was Dad.

"Hi Dad."

"Where are you, Paul?"

"I am with my friend Dad."

"You don't want to tell me, who is your friend?"

"It isn't important now Dad. Why did you call me?"

"Janet called and told me that you must come back to New York. They will kill you there."

"Did Mom tell you where I am and where I am going Dad?"

"She didn't. I think that Janet didn't know where you are and she tried to get information from me."

"Did you have sex with her, Paul?"

"They love me Dad." I and Dad laughed.

"You will do everything for Holly, Paul."

"Of course Dad. You want grandchildren. Roy called and told me about Estelle, Paul. He said that she is so rich, but you don't have a chance to marry her. I laughed a lot Paul. I know that if you want, you will marry her. I told Roy, that you will marry Holly. Do you know what Roy told me?"

"Holly is with two men. She will never marry Paul. Holly isn't a woman for Paul, Henry, but I and you will wait to see what will happens between Holly and Paul."

I don't understand why so many people don't want you to marry Holly. This is business between Holly and you, Paul. I will be waiting for you and Holly to come back to New York."

"We will be back Dad. Maybe it is good to turn off your cell phone Paul. I will tell my friend that you want me to turn off my cell phone Dad." Dad hang up.

"Do you think that I need to turn off my cell phone Morel?"

"This is a good idea Paul. Nobody needs to know where we are.

"Do you think that Estelle will tell her father?"

"I don't know Paul. This is business between Estelle and Cote. Why did you ask me?"

"Because Roy told Dad, that I need to return to New York and Holly will not marry me. Before we finish our job, Cote will not tell Roy. Cote wants Giles to die or disappear."

"Estelle too Paul."

"What will Scott do, he knows where we are going?"

"Scott will be busy with Estelle, Paul. I am kidding."

"It won't be good if Scott talks to Cindy, Morel."

"Does Cindy know your Mom?"

"No, but Scott spoke with my mom."

"I need to call Estelle, Paul."

"Hi Estelle. What is Scott doing?"

"Scott spoke with Paul's Mom, Morel. She wanted to know where Paul is. You must not allow Scott to call anybody."

"Of course Morel. If Scott tries to call somebody, you need to kill him Estelle. It will be hard for me, but I have your pistol Morel."

"Paul will turn off his cell phone. Estelle wants to speak with you."

"How are you feeling Paul?"

"I didn't feel good, after I left Paris. I am OK now. Roy told Dad that I don't have a chance to succeed Estelle."

"Roy is a greedy man Paul. Roy is afraid, because you will get to work with the money of the Cote family. I spoke many times with my father about him trusting Roy, but they are old friends. I am a new friend to you, Paul. Do you think that you and I will be good friends?"

"Of course Estelle. I am happy that you made me feel good. I want you to remember forever what happened in the bath. You want to help me to find Holly and I will not forget both Estelle. Morel doesn't need to know. You are Morel's boss. It is better for me and you."

"You are a discreet man. I like that. You want to protect my reputation. I am sending you kisses Paul."

"Do you want to speak with Morel?"

"No" and Estelle hang up.

"Can you turn off your cell phone Paul?"

"I didn't ask Gaston what kind boat he is getting for us. I will stop before we enter Marseille."

He stopped at a gas station and asked me "Do you want me to buy food for you Paul?"

"I don't want anything to eat."

"I will use the restroom."

We got back on the road and ten minutes later we were in Marseille. Morel was looking for somebody on the street we were driving very carefully. He said "I think that the man outside that house is waiting for us Paul."

Morel stopped the car few feet from the man. The man asked "Are you Morel?"

Yes, I am Gaston.

"Can you park the car inside the property? We will go with my car." Morel parked the car and we left.

Morel introduced me to Gaston. "This is Paul, Gaston."

"Lamar told me that I need to help him and he told me how much you will pay me."

"Here are thirty thousand Gaston."

"Is this OK.?"

"Yes, Morel. Lamar told me that you will pay me thirty thousand before we go."

"I will give you the rest after we finish."

"How much?"

"Ten thousand."

"I will do everything that you ask of me Morel. Can you get what you need from your car and put in the trunk of my car?"

Morel and I put our stuff in the trunk. We left with Gaston's car. He drove for a while. Gaston stopped. We exited the car. We were close to the Mediterranean. We got our bags and walked.

"We are going to a boat Morel. I got a fast boat" said Gaston.

"You are smart Gaston. We need to get fast to Ajaccio and return fast to Marseille."

"If we are lucky to return Morel."

"Did Lamar tell you?"

"He didn't want to, but I told him that I need to know why we are going to Ajaccio."

"I am a detective Gaston. Many people work with drugs, doesn't matter that they are businessmen."

"This is the business for billions of dollars Gaston. Tell that to Morel, Paul. We don't have time to speak Gaston." The boat left the bay of Marseille.

"I will try to sleep Gaston" said Morel.

"May I speak with Paul, Morel?"

"It is a long trip. If Paul wants." I was sitting next to Gaston. Morel sat behind us.

"I understand that your girlfriend was kidnapped Paul. Is that true?"

"Yes."

"Who and why did they kidnap her?"

"I know that she left the hotel with two man."

"Is this normal for her Paul.?"

Gaston laughed. I laughed too.

"Why are you laughing Paul? It is your girlfriend. If you don't love her, why do you want to get her from Ajaccio?"

"To ask her if she was happy with the two man."

"Are you going to kill them if she wasn't happy?"

"If Holly wasn't happy, I will kill them. I will tell Holly that she needs to choose better men." We all laughed.

"Hey Paul, I like you. I think that will have good time with you."

"Do you know who is my girlfriend?"

"I asked Lamar, but he didn't tell me."

"Do you know Holly Gold?"

"Of course Paul. Holly is a model. You are a lucky man Paul. Holly is beautiful. Is she is good in bed?"

"Holly makes me happy in bed Gaston."

"You are sad now because she is making happy somebody else."

"I never been jealous Gaston. If Holly is happy, I will be happy too."

"This is good for you Paul. If somebody tells me that for my girlfriend, I will kill him."

"I can't kill you, because you need to drive the boat Gaston. I will not have a chance to find Holly if I kill you."

"Lamar told me that you are a funny man, but now I am sure that you are. Do you love Holly?"

"I will marry her, Gaston. Doesn't matter that Holly is with two men."

"I understood Paul. You love her very much. I hope that Holly is alive and waiting for you."

"Where are we going to stay in Ajaccio, Gaston?"

"I have a friend there. He will help us. We will use his car and stay in his house. My friend wanted to stay with us, but I told him that it is better for him to go fishing in the Mediterranean. When we are done we will leave Ajaccio, but my friend lives there. I don't want somebody to kill him because of us. Lamar told me that I need to be ready if we need to use weapons."

"I don't have a weapon Gaston."

"I have one more pistol. Do you want it?"

"Yes, I want it."

Gaston handed me the pistol and asked me "Do you know how to use the pistol?"

"My friend in the University was a hunter. His parents live in the mountain. I have been there several times and he thought me how to use a pistol."

"Can you fire in the water Paul?"

"Morel is sleeping. When he wakes up I will fire."

"Do you have brothers and sisters Paul?"

"I am alone Gaston."

"I am alone too. I live with my parents. The house is big and I don't have problem to marry and live with me wife in the house. My dad is a good man. My mom too, but she talks a lot. If I marry and I and my wife decide to go out for dinner, then my mom will tell me that my wife needs to cook and we need to save money. Mom is right, but young girls want to go out. I will have to be between my wife and Mom all the time. They will never stop to fight, because we will live at Mom's house. I need to work two or three more years and I will be ready to buy a house or an apartment. If my wife has a problem with Mom, we will move in my apartment. I know that Mom will stop to speak against my wife and Mom will want we return in her house. Today is hard for young and old people to live together, Paul."

"I am like you Gaston. My mom doesn't want me to marry Holly. Holly has an apartment. I have one too. I will never be able to live with Mom, and I don't want to either."

"What does your father think?"

"He supports me and Holly. His name is Henry. Henry wants me to marry Holly. Henry gave me thirteen million dollars to pay the ransom for Holly."

"Oh my God. This is a lot of money Paul. Are you ready to pay the ransom, Paul?"

"I was ready, but they wanted to take my money and not give Holly back. Morel and Lamar helped me to save the money."

"I don't know Morel, but Lamar is an honest and good man. We grew up together like brothers. After he left to Paris, I was lonely Paul. Lamar wanted me move to Paris, but I don't have enough money to live in Paris. I know that Lamar will help me to find a job, but Mom and Dad will miss me. Where do your parents live?"

"They have an apartment in New York and a house in Florida, but they stay more in Florida."

"You have rich parents Paul."

"If Paul's Mom marries Alan, Paul will be richer Gaston. Alan is a rich man."

"You weren't sleeping Morel."

"I am a detective. I need to know what you and Paul were speaking about."

"Mom isn't going to divorce my dad, Morel."

"They will divorce Paul."

"Why did you give a pistol to Paul, Gaston?"

"To kill you."

"Why?"

"Because you spoke against Paul's parents."

"I was sleeping when you gave the pistol to Paul. You are a detective. I knew that when you wake up, you will say that. Every detective thinks that every person is a criminal. Do you think that I am a criminal Morel?"

"Of course Gaston. You don't have money to buy this boat. You stole the boat."

"I have one more pistol Morel. I think that the fish will be happy to eat your body. Do you think that I need to ask the fish if they want to eat a stupid detective Morel?"

"This is funny. I like you Gaston. I think that you don't have problem to kill anybody."

"Can you fire with the pistol Paul?"

"I fired. You are ready to kill too Paul."

"How many people do I need to kill Morel?"

"You need to ask Holly, Paul. She knows how many people hurt her."

"Did you hear what I and Paul spoke about?"

"Hey Gaston, I am a detective."

"Paul, we need to kill Morel, because he spied on us."

"I didn't hear everything Gaston."

"Why?"

"Because I didn't want to listen for your problem with your Mom, Gaston."

"Hey Paul, I think that I will not kill Morel, because he is joking with me."

"Do you think that this is OK Morel?"

"It is OK that your friend can't be with us Gaston. You were right. He is from Ajaccio. When are you going to call him?"

"Twenty minutes before we arrive in Ajaccio bay. His house is not far from the bay. You don't tell name him your name and he will not tell you his name, Morel. Give the money to my friend when you meet him.

"Do you know how much I need to give your friend?"

"Twenty thousand."

"You know well Ajaccio, Gaston."

"I know Morel. It will be better Morel, if we don't kill anybody when we take Holly."

"We will have to kill if they try to kill us, Gaston." The phone of Morel rang. Morel answered "I don't know Estelle. I need to ask. What time are we going to arrive Gaston?"

"After forty minutes."

The cell phone of Morel rung again forty minutes later. He said "We are close to Ajaccio, Estelle. I will Estelle. For you Paul."

"I am so happy to hear your beautiful voice lady."

"I wanted to tell you that your Mom, Janet called and asked where you are. I told her that you are waiting in bed for me."

"She told you that you need to marry me, Estelle."

"How did you know what Janet told me?"

"Mom hates Holly and she will be happy if I marry for any other woman."

"I will be happy too Paul, but Holly is a better choice for you than me."

"Why?"

"Holly is beautiful and rich. Janet ask me if I know where Scott is."

"How did Janet know Scott, Paul?"

"I told Janet that Scott is my house and I hang up. I was surprised that Roy called me and he asked for you. Frankly Roy Bell never spoke with me. I told him that I am with you in bed and I hang up. Giles called Scott and asked him If you and I had sex."

"What did Scott tell Giles?"

"That you fought with Scott and he killed you and Scott will kill me when he receives the money. It is good that nobody knows Morel. You must find Holly before Tuesday, Paul." Estelle hang up.

"Many people want to know where I am Morel."

"You spoke with Estelle for thirty seconds Morel. I understood that Estelle is your boss, because you repeated several time her name. Paul spoke with her seven minutes, but he never said her name."

"You are right Gaston. Estelle is my boss, but Paul has a good relationship with my boss."

"Is Estelle beautiful like Holly, Morel?"

"You need to ask Paul. I don't want to speak for my boss Gaston."

"Holly and Estelle are different Gaston."

"How different Paul?"

"Estelle is richer and married. She has two children."

"You are right that we need to go to get Holly, Paul. Woman with two children isn't good for you." Gaston looked at his watch and said "I need to make a call." He said "We will arrive after twenty minutes."

Gaston slowly entered the bay and he docket the boat. We took our bags and left. We walked with Gaston for five minutes when he stopped and said "We need to wait here Morel. Are you ready to give the money to my friend?"

Morel showed the envelop to Gaston. A man walked to us. The man said "Get the key of my car Gaston." Morel gave the envelop to the man. He got and checked the envelop. He said "Thanks boss" and disappeared very fast.

"Morel and Paul, follow me." We went to a parking lot Gaston found the car. We threw our bags in the trunk got in the car and left the parking. I was surprised that there were no people or cars on the streets. It was early in the morning. After five minutes were in a property. Gaston parked the car in the garage. We went to the house. Gaston said "It is good if we don't turn on the lamps Morel."

"We have light from the street lamps Gaston. I will give a lantern to Paul." Gaston showed me and Morel the bedroom, the bathrooms and the kitchen.

"The refrigerator is full. Are you hungry Paul?"

"I am OK right now. May be later I will eat."

"Do you want coffee Morel and Paul?"

"Yes, Gaston. We sat and drank coffee in the living room."

"What do we do next Morel?" Gaston asked.

"You and I will leave the house at 8:00am. We need to find Marcel's house. We will return at 12:00 o'clock Paul. You will stay in the house."

"Are you afraid to stay alone in the house?"

"You gave me a pistol Gaston. If somebody rings the bell or knock the door you don't open. It is good if you don't stay close to the window."

Gaston and Morel left at 8:00 o'clock. I was alone. I was tired. I laid on the sofa and tried to sleep. I opened my eyes and looked at my watch. It was 10:55am. I was hungry. I made a sandwich. I saw a shelf with books. I checked the books, but they were in French or Italian. If Holly was with me she would have read, I would have relaxed. Holly loves to read. I read books when I was young. After I started to work in Roy's company I stopped to read. Holly wanted to joke that I don't have a brain. You have a calculator that counts money every day Paul. You need to change your life. You need to read books. I told her "The books don't make money Holly. I need to use my calculator to make money." If I get Holly alive from here and marry her, I will try to change my life. I don't want to look alike Roy. Susan reads, Mom and Dad read too. Estelle is busy with her business. I will ask her if she has time to read books. I was at Estelle's house, but I didn't see a shelf with books. "Of course Paul, you were busy looking at Estelle's naked body," I told myself. I thought for her and I was ready. Maybe I will think for Estelle when I am in bed with Holly. I don't believe that, because Holly's body is perfect too. I had many girls, but Holly was on the top. When Holly wanted sex, she told me. "O boy, I want to make you happy in bed". Holly made me happy every time when I was in bed with her. Holly knows what to do in bed. I don't believe that Holly made Marcel happy. If Holly was happy with Marcel, why she left him. Why did Marcel needed to kidnap Holly and now I need to try to save her? Everybody who spoke with me for Holly wanted to hurt me by telling me that Holly left with two men. But I know that Holly will call me and tell me, if she wants to be with Marcel. Holly didn't call me for nine days. Dad spoke with Holly for a long time when Holly and I were in Florida or Dad and Mom were in New York. Dad knows Holly well. He gave my thirteen million and he will do everything for Holly. Dad wants me and Holly to live together. Dad has experience and knows people, but why didn't he understand that Mom and Alan have been together for such a long time? Maybe Dad is like Estelle. She loved Giles, because he married Estelle and they have two children. Estelle knew that Giles slept with girls, but she didn't divorce him. Maybe Dad is happy that he has me and he didn't care what Mom did. If I marry Holly, I will not chase Holly. If I don't believe Holly, then why should I marry her?

I looked at my watch. It was 11:50am. Morel and Gaston will back after ten minutes. I stopped to think for Holly. It was 12:20, but they didn't return. Maybe something happened with Morel and Gaston. I heard a sound. It was 1:10pm. I pointed the pistol at the door where Morel and Gaston needed to enter the house. The door opened and I saw Morel. It is good that you were ready to fire Paul. I am sorry that we are late, but Gaston bought lunch. Gaston entered too. He laughed and joked.

"Don't kill me Paul, I am carrying a lunch for you." We sat and ate. We didn't speak. After lunch Gaston cleaned the table and made coffee.

"After the coffee I want to sleep Gaston" Morel said.

"I want to sleep too Morel" said Gaston.

"What are you going to do Paul?"

"I slept for three hours on the sofa Morel. They are more in rooms in the house Paul."

"I prefer the sofa" and I laid back on it. I tried to sleep, but I didn't. I thought for Morel and Gaston. They didn't tell me what they did when they were out, but they didn't tell me that we will have a problem to get Holly. When Morel wakes up I will ask him what I need to do when we enter the house of Marcel. It was good that I didn't ask Morel and Gaston when we ate and drank coffee. I saw that they were tired. They didn't joke. Gaston woke up at 6:15pm.

"Morel is a good detective Paul. He has a plan for each of us for tonight. Morel told me that today is Sunday and Giles, Marcel and Luca will go out for dinner tonight, because Holly is locked at the studio. The second floor at north side of the house doesn't have a window. Morel thinks that Holly is there in the studio. Morel told me that we don't need to kill them, because Holly will be alone in the house."

"Do you think that Giles, Marcel and Luca will go out for dinner and spend the night in the bar?"

I understood that Morel wanted to tell Gaston that we will not kill them.

"I will go out too Gaston, if I kidnaped and locked somebody. Do you think that I have to stay twenty-four hours in the house?"

"Maybe you are right Paul, but I was them I will stay."

"People are different Gaston. Marcel and Luca sale drugs. Maybe they have drugs and they will go out to sale them."

"Morel told me the same Paul. I am happy that we don't have to kill them."

Morel woke up at seven thirty. He came to the kitchen and said "I am hungry Gaston."

"I will prepare dinner Morel. We don't know when we will eat next time."

After dinner Morel told me and Gaston what we need to do.

"Holly is on the second floor Paul. You and I will enter the house from the kitchen. If garage door is open, we will enter from there. I will stay on the first floor. When you are on the second floor you need to walk straight. You will see doors on the left and the right side. You don't go to these rooms. When the corridor ends you will see a door. Behind this door is Holly. If the door doesn't have a key, you need to open the door with your shoulder or a kick. If you have a problem to open the door, you need to use the pistol. Are clear on what you have to do Paul?"

"If I need to fire at left side of the lock. I will tell Holly to stay on the right side."

"It is good that you watch movies Paul.

"What do I need to do if somebody is with Holly?"

"You must leave the studio with Holly."

"Hey Paul, you must kill him. He is there to have sex with Holly."

"You are right Gaston. That will make me angry and I will kill him."

"Holly must get her things from the room. If the studio has a bathroom need to make sure that she takes all of her stuff from there too, Paul."

"I will check Morel."

"When you get Holly we will live the house."

"Are you clear on what you have to do Gaston?"

"I will drop you and Paul. I will leave and wait where you showed me today. When I see a light three times from your lantern, I will come to pick up you."

We left the house at 12:00 o'clock. Gaston drove carefully. There were people on the streets. Gaston stopped the car.

Morel said "Remember what you need to do Gaston."

"I will come here when I see three times the light."

Morel and I exited from the car. Gaston left. We went at end of the wall where an iron fence started. I saw a hole between the wall and the iron fence.

"It is good that Marcel doesn't have dogs, Paul. Gaston already checked."

Morel and I entered Marcel's property. We walked towards the house. The garage door was open.

"We will use the garage door Paul."

Morel opened carefully the door and we entered the house. "The kitchen is to the left Paul. You will stay at the corner. I will enter the kitchen." I heard a voice. People were speaking, very loud. in French.

"When I point to you with my hand, you need to go to the second floor, you will need to move fast Paul." I stayed on the corner waiting for Morel's signal.

Morel entered the kitchen. I saw the steps that are going to the second floor. I heard that Morel spoke with somebody. Morel spoke in English.

"What are you doing here Morel and why are you speaking English?"

"I don't want Marcel and Luca to understand what we are talking about Giles. Marcel speaks English too. How did you know that I am here Morel?"

"Marcel called the police. Marcel and Luca want the policemen to arrest you Giles. They know that you will kill them."

"Is this true Marcel?"

"I didn't call the police Giles. This man lying."

"Are the policemen coming here to arrest me Morrel?"

"They will come in the morning Giles."

"It is good that I have time to prepare for them Morel." I heard two shots.

"Marcel and Luca died Morel. What are you doing now Morel?"

"I will kill you if you don't throw your pistol Giles."

I heard two more shots. I didn't know if Morel was alive. I was happy when I saw him. Go to get Holly, Paul. I will check the living room. I jumped and run to the second floor. I saw the door when Holly was. The key was on the door. I opened it. I want to sleep Marcel. "I don't want to speak with you."

"Holly it is me Paul."

"Oh my God. I told Marcel that you will come to get me, Paul." Holly kissed me many times.

"Do you want me to make you happy Paul?"

"We don't have time now Holly. We need to leave fast. Could you collect fast your things from here? I will check the bathroom Holly."

When I returned Holly was ready to leave. "My things were in the bags Paul. I changed my bikini. I didn't change my clothes. I was waiting for you."

I checked the room. Holly got everything. We left. Holly and I walked through the corridor when Morel turned off the lamps. Holly and I were on the steps when Morel lighted his lantern at Holly's eyes. She said "I can't see Paul."

"Throw the bags to me and get Holly, Paul."

"Who is this man Paul?"

"My friend."

I took Holly. Morel lighted the steps. I was in the living room. Morel, Holly and I exited from kitchen. "I can see now Paul. I am OK now."

"That is good Holly, we need to walk fast."

We were on the street. Morel lighted the lantern three times. Gaston came fast and we entered the car.

"I was kidnapped Paul. Why did Marcel and Luca kidnap me?"

I didn't answer Holly. Gaston drove fast.

"Can you drive slowly Gaston?"

"I will Morel." Gaston stopped the car at parking where we got it.

"Can you give ten thousand more to my friend Morel?"

"Where is he?"

He is walking to the car Morel.

"You go with Holly in the boat Paul."

I took mine and Holly's bags. We walked and entered the boat.

"I feel like I am a movies Paul."

I didn't answer to Holly again.

"What happened to you Paul?"

"Why don't you answer me?"

"Why did you want to have sex when I entered your room Holly?"

"Where you waiting for Marcel or Luca?"

Holly understood that I wasn't happy.

"I am so sorry if I hurt you Paul. I didn't want to have sex with them. I was so happy that you came to get me boy. I thought that if you didn't come, they would have killed me. You don't know what I thought these days when I was alone in that room. I didn't understand why they did that to me. I have known Marcel for many years and I believed him. Marcel told me that he loves me and he wanted to marry me. Oh my God. I was ready to kill myself Paul. I love you so much Paul. If I don't marry you, I will never marry. Do you understand me Paul?"

Morel and Gaston entered the boat.

"I understand Holly." The boat left slowly the bay of Ajaccio. Then Gaston started driving the boat very fast.

"I want to sleep Paul, I am very tired."

"Could you lie on the seat and put your head of my lap Holly?"

Holly laid down and her head was on my lap. She was crying. I was feeling her tears of my leg.

"Everything is OK Holly. Can you try to sleep?"

After a while Holly felt asleep. I felt her breath. I took the pistol and gave it to Gaston.

"Did you use the pistol?"

"I didn't Gaston. Nobody was with Holly. She was waiting for me." I looked at my watch. It was 1:10am.

"We finished fast Paul what we came for."

"We did a good job Gaston. It is good that Morel didn't kill anyone Paul."

"Why did I need to kill Gaston?"

"You were in Ajaccio for that Morel. I am not stupid. Paul came in Ajaccio to get Holly. You had a plan to do something your boss wanted, but your boss listens to somebody that told her what you had to do." Gaston cleaned the piston that I gave him and threw it in water.

"I don't believe that the boss of your boss will find the pistol in the Mediterranean. You forgot something Morel." Morel gave an envelope to Gaston.

"How much is in the envelope?"

"Thirty thousand. My life costs more, but I am happy that I helped Paul. Are you happy that Holly is sleeping at your lap Paul?"

"I am sorry that you risked your life to help me Gaston."

"I didn't risk when I helped you, but I don't know what will happen in future Paul. You must think for your life too Morel. It is easy for somebody to kill one stupid detective. I will read in the newspaper. The stupid detective Morel died suddenly, but he finished good job for his boss." I didn't understand Gaston. I looked at Morel.

"I am tired and I want to sleep."

"You need to call your boss and tell her what happened Morel."

"I already spoke with her Gaston."

"Was she happy when heard the news?"

"She was and she told me to give you more money. What do you want from me, Gaston?"

"It will be better, if you go to sleep Morel."

"May I turn on my cell phone Morel?"

"Yes, Paul."

"Good night Morel. Somebody will want you and I to sleep well somewhere else, but it is good to sleep in the boat. You have a chance to wake up."

"Shut up Gaston."

"I will zip my mouth Morel, but I know that they will try to zip my moth forever."

Holly and Morel were sleeping. Gaston and I didn't speak. I started to think what Gaston told Morel. My cell phone rang. It was Dad. "Hi Dad. I was afraid Paul. I called three times." "Everything is OK Dad."

"Where is Holly?"

"She is sleeping Dad."

"Do you think that Holly is feeling good?"

"I don't know. We didn't speak about what happened, but you know me Dad. I will never ask Holly. She needs to tell me, if she wants. I am like you, Dad. Mom has a boyfriend, but you never asked her, why she loves and lives with two men. If Holly wants to have a boyfriend, I will tell her to live with him. I am stupid Dad."

"Why did you say that Paul?"

"I am feeling that Dad. Somebody used me."

"Who told you?"

"Nobody told me. I understood that ten-minute ago Dad. Holly will call you Dad." I hang up. Gaston turned his head.

"You are right Gaston. Are you afraid?"

"Hey Paul, I am a man. Holly need to take a shower and change her clothes Paul. When we arrive in my house, tell Holly that she need to take a shower." We arrived at the bay of Marseille. Holly and Morel woke up. It was early morning. We entered the car of Gaston.

"Take a shower at Gaston's house Holly."

"I need to change my clothes too Paul."

Gaston entered his property.

"I will wait in my car Paul."

"You don't like me Morel. It won't help me if I don't like you Gaston."

Holly was in the bath. I and Gaston were in the living room. I took and give him one hundred thousand.

"Morel paid me Paul. I want to help you to buy new house or apartment Gaston."

"Thanks Paul. Maybe I will have chance to use the money."

"Did Morel understand what I told him, when we were in the boat?"

"He understood, but it will be hard for him to tell Estelle. I will tell Lamar that you gave me one hundred thousand."

"Why?"

"They need to know that you are my friend and you will do everything for me."

"How did you understand?"

"Morel told me many times that he will not kill them. He didn't need to tell me, if he didn't kill them Paul. Estelle didn't want somebody to know what happened in Marcel's house. The policemen will find the bodies of Giles, Marcel and Luca. The house of Marcel will be clean and nobody will know or speak for Giles, Marcel and Luca. There will be four people that know. Holly, Morel, you and I Gaston."

"Yes, Paul. Morel needed to think before he promised Estelle."

Holly entered the living room. "You are beautiful Holly. May I kiss you?"

"Of course Gaston. You helped Paul and he saved my life."

Gaston kissed Holly.

"Did you give your phone number and your address in New York to Gaston, Paul?"

"I don't need it Holly."

"You need to have it Gaston. If you have problem in France, you need to come to New York. Paul is rich. He will pay for your trip."

"Did you hear want I said when we were in the boat?"

"I slept Gaston. The problem is that Marcel and Luca kidnapped me, but Giles told them what they had to do. May be Estelle and her family is behind it."

"Do you know Estelle, Holly?"

"Estelle is the wife of Giles, Gaston. The family of Estelle is rich, but I am rich too Gaston. Nobody knows who I am including Paul. O boy, don't be afraid that I am rich." Holly kissed me. I gave a paper to Gaston. "This is my phone number and address. We need to leave Gaston.

"Holly and I said good bye to Gaston and entered Morel's car.

"Kiss your boss Morel."

"Is she is beautiful like Holly?"

"I prefer to kiss Holly, Gaston."

"Why don't you love your boss Morel?"

"She is married."

"Estelle is free now Morel."

"I am married Gaston." We laughed. Morel drove to Paris.

"Gaston is a good man Paul."

"Morel is good too Holly. He is a detective and helped me to find you in Marcel's house."

"Where is Scott Hunter, he is my detective Paul?"

"He was in Paris when I and Morel left Paris. I don't know where he is now."

"Scott flew to America, Holly."

"How do you know?"

"Scott is my friend and he called me from the airport."

"Did Scott ask for me?"

"Scott is happy that you are free."

"I was a duck when I followed Marcel and Luca to Ajaccio, Paul. On Friday morning, I spoke with Giles and told him that I will return to New York on Sunday. Marcel and Luca came in my hotel apartment at 5:00pm. Marcel told me that I need to go at

Ajaccio. Giles will come there on Saturday or Sunday and I will sign contract with Giles there. I was happy and I didn't think, why I needed to go in Ajaccio to sign the contract Paul. I and Giles met the whole week in Paris and we didn't sign. Marcel, Luca and I left Paris with Marcel's car on Friday night. Luca drove to Marseille."

"Where did you and Marcel sit?"

"I didn't make happy Marcel, Paul."

"Shut up Paul."

"Let Holly to tell what was happened between her and Marcel."

"I am sorry Morel. You need to tell me that you are sorry Paul."

"I am sorry Holly and I kissed her."

"It is a good sorry" and Holly kissed my mouth. "We arrived at Ajaccio. I told them that I prefer to sleep in the studio. I went to sleep. I woke up on Saturday morning had breakfast and went back to the room to read. When I heard that somebody looked the door. I tried to open it, but the door didn't open. What day is today Paul?"

"Monday."

"Oh my God. I was in the studio for nine days Paul."

"You need to eat and drink water Holly."

"Marcel was the only one that came to the room. He brought me food and water. Luca watched the door when Marcel entered."

"When did you see Giles the last time, Holly?"

"In Paris, Paul."

The phone of Morel rang. He said "I am driving to Paris. We will come to your house Estelle."

"I will not go to Estelle 's house Morel."

"Estelle wants to speak with you Holly."

"Your husband kidnapped me Estelle. You must know what he did. I don't want to sign a contract."

"Give me the phone Holly. Holly we will get Holly's things from the hotel and come to your house Estelle."

"I will not go Paul."

"Shut up Holly.

"Could you buy two tickets to New York?"

"When do you want to go Paul?"

"This afternoon. I want to be in New York tonight."

"I will buy them Paul."

"See you Estelle."

"Why does Estelle wants me to sign a contract with her?"

"I need to sign with Giles."

"Do you know who is the boss Holly?"

"Estelle told me that she is the boss of Giles."

"Then why do you want to sign with Giles, Holly?"

"Giles doesn't have money. Estelle controls the money of family Cote."

"Estelle's father controls the money of family Cote, Paul."

"Do you want to meet with Cote?"

"I prefer to have business with Estelle, Paul."

"You are a good girl."

"You are a bad boy."

"I didn't leave you to call me a bad boy Holly. I had to spend money and time to get you back. I was ready to marry you."

"I will do what you want me to do Paul."

"You must think before you do something Holly."

"Do you think that Estelle wants to have business with me?"

"I think that nobody in Paris wants that Paul."

"You need to ask Estelle before you decide Holly."

"I will ask her. May I make a call Paul?"

"Why did you ask me?"

"Because I don't have a cell phone. You forgot that I was kidnapped."

"You can use my cell phone Holly?"

"Thanks Morel."

"Hi Henry. I am OK. Paul is a bad boy. I don't know Henry. I need time before I decide. I want to see you tonight. Where we will stay Paul?"

"In my apartment."

"I will see you in Paul's apartment Henry. He wants to speak with you Paul."

"I don't want."

"Paul is driving Henry. When we stop he will call you." Holly gave the phone back to Morel.

"Why did you lie to Dad?'

"You are angry with me. I don't want you to hurt Henry."

"Did you understand what you did Holly?"

"I understood boy. I lost a chance to marry you, but we I believe that we have a future together."

"Do you love me boy?"

"You know my answer Holly."

"That you love me is your answer Paul."

"You are right." We entered Paris.

"You need to stop at Citibank Morel." Holly wanted to come with me. "My new girlfriend is waiting for me in the bank Holly."

"I will stay in the car bad boy." I entered the bank. I looked for Norman.

"What are you doing here Paul?"

I turned around. It was Marion.

"I came to see my friend Norman. He works in the bank."

"Did you find your girlfriend, because if you didn't, I want you Paul?"

"I am sorry Marion. My girlfriend Holly is waiting for me." Norman came towards me and Marion. I introduced Norman to Marion. "I know her, Paul."

"I know you too Norman."

"Can you put the money in my bank account Norman? I am not sure how much is in the bag. You need to count the money."

"Oh my God. For the first time in my life, I see a man who doesn't know how much he carries with him."

"I love you Paul."

"My girlfriend will kill you if she heard that Marion. Norman is a good man too and he doesn't know how much money he has in the bank. You should invite Marion for dinner Norman."

"Do you want to go to dinner Marion?"

"Of course Norman."

"Why didn't you invite me before?"

"I saw you many times when you came to the bank, but I was afraid to ask you. I didn't know how you are."

"How long do you know Marion, Paul?"

"She is a good girl Norman. Marion is a good friend of mine. I had a problem and she helped me."

"I will go to put the money in your account Paul." I and Marion were alone.

"Is Norman rich Paul?"

"You need to give Norman a chance. He works in a bank. Do you like him, Marion?"

She didn't answer me, because Norman returned.

"This is your deposit confirmation Paul."

"This is my phone number Norman. Call me in the afternoon. I want to have dinner with you."

"I will call you Marion."

"I need to live Norman."

"Thank you for helping me."

"My pleasure Paul."

"May I see her Paul?"

"Can you come with me outside? She is waiting for me in a car with my friend?"

We left the bank. When Holly saw us, she exited the car and said "You were telling me the truth Paul. You have a new girl-friend." I introduced Holly to Marion.

"Do you love Paul, Marion?"

"Paul is rich, but you are rich too Holly. Doesn't matter if I love Paul. He wants to be with you."

Marion kissed me. "Have a good day" and she left me and Holly.

"Boy what did you do in the last nine days?"

"I looked for a new girlfriend Holly. I didn't know what you think of me, because you were with two men."

"Zip your mouth Paul." We entered the car. Morel dropped us at hotel Le Royal. I and Holly were in the lobby. Jay came to me and Holly.

"I am so happy to see you Holly" and he kissed her. "Paul promised me that he will come back to the hotel with you and you are here Holly."

"Do you love Paul. Jay?"

"He is a man Holly." Holly didn't know what to tell Jay.

"Everybody loves Paul, Holly. I am happy that you and Paul are together."

"I am too Jay."

"Are you?"

"Of course Paul. I was little disappointed when you came to get me. Marcel wasn't happy when he saw you, Paul. Marcel will have to find a new girl in south France."

"Holly and I will get our things and leave Jay. Can you prepare our check out invoice?"

"I will sign when I return in the lobby."

"It will be ready when you come back Paul." I took my luggage and returned to the lobby. Jay wasn't at the front deck. A lady gave me the invoice.

"It is for me and Holly, lady?"

"Yes, Sir." I signed. I sat at lobby and waited for Holly. Morel came and sat next to me.

"Margot wants to see you at the airport Paul."

"I don't know what time I and Holly need to be at the airport."

"I spoke with Estelle and she gave me the information. You gave one hundred thousand dollars to Gaston."

"How do you know?"

"Lamar told me."

"Did he return from London?"

"Last night. Keven told him that a very rich man paid him, but he didn't tell him the name."

"Where is Keven now?"

"He left for Brisbane, Australia. He has an apartment there."

"Does Estelle know Kevin?"

"She doesn't, but I think that her father knows Kevin." Holly came in the lobby. Jay was with her.

"Thank you for helping me Jay. Paul should have helped me."

"I was scared that you will want to do something with me in your hotel apartment Holly."

"I am not ready to do something with you, Paul."

"Of course, you were happy to do something with Marcel. If I marry you, I will not have to think for a child Holly. Marcel thought for that." Morel saw that Holly was angry.

"We need to leave Holly."

Morel and Jay put the bags of Holly in the car. We left the hotel. We didn't speak. Estelle was waiting for us outside the house.

"Nice to see you Holly and Estelle kissed Holly. Come in Holly."

"I will wait in the car Estelle."

"Come in Morel, and Paul too." We were in the living room.

"Do you want something to drink, Estelle asked us?"

"I am OK" Morel told her.

"I am OK too," Holly told Estelle.

"What do you want Paul?"

"Glass of whiskey."

"With ice or dry?"

"Dry and full class."

Estelle gave me a glass of whiskey.

"I would like to speak with you at my office Holly." They entered the office.

"It is early for whiskey."

"I don't care if it is early or late Morel. I am feeling stupid." Morel stopped to speak. Holly and Estelle returned to the living room. Estelle gave me an envelope. I opened and saw money.

"One hundred thousand?"

"Yes, Paul. My father didn't want somebody else to pay".

"How much did you paid Morel, Estelle?"

"It isn't your business Paul."

"Give me your pistol Morel." Holly and Estelle looked at me.

"Don't do that Morel. I am your boss." Morel gave me his pistol.

"Is this your father's picture on the wall Estelle?"

"Yes, it is." I fired at the picture.

I shot in the head the man on the picture. "If your father kills Morel and Gaston, I will kill him before he kills me and Holly. Can you show this picture to your father Estelle? I will never miss." Nobody spoke.

"Do you want more whiskey Paul?"

"One more glass will be better for me."

"I am not happy what Estelle told me what you did in her house Paul."

"Of course Holly. You were happier in Marcel's house."

"I didn't know why you came to get me. Now you aren't happy."

"Do you want sex with me Estelle?"

"You are drunk Paul."

"I am not Holly."

"I am married woman with two children Paul. I am so sorry I forgot for Giles."

"You are right Estelle. I need to look for a young girl. May be Gina is a good choice, but I don't like Scott, because he is Holly's detective and he will give information to Holly about what I am doing with Gina."

"Do you want one more whiskey Paul?"

"I am not in your apartment in New York, Holly. I am in the house of Estelle. She needs to ask me, but I am OK. Two glasses are enough."

"May I kiss you Holly?"

"I want you to kiss me Paul." I kissed her. Estelle and Morel laughed.

"May I see your contract Holly?"

"You need to sign a new contract before the New Year! Why did you sign a contract for five months Holly?"

"Who prepared the contract Estelle?"

"My father."

"I want to speak with him." Estelle called and she gave me the phone.

"My name is Paul Morgan. You used Holly, me, Morel, Gaston and Estelle to make Giles disappear. You and your friend think that you are smart. If something happens with Morel and Gaston, I will kill you Cote. You must see the picture of you that I shot. Next time I will not shoot the picture. I will shoot your head Cote." I hang up.

"We need to leave Estelle."

"Thank you Paul. I depend a lot on my father."

"You forgot Giles, Estelle."

"Giles isn't a problem for me Holly. I will give you an advice. Paul is the best man for you. If you listen to Paul, our life will be easy Holly."

"Do you love Paul, Estelle?"

"Of course Holly. Many people in Paris love Paul."

"What are you going to do with the money Paul?"

"We have time Morel. You need to stop at a bank."

"I will keep the money Paul."

"I don't want you have problem with your father Estelle. I know that you work hard to make and keep the money of your family."

"Paul is sick to make money Estelle."

"If you marry Paul, you will own two or three banks. Paul will buy them for you Holly, you will not have to wait to get money from your rich family."

"You know about my family Estelle?"

"Of course Holly. You are beautiful and rich. I am ugly and must work hard to get every cent from my family."

"You are a lucky woman, because you have two children Estelle."

"You will have too Holly."

"When I was in Ajaccio, I promised myself that I will have two or three children, if I marry Paul. The children will be smart like him, Estelle."

"They will be beautiful like you, Holly."

"I hope so." Estelle, Morel and I laughed.

"Oh my God. I didn't want to say that you are ugly Paul."

"Don't worry. I know who I am Holly."

"I know that Paul."

"Are you going to hire Morel to work for you when you come to Paris, Holly?"

"Morel helped Paul. I know that Paul will want Morel to look for my safety when I am in Paris, Estelle, but you and I need to start the business first. I don't want to promise, if we don't have a business."

"We will have Holly."

"I am sorry, but we need to leave Estelle. I need to stop at the bank."

"Thank you for buying the tickets for me and Paul, Estelle."

Holly, Morel and I left the house of Estelle. I put the money in the bank. Norman wanted to have dinner with Holly and me.

"Marion will come too Paul."

"We are flying to New York after 5:00pm. Next time when Holly and I come in Paris, we will have dinner together, Norman."

Morel drove us to the airport. We didn't speak. Margot waited at airport for us. She kissed Holly and me. We sat to drink coffee.

"I wanted to see you and Holly, Paul. Morel said me many good words for you. I am happy that your beautiful girlfriend Holly is with you again. I saw you in magazines, but for the first time I am seeing you alive and you are sitting next to me."

"Why do you support Estelle, Margot?" I asked.

"When we were in school, everybody laughed and said that Estelle was ugly. We were children Paul. It was so sad. Estelle was born ugly. Nobody wants to have the face of Estelle. God gave her that face. I told Estelle that she is smart. She was the number one student in the school. Estelle knew and answered easy when teachers asked her. I was so-so in school. Estelle helped me and we learned together. I knew that Estelle loved me, because I never joked with her face. Estelle and I continued to have a good relationship after we finished high school. If I had problem in my office, I called and asked Estelle. She told me fast what I needed to do."

"When I decided to marry Morel, Estelle was the one person who supported me. My whole family and my friends told me that

Morel isn't a man for me. Estelle told me. "If you love Morel with all your heart, you need to marry him." Estelle was right Paul. I have two children and a good life with Morel. He does everything what I want. Many people told me that Morel is a stupid detective and he doesn't make enough money, but some time the love is more important for family. I know that my mom and Morel will die for me. My father and brother won't Paul. Do you think that Morel is a stupid detective Paul?"

"He is smart. We found and got Holly back easy. Estelle helped me too Margot. Estelle has a good heart."

"I am happy that Morel will work for Estelle, Paul. What will Morel do for Estelle?"

"Giles disappeared and nobody know where he is. Estelle is afraid for her and the life of the children, Holly."

"I will hire Morel to work for me when I have business in France, Margot." Morel looked at his watch.

"You need to go Paul."

"Thanks Morel." We shook hands. Holly kissed Morel and Margot. I kissed Margot. Holly and I entered our gate. We flew to New York.

CHAPTER 9

My eyes were closed. I was smelling something that I like. It was coffee. It smelled the same as the one Holly made for me in her apartment. I opened my eyes. I saw a cup on front of my face.

"Do you want coffee boy?"

"Where am I, Holly?"

"In the airplane Paul."

"You make the same coffee at home."

"I made it for you here on the airplane boy. I want you to feel that you are at home with me."

I took the cup and drank. "You slept so deep and I wondered what I needed to do to wake up you."

"You did that at home when I met you, Holly. You took my power at night and the morning you woke up me with a cup of coffee in bed."

"You are right Paul."

"Why did you wake up me, I haven't sleep in the last twenty-four hours?"

"Hey boy, you slept for five hours. I didn't know what to do. You needed to think for our future." "If we have a future Holly."

"Don't say that boy. I knew that I created a big problem for you after I left to Paris. We were not together for three-weeks boy. I want to know what you did these three weeks."

"I was busy with women Holly. I was in Puerto Ricco and Gina took me in bed. It was Ok, because Gina is young, but when her Mom Cindy wanted me in bed, I didn't know what to do. Cindy is forty-five. I never been with a woman her age and I decided to try. I wanted to know what you need to do in bed with forty-five-year-old woman. Your detective Scott run after me and he wanted to kill me, because Scott wanted me to marry Gina, but I took his wife in bed. God saved my life Holly. It is a miracle that I am alive.

"What did you do in Paris, boy?"

"I arrived and asked where you are. They told me that Estelle will tell me. She called and invited me to her house. Estelle was naked Holly. I asked her why she was naked. She said "I am the wife of Giles. He slept with your girlfriend." I told Estelle that this happened four years ago and I didn't know you at that time. Estelle told me "Holly knew that Giles was married to me." I told her that she needs to have sex with you, Holly. It was hard time for me. I had to choose. To sleep with Estelle, so she helps me to find you or I return back to New York without you. You didn't return to New York, Paul. Don't think that I did something Holly. Scott came in the house of Estelle and she covered her body. Scott laughed and told Estelle that she need to do something with me or Scott will kill Estelle and me. It was a miracle that Morel came and saved mine and Estelle's life. I was alive and I saved your life Holly. You risked my life Holly."

"Estelle told me something Paul."

"Maybe she wanted to hurt you."

"If Estelle wanted, she would not have given me to sign a contract."

"This contract expires after the New Year. You will need to sign a new contract in a year."

"Do you think that Estelle wants to zip my mouth?"

"I think that Estelle's father wants to zip your mouth Holly. I told you what I did, but I don't want to know what you did with Marcel and Luca. I risked my life to save yours and I want to live with you, Holly. If you don't want me I will leave you."

"I love you, boy, but you are right. I was with two men. I didn't have sex, but I didn't know what happened when I was sleeping. I need time, before I ask you marry me. Do you agree?"

"Of course Holly. You are in my heart. We had a very good time before you left to Paris. I was ready to marry you. I wanted you to be my wife and have children with you."

"O boy. You are killing me when you say that."

"Did you believe my story Holly?"

"I didn't believe the story about the Hunter family. Estelle told me something and I was scared when you got the pistol. I thought that you wanted to kill Estelle. Maybe it that would have been good for Estelle, but not for you, Paul. When you fired at the picture of Estelle's father, I understood that you were very angry, but I didn't understand why, Paul. I am the last person that needs to ask you, what you did after I left to Paris, but it is enough for me."

"Do you like to eat? I ordered food and white wine for both of us."

"I want to tell you that I have a feeling that somebody used us, when Estelle returned the money that I gave to Gaston. If I come with you to Paris, they would not use you and me again Holly."

"O boy, you think that you are wrong."

"I am not."

"I should have discussed that with you when Marcel told me that I needed come to Paris to sign the contract, Paul." The flight attendants brought the food and two bottles of white wine.

"Do you like what I ordered for you?"

"You know that I like fish and wine."

"Cheers boy." Holly kissed me.

"I will pray to God a lot in the next two, three weeks Paul. I believe that God will help us."

"I didn't understand Holly, but she chose good food and wine for me. I ate, we didn't speak." When I finished eating Holly asked me, if I wanted more wine. We drank wine and relaxed.

"Why did you want to pay thirty-million-dollars ransom Paul?"

"I didn't have thirty million. Dad gave me thirteen million Holly."

"You came to Paris, because Henry gave you the money."

"Henry wants me to marry you and he encouraged me to do everything for your freedom."

"You didn't want to?"

"What would you do if somebody told you that I left New York with two girls?"

"I will follow you and fight to get you to be with me."

"I did that."

"I am alive, because you got me Paul. I will never forget what you did for me."

"I am not a rich person Holly. I needed to fight with rich people. They have money and power." "Estelle has money and power, but she helped you, because she loves you."

"Don't start again Holly. Her father told Estelle what she needs to do it. I understood that, when Gaston told me that somebody will kill Morel and him, but you are right that Estelle loves me and she wants to help me."

"Estelle did everything for you and me to be alive. Estelle didn't listen to her father after Morel and I left Paris. I think that somebody supported Estelle to do that. A lot of money are involved in this game. It is a miracle that we are alive. I will give you fifty million to be richer Paul. Do you think that they will stop Paul?"

"I don't have a problem in New York, Holly."

"Your problem started in America, Holly. I don't know why Mom hates you. Mom will never kill you in America. Mom knows that I will put her in jail. The goal was for you to go to France alone. You disappeared easy Holly. Cote wanted to kill Giles and they used you. The goal of Mom was to separate me with you. Cote must be happy, because Giles disappeared. I will meet and speak with Mom. They need to stop Holly."

"I will not stop to investigate, who kidnapped me."

"Marcel and Luca kidnapped you Holly."

"I want to know who paid them".

"How do you know that somebody paid Marcel and Luca?"

"I asked Marcel why he and Luca kidnapped me. He told me. I don't want to hurt you, Holly. You know that I love you and he told me that somebody paid Giles, Marcel and Luca a lot of money. He said "I don't have a choice Holly. I depend a lot on Giles and he gave me money that I never saw in my whole life.""

"Did Marcel wanted to marry you?"

"Marcel told me that he wants to marry me in his house. I told him that I want to marry in New York. Marcel understood that I wanted to leave his house. He told me "Do you think that I am stupid Holly? You want to return to America to marry Paul. Paul's Mom doesn't want you to marry him.""

"Did Janet pay you kill me, Marcel?"

He didn't answer me. After that Marcel stopped to speak to me.

"Did you offer money to Marcel?"

"Marcel told me that he will be rich after we marry. I stopped to drink water food and coffee that Marcel brought to me. I didn't believe him. I drank water from the bathroom and I ate fruit. It wasn't problem for me, because I did that so many times in my life.

I am a model boy." Holly laughed.

The airplane crew informed us that we will arrive in New York in twenty minutes. We started to get ready to get home. It was a long flight.

Holly and I were in my apartment at 10:15pm. Dad was waiting for us. He embraced Holly.

"I am happy that you are at home Holly."

"I am happy to see you too Henry."

"Paul is a man Holly. He promised me that he will return with you to New York."

"It is late to talk tonight Dad. I am tired. Tomorrow I will have a busy day in the office." I thought that Holly would came with me.

"Go to sleep Paul. I want to speak with Henry." When I woke up, Holly wasn't in bed with me in the morning. She didn't sleep in our bed. I saw Holly and Dad in the kitchen.

"Did you sleep last night Holly?"

"I didn't sleep in our bed Paul." My cell phone rang. I thought that it was Mom. It was Susan.

Hi Susan.

"Did you sleep with Roy last night?"

"Why?"

"Because Holly didn't sleep with me. If Roy doesn't want, you I will get you to sleep with me."

"O boy, you never stop to joke."

"Susan called, Holly."

"Give me Holly, Paul."

"Susan wants to speak with you, Holly." They didn't speak long. After she hung up with Susan Holly said "Susan wants to have dinner with Henry, me and you, Paul."

"Is Roy coming too?"

"She told me where we will meet, Roy and you will come from your office there."

"Do you want to see them Holly?"

"Why not Paul. Susan is my friend."

"Maybe Susan and Roy want to know what happened with you in France."

"I am in New York and I am with you Paul."

"Do you know what you need to tell them if they ask you?"

"I don't want to think now for that Paul. I have another problem that I need to resolve. Don't call me or Henry today. Why will be busy?"

"What do you think Dad?"

"You listen to what Holly tells you, Paul."

"I will Dad." I was in my office. Roy entered and closed the door.

"Are you going to kill me, because I invited Susan to come in my bed Roy?"

"It isn't time for jokes Paul. You must call Cote and apologize to him."

"Why, Because I shot at Cote's picture?"

"Because you didn't ask Cote when you used Estelle to find Holly."

"Are you kidding me Roy?"

"I am not Paul."

"If you want to fire me, you do that. Why should I apologize if you fire me?"

"We will speak for your future after your apology."

"I know Estelle's phone number. I don't know Cote's number. This is the business card of Cote." The name on the card was Viler Cote. I called "This is the house of Viler Cote. May I help you?"

"May I speak with Viler Cote?"

"Who are you?"

"My name is Paul Morgan. I am calling from New York."

"Just a Moment."

I waited for few minutes before I heard "Cote speaking."

"Did you see your picture mother faker?"

"Who are you?"

"You know very well who I am. Next time I will shoot your head Viler. You have two choices. First, you must retire and Estelle Cote will run your family. I am looking at my watch. Now is 10:15am. If Estelle doesn't tell me that she is the boss of your family before 10:15 tomorrow morning, Holly will go to the police and tell them everything that happened with her. You have twenty-four ours Viler." I hang up. I started to prepare my things to leave the office.

"What are you doing Paul?"

"I am going home Roy. You fired me."

"I didn't fire you. This is business between Viler and you. Sit and continue to work Paul."

Roy left and closed the door. I understood that I will not work for long time in Roy's company. Roy came to my office at 6:30 pm. We left the office. Roy asked me for my clients, but he wanted to know more for Nancy Jones. "I spoke with her today Roy. She was happy when I spoke with her. You know that I joke with her, but she is happy when I joke for bed and sex." "Nancy is an old woman Paul."

"Nancy told me "I am old woman Paul, but when I am listening talk about sex, I am feeling young again.""

"Does Susan feel good too Roy?"

"Why did you ask me?"

"This morning I said something to Susan, but she didn't answer me."

"Did you speak with Estelle, Paul?"

"She needs to call me Roy. If she doesn't, the family of Cote will speak with a French policeman."

"You didn't change your mind, yet?"

"I didn't Roy."

"They will arrest Alan and Janet too."

"This is a problem for Alan and Janet."

"Janet is your Mom. She must think before she does something against the law. If Janet is in jail, Henry will get a divorce easy Roy. I don't know who is wife of Alan, but she will get divorce easy too." We entered the restaurant. There were Susan, Henry and Holly. We ate, drank and spoke.

"Are going to you marry Holly, Paul, Roy asked me?"

"If Holly wants, I will marry her Roy."

"Holly was with two men Paul. You don't know what Holly did with them."

"I want children Roy, but Paul work too hard to make money for you. Paul doesn't have time to have sex with me. I got two men to be sure that I will get pregnant."

"Estelle loves Paul, Holly. Her father Viler told me that Paul had sex with her."

"I spoke with Estelle when I was in her house. You are right Roy. Estelle loves Paul. But she didn't tell me that Paul had sex with her. Frankly, I had sex four years ago with Estelle's husband Giles, but I didn't love him."

"Why do you want to marry Holly, after she had sex with Giles?"

"It was before I met her, Roy. Holly knows that I had many

girls before I met her. It is normal for young people."

"Henry, your wife is with Alan."

"Do you have problem that Janet and Alan are having a good time Roy?"

"Oh my God. I don't understand what kind person is Henry."

"I will answer you, Roy. You want to know what Alan and Janet will do in the future, because you know that Alan is my father."

"What did you say Holly?"

"Alan Goldbear is my father Paul."

"When did you find that out Holly?"

"I asked Henry, where Janet is. He told me that Janet has a boyfriend and he told me the name of her boyfriend. I was in shock Paul. I told Henry that Alan is my father and I was Hana Goldbear."

"So, Mom doesn't want you marry me, because they think that Alan is my father." I laughed.

"Why did you laugh Paul, it isn't funny?"

"This is a lot money. Alan will call and tell me 'You aren't my son, but you are my son in law. I will give you to work with the money of the Goldbear family." Holly looked at me.

"Do you want to do that?"

"Why not Holly."

"What are you going to do if Janet marries Alan, Paul?"

"It is Henry's problem Roy. Dad knows that I will never give him advice about Mom."

"Is that true Henry?"

"Of course Roy. My goal is Holly to marry Paul."

"Because Holly is from a rich family Henry?"

"Paul found out this here tonight, Roy."

We left the restaurant. Henry, Holly and I were in my apartment.

Holly said "I want to speak with you, Paul. When I was seventeen, Alan was in my bed. His hand was between my legs. He wanted to have sex with me. Mom entered and saw what Alan did. Alan left my bedroom. Mom told me that I dreamed. In the morning we had breakfast. Mom and Alan didn't speak with me. I felt that it was my fault that Alan was in my bed. Mom took the side of Alan. After I finished high school, I left the house of Mom and Alan. I never returned there. For two years I was in Los Angeles. I tried to be an actress. I met man who told me that I will never be been an actress, but I need to be a good girl in bed. He told me that I need to change my name and go to Paris. You have future there, Hana Goldbear. I moved to New York. I changed my name and went to Paris. My new name is Holly Gold. Everybody in Paris knew me Holly Gold. Nobody knew that I was Hana Goldbear."

"Do you still want to work with Alan, Paul? You don't know Alan, Paul."

"He is with Mom. Mom will tell me Holly." I and Holly laughed.

"It looks like Alan is a sick man Holly. Sometimes Alan stay in the hospital for months."

"I never heard that Alan has a mental problem Paul. You are right that sometime he wasn't at home for a long time, but Mom told me that Alan traveled for business. Who told you about Alan being sick?"

"Morel wanted to know more about Alan. I asked Roy and he told me that Alan has a mental problem, but he is smart and Alan makes the money for the Goldbear family. Do you think that Alan will want me to marry you?"

"I am sure one hundred percent Holly. Alan knows that Henry is my father."

"Who told Alan?"

"Roy told Viler Cote, and Viler told Alan. I think that the Cote and the Goldbear family have a good relationship."

"Henry and I will leave early tomorrow morning Paul. If everything is OK, I will try to speak with Mom. Her name is Lori. I haven't seen or spoken with Alan for twelve years. With Mom ten years."

"You are my hero Holly."

"Why?"

"Because you are from a rich family, but you left the family and built your life alone."

"You did that too Paul."

"Dad was there for me every time I needed him Holly."

"I love you for that Paul. I am a model and I traveled a lot. Many men were around me, but I never saw you jealous."

"This is your business Holly."

"Many men don't understand Paul. When I was somewhere for business, I counted every hour. I wanted to be with you. I loved to be with you and Henry. I felt that you were my family."

"We need to go to sleep Holly."

"I will sleep in our bed tonight Paul."

In the morning I didn't see Holly and Dad. They have already left. I was in my office. At 10:0 o'clock when Estelle called me. "Thanks Paul, I am the boss of my family now."

"Congratulation Estelle!"

"How do you feel boss?"

We laughed. "You scared many people Paul. I told them that you are a good man and you are good in the bath too."

"Oh my God. Did you tell to Holly?"

"No Paul. It is a secret between you and me. I told her that I love you and Scott pushed me to have sex with you and you saw me naked. I told Holly, because I didn't know what Scott would have told her. Did Holly ask you?"

"Now, everything is OK Estelle with Holly, but Did you know that Alan Goldbear is Holly's father?"

"I didn't Paul. My dad told me when you and Morel left to Marseille. I decided to tell you if something happens with Holly. When I saw Holly and you together, I thought that it isn't my business to tell you who is Holly's father. She had to tell you, Paul."

"She told me last night Estelle. Frankly, my mom is with Alan. They have had a sexual relationship for thirty-five years."

"Oh my God. They are crazy Paul. I thought that you were crazy when you fired at the picture of my dad. Will Alan marry your Mom?"

"I don't know Estelle, but she must divorce before she can marry Alan."

"If you want to marry me, I am a widow Paul. We don't have a problem."

"I don't want to a have boss Estelle. You are right Paul. I will be your boss." We laughed.

"I will come to New York to sign a new contract with Holly in the last week of September."

"Why do you have to wait to for the last week of September?"

"I have schedule to meet a doctor. I decided to have a plastic surgery on my face. Maybe you will want to marry me when you see my new face, but I will be looking for a rich man then Paul." Estelle laughed and hang up. I was happy for her. Estelle did everything to find Holly. I was surprised when Scott called me.

"Did you tell Holly what I did in Paris, Paul?"

"What is your problem Scott?"

"Holly wants to see me tomorrow in New York."

"Holly paid you to help her Scott. You helped and Holly is free now. You shouldn't be afraid to meet Holly."

"I will be with Gina. Do you want to see Gina, Paul?"

"I missed many days in office Scott. I need to work."

"Did you speak with Morel, Paul?"

"I told you that I am busy. I don't have time to speak with every detective I know."

"Can you ask Holly, why she wants to see me?"

"May be Holly wants to see Gina. I was with her in Puerto Rico."

"You are right Paul. Holly told me to take Gina with me."

"Don't tell Holly that I had something to do with Gina."

"I will tell Holly that you are a good and an honest man, Paul."

"Thanks Scott."

I was thinking about Scott, Cindy and Gina when Judy entered and closed the door and said "Many people in the office say that Roy will fire you."

"I don't care Judy."

"You will miss me, Paul."

"I will open my own company and I will offer you to work for me Judy."

"I will be very happy if you do that. Many people in office hate me, because I am good friends with you. If somebody jokes with you don't care Paul."

"Come close to me Judy." I kissed her on the chick.

"I don't care for anything after I got Holly back. I know that I don't have future in Roy's company, but I have future with Holly."

"Roy changed after you returned with Holly to New York, Paul. Roy spoke with you before, but now he is speaking with his old friends."

"This won't help Roy if I leave the company, Judy. You don't need to have good friends Judy. You need to have people that make money."

"I want to see that when I work in your company Paul."

"Yes, Judy."

"Do you want me to close the door Paul?"

"No, I want everybody see me that I am working Judy." She laughed and left. I know that Judy loves me and she will tell me what Roy's friends say about me. I don't care, because it will be my choice to live Roy's office. I need to keep my clients and when I decide to move to another company, they will follow me. I know that I will not have problem with Nancy Jones. She hates Roy and she will never work with him. Last night I understood that Holly can't be friends with Susan, because she didn't stop Roy when he spoke against her. I understood Susan. She is the wife of Roy, but Roy went too far when he said that Holly was with two men. This is a problem between me and Holly. Roy was stupid when he spoke for Mom, Alan and Henry. Dad thought that Roy is a good friend of his. Holly, Dad and I understood that Roy has two faces and he wants to use people. Roy used me for ten years. I know that Roy will never come and tell in my face "I am firing you Paul." He will use his friends to speak against me, so I will leave. I need to be ready when I decide to leave. I will keep my door open and I will laugh when Roy's friends joke with me. The joke will be when I leave Roy. Now the boss of family Cote is Estelle. If I call and tell Estelle that I don't work in Roy's company, Estelle will tell me that she will want to work with me. Holly prays to God. I need to pray too. If Holly is pregnant, I don't know what I am going to do. Next two or three weeks will be hard for me. For Holly too.

It was 11:45 am. Judy entered in my office and said "The lunch is ready boss. I chose the food for you Paul."

"Why didn't you buy lunch for yourself?"

"I need to lose five pounds Paul. I have a boyfriend and he told me that I am little fat. Do you think that that is polite?"

"If he loves you, he needs to tell you the truth Judy. Some men like a little heavy woman."

"You don't like them, because Holly is very thin."

"She is a model Judy, but I prefer thin women in bed."

"Your girlfriends were thin Paul. You need to eat Paul."

"Don't be afraid that Roy will fire you Judy."

"I don't care Paul. My boyfriend has money. If I don't work, I will go to the gym. I need to lose five pounds anyway. I need to look thin for my boyfriend." Judy was laughing when she left. Holly called me.

"Are you going somewhere for lunch Paul?"

"Judy bought lunch for me Holly and she brought it to the office."

"Judy wants to be with you, Paul."

"Of course Holly. If you go somewhere I need to have a girl next to me. Hey Holly, Judy will lose five pounds. She wants to be the same you."

"It will be good for her."

"What is Dad doing?"

"We finished and he wants to meet you somewhere for lunch. The good news is that doctor told me that I am OK."

"You know that I don't want to ask you, because I am not a doctor."

"Do you feel better now?"

"The doctor told me that I am psychologically and physically well."

"Don't worry Holly."

"O boy, it is easy to say that. I will be worried if my menstrual cycle doesn't start on Saturday or Sunday. Henry wants to know what you want for dinner. We will cook for you."

"Dad knows what kind fish I like."

"I will buy a special white wine for you, Paul." I was ready to leave the office when Mom called me.

"Where is Holly, Paul?"

"You didn't ask me how I am doing Mom."

"I know that you are OK."

"Thanks for saving my life Mom."

"Why did you save Holly's life?"

"Does Alan know that I am not his son?"

"You didn't answer of my question Paul."

"If Holly asks me to marry her, I will marry her Mom. Are you going to be happy if I marry Holly?"

"You know my answer. Now is different Mom. Holly isn't my half-sister."

"Where is she?"

"Holly is with Dad. They have been together for two days."

"Henry is too old for her Paul. Holly will kill Henry."

"You are jealous Mom. Did you try to kill Alan in bed?"

"I am your Mom and Henry is my husband."

"What are you doing with Alan?"

"I love Alan."

"Why don't you divorce Henry and marry Alan?"

"It isn't your business."

"I don't understand Alan, Mom. He is rich and he has money to pay for young girls."

"Alan loves me."

"Alan doesn't want to marry you, because he has a wife."

"Did you see Alan's wife Mom. Is she beautiful?"

"If Lori look like Holly, Alan will not divorce her. It will be good for you if you call Henry and ask him for your future Mom."

"Don't tell me what I need to do Paul."

"I want to help you, Mom. What do I tell Henry, when I see him?"

"That Holly is too young for him."

"Do you think that Holly is good for me?"

"I don't want you to marry Holly. She slept with many men. Holly was raped in France, Paul."

"If Holly is pregnant it will be good for me Mom. I don't need to work hard in bed to have a child."

"I know that you are crazy Paul." Mom hang up. I entered my apartment. Holly and Dad were in the kitchen.

"It smells good Holly."

"Honestly, Henry cooked, I helped him and I chose the wine."

"Did you speak with Mom, Dad?"

"Janet has a good time with Alan. I don't want to hurt Alan."

"Why, Dad?"

"Alan will think that I love Janet and I am jealous that he has a good time with her. I don't love Janet and I am not jealous. I am happy that Alan and Janet are together."

I looked at Holly. "I don't care for them too Paul. I am with Henry and you. You are my family. I want to see my mom, Paul. We need to go to California to meet her."

"I have a problem in the office Holly. We will need to go on the weekend."

"I will buy tickets for us for Friday after 7:00pm We will return on Sunday."

"This will for me Holly."

I didn't tell Dad that I spoke with Mom. I love Mom and I want to help her. Tonight I understood that Mom doesn't have a chance to live with Dad. Henry closed the door for her. I know that Alan will never marry her.

"What are you thinking about Paul?"

"For Mom and Alan, Dad."

"You need to think for Holly, Paul."

"Holly is here Dad."

"You are too. Don't think for Janet and Alan. Janet hasn't been thinking for you for thirty-three years. She lied to Alan that you are his son."

"Alan tried to have sex with Holly. I don't think that Alan loves Holly. Alan is a sick man Dad. I think that Alan will be different after he knows that you are my father."

"Why do you want to see your Mom, Holly?"

"I want to understand why she supported Alan and if she knows that Alan and Janet have a sexual relationship. I haven't seen Lori in ten years. Maybe she has changed, Paul." I and Holly were in bed.

"Do you want me to make you happy boy?"

"You told me that you aren't ready."

"I know what I need to do to make you happy Paul. Your body missed me for many days." Holly made me happy. When I woke up Holly was next to me. She was sleeping. Dad was in the living room.

"Do you want a cup of coffee Paul?"

"I will get some Dad." I took the coffee and sat next to Dad.

"What are you going to do if Holly is pregnant Paul?"

"I don't know Dad."

"Holly told me that she will commit suicide Paul. You need to speak with her."

"What do I need to tell Holly, Dad?"

"That you will accept the child Paul. You will have another child Paul."

"I am sorry Dad, but I am not ready to tell her that."

"Why?"

"I don't want people to think that I am marrying Holly, because she is from a rich family."

"Holly loves you and she is rich Paul."

"This is good for her. Many men will marry Holly and accept the child."

"You are hurting me Paul."

"It is my life Dad. I don't want to marry Holly if she is pregnant. You live with Mom for thirty-four years. Mom thought that I am the son of Alan. Why didn't you divorce Mom, Dad? Don't tell me again that you want to save my life. For ten years I haven't lived with you and Mom. You don't care what Mom did. I will care what my wife does Dad."

Henry was crying when Holly entered.

"Why are you crying Henry?"

"I told Henry that I will not marry you if you are pregnant Holly. Henry and Janet have been living together for thirty-four years like a cat and a mouse. I don't want to live with you like them."

"Don't cry Henry. I am sure that everything will be OK. Paul is right Henry. He loves me, but he doesn't want to lie to me. Are you coming to California with me Paul?"

"I promised you, Holly."

"You need to go to the office Paul. You will feel better there."

"If Roy doesn't fire me Holly."

"Roy is afraid Paul. Roy knows that you will get his business with family Cote. I know that Alan will want to work with you, doesn't matter if you marry me or not. You aren't wrong the man Paul. I am the wrong woman. Go to work boy."

Henry looked at Holly. "I can't believe, what I heard from you Holly."

"I told the truth Henry. I never lied to Paul and he never lied to me too." I left the apartment. I went to work. Judy bought lunch for me again. She said "I bought fruit salad for me Paul."

"You need to speak with Holly. She will tell what you need to eat to lose five pounds."

"Why didn't you close the door Judy?"

"I want Roy's people to see that I am your friend." Estelle called me in the afternoon.

"I spoke with Holly, Paul. I told her that I will be ready with the new contract and will come to New York. You need to support her, Paul."

"Frankly, I don't know what need to think and do if Holly is pregnant Estelle. Last night I told her that I won't accept the child, Holly needs to think Estelle."

"I understand Paul. If I am pregnant, I will never chase you. I will be happy if I have a boy, but I will never tell anybody that you are the father of the child. I will find a father who will love me and my children. I have a feeling that everything will be OK with Holly."

"Thanks Estelle."

"Do you have a problem with Roy?"

"I don't Estelle."

"If you do, call me."

"I will boss."

"You need to kiss my hand when you see me Paul."

"I will kiss your new face too Estelle."

"I will call you some time Paul. Don't think that I want something. I feel relaxed when I speak with you. I get more energy and I am feeling better. I know that my life with you will be very good, but I want you to marry Holly. Maybe Holly and I will deliver children at the same time. They will be our children Paul. I am kissing you Paul." After Estelle hang up, I started to think what she wanted to tell me. Nobody will know that I am the father of Estelle's child. If Holly has a child, everybody will think that I am the father. Three people will know that I am not. Holly, Henry and me. Maybe Mom will tell everyone that I am not the father, but who cares. Everybody knows that Mom hates Holly. I returned home. Holly was alone.

"Where is Dad?"

"He went to his apartment."

"If you have baby, I will be the father of the child."

"Did you speak with Estelle?"

"Yes I did."

"Are you sure that you will be the father?"

"Dad was right. We will have another child. Nobody knows if you are pregnant Holly."

"I am not Paul. I told you. I will know on Saturday or Sunday."

"Did you tell Estelle what you are going to do if you are pregnant?"

"I told her Paul. I don't want you to share your problems with other people Holly."

"We need to wait for three or four days Paul. I am feeling a little better now. I want to spend my whole life with you. I will never meet another man like you. I will call Henry to come back here."

"Don't call him Holly. The people who live around us must know that it is our life."

"Henry loves you so much Paul."

"I love him too, but I don't need him tell me what I need to do with my life. Henry knew that Mom hates you, but he didn't tell me. If I knew, I would have spoken with Mom."

"Janet doesn't love you, Paul."

"Janet saved my life in Paris, Holly. Janet loves me, but she loves Alan too. Janet wants to be good with me and Alan, but she doesn't understand that I am her son, Alan is her lover."

"Why does she live with Henry, when she loves Alan?"

"You need to ask Henry, why he lives with Janet for thirty-four years. You told me that Alan is sick. Why does Janet love Alan?"

"When you see your Mom, you need to ask her, why she lives with Alan."

"Maybe Mom doesn't know that Alan and Janet are together."

"This is your problem Holly. You believe what people tell you. Do you believe Susan?"

"After last night I don't. She let Roy speak what he wanted. Susan should have stopped him. Do you think that I am right?"

"No, Holly. Susan is wife of Roy and she supports him. Roy is afraid that Estelle will like to work with me. Roy and Susan will lose money. The goal of Roy was to understand If I love Estelle and I want to marry her. Roy knows that you and Alan don't have a good relationship as a father and daughter, but Viler Cote told Roy that Alan loves me and I think that now Alan wants me to marry you. If I marry you I will work with the Golgbear family. Estelle no longer will work with Roy Bell. Now the best client for Roy is Nancy Jones. If I get Goldbear and Cote families, I will have billions or trillions of dollars behind me. I will have big power. Roy Bell will be nothing for me. Susan doesn't want that and she supports Roy."

"I will support you too Paul. After I talk to Mom, I will try to meet Alan. I need to speak with him. I will ask him for fifty million dollars. I will tell Alan what kind of man you are Paul."

"Don't do that Holly. Alan knows well who I am."

"I will be happy if you speak with Alan."

"Janet will not be happy."

"Don't worry about Janet. You need to think for your Mom. You didn't see or speak with Lori for ten years. You don't know what has happened between Alan and Lori."

"I will know tomorrow Paul."

"Finally, Scott Hunter will do something for you. He got a lot of money from you, Holly."

"Come to see Gina, Paul."

"If Gina want to have sex what should I do Holly?"

"I will tell you after I see Gina, but you are right. You don't need to see Gina, Paul. I know that you didn't have sex in a long time."

"I had last night and I was happy Holly. You will be happy to-night too boy. Come to bed."

In the morning I saw Holly in the kitchen. She said "I prepared breakfast for you."

"You will be a good wife."

"I will try Paul. I am feeling better, because I stopped to think what will happen between you and me if I am pregnant. I will call Henry and take him with me Paul. I am happy when I am with Henry."

"You need to be careful with Mom, Holly."

"Why?"

"Call and speak with Mom." I laughed when I exited the apart-ment.

I got to my office by 8:20 am. "Good morning Judy."

"You are happy today Paul."

"I am happy every day Judy."

"This will be your lunch Paul."

"Good choice Judy."

"I will bring the lunch in your office at 12:00 o'clock."

"I will be ready Judy." I called an ordered a bunch of flowers. Judy entered my office at 12:00 O'clock.

"Thanks for the flowers, Paul."

"How did you know that I sent the flowers Judy?"

"You are the man that loves me Paul."

"You have a boyfriend Judy."

"He is a different man. He asked my who bought me the ring. I told him that my ex-boyfriend bought it, but he met a beautiful woman and he left me. My boyfriend didn't believe me."

"Hey Judy, you need to meet Holly with your boyfriend. Holly knows what to tell him."

"This is a good idea Paul."

I saw that Roy was on the door. "You love Paul too, Judy?"

"I love him, but Holly will marry Paul."

"Maybe!", Judy and Roy left.

"I heard what Roy told his friends Paul. He said that Holly will not marry you, because you had an affair with a rich woman in Par-is. You were in Paris to get Holly. I know that Holly will never leave you. Why did Roy lie Paul?"

"It is Roy's problem, Judy. I am not afraid that Roy will fire me."

My phone was ringing. "This is Paul."

"What are you doing?"

"I am OK Nancy. I have lunch with Judy in my office."

"Did you leave Holly?"

"Holly will stay forever in my heart Nancy. Roy called me and he wanted to speak with me."

"This is business between Roy and you, Nancy."

"You know that I don't love Roy. I will come to the office, but I want to meet with you."

"What time?"

"Three o'clock."

"It is so hot outside Nancy. I think that tomorrow morning will be better."

"I agree with you Paul. I love you and believe you, because you think for everything. I want to come today, because I want to show Roy, that I am behind you and I will follow you if you leave Roy's company. How was your trip to Paris?"

"I was in Paris to return Holly to New York. I had a little problem there, but now everything is OK. We will speak when you come to the office Nancy."

"Wait for me Paul and Nancy hung up."

"Roy spoke with your clients Paul when you were in Paris."

"I know that Judy. He will try to get my clients before I leave the office."

"Nancy will never leave you, Paul. When you were in Paris, she called the office. She spoke with Roy. I don't know what Roy told her, but Nancy called again and asked me, what you are doing in Paris. I told her that you had a problem with Holly in Paris. She called on Monday and asked for you. I told her that you haven't returned from Paris. I asked her if she wants to speak with Roy Nancy didn't want to speak with him. She called on Tuesday morning. I told her that you are in the office. I wanted Nancy to speak with you, but she told me that she is happy and she hung up. I didn't tell you, because I thought that you have spoken with her by now. What do I need to prepare for Nancy when she come to your office?"

"Nancy loves to drink green tea with honey and lemon."

"It is hot Paul."

"Doesn't matter for her. Nancy will come at 3:00 o'clock."

"I will be ready with the tea Paul." Roy entered my office at 2:00pm.

"Did you speak with Nancy Jones?"

"She will come at 3:00 to the office Roy. Come in my office when Nancy comes Paul."

"You need to tell Judy what she needs to tell Nancy, Roy. Nancy Jones is my client, but you are my boss. Nancy entered my office at 3:00 o'clock. Nice to see you my love and I kissed her. Judy entered with two cups.

"For you Ms. Jones."

"Thanks darling. I like to meet Paul any time, because I know that he will surprise me. It is hot, but I love to drink hot tea Judy."

"Paul told me what you like Ms. Jones."

"I think that Paul will take you to work for him, after he leaves his stupid boss Roy."

Nancy and Judy laughed when Roy came to the door. "I think that Paul needs to work, he doesn't need to joke."

"Of course Roy. Paul works and jokes, you count how much money Paul is making for you Roy."

"I am the owner of the company Nancy."

"Call me Ms. Jones, Roy."

"Why does Paul tell you Nancy, Ms. Jones?"

"Paul is my lover. I was jealous that he was in Paris. Do you know that there are many beautiful girls in Paris, Roy?"

"You are right to be jealous Ms. Jones. Paul had an affair in Paris. Holly will not marry Paul because of that."

"Paul doesn't have a problem Roy. Estelle is from a rich family but she has a husband and two children. Holly is from a rich family, but her father Alan Goldbear keeps the money of the family. I am rich and alone. I will marry Paul. Paul will be the richest man. You must be careful with Paul, because he will be my husband Roy."

"Do you want to come to my office Ms. Jones? The office of Paul isn't big enough."

"I feel good here, because Paul is here. Come to kiss you my love." Nancy kissed me.

"Go to work Roy, because I will take Paull with me, if you don't leave." Roy left.

"Do you think that I was honest Judy?"

"Paull will marry Holly, Ms. Jones, but I am happy that you

scared Roy."

"You are a good girl Judy. I will go to work, because Roy will fire me Ms. Jones" and Judy left. "You know that Alan is Holly's father."

"How long do you know Alan?"

"The Goldbear family is rich. I am rich too Paul."

"Do you know Viler Cote?"

"Viler called me and he asked for you, but he didn't tell me what happened in Estelle's house. I laughed a lot when Estelle told me. I am a woman and I am happy that Estelle is the boss of her family. Estelle told me that she loves you, but you need to marry Holly. Alan is crazy, but he makes money for his family. I asked Alan for you Paul. He told me that you are smart and I will never lose money."

"You chose me, because Alan told you?"

"Alan loves you Paul, but it is hard to understand a sick man. I don't know why your Mom stayed with Alan."

"I don't know too Nancy. I asked her."

"Do you support her?"

"This is a business between Mom and Dad Nancy. I love Dad so much. He is the best father, but Mom told me that she loves Alan."

"You are right Paul. Janet and Henry need to decide for their future. I came today to give you, my support Paul. Roy wanted me leave you, but he didn't tell me why. I think that Roy is afraid about his future if you leave the company."

"Why, Nancy?"

"If Alan and Estelle start to work with you, you will have two very rich families behind you. You will work with billions or trillions of dollars Paul." Judy came and asked Nancy if she wanted something.

"I need to leave Judy. Thanks for tea. I will make tea for you in Paul's new office, Ms. Jones." "You will Judy."

At 4:30 Roy called me. "Come to my office. What did Nancy decide Paul?"

"We spoke for Holly, Alan, Viler and Etsell. We didn't speak for business."

"Will Nancy continue to work with you?"

"Of course Roy."

"Can you tell Judy, that tomorrow you and I will have lunch together?"

"I want you to meet my friends." I told Judy that I will have lunch with Roy tomorrow when O was leaving the office, so she doesn't have to bring lunch for me. I was in my apartment at 8:00pm. Dad was with Holly.

"I bought the tickets for Los Angeles. We will fly at 8:30pm. Is it OK?"

"I didn't answer. Nancy was in my office Holly. She knows well Alan, Estelle, Viler, Mom, Dad and you Holly. Because you didn't tell me for your family, I looked stupid in her eyes."

"Did Nancy tell you that they love you, Paul?"

"You don't love me Holly." I laughed.

"I think that I will never meet or speak with them Paul. Now I will meet you with my mom. I am little disappointed with me, but I need to do that for mine and your future Paul. I want Alan to work with you."

"Alan loves me Holly."

"Everybody loves you. You are my hero Paul. Come to me. I want to kiss you." Holly kissed me. Holly told me that I need to tell something to Henry.

"I am sorry that I hurt you last night Dad."

"Paul was right Holly. I need to apologize to Paul, for what me and Janet have been doing. I needed to divorce her many years ago. It looks so stupid that your father is with my wife for many years."

"You did that to be with Paul, Henry. I needed to divorce her when Paul finished high school. At that time, I was fifty-five. I didn't have problem to marry somebody else. Now is too late. I am seventy Holly."

"You look very good Henry."

"I look very stupid Holly." Holly, Henry and I laughed. I woke up at 6:30am. It was Friday. I was in the office at 8:40am. Roy called me at 11:30. My friends are busy and they want to meet us on Saturday. I am busy with Holly on Saturday.

"Can you tell them to meet next week?"

"Where are you going with Holly?"

"I don't know. You need to ask Holly."

"Susan spoke with Holly and they will have lunch together. Henry will be there too. Do you want to go with me there?"

"I prefer to stay in the office Roy."

"Are you spying on Roy, Judy?"

"No. Susan called, but Roy was busy. She asked me for you. I told her that you and Roy will have lunch together. Susan told me that she has lunch with Henry and Holly. She asked me to tell Roy where he needs to come for lunch and she said that you are going there too. I know that you will not go and I ordered lunch for you, Paul. Roy and Susan are stupid Paul. Roy invited you yesterday. He was with Susan last night. Susan must have known that Roy and you have lunch together. I don't understand why did Susan call and tell me where Roy needed to go for lunch?"

"You will be very good secretary for me when I open my office Judy. You think and I like that."

"I will be happy to work in your company Paul. I know that I will get good money. I will do everything you need Paul."

"Holly will be jealous Judy. I am not talking about sex Paul." We were laughing when Roy's friends were staring at me and Judy.

"What do you want men, Judy asked?"

"Why are you laughing Judy?"

"I told Paul that I am not afraid that Roy will fire me, because Paul will take me to live with him and I will do everything what Paul wants. Is your wife good in bed John?"

"I will tell Roy, what you said Judy."

"What are you going to say to Roy if he asks you about your wife John?"

John left. His friends laughed.

"Are you leaving the company?"

"I don't have a plan now, but if Roy fires me I will open my own business Mark."

"Many people in the office will want to come to work in your company Paul. I am a good friend of Roy and I told him that he will be stupid if he fires you. Roy wasn't happy, because he wanted to hear nice words for him. Paul, I didn't believe what Roy told me. "Nobody will take Paul to work, if he leaves my company Mark.""

"He is wrong, everybody will take you Paul. You have good clients and you make a lot of money for Roy. Every owner of a company wants to have people like you that make good money for him and the company. I think that Roy is old for this business Paul. We live in twenty first century."

"Roy is here Mark," Dan told him. They left. Judy left too. I looked at my watch. It was 1:35pm. Roy didn't come to my office. He didn't call me to speak with me in the afternoon. I left the office at 5:30pm. I was at home. Holly and Dad were waiting for me. I changed my clothes fast. Holly and I were at airport at 7:20pm. We entered our gate. My cell phone rang.

"Don't answer Paul."

"It is Roy, Holly."

"If Roy fires you, I will take you to work for me."

"To be a model?"

"To be busy in bed with me, boy." Holly laughed.

"Yes, Roy."

"I want to speak with you."

"What about Roy?"

John told me what Judy told him. John left, but Mark and Dan staid in your office. I want to know what you, Judy, Mark and Dan spoke about."

"If you fire me I will open my own business Roy. I want to speak for your business Paul."

"I am at the airport Roy."

" Where are you going?"

"I don't know Roy."

"Are you kidding me, Paul?"

Holly took the phone.

"Hey Roy, this is Holly. We will go to see my relatives. I want to show Paul to them and tell them that I will marry him. If you fire Paul, I will be happy, because Paul will spend more time with me. Why don't you fire Paul? Paul will be in the office Monday, Roy. Do you want to speak with Paul?" Holly hang up.

"I think that Roy and Susan are afraid that you will leave the office. I, Henry, Susan and Roy had lunch. Roy told me that you didn't want to come to the restaurant, because you were having lunch with Judy. Roy wasn't in the office when Judy brought me the lunch in my office. Somebody called and told Roy, what you did in the office. Roy and Susan wanted to know if I will marry you and what I will do in future. I didn't tell them that I will marry you and my future is to be a model."

We entered the airplane. We continued to speak.

"You need to open your own business Paul."

"It is easy to say that Holly. I need a lot of money to open my own business."

"We will think for that after we meet with my mom. I decided to ask my mom to come with me."

"If she wants Holly."

"I know that Mom will come with me to New York."

"Where is she now?"

"In a hospital. Something happened with her. Alan put Mom in a hospital. I never heard that Mom has a mental problem."

"May be Alan put her there to be with Janet."

"Maybe you are right Paul, because Mom has been in the hospital for more than eight months. Nobody tried to help her. The Goldber family doesn't love Mom. When Lori married Alan, she didn't tell him, that she was married and she had a son. Lori told Alan after I was born. My half-brother is five years older than me. His name is Larry. I saw him when I was three or four years old. When Mom divorced her ex-husband he took Larry with him."

"Why didn't Lori take Larry with her. She is the Mom?"

"I don't know Paul. I never asked Mom. May be Mom wanted to marry a rich man."

"She did Holly."

"Your Mom didn't Paul." I and Holly laughed.

"Our families are so funny boy." I looked at Holly's face. I am not feeling good Paul. I am feeling pain in my stomach.

"What did you eat today?"

"I will go to the restroom." Holly returned. She smiled.

"It is coming Paul."

"I don't understand Holly. I will explain to you. You are angry when a lifeguard puts a red flag on the beach and you can't go to swim. You swim well and you aren't afraid of the big waves. You don't touch my body, when I raise the red flag Paul."

"You raised the red flag, because your menstrual cycle started Holly?"

"Yes, boy. Now everything is OK Paul. Are you going to marry me?"

"Of course Holly."

"Hey boy, you need to answer me."

"Yes, yes Holly." I kissed her.

"How do you feel now?"

"I am feeling like I was born again Paul. My life is changing. I promise you that I will tell you everything before I do something. It would have been disaster if I was pregnant."

"I promised you Holly."

"I know that you will care for the child, but I will feel that I am a devil Paul. You did everything for me, but I went to Paris. Let's get married for the New Year, Paul."

"Why for New Year?"

"Because people say that they start a new life on New Year. I and you will marry and we will start a new life in the New Year."

"What do you think for a baby Holly?"

"We will not wait Paul. After my menstrual cycle finishes, we will start to work on a baby. You need to be a macho man in bed Paul."

"I will try my best Holly, but if I am not, you need to look for another macho man."

"Shut up Paul. Zip your dirty mouth. Frankly, I was, but they didn't do a good job Paul. How do you feel Paul?"

"It wasn't good for me that they didn't finish a good job, because now I need to work hard Holly."

"Boy, don't joke with me. I thought to kill myself. Henry and Estelle gave me the courage, that everything will be OK."

"I will call Henry, Paul. You need to stop telling everything to Dad."

"He is alone Paul."

"Henry needs to decide when he needs to help us Holly. I know that Henry will help you a lot when we have a baby. I grew up with Henry. If Henry asks you, you tell him that everything is OK."

"I want to tell you that last week I didn't think for me Paul. I thought for you and how would you feel if I was pregnant. I didn't want to lose you and the baby."

"Hey Holly, in the future you will not have to worry about losing a baby and me."

"I know that Paul, because you will be the father of our baby. Henry told me what happened when you were six years old. I don't want you check the DNA of our baby."

"You don't want me to be like Henry?"

"We need to stop to talking about what happened in France, Paul. We need to think and speak for our future. Tomorrow, I will meet my mom after ten years. I must think what I need to tell her. I was a young girl when I left Mom. Now I am a grown woman."

"Tomorrow will be a big day for you Holly. I will be next to you and I will support you."

"Thanks Paul" and Holly kissed me.

CHAPTER 10

Holly and I were in the hospital. We walked to the patient information desk.

"My name is Hana Goldbear. I want to see my mom, Lori Goldbear."

The lady checked some file and said "I don't have information that Lori Goldbear has a daughter. Lori has a son, Larry and husband Alan." Holly gave her birth certificate to the lady.

"You need to speak with Dr. Brown." The lady called.

"The daughter of Ms. Goldbear wants to see her, Dr. Brown."

"He will come to you Hana."

"I think that I know you. Are you Holly Gold?"

"I am lady, but now I am Hana Goldbear." They laughed.

Dr. Brown came to meet Holly and me. Holly gave him the paper.

"I need to call and speak with Alan Goldbear. I don't have information that he and Lori have a daughter."

"My detective is investigating your hospital Dr. Brown. I will call him."

"Can you come to my office Hana."

"This is my fiancée. He will come with us." We entered the office of Dr. Brown.

"I don't want to create a problem for your hospital, but If I don't get Mom with me, many journalists will come here to ask questions. You will need to answer them. Me detective will speak with them before they come here."

"I will call and ask Peter, what I need to do Hana."

"Call him Dr. Brown."

"Peter, Hana Goldbear is in the hospital. She wants to take her Mom. What do I need to do?"

"Peter wants to speak with you Hana. Hi Uncle Peter. I am OK. Hey I will marry for New Year and I want my mom to meet my fiancée and take her with me. Mom will stay in New York. I don't have time now, but I want to see you in New York. His name is Paul Morgan. Uncle Peter wants to speak with you Dr. Brown." Holly, Lori and I left the hospital one hour later.

"I am happy that you came to get me Hana. I thought that I would never see you after you left the house. Did you speak with your father?"

"I didn't Mom, but I will meet and speak with him in the next two weeks."

"Do you know where Alan is, Mom?"

"I don't Hana."

"Why did Alan put you in the hospital?"

"I don't have any idea Hana, but you know your father. He does what he wants with me. Alan is my husband and I need to listen to him. It is not good for Alan and you, that you were in a hospital."

"Sometimes your father stays in the hospital too Hana. You want to see how Alan was feeling in the hospital Mom. Alan was sick when he was in the hospital. I wasn't sick when I entered the hospital. There are a lot of crazy people Hana. I am a normal person."

"Are you going to marry Paul? Is Paul rich?"

"I love Paul Mom. Doesn't matter for me if Paul is rich or not."

"You are from a rich family Hana. You must marry a rich man."

"Did you marry Alan, because he is rich Mom?"

"Of course Hana".

"Did you love Alan where you married him?"

"For me, it was more important that your father was rich."

"Why didn't you tell Alan that you have son?"

"Alan would not have married me Hana. My goal was to marry a rich man. I had a husband who didn't have money. He didn't have money, but his son grew with him. I helped him with money."

"Did Alan know that?"

"I never told him. You lied to Alan, Mom."

"Everybody lies Hana."

"Paul and I don't lie Mom."

"I don't believe that Paul doesn't lie to you."

"Because you don't believe Alan, I don't need to believe Paul."

"You didn't answer my question if Paul is rich."

"If you continue speak against Paul, I will return you to the hospital Lori."

"Do you want to go back there?"

"I want to go at to my house Hana."

"If you stay there, Alan will return you to the hospital."

"Where are we going?"

"To New York. You will live in my apartment."

"Who bought the apartment Hana?"

"Paul bought it for me Mom."

"Paul is rich and a good man, Hana."

"He is Mom." I laughed.

"Why did Paul laugh Hana?"

"Because I scared you with Alan."

"Do you know Alan, Paul?"

"My friends told me that Alan is a smart man."

"I married Alan, because he is smart Paul."

"You told me that you married for money Mom."

"I forgot what I said that Hana."

We arrived in New York at 9:30. We were in Holly's apartment.

"Tomorrow is Sunday Mom. Do you want to go somewhere?"

"I want to meet Paul's parents Hana."

"Everybody in New York knows me Holly Gold, Mom. I want you to call me Holly."

"Why did you change your name Hana?"

"I didn't want Alan to find me. I knew that you don't read books and newspapers Mom."

"Did you change your life Mom?"

"No Hana."

"I told you to call me Holly, Lori. I knew that Alan thought that you are stupid, but I don't want my friends know that Lori. You need to zip you mouth and listen to me, Lori."

"You are hurting me Hana."

"I told you the truth Lori."

"Does Paul listens to you?"

"Of course Lori. If Paul doesn't listen, he needs to leave the apartment."

"Why do you want to marry Paul?"

"Paul listens and does what I tell him Lori. Do you want something to eat or drink?"

"We had dinner in the airplane Holly. I want to sleep. I will show you the guest bedroom Mom. Tomorrow you will meet Paul's father."

I and Holly were in bed. "You are not taking a side Paul. I know what I am doing. My goal is to meet Alan. Scott must find where are Alan and Janet are."

"They are in Florida, Holly."

"They left the hotel in Florida and nobody knows where they are."

"You want to get fifty million from Alan?"

"I have information that Alan, Janet and Viler are behind my kidnapping. One of them paid Giles, Marcel and Luca. You were ready to pay thirty million dollars Paul."

"Why doesn't Alan pay me fifty million? Alan has money and he hurt me two times. First he wanted sex with me. Second he doesn't want me marry you. Maybe Alan will be happy, when he knows that Henry is my father. I don't care who is your father Paul. I want fifty million and Alan must pay. Don't think that I am greedy. This money belongs to you, because you risked your life to save my life Paul. You will be richer when I give you fifty million. Are you happy Paul?"

"Sounds good Holly. When I get fifty million, I will make more money for us."

"I am happy that you are in favor of my plan Paul."

"I will always support you when you bring money home Holly. I know what to do with the money."

"I will start to look for an office Paul. I will call you when I find a building that I like, but you have more experience and you will tell me if the building is good to open my business there."

"What do you think of Lori?"

"I think that Henry will be happy to be with Lori, Paul."

"Of course, his wife is with Alan, Holly."

"Why doesn't Henry have good time with Lori?"

"Henry told me that Janet didn't want sex with him."

"Dad is crazy telling you that Holly."

"Why, Paul?"

"Henry didn't need to tell you what he did with Mom."

"When I asked Mom, if Alan is better in bed, she told me that I am crazy and she hang up. Mom didn't want to tell me about her private life. I will never tell my friends that I am feeling good when I have sex with you, Holly."

"Are you jealous that they may want me in bed Paul?"

"It is your business if you want somebody Holly, but I don't want to speak for my private life. Do you know how many men want you in bed when they look at your all most naked body on the show?"

"I never thought for that Paul. I chose the man when I wanted sex. I made good a choice when I got you in bed. After I chose you I never looked to get another man in bed."

"I am like you Holly."

"I don't believe you, but I accepted your words Paul." Holly laughed.

"We need to sleep boy." I closed my eyes, but I thought what Holly told me. Maybe Henry told Holly that I asked him when I was in Paris, what I needed to do with a woman who didn't look good. It will be stupid if I ask Dad. When I woke up in the morning, Holly and Lori were together. They were drinking coffee.

"Good morning ladies and I kissed Holly."

"Why didn't you kiss Mom. She will be your Mom in law Paul?"

"I kissed Lori."

"What is your business Paul, Lori asked me?"

"The same as Alan's, Lori."

"Alan is a smart and makes a lot of money for the Goldbear family, Holly. Are you going to make a lot of money for Holly, Paul?"

"I think that Holly needs to work and make money for her, Lori."

"Do you know that Holly is a model?"

"I heard that now. I put a lot of money in a bank when Hana was a little girl. I thought that Hana will live with this money."

"I told you that you need to call me Holly."

"Did you give the money to Paul, Holly?"

"Paul never asked me for my money Mom. We live together, but I keep my money and Paul keep his money."

"You know that I didn't work. Alan told me that I needed to stay at home, because I needed to care for you."

"I don't remember that you did something for me Lori. I remember that people who worked in Alan's house, cared for me and I grew up with them. I remember that Uncle Peter wanted to be with me. He loved me. I don't remember that you and Alan loved me Lori." The bell was ringing.

"I will get the door Paul." I saw that Dad and Holly entered the living room. Holly introduced Henry to Lori. Dad kissed Lori's hand.

"It has been a long time since any nobody kissed my hand Holly. Henry is a gentleman. Does Paul kiss your hand too Holly?"

"Paul want to kissed my whole body Lori."

"Do you have sex with Paul, Holly?"

"Why did you ask me that Lori?"

"Because you and Paul aren't married."

"I am a virgin Mom. I will have sex when I marry Paul."

"You are thirty years old Holly. Why didn't you have sex?"

"Because I love Paul."

"How long do you know Paul?"

"One year and eight months, but I didn't have a man before I met Paul."

"I don't believe you Holly. Paul told me that you are a model. Many men are looking at your body Holly."

"They are joking Lori?"

"How did you know that Henry, I asked?"

"I and Holly spoke a lot for our past Paul."

"You said a lot for my private life Dad. I don't want you to speak for me. If Holly wants to know something, I will tell her."

"Henry is your father Paul. He needs to know everything for you."

"Do you know everything for Holly, Lori. You are her Mom?"

"Holly left me. I don't want you speak for my past Lori. It was many years ago."

"Where is your wife Henry?"

"This is good question Lori."

"She is in Florida."

"I came to New York to see you Lori. I am happy that you came to see me Henry. I am alone, because my husband is busy with his business. Holly wanted to see me and she came to get me from my home. I wanted to see Paul, Henry." Holly didn't say that Lori lied. I didn't say that Dad lied too. It was 11:30am. Lori wanted to drink wine. It is early for wine Mom.

"I don't remember seeing you drinking when I lived with you."

"I started after you left Holly. I was alone in the house." Holly said that she will order lunch and she asked what we want. We sat to eat. Holly opened a second bottle of wine. Lori, Dad and I drank, but Dad and I had only one glass. I saw that Lori was a little drunk. After lunch Lori wanted to go to her bedroom. You need to help me Henry. They entered the bed room. They will have sex Paul.

"What did you say?"

"Nothing boy. I want to relax, because I am not ready to have sex." We were in bed.

"Why didn't you tell Henry that Lori lied?"

"What is your goal Holly?"

"I want Lori to have sex with Henry. I want to hurt Janet. You aren't happy Paul."

"Janet is my mom, Holly."

"Alan is my father Paul."

"It isn't good that Mom is with Alan. Lori with Henry."

"This was my goal Paul. Henry didn't have sex in a long time, because Janet didn't want him in bed. I think that Lori too. Now Lori and Henry will be happy in bed. I am sorry that you need to wait for one week Paul." Holly laughed.

"I am happy that after one week I will have a normal life. You relax Holly. I will go to the living room and watch TV." I sat and watched TV. Dad came and sat next to me.

"I had sex Paul. I don't remember for how long I didn't have sex."

"Why didn't Mom want sex?"

"She told me that I am old and she was afraid for my health."

"Did you tell Lori that Alan and Mom are together?"

"Don't think that Lori is stupid Paul."

"Do you want to live with Lori?"

"Why not. Janet loves Alan. I will be happy with Lori." Holly came and sat next to Henry. You are a man Henry.

"I am alive Holly." Holly and Dad laughed.

"It isn't funny Holly."

"What is your problem Paul?"

"I don't approve of this relationship between Lori and Henry."

"Who are you Paul?"

"You need to think for me and you. Lori and Henry are adults.

They need to decide for their life."

"I will not take side anymore Holly. The future will tell who was right." Lori came and I stopped talking.

"Henry is a man Holly. I was happy with him. Tonight you will be in bed with me too Henry." I laughed.

"Why are you laughing Paul?"

"I hope that Dad will be alive tomorrow morning Lori."

"You need to worry about your life, not mine Paul."

"I never saw your life insurance Dad. Mom will be happy, because she will be a widow with money."

"Janet wants to get the money of Alan, Paul. You want to get the money that belongs to Holly. Henry didn't want my money. He wants to be happy with me."

"You are right Lori. It is good for me if I leave Holly."

"Do you want that Lori?"

"I will be happy, Holly too Paul."

"Shut up Lori. Paul never asked me for my money. Paul didn't know that I am daughter of Alan Goldbear."

"Why does Paul live with you Holly?"

"Paul loves me Lori."

"I think that Paul loves your money Holly. I live with Alan, because I want to get the money that belongs to him and the Goldbear family. Janet lives with Alan for that too. You don't think that Paul is different Holly."

"You are wrong Lori. Paul will never get money that belongs to Holly."

"Shut up Henry, Holly told Dad. You are right Mom, but I will marry Paul for New Year. I have time to decide if I marry Paul or not. You need to enjoy life with Henry. He is a good man and I want you to be with him. Paul too Mom." Holly looked at me. I laughed.

"Why are you laughing stupid man?"

"If I was smart I will tell that you are a good choice for Dad, Lori. You look like Mom. I understand that Dad likes women like you and Mom, but Mom is with your husband Alan. I don't approve of this sexual relationship and I will not approve your sexual relationship with Dad. It is funny Lori, so I laughed. I will go to the bedroom Holly." In the morning I saw that Dad and Lori were ready to leave.

"Have a good time Dad" and I returned to the bedroom. Holly

came in the bedroom after ten minutes.

"They left Paul. I will start to look for my office today. I will look to find office for you too."

"I have office Holly. I work for Roy Bell. When I meet and speak with Alan, I will tell him that you need to work with him. I want you to work for the Goldbear family. Estelle told me that she prefers to work with you. If you have problem with Roy, you need to leave him."

"Why are you deciding for me Holly?"

"You will be my husband. You must work for me. You don't need to work for somebody else."

"I want to open my company, but I need to have a lot of money. I will have the money. I spoke with Nancy Jones. She will follow me if I leave Roy. If I work with Alan and Estelle, I will have enough money."

"Where are Henry and Lori going Holly?"

"To Florida. I told Henry that he needs to take and keep Lori in Florida. Henry saw that Lori wanted to hurt you list night. It was good that you went to the bedroom. When I was alone with Henry, I told him what he needs to do that. Henry loves me and you, Paul. He will do everything so I marry you. Lori doesn't like that. Don't be afraid. I think for you and me Paul. I made many mistake in my past, but now I am different, because you are with me."

I left for the office. When I entered I saw Judy "Good morning Judy."

Judy said "Hi" but she didn't ask me what I wanted for lunch.

"You aren't happy this morning Judy."

"Roy told me that he will fire me."

"Is it because you bought lunch for me?"

"John told Roy something and Roy told me that I need to zip my mouth if I want to work in this office."

"Did you speak with Mark and Dan, Paul?"

"I didn't. They have a problem with Roy too."

I saw Mark and Dan. Dan said "I want to speak with you, Paul."

'Come to my office, I told them." We entered and Dan closed the door.

"Did you speak with Roy, Paul?"

"He called me on Friday after 7:00pm. He wanted to see me, but I was at the airport.

"Roy wanted to know what we spoke about."

"Yes, Mark."

"What did you tell him?"

"Holly took the phone. She told Roy, that we are going to see Holly's relatives. Holly asked Roy if he wants to speak with me, but Roy didn't want to. That is, it Mark."

"Roy lied to me and Dan, Paul. We met Roy on Saturday. He told me and Dan, that you told him everything what we spoke on Friday. To be sure that you didn't lie to him, Roy wanted me and Dan to tell him too." Mark and Dan left my office.

I closed the door and I called Morel. "Hi Morel. Hey, I heard good news for you. Holly will marry you. I don't have time to speak Morel. I have problem in my office. Holly wants to meet Alan, but he left Florida with Mom and nobody know where they went. Can you find where Alan and Mom are?"

"Is Scott investigating where they are?"

"Holly spoke with Scott. I didn't."

"I will speak with Scott, Paul."

"We need to find Alan fast, Morel."

"Maybe your Mom is keeping Alan in bed."

"It isn't time to joke Morel, but you are right. You need to look for Mom to find Alan."

"What is your father doing?"

"He is busy with Lori. She is the wife of Alan."

"This is funny Paul."

"Do you know where Lori and Henry are?"

"In Florida. Alan and Mom went there this morning."

"Will Lori and Henry sleep in the same bed in Florida, Paul?"

"I don't know Morel. You need to ask Dad." We laughed. "I wasn't happy this morning, but now I feel better about the whole think."

"I will call you, Paul." Roy opened the door.

"May I speak with you Paul?"

"Of course boss. Do you want to know what I spoke with Mark and Dan?"

"They told me. It isn't good for me what you told Mark and Dan. You work in my company and you need to tell me if you want to leave Paul."

"I am not ready to leave you, but my life changed in the last four weeks Roy. Susan spoke with Holly and she told her that Holly's Mom is in New York."

"Lori and Henry are in Florida. Morgan family wants to get the money of the Goldbear family. You are with Holly. Janet with Alan and Henry with Lori, Paul."

"What is your problem Roy?"

"I think that you want to get the money of the Goldberg family to open your business. You had sex with Estelle to get the money of the Cote family too Paul. Is it true Paul?

"Maybe you are right Roy. I have been working for you for ten years and you haven't understood that I use my brain to make money for your company. I don't make enough money. Finally, I understood that if I use sex to make money I may do better. Now I am negotiating with the families of Holly and Estelle. If I want to get money from both families, I need to marry both women, Holly and Estelle. I want to live six months with Holly in New York and six months with Estelle in Paris. Do you think that it is good for me, Holly and Estelle?"

Roy left my office. He didn't answer me. When I returned home I told Holly what I said to Roy. She laughed.

"I will ask Estelle if she likes this arrangement, because I agree with you boy. Roy is afraid to fire you, but you will have many problems at your current job Paul. If you want to leave Roy, you leave the company Paul. We have money."

"The problem is that I will lose my clients Holly. The goal of Roy is to get my clients. I need to meet you with Alan very fast, Paul."

"I spoke with Morel. I think that he will find where are Alan and Mom are."

It was Tuesday morning. I entered the office at 8:45am.

"Would you marry me?" Judy asked me and she laughed.

"Everybody in the office knows that you want to marry two rich women Paul."

I saw Mark. "Would you marry me Paul?" We laughed.

Morel called and told me that Alan and Mom arrived last night in Paris.

"They will fly to Australia on Thursday. Alan has a house in Gold Coast, Australia. I will call you again if I have more information Paul."

I called Holly. "They are in Paris and they will fly on Thursday to Australia."

"I will buy tickets for Thursday. You need to take time off Paul."

"I don't want to ask Roy, Holly."

"I will speak with Roy."

Ten minutes later Judy entered my office and sked me "Are you going to take off on Thursday and Monday, Paul?"

"Why are you asking, Judy?"

"I heard that from Roy."

"Holly spoke with Roy. I haven't"

"I don't understand what Roy wants Paul. If he doesn't want you, he needs to fire you or tell you to leave the office. Roy is the owner of the company."

"For one or two months you need to stay far away from me Judy. I don't want Roy to fire you."

"I don't care Paul. It is better for you if Roy doesn't speak with you."

Judy was right. Roy didn't speak with me on Wednesday and Thursday. Holly and I left New York on Thursday afternoon. We flew to Sidney. It was a long trip and we had a lot time to speak for our future on the airplane. It was good that Holly and I wanted to marry and have children.

"I will be ready when we arrive in Australia. I want to start to making our baby there Paul. I want to be pregnant when I marry you. Nobody will stop us to marry and have children. I don't have time to tell you that I had a big problem with my agent. He wanted me to sign to be a model for three more years. I told him that he needs cancel my schedule for the next four months and I will tell him if I want to continue to be a model before the New Year. When I visited my doctors, I was told that I have a health problem and I need to take a break from my business for four months. He told me that I am crazy, because every model wants to sign a contract to be a model for ever. I told him that I am Holly Gold. I am not like other models."

"What did he tell you?"

He understood that I have a plan and he asked me.

"Do I have future in your future plan Holly?"

I told him. "If you listen to me, you will have. He will cancel my shows and we will meet before the New Year. My life changed after Ajaccio. I understood that I lost everything that I built in the last ten years, because they would have killed me. You saved my life and you saved what I did in the last ten years. When Roy asked me why you didn't tell him that you need to take off, I was got and I asked him. Do you want Paul to leave today your company Roy? Alan will give enough money to Paul and he will open his business and I hung up the phone. Later Susan called and said that Roy has problem with you in the office, but you will be coming with me."

"Where are you going?"

"To see Alan, Susan. I want Alan to give money to Paul. Maybe Alan will retire Susan. Do you know what Susan told me?"

"It will be good for Paul and Roy. They will have more money in their business. Roy and Paul are good friends and they will have a good future, if they work with the money of the Goldbear family."

"Susan thinks that you will work forever in Roy's company. I promise you that you will have enough money and you will leave Roy before the New Year."

"You are scaring me Holly. I will not have a boss."

"I will be your boss boy. I will watch what you do with the money of my family." We laughed. On Saturday afternoon, Holly and I arrived in the Goal Coast, Australia. When we left New York it was hot, because it was summer. It was winter in Australia and the weather was little cold. We were in the hotel room.

"We will need to buy some warm clothes Holly. I feel a little chilly here."

"I checked the weather before we left New York. Open and see what I put in your travel bags." I opened. I embraced and kissed her.

"I will take a shower and wait for you in bed Paul."

"Are we starting today Holly?"

"We don't have time to wait Paul. I am thirty years old." Holly laughed.

"O boy, you scared me. I am not for one day. I don't remember how many days I didn't have sex with you Holly."

"Where do you want to go for dinner Holly?"

"I want to stay in the hotel room Paul. I am little nervous." Holly and I had dinner in the hotel room. Holly ordered a taxi for 8:30 in the morning.

It was Sunday morning. We were in the taxi at 8:30am. Holly gave the taxi driver the address where he needed to drop us. Holly told him that he needs to wait to take us back to the hotel. The taxi entered the property of Alan. I saw Mom with a man.

"Janet and Alan are on the terrace Paul."

We were exiting the taxi when Allan said "Oh my God. I don't believe that you came to see me, Hana."

"I was very lonely for the last twelve years Alan. Did you miss your daughter?"

"Sometimes."

"Alan is your father Holly."

"Shut up Janet. I will call him what I want. Do you know that Paul isn't your son, Alan?"

"When you marry Paul for the New Year, he will be my son in law Hana."

"Call me Holly, Alan."

"Come in the house." The taxi driver asked Holly, how long he will have to wait." Holly didn't answer, but gave him seven hundred Australian dollars.

"Thanks lady. I will wait as long as you want."

"Do you have a problem Holly?"

"You are smart Alan. You figured me out fast Alan. Lori needed two days for that."

"Where is Lori?"

"She is in Florida. Lori wanted to see you and Janet there, but you left."

We entered the house. Allan said "I remember that you didn't drink when I offered you something Holly."

"It was long time ago Alan. I will drink water."

"What do you like Paul?"

"I like glass of water too Alan."

"I will give them water Alan."

"I prefer that Alan gives me the water Janet. You need to give to your son."

"Peter told me that you and Paul will marry for the New Year."

"I am here to invite you and Janet."

"Are Lori and Henry coming too Holly?"

"Henry will come, but Lori doesn't love Paul and she doesn't want me to marry him."

"Why?"

"Because Lori thinks that Paul wants to marry for my family money. You needed to think when you married Lori, Alan."

Alan laughed and told Holly "You are right Holly, but Lori is your Mom."

"I want to speak with you alone Alan."

"Follow me Holly." Mom followed Alan and Holly.

"You need to stay here Janet. I want to speak alone with Holly."

My mom and I were alone. She said "Why did you come with Holly here Paul? Why are you going to marry her?"

"Dad wanted me to marry Holly."

"Henry was with Holly, Paul."

"Now Henry is with her too, Janet?"

"Why do you want to hurt me Paul?"

"I told you the truth Mom. When Henry saw Lori, he got her in bed and they had sex. Dad told me that he didn't have sex for many years."

"Henry is an old man."

"Lori is sixty years old, but she had sex with Dad. You are fifty-five years old."

"I love Alan and I don't want to have sex with Henry."

"Why don't you divorce Henry, if you love Alan?"

"I don't understand Henry, Alan, Lori and you. You and Alan have a long sexual relationship. Why did you lie to Alan that I am his son?"

"I wanted Alan to marry me."

"Alan is married Mom. You too."

"Alan will divorce. Me too."

"Why didn't you divorce Dad for so many years?"

"I didn't want to hurt you. I know that you love Henry more than me."

"Henry spent more time with me. Henry cared more for my life. Henry was my mom and dad. Why didn't you care for me, Mom? Now I know. You were busy with Alan. Alan lives in California. You live in New York and Florida.

"How did you meet with Alan, Mom?"

"Alan came to see me."

"Why?"

"I told you. Alan loves me."

"Did Alan tell you that you need to divorce Henry and marry him?"

"Alan didn't want to divorce Lori."

"Why?"

"I don't know."

I understood that Alan didn't tell Mom, what happened between him and Holly.

"Do you know something for Holly, Mom?"

"That she is a daughter of Alan and he had a problem with her when Holly grew up."

"Do you know that Alan is sick?"

"Alan works with the money of his family. If Alan is sick why the family believes him. It is billion dollars Paul."

"I don't care for Alan, I care for you, Mom. This is your life and I want to help you. Thank you for saving my life Mom. I want to save your life. Alan will never marry you, because something happened when Holly was seventeen years old. You need to speak with Alan, Mom. That you live and lie to Henry for many years, it isn't my problem. Henry is your husband and he needs to know, who you are. I love Henry and you, Mom, but I will never give advice to you and Dad."

"I wanted to tell you when you were teenager, but I didn't."

"Now I am thirty-three years old."

"If Alan leaves me, I want to go back and live with Henry."

"Could you tell Henry that, Paul?"

"No, Mom. You need to call and speak with Henry.

"Why does Henry wants Lori?"

"I never said that Dad wants Lori, but he was happy after he had sex with her."

I wanted to push Mom to speak with Dad, but Mom told me "Lori is sixty years old. I am fifty-five. Henry will call and ask me to live with him, if Alan leaves me."

I understood that Mom is crazy, because I know that Dad will never want to live with her. I told Mom "I hope so Mom. I will be happy if I see that you and Henry together."

I saw Holly and Alan. They came to me and Mom.

"I am happy that you are having a good time with Alan, Janet. Dad is a good man. That for the first time I heard Holly calling Alan, Dad."

"Of course daughter. Janet loves me and I love her, daughter."

"I will be happy if you marry Janet, Dad?"

"Will Lori marry Henry, daughter?"

"I don't know Dad, but Henry is happy with Lori."

"Don't think for us daughter. You must think for Paul. He is a good choice for you. Maybe Paull will work someday with me or with the money of your family daughter."

"The future will tell us Dad." Holly kissed Alan. She kissed Mom too. Mom didn't move. Janet laughed.

"I haven't kissed you for many months Holly. I will kiss you every time when I see you. I think that Alan will be happy when I marry him Holly."

"Dad needs to divorce first Janet. Mom is staying between you and Dad."

"Henry is staying between me and Alan too Holly."

"I love Henry, Janet. Don't hurt Henry."

"I don't want to speak for Henry, because I am with Alan, Holly. Do you want to speak for Marcel or Giles, when you are with Paul?"

"You are right Janet. See you tomorrow Dad."

"I will be happy to see you tomorrow daughter." I kissed Mom and shook hands with Alan. We returned to the hotel. I wanted to walk on the beach, but it was windy and Holly preferred to stay in the hotel.

"I will go for a walk and return for lunch Holly." I walked on the beach and thought for Holly and me. I didn't ask Holly about her conversation with Alan, because I saw that she didn't want to speak. I know Holly well. She wanted to speak when she was with me. Holly wanted to tell me what happened when she traveled. Frankly Holly had a busy life. My life was simple. I go to the office and return to the apartment. I was enjoying when I was on vacation. After I met Holly she tried to change my life. Holly wanted to see movies and shows in the New York's theaters. Holly told me that she did that in Paris. "To make money is not everything in life Paul." Holly knows many people. She has many friends. I don't. Honestly, Holly's friends were my friends, but I saw them when I was with Holly.

I liked to joke with Holly. "So many men around you, Holly, but I am not jealous."

She laughed and told me "So many women saw you when you were with me Paul. Don't get them in bed, because I will be jealous." Holly's friends loved me, because I joked a lot with them and we laughed a lot. I was very popular when I was in the university. I had a lot of friends there. My live changed when I started to work for Roy. I stayed in the office ten or twelve hours. Sometimes I worked on Saturday too. After I met Holly, I stopped to work on

Saturday. When Holly was in New York, I left the office after six or seven o'clock. Holly told me that my business was hard and I needed to relax more with her.

Holly wanted to joke with me. She told me "When you are in bed with me, you don't think that it is a hard job Paul. It is a feeling not a job." When we finished, Holly wanted to ask me. "How do you feel boy?"

I told her. "It is different Holly. When I work in the office I look at my watch when I need to leave. When I am in bed with you I want the time to stop and we stay in bed forever." My life with Holly was good. I think that in future my life will be better, because Holly will be my wife and we will have children. I returned to the hotel. Holly was ready to leave for lunch. I took a shower and we left the hotel. I spoke with people on the front desk and they told me where to find a good restaurant for lunch. After lunch we returned to the hotel. Holly ordered dinner for me in the hotel room. When I woke up in the morning, Holly was packing her luggage. I will leave at 8:40am. When I return you need to be ready to leave. I didn't ask where Holly was going, because I was sure that Alan and Holly will go to the bank. Holly returned at 10:15am. We left the hotel. In the afternoon Holly and I flew back to America.

"How do you like seventy-five million dollars Paul?"

"You told me fifty million."

"I changed my mind after I spoke with Alan yesterday. Janet created a little problem in the bank for me, because she wanted to come with Alan and me. I didn't believe it Paul. Janet said that she is the wife of Alan and she wants to see what her husband is doing in the bank. I saw that Alan got nervous and I said to the security guard to check Janet's passport. Alan laughed and told me, "You are smart daughter". Alan and I finished and we left the bank. Alan wanted to have dinner with me and you. I told him that you are busy in your office. You won't believe what Alan told me!"

"I know that Paul has a problem with Roy Bell, Holly. Paul is good at our business, but I need to check, if he is ready to work for the Goldbear family. I need to speak with your uncle Peter first."

"Uncle Peter loved me when I was a teenager, but I haven't seen him for twelve years. When we were in the hospital to get Lori, I spoke with him and he was happy to talk to me, but I don't want to call and ask him for you, Paul."

"Do you think that Lori will not want me to work for the

Goldbear family, if Alan and Peter want that?"

"Lori is not in the business of my family, but she is Alan's wife. It is good that Lori is with Henry. Maybe Alan will open his eyes that Lori isn't the right wife for him."

"Alan doesn't care what Lori does Holly, because she lied to Alan when they married. Alan will never forget that, but he will never divorce Lori."

"Because Alan wanted to have sex with me, Paul."

"If Alan divorces Lori, she will tell the court what Alan tried to do when you were seventeen. Alan knows that it will be a disaster for the Goldbear family."

"I will say that it isn't true Paul."

"I think that Lori has something that she can show in court that will prove that it was true."

"You think that it is a family secret?"

"It is Holly."

"Mom will never do that."

"Lori doesn't care for you Holly. Lori doesn't care for anybody. Lori left her son and lied to Alan. Lori didn't tell people what kind man Alan is."

"Why is Lori doing that Paul?"

"Because Lori wants to get the money after Alan dies."

"Janet wants that too Paul. Mom told me that she loves Alan and Mom isn't married to him. I don't want to speak what will happen in the future between Lori and Henry, because Dad met Lori last week. Alan and Janet have been together for a long time, but it isn't going good for them, Holly."

"You are scaring me Paul."

"The good news will be, that I and you will marry and we will have children Holly."

"O boy, I don't care for Lori and Janet. I am afraid for Henry. If Alan is alive is good for us too Paul. Alan cried and told me that he is very sorry for what he wanted to do. Alan told me "I am a sick man daughter. Sometimes I don't remember what I did in the past. You need to understand that, Holly." Now I am divided between what he did thirteen years ago and what he said now. The problem is, that I never knew that Alan was sick and my family never spoke about that, Paul."

"I think that, Lori should have told you, Holly. She is your Mom and she knows Alan well."

"I will ask uncle Peter, why my family didn't tell me, but my goal is to improve my relationship with Alan, Paul. I can't change the past, but if my family is behind me and you, it will be good for our future. Alan told me, why I was kidnapped, but I promised him, that I can't speak, about what happened in Paris and Ajaccio."

"You made a deal for seventy-five million."

"Of course boy. Now the money is more important for us. We are together and we will marry."

"Did Alan tell you something for Lori?"

"Alan told me "Lori is your Mom, you need to decide your relationship with her. I am happy with Janet and if she wants to live with me, I will be with her.""

"I think that it is good for Henry, Paul."

"Why?"

"I want Henry to live with us Paul. Henry loves you and me. He will be happy when we have a child. Henry gave you thirteen million to save my life. Henry did everything for you and me to be together."

"Will Alan be happy if he hears that we have a child?"

"Alan told me that our children will continue the business of the Goldbear family. I was surprised, because uncle Peter has two children and aunt Ann has three children. Alan told me that they only want to spend money, they don't think to make money"

"I know the children of Peter and Ann well. Peter is a good man, but he doesn't know well my business. His children too. Ann is greedy. Her children too. Peter will have big problem with Ann, if I die. I need to do something before I die Holly. I will think for Paul. I am tired and I want to stay in Australia and relax. Maybe Paul has a future in the Goldbear family."

"I will marry Paul, Alan."

"That is why I told you that I believe in your children Holly. I know that Paul will want them to take over one day Paul's business. Paul is like me. He wants to make more and more money. Paul spends a lot of time doing that. You need to support Paul when he works a lot. You don't tell him that Paul has a family and he needs to spent more time with the family. Paul is crazy like me Holly."

"How do you know that Dad?"

"I have friends in New York. They told me about Paul."

"I asked Alan do you love Paul, Dad?"

"I am a man Holly."

"You must love Paul."

"We laughed Paul. I saw that Alan was happy. He asked me "How much do you want?"""

"I told him seventy-five million Dad."

"I will give them to you, but if you and Paull need more, call me daughter. I will give you as much as you want. I have one daughter. I have enough money to live good for the rest of my life. You and Paull need to have more money. I don't Holly. God bless you and Paul and Dad kissed my head Paul."

"I had tears in my eyes. It wasn't Alan that I knew. My heart was broken. I embraced and kissed Alan. Thanks Dad that you think for me and Paul. I will never forget what you said, Dad. I asked Alan for Janet."

"When I was nineteen, your grandparents had a problem with me. I wanted to have sex. I had money and I offered money to girls, but they told me that I am crazy and they don't want to have crazy children. Janet was the first girl that I had in bed. I left her several times, because Janet wanted me to marry her. I didn't know what to do if I marry Janet. I told her that I am sick and she will have problem with me. Janet disappeared and I understood that she married Henry. I was angry that Janet married Henry, because she was my girl. The family was afraid that I will kill Janet and Henry, if I find where they are. I met Lori and asked her to marry me. She said yes and I married her, but I love Janet. You were born. I wanted to have a boy. I didn't love you, but I didn't hate you, Holly. It was a big disaster in my life when I understood that Lori was married and she has a son. Lori lied to me. I wanted to see Janet. She was married and I was too. Nobody wanted to help me to find Janet. Janet's relative told me where she was. She left Henry and we were together two months. Henry met with me and he told me that his son asked for Janet. I told Janet that she needs to return to live with her son. Janet returned, but I love her and she loves me. When I traveled to New York, I and Janet were spending time together in New York. Henry and Janet moved to Florida. I traveled there to see her. I knew that it wasn't good for Henry and Paul, but I wanted to be with Janet. Life is crazy Holly."

"Did Mom know that?"

"I didn't care what Lori knows or thinks, Holly. I never forgot that Lori lied to me."

"Janet lied to you too. She told you that Paul is your son."

"The night before I left Janet, we had sex. Henry slept with her the next day. I thought that I am the father, because I wanted to have a son Holly. I told you many times that I am a sick man."

"Do you hate Janet after you understood that Paul is the son of Henry?"

"When Viler told me I was happy, because I knew that you love Paul. I tried to call in Ajaccio, but you left with Paul. Paul is a man Holly. He wanted to pay thirty million dollars for you. You aren't his wife. You are just his girlfriend. I will never do that if somebody kidnaped Lori, who is my wife or Janet who is my girlfriend. You must love Paul. He risked his life and he wanted to pay millions of dollars to save yours."

"Are you going to do the same if somebody kidnapped me, Alan?"

"Before I wouldn't have. Now I will. I have one daughter. Many things have changed in the last twelve years Holly. Sometimes I told Peter that I needed to find you. When he asked me why, I didn't have an answer. Frankly, Peter was right. You never returned to my home. You never called me or Lori and wanted to see me or her. Peter told me that you will come and see me. You came. I am a little jealous that you saw Lori first."

"O boy, Alan joked and laughed. Alan joked that Janet prefers to live with him, because he is thirteen years younger than Henry, but Henry needs to be happy, because Lori is ten years younger than him. I asked Alan. What do you think about Janet, Dad?"

"I told you that Janet was the first girl that I had sex with. I will never forget that. I love her."

"I know that you don't love me, because I wasn't the first woman in bed with you boy." Holly laughed.

"Of course Holly. You needed to get a lot of experience before you got me in bed. You didn't lose time Holly. You weren't my first girl in bed, but I stopped to think for other women after I had sex the first time with you."

"You don't have zip on your mouth Paul."

"Hey Holly, I told you the truth. I want to have sex with you. I am feeling good in bed with you and I want to be with you, my whole life."

"This sounds good boy."

We arrived in New York. We entered the building, of Holly's apartment. The janitor told Holly that her Mom and my dad came yesterday to her apartment. We entered the apartment.

"What are you doing here Mom? You need to call me, before you come here?"

"I called on Friday and Saturday, but you didn't pick up your cell phone. We found your and Paul cell phones on the table. We were afraid that something happened with you and Paul. Where have you been Holly?"

"Alan called me to see him."

"Did you see Janet, Holly, she must to be with Alan?"

"I didn't Mom. Alan was alone."

"I don't believe you, but it is OK that you and Paul are alive."

"Do you think that somebody will kill us?"

"Henry told me what happened in France and he wanted to return to New York."

"I didn't tell you, Lori."

"I wasn't afraid for Holly, because she was with Paul. I told you that Paul would call me if he had a problem. You wanted to came to New York and find out where Holly and Paul are."

"I don't remember what you told me Henry. I am an old woman." Holly saw that Henry was angry.

"It is OK Mom. I am happy to see you and Henry. How was your vacation with Henry?"

"We had a good time, but Henry's house is small."

"You can buy a big house for Henry, Mom."

"Does Alan know that I am with Henry?"

"Alan knows everything Mom. He knows that you are in New York, but I didn't tell him that you are with Henry."

"Have you been with Alan alone Holly, because I am afraid if you were alone?"

"I told Henry what Alan wanted to do with you."

"What did Henry tell you Lori?"

"That you aren't a woman for Paul,"

"Did you know that Alan and Holly had something Paul?"

I didn't answer. I left to the bedroom. Holly followed me.

"What happened with you, Paul?"

"You didn't hear what Lori said for you and Alan?"

"I don't care what Lori says Paul."

"Lori wants to separate me and you Holly."

"It isn't news for me Paul. Janet wanted that too, but we are together."

"What do I need to do when Lori speaks against me and you, Holly?"

"Nothing. You don't answer her. It is good if Henry leaves with Lori again. I will speak with Henry."

Henry entered the bedroom. "I am so sorry Holly. Lori wanted to speak with Paul's boss. I gave her Roy's phone number. Roy told Lori that he took three days off, but Roy didn't know where you and Paul were."

Lori entered the bedroom and Dad stopped to speak. "Why did you leave me alone Henry?"

"Henry needed to speak with Paul. I will come with you, Lori." Holly and Lori exited the bedroom.

"What did you decide Dad? I met and spoke with Mom. Janet wants to return to live with you if Alan leaves her."

"This isn't possible Paul."

"Because you love Lori?"

"Lori is the same as Janet, Paul, but I need to be with her. When Holly tells me I will leave Lori. Lori is more dangerous Paul. She wants us to have sex two times per day. She wants to kill me Paul. I told Lori that we need to have sex one time per week, because I am an old man. If Lori wants more sex, she needs to find a young boy." Dad and I laughed.

"You need to listen to Holly. She knows what to do with Lori, Paul."

"I will Dad."

In the morning I saw Holly, Lori and Henry in the living room. They were having coffee and laughing.

"Did you know what Mom told me and Henry?"

"Lori will get you in bed if Henry doesn't want her."

"I prefer you Holly."

"I told Mom the same Paul."

"Do you want coffee Paul, Lori asked me?"

"I need to go to work Lori. I need to make money, because Holly will leave me."

"You are right boy. You need to leave" and Holly followed me to the door.

"Don't be angry if Roy tells you something for me and Alan, Paul. You will not work for a long time in Roy's company. Lori and Henry will go to Toronto. Lori has never been in there. They will return when I call Henry."

"You are Oster Bender, Holly. I believe that when you finish the game you will be a winner."

"You need to think positive. It is good for both of us Paul."

I was in my office. Judy told me that Roy was waiting for me in his office.

"Good morning boss." He didn't tell me good morning. I understood that Roy will try to scare me, because he didn't tell me good morning. I knew that Roy wanted to scare the people in the office when he wanted to speak with them in his office and he didn't tell them good morning or good afternoon when they told him. Roy doesn't know that I don't care for him, if he tells me good morning or not.

"I don't want you to create a problem for me Paul. I didn't know that Lori Goldbear is Mom of Holly. She called me and asked where was Holly."

"You spoke with Holly, Roy. I thought that Holly told you why I needed to take off."

"Holly doesn't work in this office. You work Paul. You needed to tell me where you are going, because I don't want to look stupid if somebody asks where you are and I don't know."

"Do you want to know what I do when I travel with Holly?"

"I don't care what you do with Holly. Lori Goldbear told me that Holly didn't want her to marry you."

"If Holly doesn't want, I will call Estelle. She is waiting for me Roy. I think that Estelle will be happy to move to New York. Can you call and ask Estelle, Roy?"

I will call. "Hi Estelle this is Roy Bell. Would you marry Paul? Estelle wants to speak with you.

"Hi beautiful lady. I am happy to hear your beautiful voce too." Estelle laughed.

"Do you have problem with Roy, Paul?"

"Roy spoke with Holly's Mom, Lori and Roy told me that Holly didn't want to marry me. I am a free man Estelle. I am looking for a woman to marry me."

"How was your trip with Holly to Australia?"

"Alan gave Holly seventy-five million and he wants me to work for him. He was happy that Holly and I will marry and wants to see grandchildren. Holly wants me to leave Roy's company and spend more time in bed with her. Do you think that this is good for me?"

Estelle laughed. "Hey Paul, I want you to call me every day. I was angry when Roy called me, because I have a problem, but now I forgot what kind problem I had. I am feeling good now. If I am in the bath with you I will feel even better. If you want, I will get the first plane and I will come with Holly to Paris."

"What will Holly do?"

"I want Holly to see that I am a good man when somebody wants to be with me."

"Oh my God. You are killing me Paul. I will call and ask Holly if she wants to see what we will do."

"Don't tell Holly what you did."

"I promised you, Paul. I will tell Holly what you and I will do in future, if Holly leaves you. Give me Roy."

I gave the receiver to Roy.

"Yes, Estelle. Paul is my good friend Estelle. I will do what you tell me, Estelle." Roy hang up.

"Does Alan wants to work with you Paul?"

"You need to ask Holly, Roy. She is Alan's a daughter."

"Why does Lori hate you and she doesn't want you to marry Holly?"

"You need to ask Holly for that too Roy."

"Do you have any more questions Roy?"

"I don't Paul. I will be happy when you get and work with the money of the Goldbear family."

"First I need to marry Holly, Roy." I left Roy's office. At 11:00 o'clock Judy called and told me that I have visitors. I walked to the front desk and I saw Holly, Lori and Henry.

"Nice to see you in my office Lori."

"How many women are in this office Paul?"

"You need to ask Roy Bell, Lori. He is the owner of the company."

"Everybody loves Paul."

"Do you love Paul, Judy?"

"Of course Ms. Goldbear."

"Did Paul buy the ring that is on your finger, Judy?"

"I bought it for her Mom. Judy is my friend. I was with Judy when I met Paul. I decided to buy a ring for her."

"You are spending my money for other people Holly."

"I have my own money Lori. You forgot that I am a model and I make money. I wanted to make Judy happy."

"Are you happy Judy?"

"I am happy that Holly is my friend Ms. Goldbear."

"Call me Lori. Every old woman wants to be called them Ms."

"I am not old. Henry is my boyfriend."

"Henry is a married man Lori. Janet is his wife. Are you going to divorce Henry?"

Dad laughed. "Maybe someday Judy."

"I want to see your office Paul."

"Follow me Lori." Lori, Holly and Henry entered my office.

"Your office is small. You don't make a lot of money for Holly."

"You are right Mom. Paul needs a bigger office to make more money."

"My office is bigger Holly." It was Roy. Holly introduced Roy to Lori.

"Nice to see you Ms. Goldbear. I spoke with you on Saturday. Paul told me that he and Holly went to see Alan. He gave Paul and Holly seventy-five million dollars and he wants to work with Paul."

"I don't believe that Roy. Alan is smart. Paul is stupid."

"Please, come to my office Ms. Goldbear."

"I want to speak with Paul, Mom."

"Tell him that he is stupid Holly."

"I will Mom. "They left and Holly locked the door.

'I love your desk Paul. I want to have sex on your desk." The voice of Holly raised.

"Somebody will hear you, Holly."

"I am feeling good Paul. I will try to be quiet."

We were ready to leave my office when Holly said "If we have a son, his name will be Desk. I will never forget your desk Paul."

Holly and I entered Roy's office. Dad looked at me and he smiled. Dad came to me.

"You forgot to zip your pants. Holly saw what I did and she laughed."

"What is funny Holly?"

"Paul needs a bigger office and a bigger desk Mom. Paul will be better on the big desk."

"I don't understand you Holly."

"Doesn't matter Mom."

"Roy invited us to have lunch together. This is a good idea Roy, but Paul needs to stay in office and work. He needs to make money for Holly. I don't love Paul, Roy."

Holly wanted to say something, but I told her "It is OK Holly. I need to work." My phone rang.

"This is Paul Morgan. Hey Paul, finally you met your father in law."

"Is that Peter?"

"Yes, it is Peter. Alan told me that he is waiting for grandchildren."

"This morning Holly was in my office and we used my desk for that Peter."

"I will tell my brother that you and Holly are using everything to have a child." We laughed.

"I wanted to tell you that Alan was excited when he spoke with me. I would like to come to your office on Friday morning Paul, is that OK?"

"I will be waiting for you Peter." When I returned home I was happy.

"Why are you happy Paul, because I will tell Roy to fire you?"

"I am not afraid Lori. I will have more time to be with Holly. Alan is waiting for a grandchild. You will be a grand Mom."

"I don't want Holly to have a child, because she will not marry you."

"If you want, I will move in my apartment Lori."

"This is a good idea Paul."

"Shut up Lori. Paul will stay in my apartment." Holly and I were in bed.

"What happen with you, Paul?"

"I spoke with Peter. He will come on Friday to my office."

"It isn't good that Lori is here Paul. You will move tomorrow to your apartment. I will tell Lori that you need time to decide if you will marry me or not. I know that Henry will do everything to get Lori out from New York."

Holly was right. On Thursday morning Dad and Lori left to Florida. Thursday night I and Holly were together.

"Tomorrow is a big day for me Holly. You need to do everything to start to work with Alan, Paul."

"I will do that Holly."

CHAPTER 11

I entered the building where I worked. I saw Roy. He was speaking with a man waiting for the elevator. God Morning boss. Peter this is Paul. I and Peter shook hands.

"Do you come to work early every morning Paul?"

"If Holly doesn't want me in bed I come Peter. I have two bosses. Holly in bed and Roy in the office." Peter laughed.

"Who is more important Paul?"

"Of course Holly. I relax and feel good in bed. In the office Roy wants me to work hard to make money." We exited the elevator. I walked to my office.

"Come with us to my office Paul." We entered Roy's office.

"Do you want to have business with me Peter?"

"Frankly, I am here to speak with Paul."

"Paul works in my company Peter."

"Paul will marry Holly and I want to find out, what are Paul's plans after he marries her."

"Paul will work here Peter."

"This is Ok if Paul want to work for you, Roy, but Alan wants to know more about Paul. You know that Alan controls the business of the Goldbear family. Alan is fifty-seven and he doesn't tell me what he thinks, but Alan is young to retire Roy. I want to ask Paul for his private life."

"Lori doesn't want Paul to marry Holly, Peter."

"This is a problem between Alan and Lori. Alan wants Holly to marry Paul and someday Paul will start to work for Alan. You know that Alan is crazy Roy. I am his brother, but sometimes I don't understand him."

"Holly and Paul met and spoke with Alan, Peter."

"Alan isn't happy that Lori is with Henry, Roy."

"Alan is with Janet, Peter."

"That is why I want to speak with Paul alone. I and Paul will go to his office Roy."

"It is OK Peter."

We entered my office. Peter closed the door and said "Roy is stupid Paul. Why do you work for him, Paul?"

"I don't have a choice Peter. Here I make good money, but I and Holly think that it is better for us if I leave Roy. Roy wants to know everything for my and Holly's private life."

"I am here to give you questions that Alan sent me. You need to answer these questions. You have two weeks Paul. When you are ready, call me. How is Holly?"

"She is busy looking to find an office for her and me."

"I know that Holly is your boss. I am happy that Holly wants to do that. Of course Holly is a model, now she need to work in an office."

"Alan knows everything Paul. He is good friend with Viler. Holly will continue in the modeling business, but Estelle will help her. Estelle is a good woman."

"She is Peter. Do you want to see Holly?"

"Next time Paul. Kiss her and say hi to her from me. You don't tell Roy what you will do."

"I know Peter."

"Lori isn't a problem for Alan, but is better if she doesn't know what we are doing."

"I will tell Holly, Peter. Lori is her Mom. Do you know Janet, Peter?"

"Your Mom is different. Janet loves Alan and you, Paul. I never heard that Lori loves somebody. I am sorry to tell you that Paul but Lori loves only the money of my brother. I will go to say good bye to Roy."

I called Holly and she said "I found a place Paul. I like it, but you need to see the place too."

"I don't have time today Holly. Peter left five minutes ago. If I leave the office Roy will think that I will have lunch with Peter."

"Just a Moment Paul. Can you come to see the space tomorrow

morning at 10:00 o'clock Paul?" "I can make it Holly."

"When I finish with the agent I will call you Paul." I looked at my calendar. Labor Day is ten days from now. It will be good if Holly and I go on vacation. I entered the office of Roy. I want to take some time off to go on vacation Roy. I want to take three days."

"Where are you going?"

"I will speak with Holly and I will tell you." Holly called me.

I told her "I want to go on vacation for Labor Day. I don't want to stay in New York. I will get three days off."

"I don't want to go to Florida, Paul. Hey boy, I want to see how many girls you have in Puerto Rico."

"This is a good idea Holly. I will make a reservation for next Thursday and we will be back on Tuesday."

"Can you buy tickets?"

"We will leave New York on Thursday morning and we will return on Tuesday afternoon. We will fly to San Juan, Puerto Rico. I will buy the tickets Paul. Do you want to go out tonight?"

"I like that Holly."

"I will stop by your office so we will go together, Paul"

After I hung up with Holly I immediately called the Marriot in Puerto Rico.

"May I speak with Pedro?"

"Pedro is speaking Sir."

"Hey my friend, what are you doing?"

"Oh my God. I thought that I will never speak with you again Paul."

"You will see me next Thursday, Pedro. I want to make a reservation. I will arrive on Thursday and leave next Tuesday."

"Do you want to stay in the same apartment?"

"If it is available."

"Of course my friend."

After I made the reservation, I went to Roy's office.

"I and Holly will be in Puerto Rico, boss. Is that OK?"

"You didn't tell me what Peter wanted."

"Alan is afraid that Lori is here. You know that Lori doesn't like me and Peter wants me to listen to Holly. It is hard for me that Lori is here and she is speaking against me. Holly isn't happy that Lori is doing that, but she is her Mom."

"If Lori calls me and asks for you and Holly, what should I tell her?"

"That Holly and I are in Puerto Rico."

Holly came in my office at 6:30pm. I told her that I need thirty more minutes to finish my paperwork.

"I will go to speak with Roy for few minutes, Paul."

Holly, Roy and I left the office at 7:20pm. Holly told me that she invited Roy and Susan. We had dinner together, but Susan and Roy were polite and careful with Holly. I didn't speak. I listened to them. We left the restaurant. I was alone with Holly. I told her what Peter gave me.

"That means that Alan doesn't trust you yet, Paul."

"Alan is right Holly. He has worked for many years to save and make money. Why should he take a risk with me if I am not ready to do what Alan does?"

I" believe that you will give provide good answers to Alan."

"I must if I want to work with Alan."

"Where are you going to work on the answers Paul?"

"I will work at home after I return from the office. I don't want Roy know what I am doing. It is good that we will go on vacation. There I will have more time to work."

"Don't forget that you need to do something in bed with me boy."

"If I forget you need to ask me. Do you want to me to make you happy boy?"

We laughed. The next day at 10:00 o'clock Holly and I met the real estate agent at the building where Holly wanted to get the office for us. The building was close to Wall Street.

"I like the place and the building Holly." The agent told Holly that she will prepare the contract and Holly needs to sign it on Monday. We had lunch with the agent. Holly wanted to do shopping in the afternoon. She bought things for our vacation in Puerto Rico. When we returned at home I started to work on Alan's questions. The questions were about our business, because I and Alan were in the same business. I have two weeks and I didn't want to answer them fast. I had to read some of the questions two or three times. On Sunday before dinner I was ready with one third of the answers. Holly and I ate. Holly asked me.

"What do you think about Alan, Paul?"

"Alan knows well this business Holly. At some point Alan and I will have different answers, because I am young and now some things have changed in our business, but in general we will should have the same answers to the questions."

"Do you have a plan if Alan doesn't want to work with you?"

"I will try to work with Nancy Jones and Estelle, Holly. I work and I am loyal to Roy, but he starts to asks too much about my private life and he is lying to me. I don't have future in Roy's company. If I open my company, I know that Alan will give me money to see how I work with the money. If I make more profit than him, Alan will want me."

"Do you want me to speak with Alan?"

"You should never do that Holly. I need to get his heart."

"It is enough that you took my heart Paul. It is better if I take the heart of Lori."

"Henry did it before you, Paul. It is good that Henry listens to me and he does everything what I want Paul."

"Can you promise me something Holly?"

"What do I need to promise you Paul?"

"You won't want to have sex two times a day when I turn seventy."

"I will get young boys to do that boy."

"Sounds good to me, but you shouldn't spend a lot of money for sex Holly. We will become poor. I don't want to return to work for your young boys."

"Don't be afraid Paul. I will be sixty-seven years old."

It was Monday morning. I was in the office at 9:00am. Peter called me at 9:30am.

"What do think Paul?"

"I am in this business Peter. Last night I finished one third of the questions. In general, the questions are about what Alan and do on the market every day. I don't work on the questions in the office. I work on them at home. Holly and I will go on vacation and there I will have more time."

"Where are you going?"

"To Puerto Rico. I was alone there and Holly wants to check how many girls I had there. Tell Alan that Holly will not marry me after she sees the girls." We laughed.

"May I tell Janet too?"

"Mom knows that I had a lot of girls before I met Holly. If you speak with Mom, tell her "They love me Mom". Mom knows what that means."

"Why did Holly wanted to live with you?"

"I don't know Peter. You need to ask her."

"Why did you ask Holly to marry you?"

"I didn't Peter. Holly asked me to marry her."

"Oh my God. You are crazy people Paul. It is customary that a man asks a woman."

"Alan and Janet are crazy too Peter. Mom wants to marry Alan. Alan is the father of Holly. Janet is my mom. What is the difference Peter?"

Peter laughed. "You have always the perfect answer Paul. It is hard for me to understand you and Holly, but I don't know you, Paul. I think that Alan knows you well."

"Of course Peter. Alan and Mom are together for thirty-five years. You need to ask Alan, if he asked Mom the whole time what I did or he had sex with her."

"Oh my God. You are killing me Paul. You speak so easy for Alan and Janet. Is Holly is like you?"

"Before she didn't, but now I don't know Peter. The life of Holly changed in the last two months. Before we didn't speak for us or our future. Now we speak a lot about that."

"Are you going to hate Alan if he doesn't want to work with you, Paul?"

"When you work with money, you must know what kind of risk you have when you invest. Alan will be right if he is afraid to risk with me. It is business Peter. It isn't feeling. I am feeling good when I am in bed with Holly, because I don't think for business. I don't want Alan to think for his money when he and Mom are in bed."

"O boy, I will tell Allan everything you said. I think that you and I will have a good time when we are together Paul. Kiss Holly from me."

"I will Peter."

In the afternoon Holly called and told me that she signed the contract for the office space.

She said "The agent will help me to find the company to clean the place and build a new office. I will call and ask Estelle for my office. You need to decide for your office Paul."

"I will use the company the same company that will fix your office Holly, but I will give them the plan of what they need to do. They need to finish your office after they will start to work on mine."

On Thursday morning Holly and I flew to Puerto Rico. It was good that Pedro was at the front desk. He looked at Holly.

"Is she with you, Paul?"

"Pedro, this is my fiancée Holly Gold. I will marry her for the New Year."

"Not so fast boy. I want to see your girls in San Juan first, after I will decide if I will marry you." "They aren't beautiful Holly. I prefer that you marry Paul."

"Do girls want to marry Paul?"

"Of course Holly. Paul is a rich man. Every girl wants to marry a rich man."

"Why didn't you tell me that Paul doesn't have girls here?"

"Do you want to me to lie to you, Holly?'

Pedro and I laughed.

"Why are you laughing boys?"

"Because I am joking Holly. Many girls wanted to sleep with Paul, but he told them that Holly got his heart."

"Did you tell them that?"

"I told them that you were busy in Paris, but I didn't want to sleep with them, because I love you, Holly."

"I will have fun time with Pedro and you, Paul."

"I will do everything you want Holly."

"Do you want to spray my back with a sunscreen Pedro?"

"I will be happy if I do and I will be happier if I touch your skin Holly."

"Paul is jealous Pedro."

"I am a friend of Paul, Holly." We laughed.

Holly and I were on the beach. I was working on answering the questions Peter gave me. Holly was laying on the beach.

"I will go in the water Paul."

"I will come when I finish the questions Holly."

Somebody asked me "Does she move her ass the same in bed man?"

I raised my head. It was a life guard. I looked at Holly's ass. I replied "Faster man."

After that everybody who saw me on the beach or the hotel told me" faster man". It was so funny when Holly asked me, why people are telling me "faster man".

"Is that a joke about my body Paul? You should be jealous, because they are looking at my body and want something."

"If they didn't look and didn't want you, I will be with another girl that they want Holly."

"What would you do If I jump in bed with some of them?"

"I will have more time to answer the questions Holly. But I will want to know, who was in bed with you."

"Why?"

"I will give him this question to see if he is smart. If the man answered good, I will know that the child will be smart."

"You will not check the DNA of our child?"

"I am Paul Morgan. I am not Henry Morgan, Holly."

"Are you serious or you are joking with me, Paul?"

"I am joking, but you are so beautiful and it is normal for people to look at you Holly."

"Thanks Paul."

"My pleasure lady."

We had a wonderful time in Puerto Rico. When we returned to New York, Holly told me "I believe that we will be a perfect family. For the first time you and I were together twenty-four hours for five days."

"We are one year and eight months together and we have been many times for more five days together Holly."

"It is true, but I was your girlfriend and you were my boyfriend. We never spoke about marriage. We didn't know that we would marry. We enjoyed that we had good time and we were together. Now you are my fiancée and I will marry you for the New Year."

"I don't see the difference Holly."

"Before I use to check your condoms. If I thought that your condoms weren't save for me, I gave you condoms that I carried with me. I was scared, not to get pregnant, because I thought for my carrier. Now I don't care for my carrier and I am not afraid that I will be pregnant. I don't want to be a model anymore. I want to marry you and have children."

"Hey, and I will be a father."

"Of course you will be. Are you afraid to be a father?"

"I never thought for that before Holly. I started to think for that when you waited for your menstrual cycle. I understood that I needed to be the father of your child if I wanted to marry you."

"You never told me why you changed your decision Paul"

"I saw that you were different after we returned from Paris. I wanted to marry you, because I love you so much. I had two choices. To accept the child or separate with you. I wanted to be with you and I told you that I will be the father of the child. Honestly, it wasn't an easy decision."

"Did somebody help you?"

"Yes, Holly."

"It is good that you never lied to me Paul."

The cell phone of Holly rang. "Oh my God. It is Mom. She called me many times."

"Hi Mom. I and Paul were in Puerto Rico. I didn't speak with Alan or Peter. My cell phone was in my apartment Mom. You don't tell me what I need to do Lori and Holly hang up."

"I don't understand what Lori wants Paul. She must stop to speak against you. You are my fiancée boy."

"I need to call Peter. I am ready with the questions." I called.

"Hi Peter. This is Paul.'

"Did you have good time with Holly in Puerto Rico?"

"We had. I am ready Peter."

"Do you want me to send you an e-mail?"

"I will come to New York on Thursday and I will get the questions and your answers. I want to see and speak with Holly when I come to New York."

"How many days are you planning to stay in New York?"

"I need to return to California on Saturday, Paul."

"Where are you going to stay in New York?"

"I will decide tomorrow Paul."

"Holly wants to speak with you, Peter."

"Hi Uncle Peter. I want you to stay in my apartment. Lori is with Henry. I will tell Henry to keep Lori far away from New York. See you on Thursday Uncle Peter. I need to speak seriously with Lori when I see her, Paul. She scares everybody. Lori doesn't know who I am "

I was in the office at 8:30 on Wednesday morning. It was good that I didn't meet Roy when I entered my office. I closed the door. Nobody called or entered my office before 12:00 o'clock. Judy opened the door at 12:00. The lunch is ready Paul. Holly called me and told me what I need to buy for lunch. She told me that you had a good time in Puerto Rico. We joked a lot for you Paul. Roy came in my office. You are together again Judy. Paul missed me Roy, but I was happy that Paul worked hard in Puerto Rico.

"Why did Paul work hard in Puerto Rico, Judy?"

"Holly told me that she wants two boys, but if she has three, Paul won't have to work hard in the future. Paul will relax in the house that Holly will buy."

"You need to work Judy."

"It is lunch time Roy. Holly told me that I need to clean Paul's desk after he finishes lunch. If you fire me, Holly told me that I will work in her company. Do you think that I will be better there Roy?"

Roy didn't answer. He left. Roy didn't come to my office on Thursday. It was good for me. Peter was at Holly's apartment when I returned from my office. He was drinking whiskey. Holly stopped to drink alcohol after I stopped to use a condom. I gave the paper with the questions and the answers to Peter.

"I need to speak with Alan, Holly."

"Follow me Peter." They entered the room that Holly used as an office. Holly returned and she asked me if I wanted to drink.

"One glass of whiskey will be good for me Holly." Holly gave me a glass and sat next to me.

"Don't be afraid. I spoke with Peter for your future Paul."

"I am not afraid Holly, but it will be good for me if I work with Alan. It will be easy to leave Roy."

"You didn't tell me what is Roy doing in office Paul."

"In the last two days we spoke for your future office and business Holly. I am happy that you changed your mind fast and you don't want to be a model anymore. I was happy that you chose my lunch for the last two days."

"Is Judy a good secretary Paul?"

"Judy did everything you told her. I want to tell you that it will be hard if I decide to change my business."

Peter came and he gave me his cell phone. Allen was on the line and he asked me "Why do you want to risk in an international investment Paul?"

"I want to build small group in Japan or Hong Kong and one group in Europe. If a problem on the market starts there, I will have time to do something in America. I will invest in real estate there Alan. I will not risk cash money."

"This is new for me Paul."

"You are older than me Alan. I have different vision than you."

"Give me Peter." Peter went back to Holly's office.

"Why doesn't Peter speak here Paul?"

"Alan doesn't want me to hear what they are talking Holly."

"What is the problem if you work with Alan?"

"He is from an older generation Holly. They don't understand that today is easy for somebody get your information, because you use computer, you send e-mail and you use cell phone."

"Can you help me prepare dinner Paul?"

Holly and I were in the kitchen. Peter came there.

"You are looking so lovely Holly."

"We are uncle Peter. When I met Paul I wanted to stay at home, because I wanted to be alone with him. I taught Paul what to do when he helped me to prepare lunch or dinner."

"Who taught you, Holly?"

"In France I lived with a roommate for two years. She grew up with her grand Mom in south France. Her grand Mom taught her and she taught me."

"You didn't have money to eat out?"

"I didn't have enough Peter."

"Your Mom told me that she put a lot money for you in the bank."

"I didn't have permission to use this money when I was twenty-years-old, but I don't regret that, because I learned something that your or Ann's children are ashamed to do, because they are from a rich family. I wasn't."

"You will get a lot of money from the Goldbear family, when Alan dies. I want Alan to live long and I want to make my money. Everything that I will get from the Goldbear family, I will give to Paul. "

"Do you hate your family Holly?"

"A hate isn't a good word Peter. When I grew I didn't feel that I had a Mom and father. I didn't feel that I had relatives. You were the only person that loved me and tried to understand me. In your life you have chance to choose everything you want."

"You don't have a chance to choose your Mom, father and relatives Holly."

"You are right Peter. I chose Henry to be my father and Paul to be my husband. I wanted Janet to be my mom, but she chose to be with Alan."

"Lori is your Mom, Holly. She will never be my mom, because she hates Paul."

"Lori loves Henry and she is with Henry."

"Lori never loved anybody, Peter. She is with Henry, because Lori uses Henry to separate Paul with me. Lori doesn't know that I told Henry to be with her."

"Do you think that someday you and Alan will have a good relationship like a father and daughter?"

"I don't have a choice Peter. I want Alan and Paul to work together. Frankly, Alan is different now. He told me that he was sorry and I accepted his apology. I know that Alan will be happy when he hears that I and Paul have a child. Lori will never accept my baby, because she will be afraid that Alan will give everything to my baby. Alan will be right if he does that, because Paul and I will make good money. We want to work hard Peter. Paul and I don't wait somebody to give us money. You know what your and Ann's children say."

"You are a model Holly. What are you going to do after you are pregnant and have a child?"

"I will have my own business. I am building my office and after September, I will open my business. I will be the boss of Paul, because my office will be above Paul's office."

"You will leave Roy and start your business Paul?"

"I will Peter, doesn't matter if Alan wants or not to work with me."

"Alan wants to retire Paul. Alan told me the name of the new company. The name is Goldbear& Morgan financial group. Do you like the name Paul?"

"I am happy to hear that Peter. Welcome to the Goldbear family Paul. I will tell our family lawyer to prepare the documents for new company."

"Thanks Uncle Peter."

"I know that my dad loves me."

"I need to improve my relationship with Alan, Peter."

I was in the office at 9:00am. "Good morning Paul."

"Good morning Judy. May I kiss you Judy?"

"Don't get me in bed Paul, Holly will kill me." We laughed.

"I will get you to work in my company Judy. Are you going to follow me if I leave Roy, Judy?"

I" will be happy to work in your company Paul."

"You need to be ready after the New Year, Judy."

"Oh my God. I will be ready any time Paul. You need to give

me a signal."

"I will Judy." I was in my office. My cell phone rung. It was Mom.

"Are you happy now son?"

"I am Mom. I didn't believe that someday I will have my own company. I am happy that I met Holly."

"Are you going to marry her Paul?"

"You know my answer Mom. Hey Mom, I work hard so you become a grand Mom."

"What are you going to tell your child if I marry Alan?"

"So many people divorced and married again Mom, but it will be hard to tell my child that you are my mom and Alan is the father of Holly."

"If Henry marries Lori, it will be OK Paul."

"I don't believe that Dad will marry Lori, Mom."

"Is Henry waiting for me?"

"I don't think so Mom. Holly and Henry have a good relationship. She accepts Henry as her father. I think that Holly will want Henry to live with us."

"Do you think that it is good, because Alan is the father of Holly?"

"I don't know Mom, but I love Henry and Holly. I will do what they want. Holly is different now Mom. She doesn't want to be a model. Holly wants to be a Mom."

"Holly is crazy Paul. Every girl wants to be a model."

"Holly was right, when she said, "I don't want to be model like them. I am Holly Gold"."

"Where is Henry?"

"I don't know Mom. He is somewhere with Lori."

"Do you want to speak with Alan?"

"Of course Mom. Hi Paul. Thanks you for believing in me Alan."

"I don't have choice Paul. Holly will marry you."

"You don't think that I am not good in our business."

"I am kidding Paul. I know that my family will not lose money. I want to retire after the New Year."

"Hey Alan, you will have a lot of free time. Take Mom to bed." We laughed.

"I am afraid that Janet and I will have a child Paul. What do I tell the child Paul?"

"That I am half-brother and Holly is half-sister of the child."

"It will be so funny Paul."

"Life is good when people laugh Alan."

"Maybe you are right Paul. I need to think about that."

"If you think you will never have a result, then you need to do something in bed with Mom."

Alan laughed. "I will tell Janet to be more attractive Paul. Is Lori attractive to Henry?"

"I will ask her. I know that Henry will not tell me, Alan. Hey Alan, Holly will be my boss, because her office will be above my office."

"You need to listen to your boss, because the boss will fire you, Paul. If Holly fires me I will be a free man Alan."

"I will tell Holly that I want you to be my son-in-law, because you will make good money for the Goldbear family."

"I must do that, because I will marry in the Goldbear family Alan." We laughed.

"I will come to the wedding, Paul."

"I will be happy to see you there Alan." Alan hang up. Holly called and told me that the people started to work on her office.

"I want to go out for dinner Paul. You saved a lot money and I want to spend them."

"I didn't save any money Holly. I bought everything you wanted."

"You aren't paying for condoms now and you are saving money boy."

"I calculate every dollar that you save."

"You don't want me to be rich Holly?"

"You will be rich, because I will be your wife boy."

"Hey Holly, I have a question can you work and I will stay at home and raise the children?"

"Why not Paul."

"This is a great idea. You will be a good babysitter."

"I thought that you will tell me that I need to work." We laughed.

"I spoke with Mom and Alan."

"What did they say?"

"Mom called me. Looks like she has mixed feelings. She asked me for Henry and Lori. Alan was happy. We joked. Alan promised me that he will come when you marry me."

"Alan will come Paul. The problem are Janet and Lori. I don't want to think what will be happen if they are together at our wedding, but there are three months until the New Year."

Holly was busy and she spend a lot of time on her office. Holly wanted to finish it before Estelle was coming in the last week of September. After I spoke with Alan, I started to meet and speak with young people that work in my business. I wanted to select people who will work in my office after the New Year. I met with them on Saturday or Sunday. I didn't want Roy to know what I was doing. It was good that Henry kept Lori out of New York.

Estelle came to New York the last Thursday of September. She was with her boyfriend Byron. Holly and Estelle were busy with their business. It was good that Byron was with them. Holly, Estelle and Byron came to my office on Friday afternoon. Estelle introduced me to Byron. Byron was surprised that my office wasn't bigger and I don't have a secretary.

"Estelle told me that you work with billion dollars Paul."

"I am a politician and I have a big office and a secretary."

Holly told Byron "I don't want Paul to have a secretary and a big office, because Paull will not work to make money. He will spend a lot time with the secretary in his big office Byron".

"Why Holly?"

Estelle and Holly laughed.

"I don't know Byron. You need to ask Paul."

"Holly was trying to say that I will have sex in the big office with my secretary. She is jealous Byron."

"Do you have something going on with your secretary in your big office Byron", Estelle asked?

"I love you Estelle."

"I know you for one month Byron." Byron didn't know what to say, so I helped him.

"Byron will never look at another woman, because your face looks so pretty and your body is perfect. You are a new person Estelle."

"Do you like my new face Paul?"

"I just told you all that Holly is jealous Estelle. I don't want to have problem with her."

"Could you kiss Estelle, Paul?"

"I need to ask Byron, Holly."

"I don't have a problem with it", Byron told me. I kissed the new face of Estelle.

"Do you think that Estelle is different Paul?"

"I don't know Holly. I never kissed Estelle before. It is first the time that I kissed her." I saw that Estelle wasn't happy that Holly asked me, if I have kissed her before. I didn't want Byron to be jealous like Holly, but Holly needed to think before she asked me about Estelle. Holly understood that Estelle wasn't happy and she told Estelle "I never saw Paul kissed another woman after I met him. I am sorry if I hurt you Estelle".

"You didn't hurt me Holly. Maybe you hurt Byron." Estelle and Holly laughed, "because he loves me".

"It is Ok if Paul kissed you before Estelle. Paul saw you naked too Estelle."

"Who told you that Holly?"

"My detective Scott told me, but I didn't care for that, because Paul saw many naked women before I met him. Paul is a man Byron."

Roy entered my office and said "Nice to see you Estelle. You didn't tell me that you will be coming to my office."

"I have business with Holly and she wanted to introduce my boyfriend Byron to Paul." Estelle introduced Byron to Roy.

"Come with Byron to my off Estelle. There is more space. The office of Paul is small and Paul needs to work. I don't want to fire Paul."

Estelle looked at me. "Roy is right. Paul needs to work, because he will be a father."

"What did you say, Estelle asked Holly?"

"I am pregnant Estelle."

"Oh my God." Estelle embraced and kissed Holly.

"Goldbear family will have one more child Holly."

"Alan will be happy when he hears that I am pregnant Estelle. Alan wants to work with Paul when I marry him."

"I want too Holly. I know that my father wants Roy, but now I make the decisions."

"I embraced and kissed Holly. Thanks Holly."

"You need to be proud with you, Paul. You worked very hard and we have a result."

Estelle and Byron laughed. "I worked hard too and Estelle is pregnant", Byron told us.

"Oh my God." Holly kissed Estelle.

"Is your father happy Estelle?"

"He is Holly and he loves Byron." Holly, Estelle and Byron walked to Roy's office. Roy wanted me to come in his office, but I told him, that I have a lot of work and I need to finish before I leave the office. When they left I closed the door. I thought for Holly. She was a little jealous when she asked me for Estelle, but Holly loved me. Holly scared Roy with Alan. Holly wanted to tell me that she is behind me and Roy is nothing for her and me. Estelle scared Roy too when she said that she is decision maker now for the Cote family. It was good that Byron will be the father of Estelle's child. I don't want somebody think that I am father of her child.

"Why did Estelle told me that she knows Byron for one month?" I don't need to think for Estelle and Byron. I know that Estelle will never tell anyone that I am the father. She promised me.

Holly opened the door of my office and said "We are leaving Paul. Roy invited us to have dinner with him and Susan. Roy will tell you where you need to come. I think that Roy will come with you to the restaurant. Don't be angry with Roy, Paul. Your future is with Alan."

"May I kiss you, Holly?"

"Of course boy." Holly came and sat in my lap. I was kissing Holly when Estelle and Byron entered.

"Do you see what Paul does with his secretary Byron?"

"I want you do the same when I come to your office." Holly laughed.

"I used this desk to have sex with Paul, Estelle."

"I want you to do as Paul does, Byron." Roy came and Holly, Estelle and Byron left the office.

Roy and I left the office at 7:00p. Roy wanted to know what Alan was doing.

"I don't know Roy. Holly told me that Alan wants to work with you."

"Alan is a sick man. You never know what will decide tomorrow Roy." We entered the restaurant. Susan asked Holly what Alan was doing.

"Alan is OK Susan. He has good time with Janet and he wants to retire."

"Will Paul will work for the Goldbear family Holly?"

"Of course Susan. Paul will be in my family after the New Year. I am pregnant and Paul will be a father."

"I know that your Mom Lori isn't happy that you will marry Paul."

"Alan controls the money of my family Susan. I know that Alan will be happy that he will be a grandfather."

"Janet will not be happy, because she did everything to separate you with Paul."

"You need to ask Paul for Janet, Susan."

"How do you know that Susan, Estelle asked?"

"Your father Viler told Roy."

"I never heard my father to speak for Janet, Susan. I know that Alan is married to Lori. Who is Janet, Susan?"

"She is Paul's Mom, Estelle. You didn't know Estelle!"

"I didn't Susan."

I told Estelle that Janet is my mom and she was with Alan, but I didn't tell Susan that Estelle knows Mom. I understood that Estelle will leave Roy Bell and she wanted to make Susan and Roy nervous. Estelle did that very well. When we left the restaurant Roy wanted to speak with Estelle. She told Roy that she is tired to speak now.

"I will speak with you when I come next time to New York, Roy."

Estelle and Byron left to their hotel. They promised Holly that tomorrow morning at 10:00 o'clock they will come to Holly's apartment. They will leave New York in the afternoon. Estelle and Byron came at 10:00am. Byron wanted to look around the apartment. Holly showed it to Byron. Estelle and I were alone.

"I was happy that you kissed me yesterday Paul. I saw that Holly was jealous. I didn't tell her Paul."

"I asked my dad what I need to do Estelle. He spent a lot of time with Holly after we returned to New York, but I did everything to save Holly's life."

"Don't be afraid that I am pregnant. I told Byron that I am pregnant and that Giles is the father. I will marry Byron. We decided to marry in February next year. It will be six months from Giles's disappearance."

"What is Morel doing?"

"He is OK. Margot is happy that he works and make more money for her."

"Is anybody asking what happened in Ajaccio?"

"Alan wanted to know and he asked my father. Your Mom looks good Paul. I saw her when she was with Alan in my dad's house.

"Why did you lie last night?"

"Who is Susan to ask me questions like that Paul?"

"The Bell family makes a lot money from my family. Roy Bell uses my father. Viler told me "Daughter, Bell is my best friend." I told him that Bell uses him to make money. I want to see what kind of friend is Roy of Viler, when I start to work with you, Paul."

"Are you going to work with me?"

"Yes, after you open the Goldbear & Morgan financial group."

"Did you tell Holly?"

"You forgot that Alan and Viler are good friends, but Alan didn't use Viler to make money."

"Do you think that Roy knows too?"

"Only, if Viler told him. Don't worry Paul. I saw that the construction people are working hard and your office will be ready after one month." Holly and Byron came to the living room where I and Estelle were.

"You look so lovely."

"You are Holly" and Estelle kissed me.

"Now you know that I love Paul, Holly."

"I don't care for that Estelle. I know that Paul will be my husband."

"He will be Holly" and Estelle kissed Holly. I will send people from Paris to help you, Holly. "The people that you have chosen don't have experience, but they are young and hard working. It is good for you, Holly."

"Thanks for your help Estelle. It is different business. Before I used and showed my body. Now I need to use my brain."

"You are smart Holly. You made a lot of money when you showed your body. Now you will show that you have brain in your head. If you think for your business is better Holly. I will have business with you and Paul. You don't need to look into what I and Paul are doing. Byron will be my husband. Paul will be your husband. Do you agree Holly?"

"You are right Estelle. The past is past. I will be happy if you and Paul work together. Paul will make more money for your family Estelle, but Paul will make money for me too. I am not greedy, because I have money and my family is rich too."

"If you are jealous, I will not work with Paul, Holly. I don't want you think that I meet Paul in his office to have sex on Paul's desk. I am from France. I will do something that Paul will feel good. The man who lived with me and I have two children from him told me that you were better in bed, but I made him feel good when I was using my mouth." You didn't Holly. Byron looked at Holly and Estelle. "I am joking Byron, Giles dreamed to be with Holly in bed and he told me that he thought for Holly, when he was in bed with me. Are you jealous Paul?"

"I am not Estelle."

"What do you think Holly?"

"I must zip my moth if I want you to work with Paul." Estelle walked and embraced Holly.

"We will be partners Holly. You must trust me when I am with Paul." Holly kissed Estelle. "Thanks Estelle. I trust you." Estelle and Byron left New York in the afternoon.

Later that day Holly told me "I was stupid when I wanted to hurt Estelle, Paul."

"Do you trust Estelle now Holly?"

"I don't have a choice, but she was right. I slept with Giles. Henry told me that you asked him, but you didn't tell him. It is good that I trust you Paul. O boy, I am pregnant. I will marry you. Why I needed to think about what happened in Paris. If I was with you, you wouldn't have met Estelle. Everything will be different Paul."

"Do you regret that you went to Paris?"

"No Paul. After Paris, I know that Alan is a sick man and I don't hate him now. I know well Lori and Janet. I know what I want. Come with me boy. I want to make you happy in bed." After we finished, Holly told me "Don't think for Estelle when you are with me in bed boy."

"I don't think Holly."

"How do I know that Paul?"

"I will not be ready to have sex if I think for her." We laughed.

"Frankly, Estelle looked good after she had the plastic surgery Paul."

"You are beautiful Holly. I am happy that I am with you. You need to think positive for our future life Holly. You and I had good and busy life with other people in our past. God wanted you and I to be together and we are. What do you want more Holly?"

"You know what you need to tell me Paul. Henry, Estelle and Alan told me that I need to listen you, Paul. You will make my life to be easy and good. I am happy that I am pregnant. You did easy that boy."

"I spent many hours in bed with you, Holly."

"I know that you were happy boy."

"Do you think that I need to stay away from you Holly?"

"No boy. You don't have chance to stay away now. I will tell you when you need to do that in four or five months from now. You don't think to go in bed with another woman boy." We laughed.

On Monday when I went back to work, Roy called me to come to his office.

"Does Lori know that Holly is pregnant Paul?"

"I don't know Roy. Holly needs to tell Lori."

"I spoke with Lori this morning and I told her."

"It is good that Lori knows Roy."

"Lori wasn't happy when I told her."

"What is your problem if Lori isn't happy Roy?"

"Lori is Holly's Mom. When Susan was pregnant her Mom was happy that Susan and I will have a child."

"I don't understand you, Roy."

"Lori doesn't want Holly and you to have a child Paul."

"Can you call and tell Holly, what you told me Roy?"

"I will be happy to hear Holly's answer."

"You need to tell Holly. I am your boss Paul." I called.

"Hi boy, what are you doing?"

"I am in Roy's office. He told me that Lori isn't happy that you and I will have a child."

"Give me Roy, Paul."

"I am going to work boss" and I gave the receiver to Roy. Roy didn't come to tell me what he spoke with Holly. When I returned at home, Holly didn't tell me too.

"Did you speak with Henry, Paul?"

"Dad hasn't call me after they left the apartment Holly."

"If Lori and Henry return tomorrow, you don't speak with Lori. I will speak with her."

It was Tuesday morning. I entered my office.

"Roy isn't happy Paul. It is Roy's problem Judy. He went too far in my private life."

"What happened yesterday Paul?"

"I saw Roy before you this morning and he told me "Paul will not work very long in this office Judy"."

"Roy is right Judy. I will be happy if he fires me." It was good that Roy didn't call or came to my office the whole day. I returned home. Lori and Dad were there.

"I am not happy that Holly is pregnant Paul."

"What do you think Dad?"

"I am happy that I will be a grandfather Paul."

"Shut up Henry. Paul needs to listen and do, what I tell him Henry. You need to support me, if you want to marry me."

"I need to divorce Janet after I can think to marry you, because you need to divorce Alan."

"I will never divorce Alan, Henry."

"Somebody has mental problem, but I will listen to you, Lori." Henry looked at me and he smiled. Dad was on Holly and my side.

"Why is Holly pregnant, you needed to use condoms Paul?"

"Holly and I decided to save money Lori. I didn't buy condoms and we are rich now."

"You don't speak for sex with me, I am an old woman, Paul."

"Did you have sex with Henry, Lori?"

"It isn't your business Paul. I don't think that it is your business to ask me why I have sex with Holly, Lori." Holly and Henry laughed.

"Why did you laugh Henry?"

"Because I didn't use condoms, but you aren't pregnant Lori."

"I am an old woman to be pregnant Henry."

"I had a lot of sex in the last two months Lori. I wanted you to be pregnant."

"You are crazy Henry. What I will tell Alan if I am pregnant?"

"Why did you want sex with me Lori?"

"Because Alan is with your wife Henry."

"Maybe Janet doesn't have sex with Alan."

"Did you ask Janet what she did with Alan?"

"They had sex, but Alan used condoms Lori. You didn't want me use them."

"Next time you will use Henry."

"If I want to have sex Lori."

"Do you love me Henry?" I saw that Holly looked at Dad.

"Of course I love you Lori. I will do everything you want Lori."
You are a good man Henry. Holly and I were in bed.

"Why are you pushing Henry to stay with Lori, Holly?"

"If Lori is alone, she will create a big problem for me, you and Alan. Alan will divorce Lori. I think that Lori keeps a document or a picture of what Alan did when I was a young girl Paul. I am not sure, but Alan told me that he is afraid to divorce Lori."

"If Lori has something, she is keeping it somewhere. Alan needs to find it."

"Alan lives in Australia, Paul."

"May I speak with Peter, Holly?"

I called. "Peter, it is me Paul."

"Does Alan know that Lori has evidence about what happened between Holly and Alan, before Holly left Alan's house?"

"Does Holly want to know Paul?"

"Holly is here Peter."

"Alan told me and we looked everywhere, but we didn't find anything. I and Alan didn't want to involve other people. You know this is family business Paul."

"We need to find what Lori has before Alan and I start to work together Peter. Lori doesn't love me. Holly is pregnant. Lori doesn't want Holly and I to have a child."

"Oh my God. Lori is crazy Paul. Everybody wants to have a grandchild. Can you speak with Larry, Paul?"

"Larry has children. Lori is a grand Mom already. I will give you the phone number of Larry." I wrote it down.

"Do you have an idea what Alan and I need to do to find what Lori has Paul?"

"I have a detective friend. He lives in Paris. His name is Morel. He helped me to find Holly alive very fast. If he didn't help me they would have killed Holly."

"Alan knows that Peter. I am sure that Morel will never tell anybody what he does with Alan and you, Peter. It is good that Lori is with Henry, Peter. I will tell Henry to keep Lori busy. If Lori wants to return to California Henry will tell me. I will call Morel and tell him that you and Alan need to find something in California. Morel knows Alan, Peter. You keep your cell phone with you, Morel will call you."

"I will Paul."

I called Morel. "Are you alive Paul?"

"I am Morel. Listen, you need to help of Holly's uncle Peter and her father Alan. I will give you Peter's cell phone. He is waiting for your call." I gave it to Morel.

"Estelle told me that you and Holly will marry for New Year."

"Holly's Mom Lori doesn't love me and she doesn't want me to marry Holly. Lori keep something against Alan. If you find it, I will marry Holly. If you don't I will not marry Holly."

"I will find it Paul. I want you to marry Holly. I will call Peter now."

"Morel will find everything that Lori has against the Goldbear family."

"You need to call Larry, Holly. Ask him, what Lori did when his wife was pregnant."

Holly called. "Hi Larry, this is your half-sister. Yes, Larry I changed my name. Was Mom happy when your wife was pregnant? I am pregnant and Lori isn't happy. Yes, Larry. I will marry Paul for New Year. I will invite you, Larry."

"What did Larry tell you, Holly?"

"Lori told Larry that she was happy, but Lori doesn't love his wife. Larry told me that Lori wants to get a lot of money from the Goldbear family."

"Lori didn't care for me or you, Holly. I grew up with my father, you left and didn't return in her house. You shouldn't care what Lori tells you. You must care what you and Paul want. I and my wife will be happy when you marry Paul."

"Larry knows who you are Paul."

"Do you know where Henry and Lori are, Holly?"

"I think that they are in Florida, but I didn't spoke with them for two days. You need to call Henry and tell him. If Lori wants to return to California, Dad must call me immediately. "

"I will call and speak with Henry tomorrow Paul."

"Tell Dad to call me."

"Why don't you call Henry?"

"Lori needs to think that I am angry that Dad is with her. It is good for me and Dad. I know that Lori will push Dad to tell me that I need to separate with you, Holly."

"I am pregnant Paul. Now, Henry is playing well this game and I want Lori to believe him." Henry called me the next day. "I am glad that you trust me Paul."

"Dad, do you think that one woman will create problem between us?"

"Never Paul. Lori hates you Paul. She told me that I needed to tell you that you need to leave Holly."

"You tell Lori that I promised you that I will leave Holly, before New year. I need time Dad. Lori must stay out of California, for one or two weeks."

"Holly told me Paul. You don't call me. If I need I will call you, Paul."

It was Saturday afternoon. Holly and I were at home. The phone rang. I picked up.

"We found what we were looking for Paul. Morel is smart."

"Did Morel see what he found?"

"No Paul. Morel showed to me and I took everything. I was alone when I did it. Lori is a devil Paul."

"Hey Peter don't say that, because Dad is with her."

"Henry is a hero Paul. Alan told me many times that Lori is a devil. I thought that Alan spoke against Lori, because he wanted to be with Janet. Now I believe that Alan was right."

"What are you planning to do with evidence Peter?"

"I will burn them. I don't want Alan or Holly to see them."

"This is a good idea Peter. It is good if you don't tell Alan and Holly what you found."

"What did you say Paul?"

"Be quite Holly."

"Did Holly hear what I said?"

"No Peter. She is sitting on the sofa."

"I will not tell Holly, but I need to tell Alan. He needs to change his will, if he dies suddenly." "This is a good idea Peter."

"Do you want to speak with Holly?"

"Not now Paul. I need to speak with Alan. Say hi to her and kiss her from me Paul."

"I will Peter."

"Why did you hang up Paul?"

"Peter needs to speak with Alan, Holly. He will call you later."

"Are you keeping a secret from me Paul?"

"I am not Holly. Morel found something that Lori was hiding in California."

"What was Morel doing in California?"

"I don't know Holly. Peter spoke with Morel and he was in California. It is bad for Alan and you Holly."

"I want to speak with Peter."

"Not now Holly. I told you. Peter will call you."

Peter called on Sunday morning. He spoke with Holly. After she hung up she said "I can't believe it Paul. Lori is a monster. I will call her."

"Don't do that Holly. Lori must think that she has in her hand the Goldbear family with these pictures. Alan needs time to change his will. If you call Lori she will go back to California. When she doesn't find the pictures, she will try to divorce Alan to get money."

"That is good for your Mom Paul. Janet will marry Alan."

"Don't think for my mom, Holly. You need to think for you. Lori will go and speak with journalists and tell them what happened thirteen years ago. I don't want to read in the newspaper about it. You will be my wife."

"What will be different between now and after we marry?"

"Alan will zip Lori's mouth."

"OK boy, I will not tell Lori what I think for her now. I will tell her after we marry."

It was October 18th. Dad called me. "Lori and I are going to London. She spoke with a man and he wants to see her in London. I will call you when I return back."

"OK Dad."

Holly and I were happy that Lori left to London. The construction workers finished with Holly's office and they started to work on mine. People that work for Estelle came to help Holly. Holly was busy with her office, I was busy at work and finding people who will work in the Goldbear & Morgan financial group.

Dad called me and said "I am back in Florida, Paul. Lori left for California."

"How was your trip Dad?"

"I don't know what I need to tell you, Paul. Janet is crazy, but Lori is a dangerous woman. I am happy that she left for California. I will never live with Lori again Paul. When I see you, we will speak. What is Holly doing?"

"She opened her office and she is busy, but she is feeling good Dad. Hey Dad, Holly told me "If we have a boy, his name will be Henry Morgan Junior". Holly didn't give me a chance to choose the name, but I will be happy to have a boy and he has your name Dad. Holly is the boss Dad."

"I love you so much Paul."

"I love you too Dad." I heard Dad crying and he hang up. I never heard Dad crying before. I had a feeling that something will happen, because Lori left for California and Dad didn't come to New York.

CHAPTER 12

It was Thursday morning, November 2nd. I will never forget this day. I took a shower dot dressed and entered the living room. I saw Holly crying. When she saw me she said "Alan and Janet are death Paul."

"What?"

"Peter called me. He told me that a policeman from Australia called and told him, that friend of Alan found Janet and Alan death. They think that Alan killed Janet and he committed suicide. I don't believe that Paul. Peter will come tomorrow to New York. He wants to see you at this address. Aunt Ann is going to Australia. This is changing everything that you and I planned."

"It is too early to think for that Holly."

"I want you to stay with me Paul."

"You need to go to your office and tell your manager what he needs to do in the next two or three weeks Holly."

"I will go to the office too. I will return for lunch here. Janet and Alan are death died. We don't need to stop our life."

"I am afraid to think about what happened Paul. I think that Lori knows something, because she returned to California."

"Stop to think negative Holly. You need to get ready to go to your office. You need to be strong there."

Holly and I left the apartment. I was in the office.

Judy saw me and said "Roy wants to see you Paul. He was happy this morning. I don't know why. I never saw Roy happy before."

"Somebody found death my mom and Holly's father Judy."

"Oh my God."

"It was bad news for me this morning, but I need to accept what happened. I must fight for my future."

"Can I help you, Paul?"

"I will tell you what you will do after I meet with Roy." I entered Roy's office.

"Did you hear the bad news this morning Paul?"

"Holly told me Roy."

"Your chance to open your company disappeared after Alan died Paul. You will have to work in my company forever."

"I need to get two weeks off. We will speak for my future in your company after I return Roy. I will get my paperwork with me at home. I will work there for two weeks."

"See you after two weeks Paul." Roy laughed. I took what I needed. I took many papers.

"Did Roy fire you Paul?"

"No Judy, but I will never return to this office. I got two weeks off and I took this paperwork with me, but I have more in my office. You need to help me to get it Judy."

"What do you need me to do Paul?"

"Every day you will get paperwork from my office and put it in your apartment. I will come and get the paperwork from your apartment. Slowly you need to clean my office. This is the key to open the door. Tomorrow I will know what I will do in the future." I left the office.

I called Nancy. "It was so sad to hear the bad news Paul."

"Do you have information about what happened?"

"I don't, but I want to see you."

"Came to my apartment Paul." I took a taxi and got there. I rang the doorbell.

Nancy opened the door and said "Come on in Paul"

I entered her apartment and said "I left Roy, Nancy".

"This is good for you, Paul. I will follow you where you go."

"I am meeting Peter tomorrow."

"It is good that Goldbear family wants to meet with you, Paul. Are you ready with your office?"

"Almost Nancy. The office will be ready after two weeks, but I will use Holly's office."

"You need to tell your clients what you are planning to do in the future."

"I spoke with them already Nancy. I have ten people who are ready to work for me."

"You will have hard time, but is normal when you open a new business Paul."

"I am sorry I can't stay long. I need to go back home to be with Holly right now."

"You are a man and you need to be with Holly. She is pregnant Paul."

"Thank you for thinking for Holly and me, Nancy."

"Call me if you need help Paul."

I was at home. Holly was there.

"I spoke with Henry, Paul. He is afraid to call you."

Don't worry I will call him right now. "Hi Dad. I know Dad. You must come to New York."

"I didn't believe that Janet wanted that Paul."

"I don't want to speak on the phone Dad. We will speak when you return to New York." I hang up.

"Peter called me again Paul. He wanted me to go with him to California tomorrow. Can you come with me Paul?"

"You forgot that my mom died too Holly. I need to be in New York. Dad will return late tonight to New York. He will be in his apartment. I will have to be with him."

I met Peter on Friday morning. We met at his friend's office.

"It was sad news for me Paul. I don't believe what the policemen told me, because Lori asked the lawyer of my family to see Alan's will yesterday." A man entered the room.

"This is Gary Lee. Gary this is Paul Morgan." We shook hands.

He said "You need to sign this document Paul. Do you want to read it?"

"I don't Gary. I trust you. Where do I need to sign?"

Gary showed me where to sign and I did it.

"I need to leave Peter."

"I will call you later to tell you how long we need to wait to open the Goldbear & Morgan financial group. It is good that you have an office and we have an address for the new company. I will stay in New York today. Where do you work Paul?"

"Today I am planning to be here Gary."

"If I need something I will call you, Paul." Gary left the room.

"Did you speak and meet with Henry, Paul?"

"I spoke with him last night. I will meet him tonight. Lori and Henry were in London. They returned to America, but Lori went to California. Henry went to Florida."

"Maybe Henry knows something Paul."

"I am sure that Dad will never kill anybody Peter. I was ready to kill when Holly had a problem. Henry is quite and loving man Peter."

"Holly told me that she is planning to come with you to California. Can you keep her safe, because she is pregnant Peter?"

"Don't be afraid for Holly, Paul. I promise you that Holly will back in New York safe after the funeral of Alan. Frankly, Alan was so happy that he would been a grandfather. That is why I didn't believe that he committed suicide Paul. I will give you copies of the papers that Alan sent to me before he died. If you have questions you need to call me. I need to get Holly and go back to California." Peter left.

I called Holly. "Peter will come to get you. I will not see you Holly. You must be careful, because you are pregnant."

"O boy, I don't know what to do. You must go to California to help Peter. I think that he will have problem with Lori. You are the daughter of Alan, Holly. You don't know what Alan wrote in his will."

"I don't want to get anything from the Goldbear family Paul. Everything will belong to you if Alan give me something in his will. I love you so much Paul. I will miss you, but you are right. I need to help Peter if he has problem with Lori. I am kissing you, Paul."

"I am kissing you too Holly." I spent the whole day in the office of Peter's friend. The secretary of his friend bought a lunch for me. I left the office late in the afternoon.

I called Dad "I will be in my apartment in few minutes Dad."

"Where is Holly?"

"She went to California with Peter. Holly wants to help Peter if he has problem with Lori."

"Lori is a devil Paul. Hey Dad, you slept with the devil."

"You are right Paul. Maybe, I am a devil too." I laughed.

"Don't say that Dad. You did everything what Holly wanted. You helped Holly and me because you kept Lori with you."

"I will come to your apartment Paul." I and Dad sat and drank whiskey. I didn't' ask Dad. I knew that he will tell me everything.

"When we were in the hotel room in London somebody called.

I heard when Lori said "I will give you four million Kevin, but you must kill them". The next day, Lori told me that she need to meet with somebody alone. We were in London seven days after she met that person. Lori told me that we need to return to America, but she is going to California. I bought a ticket to Miami. That is what I know Paul. I was surprised when somebody called me and told that Janet died. I called Lori and asked her, what she paid four million dollars for? Do you know what Lori told me?"

"Your stupid wife paid two million to somebody to kill us. I paid four million Henry and he finished a good job. I want to marry you after Alan's funeral. We are free now. I love you Henry, but you must stop Paul to marry Holly."

"I hang up Paul."

I looked at my watch. It was 10:45pm. I called Morel. "You need to find Keven. Tell him that I want to speak with him or I will kill him."

"I will Paul."

"Why is that Paul?"

"Kevin saved my life. I don't believe that he killed Mom and Alan but I want to be sure Dad."

"I am sorry that I created a problem for you Paul."

"You didn't Dad. What are you planning for Mom's funeral?"

"I spoke with your aunt Becky and told her what happened with Janet. Becky told me that I don't need to invite a lot of people at Janet's funeral, because people will ask me, why Janet was with Alan in Australia. Aunt Becky is right Dad. I think to invite Becky, her husband, Janet's brother Tom and his wife. They live in Ohio. I will not invite people from New York and Florida, Paul."

"This is good Dad. I don't want people to ask me for Mom. Who will deliver Mom's body?"

"Ann Goldbear. I spoke with her. Ann will deliver the body to New York."

"Does Ann know Mom?"

"Everybody in the Goldbear family know her name, but Ann and Peter know Janet well."

"How do you know that?"

"Lori told me, but I asked Ann if she knew Janet. Ann told me that she met Janet many times when she was with her brother."

"I thought that Janet was a better choice for Alan, Henry."

"I took two weeks off, but I will not return to work for Roy,

Dad. I met with Peter. We will open a new company. The name is Goldbear & Morgan financial group."

"The name is good Paul. I know that you and Peter will be good friends. From Saturday to Tuesday I worked from my apartment. Dad was with me and he cooked for me. I spoke with Holly shortly about three times. On Wednesday, they called Dad to inform him that the coffin with Mom's body will arrive on Thursday. Dad called my relatives in Ohio and told them that funeral of Mom will be on Friday.

"They will come tomorrow to my apartment Paul. I need to go back to my apartment."

"Do you want me to stay tonight here Paul?"

"No Dad." He left. Kevin called and told me that he was in New York. I gave him my address and told him that I will be waiting for him.

"I thought that I will never see you, Paul."

"Me too Kevin. I want to know what happened at the Gold Coast."

"Janet paid me two million dollars to kill Lori and Henry. I met with Lori and Henry in London. Lori paid me four million to kill Janet and Alan. Frankly I didn't want to kill them Paul. I was in London. I called Alan and told him, that I had problem with Janet and Lori and I want to meet him in London."

"I want to stay in the Gold Coast, Kevin. Tell me what is your problem with Janet and Lori."

"I don't want to speak on the phone Alan. I will come to your house after two days." I was at Alan's house at the Gold Coast. I told him what Janet and Lori wanted and how much they paid me. Alan was angry and told Janet. "It is over Janet. I want to see a grandchild. Holly and Paul will marry for the New Year."'"

"I want to marry you Alan. I spend thirty-five years for that to happen."

"I will not marry you, because you are married to Henry, and I am married for Lori. I and you will stay and live together here. I am with you and I love you Janet. If Lori and Henry want to divorce and marry, then I will marry you, Janet."

"If Lori and Henry don't want to divorce, what are we going to do Alan?"

"How does it matter if we marry or not Janet?"

"You will never go back to live with Henry. I will never go back to live with Lori." I saw that Janet had a pistol in her hand. She put the pistol at Alan's head. Are you going to kill me Janet?" "You lied to me for many years Alan" and Janet fired at Alan's head. I thought that Janet will kill me, but she moved the pistol and put it in her mouth. Janet fired Paul. I checked the body of Alan and Janet. They were death. I took and cleaned the pistol. I put the pistol in Alan's hand. I knew that the policemen will think that Alan killed Janet and he committed suicide. I am so sorry for your Mom Paul. I know that If I didn't get the money that Janet gave me, maybe they will be alive. Alan didn't deserve to die Paul. I know him for more than twenty-five years. Alan was crazy, because he was sick, but he was a good man, Paul. I didn't know well your Mom."

"Who paid you to save my life?"

"Alan paid me. You need to change your identity Kevin. You need to call Morel every week. If I need to meet you, Morel will contact you. You know where to come. This is my apartment. I will return the money that I got from Janet and Lori."

"I don't need this money Kevin. Keep the money". Kevin left my apartment. I thought for Mom.

"Why did she kill Alan?"

Alan loved her and wanted to live with her. Mom didn't want me to marry Holly, but she killed Alan, because he didn't want to marry her. When Holly returns from California and tells me that she doesn't want to marry me, I will not kill her, because I love her. Mom loved Alan, but she killed him.

"What kind of love was this?" She needed to enjoy that she was with Alan.

It was Friday morning, I entered Dad's apartment. There were Becky, Tom, Frank and Sara. I said hi to them.

"Oh my God. You are a big boy Paul. I haven't seen you for a long time."

"I haven't too aunt Becky."

"Sit next to Tom. I will prepper the same breakfast for you when you were in my house Paul."

"Do you know how Janet died Paul?"

"I want to know, because I am her brother."

"I don't know uncle Frank. Why was Janet in Australia?"

"Mom had a boyfriend. She lived with him in the last eight or nine months."

"What kind of man are you Henry?", uncle Frank asked Dad.

"What is your problem to ask Dad like that, uncle Frank? This was the life of Henry and Janet. How many years you haven't seen Mom uncle Frank? Why didn't Mom want to see her relatives in Ohio? Now you are in Henry's apartment and you are asking him for Mom? You are my mom's brother. You need to know what kind of woman was your sister Janet. Mom never knew that I was in Ohio. Frankly I never slept in your house uncle Frank. My grand Mom wanted me to stay in her house, but you didn't want me, because you thought that you were the owner of the house. Where does grand Mom live now uncle Frank?"

"I love you for that Paul. You aren't afraid to ask my brother Frank."

"Shut up Becky."

"Don't tell me to shup up Frank. Mom lives in my house Paul. Frank wants Mom to live with me, doesn't matter that she has a house and Frank lives in her house."

"This is enough Becky", uncle Tom told her. After breakfast we went to the cemetery. We didn't stay for a long time there. I understood that nobody loved Mom. I had tears in my eyes. Nobody else had. We returned at Dad's apartment. Uncle Frank wanted to drink.

"Henry told me that you have a nice apartment Paul. I want to see it."

"Of course aunt Becky."

"Are you ready to go now?"

"I want to go Paul." Becky, Tom and I left. I saw that Dad wasn't happy, but I didn't like uncle Frank. We were in my apartment.

"Do you want to drink Tom?"

"Now I want Paul. Thanks that you got us out of Henry's apartment. I didn't want to stay with Frank. Sara is a good woman, but Frank is a bad man."

"I heard that you will marry for the New Year, Paul."

"I don't know what I need to tell you Becky. Many things have changed after Mom and Alan died."

"You tell Holly that if she doesn't marry you for New Year, she will marry you when her belly is big or she will carry the baby in her hands when she marries you."

"It is good idea aunt Becky. Holly is looking at her body many times a day." I wanted Becky and Tom to stay few more days in New York.

"We need to return to Ohio, Paul. Your grand Mom is waiting for us."

"Is she OK?"

"I don't know what people feel when they are eighty-five, but she doesn't complain. Janet was a disaster for Mom, me and you, Paul. She separated us. Janet never returned to Ohio after she married Henry. I helped Henry to find Janet when you were six years old. I couldn't believe that Janet left you and Henry to be with Alan. Janet was greedy Paul."

"Shut up Becky. Janet is dead."

"You shut up Tom. Paul needs to know what kind of Mom Janet was. Holly and you need to decide who you will invite to your wedding, but I want to see your baby."

"I will call you to come when Holly delivers the baby, Becky." Aunt Becky and uncle Tom left New York on Saturday morning. After they left, I called Holly.

"What are you doing boy?"

"My relatives from Ohio left New York and I decided to call you. What do you think for our marriage Holly?"

"It isn't good time to speak for that Paul."

"My aunt Becky told me that if we don't marry for the New Year, you will be with big a belly or carry a child when we marry."

"Oh my God. I didn't think for that Paul. Becky is right. I will be ashamed when I look at my wedding pictures. I will tell Peter that we will marry for the New Year. Thanks that you opened my eyes boy."

"I think for you all the time, Holly."

"I am returning to New York with Peter on Tuesday, Paul. I don't feel good here. Noting has changed after twelve years. Everybody thinks that I am here to get money. Lori is afraid that my name will be on Alan's will."

"What does Peter think?"

"He told me that I shouldn't care what they think and say. I must think that the Goldbear family will have one more child."

"You must think that you are pregnant Holly."

"Frankly, I don't think for them. I think for Henry and you, Paul. You are my family."

"Lori is walking towards me Paul. I will call you tomorrow after the funeral boy." I was in my apartment. Dad came to see me.

"Where are Becky and Tom?"

"They left for Ohio Dad."

"Did you speak with Holly?"

"I spoke. Frank wanted you to marry Holly after one year, because your Mom died Paul."

"Aunt Becky told me that I must marry for the New Year, Dad."

"Why didn't you tell Frank to put his finger in his ass Dad?"

"It is business between me and Holly. I don't understand why people need to decide for me and Holly. First was Mom. Second Lori. After Roy. Now Frank."

"Do you know that Mom killed Alan, because he didn't want to marry her?"

"Who killed Janet, Paul?"

"Janet committed suicide Dad. Janet killed herself, because she loved Alan. Janet didn't care for you and me. Nobody loved Janet in Ohio Dad. Janet dreamed to marry Alan, her whole life. This is crazy."

"Janet is dead Paul. We need to think for us."

"I don't want you to live with Lori. If you want to do that, then I don't want to see you Dad.'

"I promise you that Lori will not return in my life. I closed the door with Lori, Paul. If Holly wants that, then I will stop to speak with Holly. Holly needs to decide who is more important for her. Lori or me."

"Tanks Dad."

"Hey we need to celebrate Paul."

"You are right Dad. Mom paid one million for somebody to kill you, but you are alive. Mom died. You need to be happy and enjoy."

"We will have one shot and I need to return to my apartment Frank and Sara will leave tomorrow Paul."

"We will celebrate tomorrow Dad."

"Will anything change between me and you after your mom's death?"

"No Dad. You are my hero, because you lived thirty-four years with her, but you are alive."

"It is a miracle that Janet didn't kill me, Paul."

"It is Dad."

"See you tomorrow Paul."

I was alone. It wasn't for the first time. I was alone for many years before I met Holly. I am happy that in future I will be with Holly and our children. The next day, Dad came at four o'clock. We sat down and got ourselves a drink at six o'clock. Holly called me around eight o'clock. I was a little drunk.

"Are you are drunk, because Janet is death Paul?"

"No, we are celebrating that Dad is alive."

"This isn't funny, because your Mom died Paul."

"If Henry died, it wouldn't have been good for you Holly. Mom will never have wanted me to marry you. I am alive and I will marry you, but I can't be sure, because Lori may kill me, Holly. Henry wants me to marry you. He promised that he will never kill me Holly. We are celebrating that."

"You are drunk Paul. Give me Henry."

"If you don't want to marry me, you don't tell Henry to kill me. I want to see my child Holly. After that I don't care if somebody kills me."

"You are stupid Paul."

"I am, but I love you Holly. I gave the cell phone to Dad."

"He is OK Holly. Paul told me something that I didn't believe, but you know Paul. He never lies."

"Give me the cell phone Dad."

"If you go to Hawaii, I don't want Scott to tell me that you went with two men Holly. One is enough."

"I promise you boy. I will go everywhere with you." Holly was laughing when she hung up.

"Paul, why did you say that to Holly?"

"I need to be sure that Holly loves me and she will marry me Dad."

Holly returned on Tuesday, but Peter didn't come with her.

"Peter and Gary will stay in a hotel. Peter wants to see you in my office at 9:00 tomorrow morning. I have good news for you, Paul. My name was in the will of Alan. I got one third of the money that the Goldbear family has. I am a partner with Ann and Peter."

"What did Lori get?"

"I need to pay her one million dollar every year and Lori gets the house that belonged to Alan. This news surprised everybody in my family. Lori told Gary that she has evidence that Alan kissed my naked body everywhere. If the family didn't give her the money that belonged to Alan, she will give the pictures to the newspapers. Peter and Ann didn't want to see what Lori has. Gary laughed and toll Lori that he wants to see the pictures. Lori didn't show it and she signed everything that Gary gave her. Ann told me that I need to kiss you and she is happy that you will continue the business that Alan had. Ann told me "Paul's friend was here and he did a good job. I trust Paul, Holly. I know that the family will never lose the money." Paul is in our family aunt Ann. "He is Holly and you must marry Paul for New Year. My brother will never return, but I know that he will be happy when you marry Paul and you deliver a child. Alan was different after you went and spoke with him, in Australia."

"You made me rich Holly."

"Of course boy. Come in bed with me. I want to make you happy there too."

Holly and I were in her office at 8:30 am. Peter came at 9:00am. Holly didn't have a secretary. She made coffee for Peter, me and her.

"Why don't you have a secretary Holly?"

"I don't want Peter."

"I will ask Judy to be my secretary, but will not have my office ready for two-weeks Holly."

"Why don't you use Judy for two weeks Holly? She is waiting for me to call her when I am ready."

"This is a good idea Paul. I will call and tell Judy to come tomorrow in my office Paul." Peter gave me all of the papers that Alan had.

"My brother didn't want to keep a lot of papers Paul."

"I don't want too Peter."

Gary came at 11:15am. He showed me and Peter the papers of the Goldbear & Morgan financial group.

"Is everything OK Gary?"

"Of course Peter. Paul is ready to start now."

Holly opened a bottle of champagne. We drank and spoke.

"Before Alan died, he called me and said "Gary, you need to be happy that I will retire. You will not have to spend a lot time in court, because I have many problems with people that I work with and they want to sue me. Paull won't do what I do so you will have a lot of free time. You need to find a girlfriend." Alan and I laughed a lot."

I told him "You forgot Lori, Gary. She will keep you busy in court to get more money from the Goldbear family."

"You are right Paul. I forgot that."

Peter and Gary returned to California on Friday. On Monday I was in Roy's office. Judy has left the company. She ws starting to work for Holly today. I walked to see Roy.

The receptionist asked me "Who are you and where are you going Sir?"

"I am Paul Morgan, lady. Roy fired you and he doesn't want to speak with you."

"Can you take the key of my office, because I have a big office at my company?"

"Give me the key Sir."

"This is the key and this is my business card lady. Give it to Roy." She said that she will call Roy.

"I don't want to speak with Roy, lady."

I left Roy's office. I was happy that I didn't see and speak with Roy. The following Monday I opened the office of Goldbear & Morgan financial group. I had ten people that worked in the office. I was surprised that many people wanted to work at Goldbear & Morgan financial group. They knew me well. I didn't know them well. I interviewed the people, but Judy choose many of them. Judy had big power in the office. Holly joked with me that Judy was the boss. Frankly, Judy chose the right people, that had experience and they were loyal to me. Judy was my personal secretary. I let Judy to do what she wants, because I didn't have administrative experience. Judy had. Holly and I married for the New Year. Holly invited Peter with his wife, Ann, her husband, Gary, his wife, Estelle, Byron, Morel, Margot. I invited aunt Becky, Tom, Larry, his wife, Susan, Roy, Judy, her boyfriend, Henry and Lori. It was so funny. We drank, ate, danced and joked. Aunt Becky joked with Holly that her bally looked good, but Estelle's belly was bigger. Susan joked with Roy, that he needed to work for me, because I will make more money for her. Gary told Lori, that she needs to be happy that Holly married me and I work with the Goldbear's family money, because Lori is looking to get one million every year. Lori told him that she will get the money that belonged to Alan. Gary laughed and told her.

"If Alan calls and tells him then he will give you the money."

Ann wasn't happy and told Gary that he needs to stop saying that name. Holly laughed and told Ann that Gary is OK.

Holly told Ann "Alan is looking at us and he is happy that I married Paul. Maybe Alan will give Lori more money, if she stops speaking against Paul and me."

Peter joked with Dad that he will not marry Lori, because Alan didn't give her a lot of money and Lori is not so rich. Dad laughed and told Peter that Lori wanted a lot of sex and she forgot that Dad is seventy years old.

"Maybe Alan did, but he was fifty-seven Peter."

Ann understood that people wanted to speak for Alan, because he deserved to be here and she told Henry "Alan told me that he wanted to have more sex with Janet, because she was five years younger than Lori and Janet was more attractive in bed." Henry laughed and told Ann "I know well that Ann. I and Janet have a son, Paul and my son now married to Alan's and Lori's daughter. I think that this is a good choice for my son. What do you think Lori?"

"I didn't want Paul to marry Holly, Henry. I will never accept that."

"Can you say that to Holly, Lori, you are her Mom?"

"I will tell Holly latter Henry."

It was 12:00 o'clock. Everybody said happy New Year. Holly embraced and kissed me.

"I am happy that I am with you that I married to you and we will be together for ever Paul. Can you promise me that you will not look for another woman?"

"If you don't leave me Holly."

Holly laughed and told me "Just say yes boy."

"Yes, Holly. I love you and I will never look for another woman." I kissed Holly.

"Happy New Year my children."

"Happy New Year Dad." Henry kissed me and Holly. Morel, Margot and I were at the airport.

"May I speak with Morel alone, Margot?"

"Of course Paul."

Morel and I walked away from Margot.

"Tell Kevin that he doesn't need to call me anymore Morel."

"Thanks Paul. It is good for everybody, but I want to know where Kevin is, if I need to use him." "You decide for Kevin, Morel."

They left for Paris. Estelle and Byron stayed on week after the New Year in New York. Gary prepared a contract between Goldbear & Morgan financial group and the Cote family. Estelle, Gary and I were in the office. Judy gave us coffee.

"Does Paul uses the desk for work Judy?" Estelle asked.

"Do you think that Paul works on the floor Estelle?"

Estelle and Judy laughed.

"Oh my God. You are a dangerous man Paul."

"He Is Estelle."

Estelle and I signed the contract. After the New year, Holly's and my life were busy with our business and travel. Estelle and Byron married in February and I and Holly were for one week in Paris for their wedding.

Lori sold her house in California and bought a big house in Florida. Lori wanted Dad to live with her, but Henry didn't want to. Holly and I were at Lori's house in Florida. Henry didn't come there.

Lori came to New York to see Holly. She was with her new boyfriend. His name was Rios Espinosa. He was twenty-nine years old. Holly was surprised that Lori had a young man for a boyfriend. I wasn't. I knew that Lori wanted to hurt Henry. I told Dad about that. He laughed and told me that "Lori will have more sex now. I don't care what Lori is doing Paul. I want to see my grandson."

Judy married in April and Holly and I were at her wedding. Holly and I bought a new house in Long Beach. We wanted the boy to live in a new house. Estelle delivered her boy on twentieth of April. Henry Morgan Jr. was born on May twenty-sixth. Henry was so happy that he saw his grandson. I didn't have words to tell what I was feeling. Peter and Ann were very happy too. Ann told me that the Goldbear family has one more man. I promised her that if Holly and I have a second boy, his name will be Alan.

"You will never forget my brother Paul."

"I saw him one time, but he will stay in my mind forever. Alan gave me everything that belonged to him Ann. I have a beautiful wife and son. I opened the business with Goldbear family. Alan did that Ann."

"Thanks for remembering my brother Paul. Many people forgot Alan very fast."

After Henry was born, Holly and my life were busier than ever.

Holly was a hero for me. She had four people to help her at home, but Holly spend a lot of time with our son and she worked hard in her office. Holly and I decided to celebrate one year for our wedding anniversary and New Year at Henry's home in Florida. Lori called and she wanted Holly and I to go to her house, because she had a party with many people. Holly told her that she didn't want to have a lot people, because she wants to spend time with Henry Morgan Jr.

"My son will go to bed early Mom."

"Did you know what Lori told me Paul?"

"That I wouldn't have had this problem if I didn't have a child."

Holly, our son, me Henry and his neighbor Emma were having dinner. We ate and drank and were waiting for the New Year. It was 9:30pm, when Lori and Rios entered Dad's house. Dad introduced Lori and Rios to Emma. Lori looked at Emma.

"Your girlfriend is old Henry."

"I am not Henry's girlfriend. My husband died seven months ago Lori."

"What are you doing here if your husband is died Emma?"

"Henry invited me, because I was alone at home Lori."

"Mom who are you to ask Emma?"

"Shut up Holly. You need to take care of your stupid husband and son."

Holly laughed and told Lori." I am pregnant Mom. I will have one more stupid child. Are you happy now Lori?"

"Of course Holly. I want to tell you that your loving father kissed your naked body everywhere." "You want to hurt me Lori. Alan loved me and he gave me everything that belonged to him. I don't believe that Dad did that with me. Frankly, Paul does that with my body Mom. Paul is happy when he does that. I am wondering how Rios kisses your naked body? Are you kissing Mom's naked body Rios?"

"You don't talk like that Holly! Lori is old for me to do that. I am kissing the bodies of young girls."

"Why did you tell me that you love me Rios?"

"Are you lying to me, Rios?"

"Why did you tell me that you have billions of dollars after your husband died Lori? I am with you, because you promised to give me millions of dollars. Now I know that Holly got the money. I want to live with Holly, because she will give me million dollars,

Lori."

"I am sorry Rios, but I gave my money to Paul. If you want to get millions you need to live with Paul."

I looked at Rios. "He looks good Holly." We laughed a lot.

"You are a funny family. I love you."

"You must love me Rios."

"You don't have enough money Lori."

It was 12:00. The New Year came. We went outside to watch the fireworks. Everybody said happy New Year and cheers. I kissed Holly, Dad, Emma and Rios. Lori didn't want to me kiss her. Holly went back to the house. Lori wanted to take Rios back to her house, but he told her that his friend will come to pick up him.

"I don't want to see you anymore Lori."

Lori left. Rios friend came and picked up him.

"May I stay at your house tonight Henry?"

"Of course Emma. My house has four bedrooms."

In the morning I saw Emma exiting Dad's bedroom. Emma started to live in Dad's house. Holly, Henry Morgan Jr. and I returned to New York. Henry called me in February and he told me that Lori came drunk three times in his house after the New Year. I told Holly about that.

"I know that Lori drinks a lot Paul. I spoke with Larry. Lori called in the middle night and wanted to speak with Larry. She was drunk. I don't know what to do."

"Can you speak with Lori, Holly?"

"I spoke to her, but she told me that it is her life Paul."

On March 8th, Henry called at 7:30 am. He told me that Lori had a car incident and she died. Henry heard the news on TV.

"There was an incident and two people died. I saw that one of cars looked like Lori's. I called the police and asked them. They told me that woman that died was Lori Goldbear. It isn't good news for Holly, Paul. She is pregnant. Don't let her to go to California, Paul."

Holly agreed with Henry and I went to California for Lori's funeral. It was like Mom's. Everybody wanted the funeral to finish fast. I was surprised that Larry didn't say something at the funeral. We were at Peter's house when Larry came to me. I spoke with Ann, Paul. She told me that you will help me. I am afraid to ask Peter and I need you to speak with him.

"What do you want Larry. I will help you?"

"Ann told me that you don't like politics. I want to be run for the mayor of my city."

"Ann is right. I don't like them, but I will speak with Peter. Follow me." We came to Peter.

"Peter, Larry wants to be the mayor of his city and he wants somebody help him."

"You know that I don't like to give money to politicians, but I will help you Larry. I will give you money and I will speak with people of my party in your city. Believe me, they will vote for you, Larry."

"Thanks Peter."

"Hey Larry, you are half-brother of Holly. You know that I love Holly. You call me when you need help." Peter left and Larry and I were alone.

"How is Holly?"

"She is OK."

"My wife told me that Holly made the right decision not coming, because she is pregnant."

I returned to New York the next day. Mine and Holly's life were almost the same. Go to the office, then return home and spend time with Henry Jr. Holly delivered a second son on August 10th. Holly wanted his name to be Paul. I told her that the name of the boy will be Alan. Dad laughed and told Holly that the third boy will be Paul. Ann was so happy when she heard that Holly and I have a boy and his name is Alan.

Henry told me that he wants to live with Emma.

"Of course Dad. Emma isn't from the Goldbear family. If you decide to marry Emma, I will support you, Dad." Henry married Emma.

Holly and I bought a big house in Florida. Dad kept his house, but he and Emma came to see us always when Holly, I and the boys were in Florida. I am happy that I have a beautiful wife, two boys and money. I have one goal in my life, to keep my family together. I was doing everything I can to spend more time with the boys. I was with Holly all the time, because we went together to the office. We had lunch together and of course we were in bed together. Frankly my life was simple. I asked Holly what she tough of her life.

"My life is busy Paul. Sometimes I don't want to have sex. I want to sleep boy, but I don't want to hurt you."

"You need to tell me Holly. After sex I fall asleep very fast boy. You are my sleeping pill for a good night sleep." Holly wanted to joke with me and I was happy that she did it. I was surprised when Morel called me. I haven't heard from him in a long time.

"I don't believe that you remember me Morel! What are you doing?"

"I have a problem Paul."

"Can I help you Morel?"

"If you want to spend time with Margot it will be Ok with me Paul."

"What happened Morel?"

"Margot wants one more child. Now I have to work very hard every night. If somebody takes Margot with him I will be free Paul."

"Aren't you going to be jealous?"

"I won't be Paul." We laughed.

"How is Holly doing Paul?"

"She is busy and I need to be happy that Holly doesn't want one more child Morel."

'We have a problem Paul. Somebody wants to know what was happened with Giles, Marcel and Luca." My first thought was for Gaston and I asked Morel for Gaston.

"Is Gaston OK?"

"He is, but he needed to go to live with his wife and son for four months in Spain."

"Where is he now?"

"The Cote family has a hotel in Mallorca, Spain. Gaston is the manager of the hotel and he is happy, because he makes good money."

"I know that Gaston likes money, doesn't matter that the money will kill him Morel." We laughed.

"He lives with his family there and he is happy as a manager of the hotel. He told Lamar "Maybe someday Paul, Holly and Morel's boss will give me money to buy a hotel Lamar"."

"Does Gaston know Estelle?"

"He doesn't and Gaston is smart Paul. He never asked Lamar, who was my boss. It is good for Estelle, Paul."

"Why didn't Estelle call me?"

"She thought that after Gaston left France everything will be OK. But now it isn't OK. For that reason, I called you, Paul."

"Don't tell Estelle! I will send you an envelope. You know what to do after you see what is in the envelope. Say hi to Holly from me."

"I will Morel. Hey Morel, you need to ask Margot if she wants me to help you. I think that she will be happy."

"I will be too Paul." We laughed when Morel hang up. I thought for Gaston. He was involved and he risked his life. Now Gaston is risking the life of his wife and son. Holly entered my office.

"Do you need something Holly?"

"Estelle called and told me that she and Byron will come on Friday to New York. I tried to ask her, but Estelle hang up."

"Did you speak with Estelle?"

"I spoke with her two weeks ago, but Estelle didn't tell me that she had planned to come to New York."

"Do you want to use my desk Holly?"

"Not now. I need to return to my office Paul, maybe next week Paul" and Holly left.

The next day I received an envelope from France. I opened it. I saw pictures of Byron. I understood that Estelle had a problem with Byron. Estelle and Byron were living together for more than two years and I never heard that they had problem between them.

"Why does Byron want to know about Giles, Marcel and Luca?"

Nobody knows where they are and nobody spoke about them for more than three years. It will be stupid if I call and ask Estelle. She needs to call me if she needed me to help her. Maybe Estelle wants me to do that on Friday. She will come with Byron to New York. "I am ready for you, Byron", I told myself. Estelle called me at 10:15 on Friday morning.

"Byron and I are in New York. I want to have lunch with you and Holly" and Estelle told me where we will meet at 12:00 o'clock.

"Maybe I will not stay in New York tonight Paul."

I and Holly entered the restaurant where I and Holly needed to meet Estelle and Byron. I shook hands with Estelle and Byron. Holly kissed them. We ordered lunch. I saw that Byron was nervous and he looked at the people who entered the restaurant.

"Are you waiting for somebody Byron?"

"I am not Paul, but I want to see who enters the restaurant."

"People who want to have lunch are entering Byron."

"Did you choose the restaurant Paul?"

"Estelle told me to come here Byron. I prefer another restaurant, but this restaurant is quiet and good if you want to speak with somebody for business. I prefer to speak in my office for business Estelle."

"I don't have business today with you. Byron wants to speak for business with you, Paul."

"I am not a politician Estelle. I don't have business with Byron."

"Can you tell Paul what you want Byron?", Estelle told him.

"I want one hundred million Paul."

"You didn't tell Paul if you want French francs or dollars Byron."

"You know that I want dollars Estelle."

"I know, but Paul doesn't.'

"Why do I need to pay you one hundred million dollars Byron?"

"Do you want to be the president of France?"

Estelle laughed. Holly looked at Estelle.

"One hundred million dollars are a lot of money Byron."

"For you and Estelle are nothing Paul. You will give me fifty million. Estelle will give me fifty million."

"Estelle is your wife Byron. You and Estelle have a son. He isn't my son. It is your son Paul."

"How do you know that Byron, Holly asked?"

"When you were with Giles, Marcel and Luca in Ajaccio, Paul and Estelle had sex in her house. Maybe your first son is son of Giles, Marcel and Luca, Holly. You had good time with them in Ajaccio."

"I have never been in Ajaccio and I don't know where Ajaccio is."

"Can you tell me where Ajaccio is, Byron?"

The waiter brought food and we stopped to speak. When the waiter left, Byron asked Holly.

"Do you know Gaston, Holly?"

"Of course Byron. I was in Gaston's house, when I was in Marseille."

"Why did you stay there, you are rich Holly?"

"I was alone and Paul told me to stay at Gaston's house. Gaston was my bodyguard Byron. He is a funny man. I had a good time with Gaston. Maybe Gaston is the father of my first son Byron, but Paul was happy and he didn't check the DNA of Henry Morgan Jr. Paul told me that he is happy that we have a son. You must be happy that Estelle and you have a son Byron, doesn't matter that you think that Paul is the father. Everybody knows who is the Mom. For the father you need to check the DNA of the child Byron. Did you check the DNA of your son?"

"I didn't Holly, but I don't care who is the father."

"Then don't say that Paul is the father of Estelle's son Byron."

"If Paul and Estelle give me one hundred million, I will not say what happened in Ajaccio and who is the father of Estelle's son Holly."

"If they don't, what are you going to do Byron?"

"I will tell the police that Giles, Marcel and Luca kidnaped you and they kept you at Marcel house in Ajaccio, Corsica. Paul killed them and got you back to America, Holly. Paul paid thirty million dollars for your freedom Holly."

"Why did you said that Paul killed them, if he paid thirty millions ransom Byron?"

"Paul was jealous that Giles, Marcel and Luca raped you many times."

"Who took the ransom Byron?"

"I don't know Holly, but I want one hundred million dollars."

"Why did you marry Estelle?"

"I needed to live in her house to find information, about Giles, Marcel and Luca. It took me two years Holly. I wasn't happy when I was in bed with Estelle, but I needed to have sex with her. I felt that I was Giles, Estelle. Giles had sex with you to for your money, I had sex to find information Estelle."

I saw that Estelle was angry and she tried to say something to Byron.

"Shut up Estelle. You needed to think when you married for Giles and Byron."

"Can you show me what you found in Estelle's house Byron?"

"I told you that if you and Estelle don't give me the money that I want, I will tell the police that you killed Giles and Estelle gave you a lot of money."

"Nobody has found the bodies of Giles, Marcel and Luca, Byron"

"Gaston told his friend that you killed them and you paid good money to Gaston, Paul."

I understood that Byron doesn't have information about Ajaccio. Byron wanted to scare Estelle and me to get money.

"You don't have information for Giles, Marcel and Luca, Byron. I have information about what kind of politician you are Byron" and I gave him the pictures that Morel sent me.

"You have sex in your office with your secretary and you buy and use drugs."

"How did you get this picture Paul?"

"I am a French politician. I will sue you that you spayed on me in my office. You are an American businessman. They will put you in jail Paul."

"You must tell in court, why you had sex in your office with your secretary and why you used drugs if you are a French politician Byron."

"You must think for yourself. You don't think for me. My lawyer will think what he needs to say in court. I don't want you give me fifty million dollars Paul. I am joking."

"Do you want me to give you fifty million Byron?"

"No Estelle. You are my wife and I love you."

"I don't love you Byron. I don't want you to return to my house. You will meet my lawyer. He will give you the divorce papers. Paul was right. I must think before I raise my lags. I need to return to Paris, Holly." Estelle stood up.

"I don't want you to follow me Byron. I don't want to see you anymore."

"Paul will come with you, Estelle."

"You need to keep Paul, Holly. You chose the right man. I didn't, but Paul will stay in my heart forever Holly. See you next time Holly."

"I will call you tomorrow Estelle."

"Sounds good Holly."

"Why did you do that Byron?"

"It is a long story Holly. I thought that Paul is stupid, but he isn't. I know that they will kill me, but I needed to think before I started this game. Now is too late Holly."

"You are a politician Byron. If Paul gives this pictures to the newspapers, I will not be a politician tomorrow."

"Paul will not give them to the newspaper Byron."

"I know that Holly. Paul doesn't want to have problem with the Cote family, but I can't have the support from Cote family. They will never forget what I tried to do with them. Fifty million dollars are a lot of money Holly."

"I will speak with Estelle tomorrow Byron. You don't say my name and speak for me Holly."

"Why?"

"Estelle will hang up and she will never speak with you. I know well Estelle, Holly. I know that you and Paul will never hurt me or try to create a problem for me after I leave New York. But I will return in France. The Cote family will be there waiting for me. Don't be surprise if I am death Holly, but Cote family is right. They helped me a lot in the last three years, but I am a greedy man. I deserve to die." Byron stood up. "Good bye Paul and Holly."

Byron left the restaurant. Holly was crying.

"We need to leave Holly. I have a lot of work in the office."

That night when we went home I asked Holly "Where do you want to go with children tomorrow Holly?"

"We will decide when we wake up Paul. I don't want to think now for tomorrow."

"Are you thinking for Byron?"

"Yes, Paul. I will call and tell Estelle that she needs to speak with Byron."

"You will create a problem for me with Estelle, Holly."

"I don't think so, because Estelle loves you."

Later that night we were in bed when Holly said "I want to have a third child Paul."

"Oh my God. I thought that you will not want sex with me, after you heard what Byron said."

"I don't care what people say for you. I know who you are. I know that if I followed you to Florida, many people would have been alive Paul."

"I don't want to think for the past Holly."

"Can you start to work for our future Paul?"

"I will be happy if I have a third son."

"I prefer a daughter Holly."

"God will decide, but you need to do something Paul."

In morning Morel called me and said "You did a good job Paul".

"Does Byron have chance to be alive Morel?"

"I don't know Paul. He had everything."

"Why did Byron do that?"

"I know that you will never punish Byron, but I don't know what Estelle thinks."

"She is my boss, but I will not do anything against Byron, Paul. He is different from Giles."

"Hey Morel, is Margot is pregnant?"

"She hasn't told me that she is Paul."

"Why did you ask me?"

"Because last night I started to work hard for a third child."

"Who wants a child?"

"Holly, but I want that too."

"Are you afraid that somebody else may be helping her?"

"Maybe you are right Morel."

We were laughing when Holly came to me and asked "Who are you talking to Paul?"

"Morel. He is works for a third boy."

"Hey, Paul, I am hoping for a daughter."

"Me too Morel."

"Give me the phone Paul."

"Is Margot happy Morel?"

"I think so Holly, but you need to ask her."

"Can I speak with Margot, Morel?"

I was happy that Holly took the phone to speak with Margot, because I didn't know what to tell Morel to save Byron's life. When I spoke with Estelle for business, she wasn't. I know that Estelle was angry that Byron tried to get money and he said that he needed to have sex with her to live in her home. He was her husband. He should have been happy when he had sex with her. I know that Estelle will never forget that.

Two months later Morel called me and said "He is death Paul. Byron used a lot of drugs after he separated with Estelle. This way is good for everybody Paul." For a minute, new didn't say anything then Morel broke the silence "Hey Paul, Margot is pregnant. I will be a father again."

"Congratulations Morel."

"Is Holly is pregnant?"

"She hasn't told me, but I hope that she will be soon Morel. I am spending a lot of time in bed."

"Do you sleep or have sex Paul?"

"Both Morel." We laughed.

"Did Gaston return to France?"

"I don't think that he wants to. Gaston told Lamar that he and his family are happy in Mallorca."

"What is Gaston Mom doing?"

"His Mom and Dad moved to Mallorca too."

"What will Estelle do if I decide to buy a hotel in Mallorca?"

"I don't know Paul. Frankly I am afraid to ask Estelle what will she do if you move Gaston to your hotel. Why do you want to do that Paul?"

"Because Gaston risked his life and the life of his family Morel. If Gaston wants to live in Mallorca, I will buy a hotel there and Gaston will own thirty percent of it."

Morel laughed and told me "If you were my boss, now I would have had already a private building in Paris and many people working for me. I would have been the boss Paul."

"Don't say things like that, because you may die Morel. Your boss will never give you a chance to leave her. She paid you a lot of money when you left her office." We laughed.

"You are right Paul. I will work forever for the Cote family."

"Gaston is smarter. He will be an owner and have a good business with you. I will call Lamar and tell him, what you want to do. I know that nobody will try to kill Gaston, because you are behind him Paul. Honestly, Margot loves you so much Paul. It is good that your boss doesn't love me Morel. Nobody knows that Paul, but I will be happy if Estelle doesn't love you. You need to stay far away from her if you want to be alive. Byron was greedy, but he was a good man. I knew him very good Paul. When I have answer from Gaston, I will call you, Paul."

I sat on the chair and thought for Gaston. He did everything to get Holly from Ajaccio. He was smart too. He figured out first that somebody would prefer to kill him, Morel, Holly and me after we left Ajaccio. Viler didn't want anybody to know what happened with Giles, Marcel and Luca. Holly entered my office and said "Estelle told me that Byron died and we won't have any problems in future Paul."

"Why did Estelle kill Byron?"

"He asked for money, but he was honest after he understood that he lost the game. Estelle is a devil Paul."

"Did you tell that to her?"

"The problem is that I depend a lot on her and I don't want to have problem with her Paul."

"Do you want to have a hotel at Mallorca, Holly?"

"Where is Mallorca, Paul?"

"It is an island in the Mediterranean."

"Is it a French island?"

"Mallorca is a Spanish island."

"Why do you want to buy a hotel there? Isn't it better in the Caribbean?"

"I will buy it for Gaston. We will own seventy percent. Gaston will own thirty percent."

"You know that I love Gaston, Paul. I will be happy if you help him."

"Doesn't Gaston live in Marseille?"

"He is a manager of a hotel that belongs to the Cote family. It will be better if Gaston works for the Morgan family. He has a chance to be alive."

Morel called me a week later and said "Gaston wants to work with you Paul. He will find a hotel and he will call you."

"Do you think that this is dangerous for him?"

"After Byron's death it isn't Paul, but it will be better if you need to speak with Estelle about it."

"Hey Morel, Holly is pregnant."

"This is good news Paul."

"I will tell Margot that Holly will be a Mom again, because Margot told me that you weren't doing a good job and I may have to help you."

"I will call Estelle, Morel."

"Hey buddy, are you jealous?"

"I am not Morel, but I need to speak with your boss. You know that she loves me. Will Estelle be happy when I tell her that Holly is pregnant?"

"Maybe Estelle wants to be too Paul. Don't say that Morel. Holly will kill me."

"Where Paul?"

"Of course in bed. Holly will want to get all of my strength."

"You will not have any left to have sex with Estelle, Paul."

"You are right Morel." I laughed and hang up.

I called Estelle and said "Hi boss."

"Are you happy today Paul?"

"Holly is pregnant Estelle. I spoke with her yesterday. She didn't tell me that Paul."

"Holly was a little disappointed about Byron. You know that Holly is different from me and you, Estelle."

"Why did you call me?"

"I will buy a hotel in Mallorca. I want Gaston work for me."

"Are you afraid for Gaston, Paul?"

"I am not, but Holly and I love the Gaston family and we would like to help them."

"I don't have a problem if you want to Gaston to work for you, Paul."

"I will buy a hotel, but thirty percent the hotel will be Gaston's, Estelle."

"I know that you are a man and you think for the people that help you. I will never be against you, when you decide to do something Paul."

"Thanks so much Estelle. I love you, Paul, but Holly love you so much." Estelle hang up.

The next day Gaston called me "What are you doing with my future boss?"

"I was busy with Holly, Gaston."

"Lamar told me that Holly is pregnant Paul. You have two boys Paul. I have one. I need to think for one more."

"You don't need to think. You need to keep busy your wife in bed Gaston."

"Hey Paul, you are right. I need to have more children, because they need to help me in my future hotel. I know that someday I will own it one hundred percent of it."

"You will Gaston. Holly, I and our boys will be happy to visit your hotel."

After three months Gaston and I bought the hotel. It needed improvement, so Gaston hired the people to do that. Margot delivered a girl. Muriel was happy. Holly delivered a boy after two months. Holly wanted to name him Paul Morgan Jr. I told her that we have Henry Morgan Jr. I want the name of the boy to be Paul Morgan. Holly agreed with me. Dad laughed and told Holly that she needs to think for a daughter.

Holly said "The last four years of my life have been very busy Henry. I delivered three boys. I am busy with my business. I will take some time off and I will think for another child before I am forty years old."

Gaston and I opened the hotel. The name of hotel was Holly Gold Spa and Resort. Gaston chose the name. On the opening day, there was Gaston's family, myself, Morel, Lamar and people from Mallorca. Holly and Margot didn't come. They were busy with the children. Holly and Margot promised me and Morel that we will have a vacation there together. Estelle told me that she was busy. We had a big party. I and Morel understood that Gaston has a big heart and that the people in Mallorca loved him for that. People from different place of the island were there for the opening celebration.

It was at 2:30 am. In restaurant of the Holly Gold Spa Resort were Morel, Gaston and I. Lamar left. We were sitting and drinking. Gaston said "Hey Paul, we are like the three Musketeers. I am Athos, Morel is Aramis you are Porthos, but D'Artagan missing."

"Lamar was tiered Gaston."

"Lamar isn't D'Artagan, Morel. Your boss is D'Artagan."

"You need to be happy that you are alive Gaston."

"You too Morel."

"Now I am not afraid for my life Morel, because Paul is my boss. Your boss will be afraid to kill me, stupid detective."

"Why did you call me a stupid detective Gaston?"

"I did everything to save your life."

"Your boss has billions, but you don't have million dollars Morel."

"My boss has billions, but I have millions of dollars. You needed to think before you choose your boss Morel. That is why I called you a stupid detective. I love you that you saved my life. You and Paul are my brothers."

"You are smart and loyal friend Gaston. You never told anybody that I and Paul were in Ajaccio. My boss wanted to kill you, but I told her that she needs to kill me, but she needs to remember that Paul is behind us and he will kill her. She laughed and told me that Paul loves her. She understood that she went the wrong way when she said that Paul loves her and she told me that I need to save the life of Gaston. After that she never mentioned your name when I was with her. This was one and half year ago Paul."

"Does Margot know Morel?"

"You know that I tell Margot everything, Paul."

"What did Margot say when you told her?"

"That my boss will listen to what you tell her."

"Oh my God. I know that Paul is the boss of your boss Morel."

"Cheers for your and my boss Morel."

We left the restaurant at 5:00 o'clock in the morning. We were drunk. Morel, Lamar and I left Mallorca the next day for Paris. Many people came to say good bye at the airport. We were in the plane when Morel said "You are the king of Mallorca, Paul."

"He is Morel, not me."

Lamar said "I know well Gaston, Paul. Next time Gaston will invite more people to the party."

"Gaston knows this business Lamar. More people will come to stay in the hotel. I never spoke with you for Gaston. Now I have a chance to thank you for asking Gaston to help me."

"I don't need a hotel Paul."

"Does Morel give you good money?"

"I am happy that Morel is my boss Paul. He gives me everything that I need."

"If you need something you need to call me Lamar."

"I will never forget that you told me exactly what to do when I had to enter Park Moncean."

"I will tell Morel if I need something Paul."

"It isn't my business, but I think that you need to get married Lamar."

"I am planning to marry next year Paul."

Morel insisted that I stay for one night in his new apartment. Margot was very happy when she saw me.

"You surprised me Paul. I don't believe that you wanted to see me."

"If I was alone it would have been better for us Margot."

"Do you think that Holly will be jealous Paul?"

"I don't know, but Estelle will be jealous Margot, Morel answered."

"I know that Morel. Estelle loves Paul."

"Did she tell you that?"

"Many times Paul. I told her that she is crazy, because you love Holly."

"Do you want to speak with Estelle, Paul?"

"I will call her Margot. Hi Estelle, it is Paul."

"Where are you, Paul?"

"At Margot's apartment."

"Do you want to see me tomorrow Paul?"

"I will be waiting for you at Margot's apartment. I will leave Paris in the afternoon Estelle."

"I prefer you that you come to my house. I will be alone Paul."

"Holly is my wife and we have three boys Estelle."

"I am joking Paul. I will come at 10:00 tomorrow morning to Margot's apartment."

In the morning Margot, Morel and I were having coffee. I told them that Estelle will come to see me here at 10:00 o'clock.

"It is good for you, Paul."

"Shut up Morel."

"Why Margot?"

"Estelle went too far when somebody killed Byron."

"Byron overdosed on drugs Margot."

"It was good news for a stupid detective. I think that Estelle paid somebody to kill Byron."

"Holly thinks the same as you Margot. Holly was disappointed when she heard that Byron was death."

"It was good for everybody Paul."

"It wasn't for me Morel."

"Did you think that I killed Byron?"

"I don't Morel."

"If you and Estelle wanted to kill Byron, then why did you send me the pictures?"

"Why did you think that Estelle killed, Byron?"

"Estelle isn't a killer. She paid somebody. Estelle was angry when Byron told her that he married her, because he needed to live in Estelle's house. Byron used Estelle like Giles did."

"Estelle was right when she told me that you are smart and a dangerous man."

"Of course honey. Now I understand why people told me that I was married for a stupid detective."

"Morel isn't stupid Margot. Estelle is Morel's boss. He needs to listen to her if he wants to get good money. Frankly, Morel gives you the money. Morel works for you, Margot."

"Thank you for being on my side Paul."

"It is the truth Morel. I didn't take a side. Estelle used me, but I got information to find Holly and Gaston, you and I saved the life of Holly."

"Did you sleep with Estelle, Paul?"

"This is Paul's privacy, Margot. Paul doesn't need to answer you darling. I didn't take a side. I told the truth Paul." We laughed.

Estelle came at 10:00am. She was with a short and thin man around seventy years old.

"This is my father Viler, Paul."

"Why are you here Viler?"

"Are you going to kill me because I came here Paul?"

"I didn't want, to come. I was afraid after I saw my picture, but Estelle wanted me to come."

"This was a long time ago Viler. I know that you were Alan's best friend. I want to ask you about him."

"You are right Paul. I will never forget Alan, doesn't matter that he is death. Alan will be forever in my heart. What do you want to know about Alan?"

"I met Alan one time, but I felt that Alan loved me."

"Of course, he was with your Mom Paul. You should have hated him about that."

"It was a problem between Mom and Dad Viler."

"May I sit next to you, Paul?"

"Can you leave Paul alone Dad?"

"We came here to see Margot's baby daughter."

"You don't need to lie Estelle. You wanted me to meet Paul."

"Sit next to me Viler and tell me about Alan?"

"In business Alan was crazy man like you, Paul. Alan wanted to make more and more money. In private life Alan was different. When he was sick he stayed in a hospital. When he was healthy he spent all his time with women. I will tell you a story. Alan and I were in a restaurant. A beautiful actress entered the restaurant. I don't want to tell her name, because she is alive Paul. Alan told me that he will be with her that night. I didn't believe him, because I knew her well. Alan invited her to dance. When I was ready to leave, I didn't see Alan. I didn't see the actress too. The next day I meet Alan. He laughed and told me "I paid one hundred thousand, but she was good in bed Viler." This is a lot of money Alan. "If she wanted one million, I was ready to pay her that Viler." I saw that Estelle, Margot and Morel looked with open mouths Viler."

"How did you meet Alan?"

"Alan's sister Ann was my girlfriend. Alan saw me and Ann in bed. We had sex. I was twenty-three, Alan was eleven. Alan didn't tell his parents what he saw us."

"Why didn't you marry Ann?"

"Ann's father told her that I am a short man for her. Ann married another man, but when Alan grew up she called and told me. Alan wants sex Viler, but girls don't want him. My family doesn't know what to do. "Tell Alan to offer money to them. Some girls will want sex for money." I was married, but when Alan came to Paris, we went out and spend time with women. I will tell Mom, what you say Dad. Your Mom knows that Estelle, but she loves my money. She will never divorce me. Viler laughed. I laughed too, because Lori was the same."

"Why does my father hate you Viler?"

"He saw me when I grabbed the ass of your Mom Margot. Your father was angry, but your Mom was happy. Frankly I preferred to kiss her ass Margot."

"Did you have sex with her Viler?"

"You need to ask your Mom Margot. I Morel and Viler laughed."

"I like you Viler. You opened my heart. I never knew that you were a funny man."

"I spoke with Alan one week before he died. He told me "When Paul marries Holly, I want you and Paul to meet at my place in the Gold Coast. Paul is funny man like me and you Viler. We will have a good time together." Alan loved you so much Paul. I am ready to leave Estelle. I know that you invited me to create a problem for Paul, but now Paul knows what kind of man I am. I will give you advice daughter. Next time when you decide to get in bed the first man from street you need to tell Margot and Paul. They will tell you if you need to marry him. Two of your ex-husbands are death. I don't want a third to be death too."

"I want you to come to New York to meet Holly and my children Viler."

"I will come Paul. Now I am not afraid to see you." Estelle and Viler left the apartment. Margot, Morel and I didn't speak.

Morel looked at Margot and he told her. "Viler is a good man Margot."

"Do you think that Estelle is a bad woman Morel?"

"I don't want to answer that."

In the afternoon, I left to New York. Finally, I understood that Estelle was dangerous, not Viler. I need to be careful with her, if I don't want to have problem with Holly. I will tell Holly that she needs to be very careful with Estelle when she come to New York. Estelle needs to understand that I will never have sex with her again.

I was happy when I made it home. I kissed Holly and my boys. I was surprised that Holly followed me everywhere in the house.

"What is your problem Holly?"

"I don't know Paul, but I was little jealous when Margot told me that Estelle came to her apartment."

"Morel, Viler and the children of Margot were there, Holly."

"I am afraid when Estelle wants to see you, Paul. It was good that she didn't come to Mallorca. Maybe I would have gotten the first flight to come there too."

"You think that I will have sex with Estelle."

"No Paul, I am afraid that Estelle will kill you."

"Why?"

"I don't have anything specific to tell you but you need to be careful with Estelle comes to see us."

"I agree with you Paul."

Viler called me after three weeks. He said "I will be in New York next Friday, Paul."

"I would be happy if you stay in my house Viler. I and Holly want to speak with you about Alan."

"Thank you for inviting me to your house Paul."

"Hey Paul, I will come straight to your office when I arrive in New York."

Viler was in my office on Friday afternoon. I was happy when Viler entered.

"I will call Holly to come here Viler." He was surprised that Holly embraced and kissed him.

"Don't do that next time Holly, I am a man." Holly told Viler that she didn't have a man in long time. We laughed. Holly, Viler and I were at the house.

"Can I call Ann, Holly?"

"Of course."

He called "Hi Ann. Of course I am. You know that I love you." I and Holly laughed.

"Holly and Paul are laughing Ann. I am in their house. I will be happy to see you Ann. Hey Holly, my old love will come to see me. If her husband calls and ask for Ann, you don't tell him that I am here. He will want to come too."

We were surprised that Viler wanted to play with the boys.

"They Alan's are grandchildren, Holly. I know that Alan is looking at us and he is happy."

We had a fun dinner. The next day Ann arrived at my house. I didn't believe that Ann embarrassed and kissed Viler many times.

"If you aren't short I would have been your wife, but you will be forever in my heart Viler."

The phone rang. I picked up. "I want to have dinner with you and Holly, but tell Viler to come too Paul. I need to ask Viler, Susan."

"Susan and Roy want to meet you, Viler."

"I will be happy to see Susan, but tell her that I will be with Ann."

I told Susan. She laughed and told me where she and Roy want to meet us. We were in the restaurant. Susan sat next to Viler. I saw that Susan looked at Viler lovingly. I understood why Roy worked with the Cote family money.

"Why did you came to New York Viler, Roy asked?"

"I wanted to see the grandchildren of Alan. When I saw them, I felt that Alan was next to me, Roy."

"Alan died four years ago Viler. He killed Paul's Mom."

"Alan will never be death in my heard and I didn't know that Alan killed Janet, Roy."

"Maybe Alan didn't want anybody else to be with Janet, Viler."

"Now I understood why you haven't killed Susan. You want Susan to be with somebody else Roy."

"You are right Viler. My husband didn't kill me when he understood that I was with you."

"I will tell your husband what you say Ann."

"I don't care Roy. I will divorce him and marry Viler. He is my old love."

"Is he Ann?"

"Of course Susan, but you don't be jealous. You will never leave your stupid and greedy husband. He needs to think when he speaks about my death brother." Holly and I looked at this old people who spoke easy for their past and sexual relationships.

"Why didn't you marry Susan, Viler?"

"I was a short man for her, Roy." Ann, Susan and Viler laughed. Viler stayed in our house for five days. Holly and I were happy that Viler told us what kind man Alan was. We were at the airport.

"I will speak with Estelle, Holly. She needs to stop chasing Paul. I know that you are afraid that Estelle will try to get Paul in bed. I promise you that Estelle will never have sex with Paul. I don't want to hurt Alan, Holly."

I was in my office. Holly entered and told me "I spoke with Estelle. In the future, Viler will meet and speak with you for the business of the Cote family. When Estelle comes to New York, I will be with her Paul."

"Thank God!" Holly laughed.

I never met Estelle after that. I met Viler when he came to New York or I was in Paris. Viler introduced me to his friends and they started to work with me too.

"Why didn't Alan work with them Viler?"

"Alans asked my friends. "Are you going to kill me if I lose your money?" How would you feel if somebody tells you that Paul?"

"I want to tell you that I feel that I am with Alan, when I am with you, Paul. Maybe that hurts you, because Alan was a crazy man."

"You are not hurting me Viler. I am turning forty. In a way, I am happy that I remaining you of him, because he trusted me with the future of his family and everything he has built."

Holly was joking with everyone that I am an old man and she needs to look for a young boy. I told her that she has three boys. Henry Morgan Jr. was going to school. Holly didn't want anybody to drop and pick up Henry from school. She did it. It was hard for her and I called Dad to return to New York to help her. Dad started picking up Henry Morgan Jr. from school. He told me that the boys in the school were telling him that his Mom is beautiful, but his Dad is old. Emma came to New York too. She wanted Dad to go back to Florida or she will divorce him. Dad divorced Emma.

I and Holly were in bed. I asked her "Do you want another child Holly?"

She laughed. "I am not ready. Maybe after one or two years, Paul."

Holly was sleeping. I thought for her. Holly was a hero for me. She quit her modeling and delivered three boys. She worked hard in her business. Honestly, Holly did everything to make me happy. I had a life with her in the past. I have a good life with her now and

I know that I will have a good future with her, Dad and the boys. I live with people who love me and I love them. My life is simple and like it that way. I know that every day will be the same, but Holly, Dad and the children make me very happy, because I will see them every day. I will never know if Mom or Alan paid for Holly's kidnapping, but I don't care for that, because I saved her life. I married Holly and she is sleeping next to me. I kissed Holly and closed my eyes.

www.ingramcontent.com/pod-product-compliance
Lightning Source LLC
Chambersburg PA
CBHW071844020726
47502CB00003B/600